Reason to Breathe

Rebecca Donovan

ISBN-13: 978-0615581927
ISBN 10: 0615581927

CONTENTS

For my intuitively perceptive friend, Faith,
~ we were friends before we met ~
you helped me discover who I have always been... a writer

1. NONEXISTENT

BREATHE. MY EYES SWELLED AS I SWALLOWED AGAINST THE LUMP IN my throat. Frustrated with my weakness, I swiftly brushed the tears that had forced their way down my cheeks with the back of my hand. I couldn't think about it anymore—I would explode.

I looked around the room that was mine, but had no true connection to me—a hand-me-down desk with a mismatched chair against the wall across from me with a three tiered bookcase that had seen too many homes in too many years next to it. There were no pictures on the walls. No reminder of who I was before I came here. It was just a space where I could hide – hide from the pain, the glares and the cutting words.

Why was I here? I knew the answer. It wasn't a choice to be here; it was a necessity. I had nowhere else to go, and they couldn't turn their backs on me. They were the only family I had, and for that I couldn't be grateful.

I lay on my bed, attempting to divert my attention to my homework. I winced as I reached for my Trigonometry book. I couldn't believe it was sore already. Great! It looked like I'd be wearing long sleeves again this week.

The aching pain in my shoulder caused the images of the horrific exchange to flash through my head. I felt the anger rising, making me clench my jaw and grit my teeth. I took a deep breath and allowed the dull wash of nothingness to envelop me. I needed to push it out of my head, so I forced myself to concentrate on my homework.

I was awoken by a soft tap at my door. I propped myself up on my elbows and tried to focus in my dark room. I must have been asleep for about an hour, but didn't remember dozing off.

"Yeah," I answered, my voice caught in my throat.

"Emma?" the small cautious voice called out as my door slowly opened.

"You can come in Jack." I tried to sound welcoming despite my crushed disposition.

His hand gripped the doorknob, as his head—not much taller than the knob—peaked in.

Jack's enlarged brown eyes scanned the room until they connected with mine—I could tell he was nervous about what he might find—and smiled at me in relief. He knew way too much for his six years.

"Dinner's ready," he said, looking down. I realized it wasn't the message he wanted to be responsible to give me.

"Okay, I'll be right there." I tried to smile back to assure him it was okay. He walked toward the voices in the other room. The clatter of platters and bowls being set on the table along with Leyla's excited voice awaited me down the hall. If anyone were to observe this routine, they would think this was the picture perfect American family sitting down to enjoy dinner together.

The picture changed when I crept out of my room. The air became thick with discord with the crushing reminder that I existed, a blemish to their portrait. I took another deep breath and tried to convince myself I could get through this. It's just another night, right? But that was the problem.

I walked slowly down the hall and into the light of the dining room. My stomach turned as I crossed the threshold. I kept my gaze down at my hands that I twisted in anticipation. To my relief, I wasn't noticed when I entered the room.

"Emma!" Leyla exclaimed, running to me. I bent down, allowing her to jump into my arms. She gave me a tight embrace around my neck. I released a breathy grunt when the pain shot up my arm.

"Did you see my picture?" she asked, so proud and excited of her swirls of pink and yellow. I felt the glare on my back, knowing that if it were a knife, I'd be incapacitated instantly.

"Mom, did you see my drawing of Tyrannosaurs Rex?" I heard Jack ask, attempting to distract the attention away from my disruption.

"That's wonderful, honey," *she* praised, redirecting her attention to her son.

"It's beautiful," I said softly to Leyla, looking into her dancing brown eyes. "Why don't you go ahead and sit for dinner, okay?"

"Okay," she agreed, having no idea that her affectionate gesture had caused tension at the dinner table. How could she? She was four, and to her I was the older cousin she idolized, while she was my sun in this dark house. I could never blame her for the added grief her fondness for me caused. The conversation picked up and I thankfully became invisible once again.

After waiting until everyone was served, I helped myself to the chicken, peas and potatoes. I could sense that my every move was being scrutinized, so I kept my focus on my plate while I ate. I knew that what I'd taken wasn't enough to satisfy my hunger, but I didn't dare take more.

I didn't listen to the words coming from *her* mouth as she went on and on about her trying day at work. Her voice raked through me, making my stomach turn. George responded with a comforting remark, attempting to re-assure her as he always did. The only acknowledgement I received was when I asked to be excused. George looked across the table with his ambivalent eyes and dryly granted my request.

I gathered my plate, along with Jack and Leyla's, since they'd already left to watch TV in the living room. I began my nightly routine of scraping plates and placing them in the dishwasher, along with scrubbing the pots and pans George used to prepare the dinner.

I waited for the voices to move into the living room before I returned to the table to finish clearing. After washing the dishes, taking out the trash and sweeping the floor, I headed back to my room. I passed by the living room with the sounds of the TV and the kids laugher in the background. I slipped by unnoticed, as usual.

I lay on my bed, plugging in the ear buds to my iPod, and turned up the volume so my mind was too preoccupied with the music to think. Tomorrow I would have a game after school that would keep me late, missing our wonderful family dinner. I breathed deep and closed my eyes. Tomorrow was another day – one day closer to leaving this all behind.

I rolled on my side, forgetting about my shoulder for a moment, until painfully reminded of what I was leaving behind. I shut off my light and let the music drone me to sleep.

3

I grabbed a granola bar on my way through the kitchen with my duffle bag in hand and backpack slung on my shoulder. Leyla's eyes widened with delight when she saw me. I went over and kissed the top of her head, making a conscious effort to ignore the penetrating glare I was receiving from across the room. Jack was sitting next to Leyla at the island eating cereal—he slipped me a piece of paper without looking up.

"Good Luck!" was written in purple crayon with an adorable attempt at a soccer ball drawn in black. He glanced at me quickly to catch my expression, and I flashed a half smile, so she wouldn't pick up on our interaction. "Bye guys," I said, turning toward the door.

Before I could reach it, her cold hand gripped my wrist. "Leave it."

I turned towards her. Her back was shielding the kids from witnessing her venomous glare. "You didn't ask for it on your list. So I didn't buy it for *you*. Leave it." She held out her hand.

I set the granola bar in her palm and was instantly freed from her crushing grasp. "Sorry," I murmured and rushed out of the house before there was more to be sorry for.

"So… what happened when you got home?" Sara demanded in anticipation, lowering the volume of the fast beat punk song when I entered her red convertible coupe.

"Huh?" I responded, still rubbing my wrist.

"Last night, when you go home," Sara prompted impatiently.

"Not much really—just the usual yelling." I replied, downplaying the drama that awaited me when I got home from practice yesterday. I decided not to divulge more as I casually rubbed my bruised arm. As much as I loved Sara and knew she would do anything for me, there were some things I thought best to save her from.

"So, just yelling, huh?" I knew she wasn't completely buying it. I wasn't the best liar, but I was convincing enough.

"Yeah," I mumbled, clasping my hands together, still shaking from her touch. I kept my eyes focused to the side, watching the trees fly by, broken up by the oversized homes with their landscaped lawns, feeling the crisp late September air whip against my flushed face.

"Lucky for you, I guess." I could feel her looking at me, waiting for me to confess.

Sara turned up the music, recognizing I wasn't going to give her more, and started yelling while thrusting her head to a British punk band.

We pulled into the school parking lot, receiving the usual turning of heads from the students and the shaking of the heads from the faculty. Sara was oblivious, or at least acted like she could care less. I ignored it, because I really could care less.

I slung my backpack over my left shoulder and walked across the parking lot with Sara. Her face beamed with an infectious smile as people waved to her from across the parking lot. I was barely noticed, but I wasn't bothered by the lack of recognition. It was easy to be overshadowed by Sara's charismatic presence with her mane of gorgeous fiery hair that flowed in layers to the middle of her back.

Sara was every high school boy's fantasy, and I'm sure some of the male teachers' as well. She was startlingly attractive and had the body of a swimsuit model, filled out in just the right places. But what I loved about Sara was that she was real. She may have been the most desired girl in school, but it didn't go to her head.

"Good morning, Sara" could be heard from just about everyone we passed as she walked with a bounce of energy through the junior halls. She'd return these welcomes with a smile and a similar greeting.

There were some greetings thrown my way as well, to which I would respond with a quick glance and a nod of my head. I knew the only reason they even acknowledged me was because of Sara. I actually wished I wasn't noticed at all as I slunk through the halls in Sara's shadow.

"I think Jason's finally coming around to realizing I exist," Sara declared while we gathered what we needed for our first class from our adjacent lockers. By some miracle, we were in the same homeroom together, making us practically inseparable. Well, that was until our first class when I headed to Advanced Placement English and she was off to Algebra II.

"Everyone knows *you* exist, Sara," I responded with a wry smile. Some too well, I thought, holding my smile.

"Well, it's different with him. He barely looks at me, even when I sit right next to him. It's so frustrating." She collapsed back against her locker. "You realize guys notice you too," she added picking up on my emphasis, "but you can't look up from your books long enough to notice *them*."

5

My face turned red and I looked at her with a questioning scowl. "What are you talking about? They only notice me because I'm with you."

Sara laughed, her perfect white teeth gleaming. "You have no idea," she scoffed, still smiling in amusement.

"Enough. It doesn't matter anyway," I replied dismissively, my face still hot. "What are you going to do about Jason?"

Sara sighed, holding her books to her chest while running her blue eyes along the ceiling as she looked distant, lost in thought.

"I'm not sure yet," she said from that far off place that kept the corners of her mouth curled up. It was evident she was picturing him and his swept back blond hair, intense blue eyes, and drop-dead smile. Jason was the captain and quarterback of the football team. Could it get any more cliché?

"What do you mean? You always have a plan."

"This one's different. He doesn't even look at me. I have to be more careful."

"I thought you said he finally noticed you?" I asked, confused.

Sara turned her head to look at me, her eyes still sparkling from that place she was slowly returning from, but the smile was lost.

"I don't get it really. I made sure to sit next to him in business class yesterday, and he said 'hi', but that was it. So he knows I exist. Period." I could hear the exasperation in her voice.

"I'm sure you'll think of something. Or maybe he's gay." I smirked.

"Emma!" Sara exclaimed with wide eyes, punching my right arm. I forced a smile while gritting my teeth, hoping she hadn't noticed my shoulders tense with the impact of her harmless blow. "Don't say that. That would be devastating—for me at least."

"Not for Kevin Bartlett." I laughed, causing her to scowl.

To see Sara so distracted by this guy was amusing and disarming at the same time. She had a way with people—the results almost always ended in her favor, especially with guys. It didn't matter who she was trying to persuade, she would put an endearing spin on what she wanted so that the person was actually eager to accommodate her.

Sara was obviously flustered by Jason Stark. It was a side of her I almost never saw. I knew this was new territory for her, and I was interested to see what she was going to do next.

The only other people who have given her a greater challenge have been my aunt and uncle. I kept assuring her that it had nothing to do with her, but it only made her more determined to win them over. In doing so, she hoped to make my personal hell a little more livable. Who was I to stand in her way? Even though I knew it was a lost cause.

We parted after homeroom. I entered A.P. English and sat in the back of the room as usual. Ms. Abbott greeted us and began the class by handing back our most recent papers.

She approached my desk and greeted me with a warm smile. "Very insightful, Emma," she praised as she handed me my paper.

My eyes met hers with a quick, yet awkward, smile. "Thank you."

The paper was marked in red pen with an "A" at the top. There were additional positive comments written in the margins throughout the paper. It was what I anticipated and what my peers expected of me. Most of the other students were leaning over to see what the person sitting next to them received in comparison to their own marks. No one looked at my paper. I tucked it into the back of my binder.

I wasn't embarrassed by my grades or what other students thought of my high marks. I knew I earned them. And I also knew that they were going to save me someday. What no one understood, besides Sara, was that all I really cared about were the days I counted down until I moved out of my aunt and uncle's house to go to college. So if I had to put up with the whispers behind my back as I received the highest marks in the class, then so be it. They weren't going to be there to save me if I did anything but succeed, so I didn't need to get involved in the gossip and typical teenage tripe.

Sara was the closest I was going to get to any semblance of the high school experience, and she definitely kept it entertaining. She was admired by most, envied by many, and could discretely seduce a guy with a grin. What mattered most to me was that I trusted her with my life—which was saying a lot, considering the unpredictability that awaited me at home each night.

"How's it going?" Sara asked when we met at our lockers before lunch.

"Nothing new and exciting here. Any progress in Business class with Jason?" This was Sara's class right before lunch, so it usually gave her enough to talk about until we reached Journalism after.

"I wish!" she exclaimed in annoyance. "Nothing – it's so frustrating! I'm not being overly aggressive, but I am definitely putting the obvious signals out there that I'm interested."

"You don't have what it takes to make him interested," I teased with a grin.

"Shut up, Em!" Sara looked at me with stern eyes. "I think I'm going to have to be more direct. The worst he can say is -"

"I'm gay," I interrupted and laughed.

"Laugh all you want, but I am going to get Jason Stark to go out with me."

"I know you will," I assured her, still smiling.

I purchased lunch with my weekly stipend from the money I earned during the summer – money that was strictly regulated without allowing me direct access. Just another irrational rule I had to live with for the next six hundred and seventy-three days.

We decided to have lunch outside at the picnic tables to take advantage of the Indian summer day. Fall in New England was very unpredictable. It could be frosty and cold one day, and the next would be warm enough to pull out the tank tops. But once winter hit, it stuck around for longer than it was welcome.

As most of the other students were shedding clothes to take advantage of the warmth, I could only push up the sleeves of my shirt. In contrast, my wardrobe revolved around the colors of the healing bruises on my arms, and had nothing to do with the temperature.

"What did you do to your hair today? It looks good. It looks straighter. Very chic."

I looked at Sara sideways as we headed outside, knowing the only reason my hair was in the ponytail was because I ran out of my allowed five minutes in the shower this morning, and didn't get to rinse the conditioner out of my hair before the water was turned off. "What are you talking about?" I asked incredulously.

"Forget it. You can never take a compliment." Changing the subject, she asked, "So will you be able to go to the football game tomorrow night?"

I just looked over at her with my eyebrows raised, taking a bite out of an apple.

Realizing I wasn't going to answer the obvious, Sara picked up her soda, stopping with the can raised to her lips.

"Why is he torturing me?!" Sara whispered, slowly lowering the can with her eyes fixated on something behind me.

I turned to see what had captured her attention. Jason Stark and another well-built senior had their shirts off, tucked into the backs of their pants, and were throwing a football back and forth. The attention he captured was painstakingly obvious. I watched him for a minute as Sara moaned behind me. Oddly, he seemed oblivious to all of the girls drooling over him – interesting.

"Sara, maybe he doesn't realize he's as wanted as he is," I observed objectively. "Have you ever thought of that?"

"How could he not know?" she questioned in disbelief.

"He's a guy," I said with a resigned sigh. "Have you ever seen him out with anyone other than the two years he was dating Holly Martin? Just because we think he's a god, it doesn't mean he puts himself on the same pedestal."

We looked over at the tall figure with the defined muscles and playful smile. Even I couldn't help but get lost in the details of his tanned body. Just because I was focused on school, it didn't mean I was dead. I still noticed—well, sometimes.

"Maybe," she considered with a devious smirk.

"You guys would make an amazingly beautiful couple," I sighed.

"Em, you have to go to the game with me tomorrow!" she pleaded with an edge of desperation.

I shrugged. It wasn't like it was my choice. I had no control over my social life; hence, I had no social life. I was holding out for college. It's not like I wasn't participating in the high school experience. I just had my own version—three varsity sports, editor of the school paper, along with participating in the yearbook, art and French clubs. It was enough to keep me after school every day, and sometimes into the evenings when I had games or deadlines with the paper. I needed to create the ideal transcript for a scholarship admission. It was the *only* thing I felt like I had control over, and it was honestly more of a survival plan than an escape plan.

2. FIRST IMPRESSION

WHILE SARA AND I WALKED TO JOURNALISM CLASS, I COULD TELL THE lunch performance was still lingering. She looked enchanted, and it was a little eerie. I paced alongside her in silence, hoping she'd snap out of it.

Upon entering class, I went straight to the computer with the oversized screen and pulled up the latest draft of this week's *Weslyn High Times*. Focused on the screen, I zoned out the scraping of chairs and murmuring voices as everyone found their seats. I had to get this edition to the printer before the end of class so it could be distributed in the morning.

Faintly, I heard Ms. Holt gather everyone's attention to review the progress of the assignments for next week's paper. I blocked out the conversations. I continued scrutinizing the formatting, moving ads to accommodate article space and inserting the photographs to compliment the featured articles.

"Is it too late to consider another article for next week's paper?"

The voice distracted me. I didn't know this voice. The guy spoke without hesitation, with a sense of purpose and confidence. I stared at the computer screen without seeing what was in front of me, waiting. The room was silent with anticipation. Ms. Holt encouraged him to continue.

"I wanted to write an article about teenagers' self-image and if they're able to accept their flaws. I'd like to interview students and hand out surveys to find out what part of the body they're most self-conscious about." I turned my chair around, interested in who would think of such a controversial topic. "The article could reveal that despite a perceived social status, everyone's insecure about something." He glanced over at me during his explanation, realizing I was paying attention. Some of the other students also noticed I was no longer working on the computer and were watching me, trying to decipher my pensive expression.

The voice belonged to a guy I'd never seen before. As I listened to him finish, I was irked by his request. How could someone, obviously without flaws, think it would be okay to interview emotionally vulnerable students to reveal something they didn't like about themselves? Probably confiding an insecurity they had a hard time admitting to themselves. Who'd want to openly discuss their embarrassing whiteheads, or admit that they wore an A cup, or that they had the muscle structure of a ten year old? It sounded cruel. The more I thought about it, the more irritated I became. Honestly, who was this guy?

He sat in the back of the class wearing an untucked sky blue collared shirt and a pair of perfectly fitted jeans. His sleeves were rolled up and the buttons undone enough to reveal his smooth skin and a hint of a lean muscular frame.

The shirt complimented his steel blue eyes that moved across the room, connecting with his audience. He appeared relaxed, even though everyone in the class was staring at him. He probably expected people to take notice of him.

There was something else about him that I couldn't quite put my finger on – he seemed older. He definitely looked like he was either a junior or senior. He had a youthful face with a strong jaw that extended to the angles of his cheekbones, complimenting his brow line and straight nose that pointed to his perfectly defined lips. An artist couldn't have chiseled a better bone structure.

When he spoke, he easily captured everyone's attention. He obviously got me to stop and take notice. The projections in his tone made me think that he was used to talking to a more mature audience. I couldn't decide if he seemed distinguished or just arrogant – he was so confident. I leaned towards arrogance.

"Interesting idea…" Ms. Holt began.

"Seriously?" I interjected before I could stop myself. I could feel fourteen pairs of eyes shifting toward me. I even caught a couple of mouths dropping open out of the corner of my eye. My gaze remained focused on the source of the voice. I found the perplexed smoky eyes looking back at me.

"Let me get this straight, *you* want to exploit the insecurities of a bunch of teenagers so that you can write an article exposing their flaws? Don't you think that's a little destructive? Besides, we try to write news in our paper. It can be entertaining and witty – but it should always be news, not gossip." He raised his eyebrows in what appeared to be shock.

"That's not exactly –" he began.

"Or are you planning to write an exposé on how many girls want bigger breasts and the number of guys who want bigger…" In my pause, I heard a few shocked inhales. ".. um, muscles. Superficial and sleazy may work for tabloids, or maybe that's what you're used to where you come from. But I give our readers the benefit of assuming they have brains." There were a few muffled laughs. I didn't flinch—I stared intently into the unwavering blue eyes. There was a slight smirk on his face. Was he amused by my verbal assault? I set my jaw in preparation for his attack.

"I take my assignments seriously. I'm hoping my research will uncover how much we all have in common, regardless of our popularity or conceived attractiveness. I don't think the article will exploit anyone, but assure us that everyone has insecurities about their appearances, even those who may be considered perfect. I respect the confidentiality of my source, and I understand the difference between a puff piece and actual news." His voice was calm and patient, and yet I thought it was patronizing. I could feel the heat rising in my cheeks.

"And you think you will get honest answers out of people? They will really talk to *you*?" There was a bite in my tone that I was not used to hearing, and by the silence in the room, it was a surprise to everyone else as well.

"I have a way of getting people to open up and trust me," he said with a smile full of conceit and narcissism.

Before I could rebut, Ms. Holt interrupted, "Thank you, Evan." She looked at me cautiously. "Emma, since you seem to have reservations about this article, as the editor of the paper, would you be willing to permit Mr. Mathews to write the article, and then you can have the final say as to whether it makes the cut?"

"I can agree to that," I stated methodically.

"Mr. Mathews, is that acceptable to you?"

"I'm comfortable with that. She is the *editor*."

Oh, he was pompous, wasn't he?! I couldn't stand to look at him any longer. I turned back to the computer.

"Great," Ms. Holt replied with relief. Then she directed her attention back to me. "Emma, are you just about done with the computer? I'd like to begin today's discussion."

"I'm sending it now," I confirmed without looking back.

"Wonderful. Would everyone please open your textbooks to page ninety-three, with the heading *Journalism Ethics*?" Ms. Holt attempted to redirect the attention to the front of the class. I took my seat next to Sara, feeling the lingering stares of shock upon me. I kept my eyes glued to the book, unable to concentrate.

"What was that about?" Sara whispered, just as shocked. I shrugged, not looking over at her.

After what felt like the longest fifty minutes, Journalism was finally over. When we were released into the hall, I couldn't hold back any longer. "Who does he think he is? How completely arrogant can a person be?!"

Sara stopped when we rounded the corner, heading to our lockers. She gawked at me like she didn't recognize me. Not acknowledging her confounded stare, I went on, "Who is he anyway?"

"Evan Mathews," his voice said from behind me.

My back tensed, and I stared at Sara, mortified. I slowly turned toward the voice with a reddened face. I couldn't say anything. How much had he heard?

"I hope I didn't upset you too much by suggesting the article. I wasn't trying to offend you."

It took me a minute to compose myself. Sara stood beside me, unwilling to miss out on the front row seat of our confrontation.

"I wasn't offended. I'm just looking out for the integrity of the paper." I tried to sound aloof, as if the interaction in class hadn't bothered me.

"I understand. That's your job." He actually sounded sincere, or was he patronizing me again?

I changed the subject. "Today your first day?"

"No," he said slowly, appearing baffled. "I've been in class all week. Actually, I'm in a few of your other classes too."

I looked to the floor and quietly said, "Oh."

"I'm not surprised you didn't notice. You seem pretty intense in class. It's obvious school's important to you. You don't seem to pay attention to anything else."

"Are you accusing me of being self absorbed?" I shot my eyes back up at him, feeling my entire face flame up.

"What? No." He smiled in amusement at my reaction.

I stared at him in offense. He held my glare, unblinking with his cold gray eyes. How did I ever think they were blue? He was full of himself, and it repulsed me. I shook my head slightly in disgust and walked away. Sara could only stare with her mouth ajar, as if having witnessed a horrific car wreck.

"Where the hell did that come from?" she demanded, her wide eyes glued to me as she strode alongside me. "I've never seen you act like that before." I couldn't get over her astonishment. She almost sounded disappointed.

"Excuse me?!" I shot back defensively, unable to look at her for more than a second. "He's a conceited jerk. I don't care what he thinks of me."

"I thought he was just concerned that he hadn't offended you in class. I think he might even be interested in you."

"Yeah, right," I replied dismissively.

"Seriously, I know you're extremely focused, but how did you not notice him before today?"

"What, do *you* think I'm self absorbed too?" I snapped, regretting it as soon as I said it.

Sara rolled her eyes. "You know I don't, so stop being stupid. I get why you shut everyone out. I know how much you need to get through high school, like every breath depends on it. But I also get how it looks to everyone else.

"It's just accepted that this is who you are, so no one really pays attention anymore. Your lack of," she hesitated, looking for the right word, "*interest* is expected. I think it's amazing that a guy, who's only been here a week, has picked up on your intensity. He's obviously noticed *you.*"

"Sara, he's not that perceptive," I accused. "He was just trying to recover from the blow he took to his ego in class."

She let out a quick laugh with a shake of her head. "You're impossible."

14

I opened my locker, then looked over at Sara before putting my books away. "He's really been here all week?"

"Don't you remember when I mentioned the hot new guy during lunch on Monday?"

"That was *him*?" I scoffed, shoving my books in my locker and flinging the door shut. "You think he's good looking?" I laughed like the thought that he could be attractive was insane.

"Yeah," she responded emphatically, like I was the one who was insane, "along with like every girl in school. Even the senior girls are checking him out. And if you try to convince me that he's not gorgeous, I'm going to slap you."

This time, I rolled my eyes. "You know what—I really don't want to talk about him anymore." I was oddly exhausted by the outburst of emotion. I was never out of control, especially in school—with witnesses.

"You know everyone in school will be talking about it. 'Did you hear Emma Thomas finally snapped?'" Sara teased.

"Nice. I'm glad you're finding this funny," I shot back before walking past her down the hall. Sara jogged to catch up, still smiling.

As much as I wanted to forget it, I couldn't help but replay the entire scene over in my head while we walked to study period in the cafeteria. We continued through the caf, where I could already hear the whispers, and out the back doors that led to the picnic tables.

Seriously, what happened? Why did this guy bother me so much? I shouldn't care enough to be this upset. Honestly, I didn't even know him. Then my overreaction sunk in.

"Sara, I'm an idiot," I confessed, feeling truly miserable. She was lying down on the bench, taking in the warm rays, peeling back the straps of her tank top to avoid tan lines – messing with every guy within eyeshot. She sat up curiously and took in my agonized expression.

"What are you talking about?"

"I have no idea what happened to me in there. Really, why should I care if this guy writes an article about the imperfections of being a teenager? I cannot believe I acted like that and then made a scene in the hall. I'm completely humiliated." I groaned and put my face down in my folded arms.

Sara didn't say anything. After a moment, I looked up at her, questioning. "What? You're not even going to *try* to make me feel better?"

"Sorry, I've got nothing. Em, you were pretty crazy in there," she remarked with a smirk.

"Thanks, Sara!" I connected with her smiling eyes and couldn't hold back. We simultaneously burst out laughing. It came out so loud that the table next to us stopped mid-conversation to stare. I definitely looked like I'd lost my mind now.

It took a full minute for me to break through the hysterics. Sara tried to stop, but small bouts of laughter would escape whenever she'd look at me.

She leaned toward me and lowered her giggling voice, "Well, maybe you can redeem yourself. He's on his way over here."

"No way!" My eyes widened in panic.

"I hope the laughing wasn't about me." It was that same confident, charming voice. I closed my eyes, afraid to face him.

I took a calming breath and turned to look up at him. "No, Sara said something funny." I hesitated before I added, "I shouldn't have gone off on you. I'm not usually like that."

Sara started laughing again, probably replaying my mortifying moment in her head. "Sorry, I can't help it," her eyes watering from trying to hold it in. "I need to get some water."

She left us alone. Oh no—she left us alone!

"I know," he responded to my indirect apology. His perfect lips curled up into a soft smile. I was surprised by the casualness of his response. "Good luck in your game today. I heard you're pretty good." Without allowing me to respond, he walked away.

What just happened? What did he mean *he knows* I'm not usually like that? I stared at the spot where he stood for half a minute, trying to comprehend what just played out. Why wasn't he upset with me? I couldn't believe I was so worked up, especially over a guy. I needed to shake it off and be over it—stay focused.

"He's gone? Please don't tell me you insulted him again!"

"No, I swear. He wished me luck in the game today and walked away. It was… strange." Sara raised her eyebrows, grinning.

"Oh, and I guess you could say he's decent looking," I mumbled. Sara's face lit up with a huge smile.

"He's so mysterious, and I think he likes you," she taunted.

"Come on, Sara. Now you're being stupid."

Somehow I completed the homework that was due the next day, despite glancing around and searching for him every other minute. I couldn't get to the longer term assignments. I saved them for the weekend. It's not like I had anything else to do.

"I'm going to the locker room to get ready for the game."

"I'll be down in a minute," Sara replied, from her meditative spot on the bench.

I gathered my books and walked through the cafeteria. I did everything I could to stare straight ahead so I wouldn't look for Evan — unsuccessfully.

3. DISTRACTION

"YOU WILL NEVER BELIEVE WHO JUST ASKED ME…"

I wasn't able to throw my varsity jersey over my head in time. I closed my eyes and took a breath in preparation for her reaction.

"Shit," Sara whispered, still frozen at the door of the locker room.

I didn't turn around. I couldn't bring myself to say anything. I knew the large circular bruises that covered my right shoulder and continued to the middle of my back said more than enough.

"It's not as bad as it looks," I mumbled, still not having the heart to face her.

"Looks pretty bad to me," she murmured. "I can't believe *that* was for forgetting to take out the trash." We were interrupted by voices and laughter, as a few girls entered the locker room. The girls brushed past Sara, who remained unmoving in the doorway.

"Hey, Emma. We just heard about you telling off the hot new guy," one of the girls exclaimed when she noticed me. "He must have totally pissed you off," added another as they began to change.

"I don't know. I guess he caught me on a bad day," I mumbled, my face changing color. I picked up my shoes, socks, and shin guards and left the room before anyone could say anything else, especially Sara.

I sat at the top of the steps leading to the fields in the back of the school and proceeded to put on my shin guards and shoes. I needed to gather myself after everything that had happened in under two hours. This was not how my days were supposed to go. No one tried to get involved with me, and I kept to myself. This was the place where

18

everything was supposed to be safe and easy. How could Evan Mathews unravel my constant universe in just one day?

That's when I heard his voice again. What was with this guy? First I didn't notice him for almost a week, and now I couldn't avoid him. He exited the guys' locker room below the steps, talking to another guy I didn't know about giving him a ride to the football game the next night. I caught his eye, and he nodded to me in recognition. Why wasn't I invisible to him like I was to everyone else? To my relief, he continued to jog toward the practice fields with a small black bag in his hand. From his attire, I realized he was heading to the guys' soccer field. Great, he played soccer.

The sun danced off the glints of gold in his tousled light brown hair as he jogged further away. Lean muscles along his back brushed against his over-worn t-shirt. Why did he have to look like he just stepped off of an Abercrombie bag?

"Nice," Sara exhaled looking after the same image. I turned with a start, not realizing she was next to me. Heat spread across my cheeks, fearing she could read my thoughts. "Stop it—he's hot. It's just taken you way too long to notice."

Before I could defend myself, a bus pulled up along the dirt road that circled the school, separating the fields from the building. The open windows carried the synchronized chanting and hollering that were indicative of a high school sports team.

"Who are we going to beat?" several boisterous voices screamed.

"Weslyn High!" the bus rumbled in response.

"Don't think so," Sara stated. I smirked and jogged with her to the field.

∞

"Omigod!" Sara screamed, as we drove home. "Stanford! Emma, this is so amazing!"

I couldn't find the words to say anything. The stunned smile on my face said it all. I was soaring from our win, then taken to a different level when I discovered four colleges were scouting the game in which I happened to score three out of the four goals.

"I can't believe they're going to fly you out there this spring," she continued in a rush. "You have to take me with you! California! Can you imagine?"

"Sara, he said that they'd be *interested* in setting up a visit, depending on next quarter's transcript."

"Come on, Emma. That's not going to change. I don't think you've received less than an 'A' your entire life."

I wanted to be as confident, but then we pulled into my driveway. I was immediately grounded – the win and the scouts dispersing like I woke from a dream into a nightmare.

Carol strolled up the driveway from the mailbox, pretending to get the mail. She was up to something, and my heart sank into my stomach. Sara glanced over at me, just as concerned.

"Hi, Sara," she said, completely ignoring me as I got out of the car. "How are your parents?"

Sara smiled her dazzling smile and replied, "They're wonderful, Mrs. Thomas. How have you been?"

Carol sighed her exasperated, pathetic sigh. "I'm surviving."

"That's good to hear," Sara returned politely, not falling for the *woe is me* bullshit.

"Sara, I feel terribly uncomfortable asking you without speaking to your parents directly." I froze in anticipation. "But I was wondering if it would be a bother to allow Emily to stay the night tomorrow night. George and I are going out of town, and it would be easier if she were with someone who was responsible. But I don't want her interrupting your plans." She spoke of me as if I weren't standing next to the car, listening.

"I don't think that'll be a problem. I was planning to go to the library to work on a paper. I'll check with my parents when I get home." Sara smiled, playing along with Carol's façade.

"Thank you. We would be so appreciative."

"Good night, Mrs. Thomas." Carol waved back as Sara drove away. She turned her attention to me in disgust.

"You have no idea how humiliating it is to have to beg people to take you just so that your uncle and I can spend some time together. It's a good thing Sara pities how pathetic you are. I have no idea how she can stand to be around you."

She turned and walked back to the house, leaving me standing in the driveway. Her words circled me like cutting barb.

There was a time when I thought she was right. That Sara was only my friend because she felt bad for me. Honestly, all you had to do was look at us standing next to each other to easily conclude the same thing.

Sara, in all her gorgeous brilliance, compared to me in my ordinary plainness. But I learned that my friendship with Sara was probably the only thing I could really trust.

I entered the house to find life waiting for me with the sink full of dishes and pans from dinner. I set my bags in my room and returned to clean up. I didn't mind the monotony of washing the dishes, especially tonight – engrossing myself in scrubbing to keep from smiling.

∽

When I woke the next morning, I felt more optimistic than I'd felt in a long time. I had my backpack over one shoulder and a tote bag full of clothes in my hand.

Then reality came crashing down with a jolting tug of my hair. "Don't embarrass me," seethed into my ear. I nodded—my neck tense, resisting getting any closer to her as she tightened her hold of my hair with her hot breath scorching my skin. And just as quickly as it happened, she was gone – calling sweetly to the kids to come down for breakfast.

Sara was giddy when I entered the car. She gave me a hug and exclaimed, "I can't believe you're going to the game tonight!"

I pulled back, still shaken by the threat. "Sara, she's probably watching. We'd better get going before she changes her mind and locks me in the basement for the night."

"Would she do that?" Sara appeared concerned.

"Just drive." *Yes. She would*, was the answer I couldn't say out loud.

Sara drove off. The top was up since the brisk fall air was finally catching up with us as we headed into October. The leaves on the trees were beginning their yearly change to the vibrant hues of red, orange, gold and yellow. The colors looked brighter to me today, maybe because I was actually paying attention. Despite Carol's threat, I was still floating from our team's win along with the positive comments from the Stanford scout. And knowing I was going to the game with Sara tonight eased a smile on my face that actually felt comfortable. This would be my very first football game – it only took me three years.

"I've decided that before we go tonight, I'm going to pamper you a little."

I looked at her cautiously. "What are you planning?"

"Trust me, you'll love it!" Sara beamed.

"Okay," I gave in. I feared my idea of being pampered was going to be completely different than what Sara had in mind. I preferred to hang out, watch movies and eat junk. While that might seem very predictable and boring to most teenagers, this was a true luxury to me. I decided not to worry about it. She knew me, so I trusted her.

"I'm going to ask him out tonight after the game," Sara declared while we walked to the school from the parking lot.

"How are you going to do it?" I was finally able to ask after tunneling through Sara's entourage and their gleeful morning acknowledgements. I couldn't believe how matter of fact she was about putting herself out there. But then again, who would say no to her? "No" didn't seem to be in Sara's vocabulary, whether it was receiving it, or saying it.

"I was thinking, but only if it's okay with you," she gave me an apprehensive glance, "that after the game we would go to Scott Kirkland's party, and I'll ask Jason to meet me there."

A party?! I'd never been to a party before either. I overheard the gossip about them in the halls and locker room and even saw the mementos hanging in the lockers throughout the junior and senior halls. It was a rite of passage I wasn't privy to and wasn't sure I was ready for. A wave of panic surged through me just thinking about walking through the doors and having everyone stare at me.

Then I looked into Sara's anxious blue eyes and knew this was important to her. I could make meaningless small talk with people I'd been in school with for the past four years, yet knew nothing about. This would definitely be interesting.

"That sounds great," I said, forcing a smile, falling in line with all the others unable to disappoint Sara.

"Really? We don't have to go to the party. I could figure something else out. You looked pale when I mentioned it."

"No, I want to go," I lied.

"Perfect!" Sara exclaimed, hugging me again. She was very affectionate today; it was throwing me off. I think she realized it too because she pulled back. "Sorry, I'm just so excited that you're going with me. I don't think I could go through with it if you weren't there. Besides, we hardly ever get out of school time together, so this is going to be the best."

I smiled awkwardly, my stomach still twisting with thoughts of the party. It was for Sara. I could get through it. What was the worst that could happen? Well... people might actually try to talk to me. My stomach turned again just thinking about it. This was going to be terrible. I swallowed hard.

More than ever, I needed to retreat to Art class to recover from panicked thoughts of the party. Art was the rotating class that moved through my schedule. Today it took the place of English, as my first class—thankfully. I was desperate to escape in my work.

I walked into the open space of the Art room, inhaling the calming scents of paints, glue and cleaning chemicals with a gentle smile. It was inviting and warm with its tall yellow walls covered with art projects and the oversized windows that glowed with natural light. I breathed easier in this room. No matter how my day was going or what I left behind at home, I gained control over it in here.

Ms. Mier greeted us as we sat at our stools at the tall black work tables. Ms. Mier was the sweetest, kindest person I'd ever met. Compassion exuded from her, which made her an amazing artist and an inspirational teacher.

She invited us to continue working on our assignments from last class, replicating a picture with movement we tore from a magazine. There was some murmuring, but it was fairly quiet as the attention was primarily focused on the art. The quiet was another reason I loved this class so much.

My heart skipped a beat – amongst the murmurs, one stood out. I didn't want to look but was drawn to the smooth voice. There he was, standing at the front of the class, talking to Ms. Mier while holding a camera. She flipped through a book of what appeared to be photographs, making comments. He glanced up and grinned when he saw me. I shot my eyes back to my canvas. I wished I really were invisible.

"So I guess you *are* pretty good," Evan said from beside me. I looked up from my canvas. My heart was behaving insanely, beating at a pace that didn't coincide with sitting still. Calm down – what was wrong with me? He continued when I could only stare up at him blankly. "Soccer. That was quite the game yesterday."

"Oh, thanks. Are you in this class too?" I felt the heat rise in my cheeks.

"Sort of," he responded. "I asked to switch to this class if I could work on photography projects instead. Ms. Mier agreed, so here I am."

"Oh," was all I could mutter. He grinned, which sent more color to my face. My body was betraying me – between my hyperactive heart and my fiery face, I had no control. It was not like me, and it was driving me crazy.

To my relief, Ms. Mier interrupted us before the possession could completely humiliate me. "So you know Emma Thomas? That's wonderful."

"We met yesterday," Evan replied, glancing at me with a smile.

"I'm happy to see that you've made some connections. Emma, would you mind showing Evan the photo lab supplies and the dark room?" My heart went from being on speed, to a dead stop, but my face kept beaming red. It must have been radiating heat by now.

"Sure," I said quickly.

"Thank you." Ms. Mier smiled in appreciation. Why was she, of all people, torturing me?

Without looking at Evan, I stood and walked to the back corner of the room. I slid open one of the cabinets that hung above the counter.

"This is the cabinet with all of the photo supplies. There's paper, developer, whatever you need." I slid the door shut, with my back to him.

On the counter below I pointed to the paper cutter and sizing equipment. We crossed the room to the dark room, where I explained the developing light and the switch on the inside wall to turn it on.

"Do you mind if we look inside?" he asked.

I stopped breathing for a few seconds. "Sure," I replied, glancing at him for the first time.

We walked into the small rectangular room. In the center was a long metal table lined with trays for developing pictures. There was a sink in the back right corner. Cabinets lined the long wall on the right and to the left were two rows of wires with black clips for drying the developed pictures. Even though the developing light wasn't on, the space seemed unnaturally dark – not a place I wanted to be alone with Evan Mathews.

"Here it is," I declared, holding my palms up to present the room.

Evan walked past me toward the cabinets and started opening them, examining their contents. "Why don't you talk to anyone besides Sara?" I heard him ask from behind the cabinet door. He closed the door, anticipating my answer.

I remained frozen. "What do you mean?" I shot back, sounding defensive again.

"You don't talk to anyone," he stated. "Why not?"

I didn't answer. I didn't know how to answer.

"Okay," he recognized my stalling. "Why don't you talk to me?"

"That was direct," I accused. He smiled, causing my heart to attempt another escape from my chest.

"Well..." he pushed.

"Because I'm not sure I like you," I blurted without thought. He looked at me with that devious, amused grin. What kind of reaction was that?! I couldn't stay in the confined space with him any longer. I turned abruptly and walked out of the room.

Concentration evaded me for the remainder of class, leaving my art piece unfinished. Evan left to take pictures of whatever he took pictures of, but his presence lingered. This class was supposed to be my sanctuary, and leave it to Evan to turn it upside down.

Sara noticed my agitation when we were switching books at our lockers.

"Are you okay?" she asked.

"Evan Mathews is in my Art class," I fumed.

"And..." Sara looked confused, waiting for me to continue.

I shook my head, unable to find the words to explain how disruptive he was to my predictable day. As much as Sara understood me, I wasn't ready to talk about it. My blood was still surging; I was having difficulty collecting my thoughts.

"I'll talk to you later," I said in a rush and walked away. I couldn't make sense of what was happening to me. I survived by keeping my emotions in check – by maintaining my composure and tucking it all away. I managed to stay under the radar, skating through school without anyone truly remembering I was here. My teachers acknowledged my academic successes and my coaches depended upon my athletic abilities, but I wasn't important enough to make a recognizable social contribution. I was easily forgettable. That's what I counted on.

There were times when people tried to befriend me by talking to me or inviting me to a party, but that didn't last long. Once it was obvious I wouldn't accept the invitations, or provide more than one or two word answers, I wasn't interesting enough to acknowledge any longer—making my life easier.

Sara was the only one who stuck by me when I first moved here four years ago. After six months of Sara persistently inviting me over,

Carol finally said yes. She wanted to go shopping with a friend and didn't want to bring me along, so the invitation was convenient for her. That serendipitous moment sealed our friendship. I've been permitted to go to Sara's on occasion, and I got to sleep over on rare occasions when it suited Carols' social schedule. It helped that Sara's father was a local judge, so Carol relished the prestige through affiliation.

Last summer I was even allowed to go to Maine with Sara and her family for a week. It coincided with a camping trip George and Carol had planned with the kids. When Sara's parents invited me, they made it sound like they were inviting the entire soccer team and were obligated to include me, which made it easier for Carol to agree. I ended up paying for it when I returned home – I guess I wasn't grateful enough.

But the bruises couldn't take away the best week of my life. It was during that week I met Jeff Mercer. Jeff was a lifeguard at the beach that was walking distance from the lodge. His family owned a summer house on the lake, so he stayed for the season and worked as a lifeguard.

For two days, we went to the beach and drooled over him. After his shift on the second day, he invited Sara and me to a bon fire party at a private beach.

When Jeff introduced us to his friends, I lied and said I was Sara's cousin from Minnesota. That lie developed into a more elaborate story that Sara and I pre-fabricated before the party. My false life revealed itself comfortably, allowing me to be anyone I wanted and no one knew the difference. I didn't have to be invisible, because I really didn't exist.

Swept up in my story, I allowed Jeff to get close to me. I was able to talk and laugh with ease. Jeff and I ended up having a lot in common—he played soccer and we listened to a lot of the same music. He was an easy person to like.

At the end of the night, while everyone was sitting around the fire either coupled off, or involved in conversations, Jeff sat next to me on the sand, leaning against a large log, intended to be a bench. In the midst of the calming mood, with the sounds of a few guys playing guitar in the background, he put his arm around me, and I leaned against him. Being against him was oddly comfortable considering this was the closest I'd ever been to a guy.

We talked and listened to the music. He shifted his body to face me and casually leaned down to kiss me. I remember not breathing for a minute, paralyzed with fear that it was obvious I hadn't kissed anyone before. He was gentle as his soft, thin lips touched mine.

It wasn't easy saying good-bye, with false promises of emailing; but it wasn't hard either. Not for Emma Thomas from Weslyn, Connecticut – the overachieving, self-contained shadow who roamed the halls of Weslyn High. It wasn't hard because that girl didn't truly exist to Jeff.

That's what was bothering so much about Evan Mathews. He knew I existed. He was determined to pull me out from the shadows, and I couldn't get away from him. He wasn't deterred by my one word answers or abrupt responses. He wasn't supposed to be paying attention to me, and I was trying, without success, to ignore him. But he was getting to me, and I think he knew it – and it seemed to amuse him.

I took a deep breath before entering my A.P. European History class, prepared to see him as I walked in the room. He wasn't there. I looked around in surprise and felt my heart sink. That was another problem. My heart was beating, stopping and sinking like it had a mind of its own, not to mention the absurd flushing that was overtaking my face. I was beyond annoyed!

Evan wasn't in my Chemistry class either. Maybe he wouldn't be everywhere as I feared. Distracted with retrieving my homework assignment during Trig, I tensed at the sound of his voice, inciting the rapid beating in my chest.

"Hi."

I continued opening my notebook for today's lesson, refusing to look at him.

"Not talking to me at all now, huh?"

Angered by his antagonism, I couldn't contain myself any longer. I turned to face him.

"Why do you want to talk to me? *What* could you possibly want to talk to me about?" I snapped.

He raised his eyebrows in surprise but quickly replaced the look with his taunting, amused grin.

"And why do you keep looking at me like that?!" My face flushed as I tightened my jaw.

Before Evan could answer, Mr. Kessler walked in to begin class. I stared at my book and the front of the classroom throughout the period. I could feel him looking over at me every so often—it kept me on edge the entire class.

As I was gathering my books to head to Anatomy, I heard him say behind me, "Because I think you're interesting."

I slowly turned around, with my books clutched firmly to my chest.

"You don't even know me," I replied defiantly.

"I'm trying."

"There are so many other people in this school—you don't have to know me."

"But I want to," he replied with a grin.

I walked out of the class, confused. He never said what I thought he should. What was I supposed to say? I started to panic.

"Can I walk with you to Anatomy?" I was too distracted to realize that he'd followed me out of the room.

"You are not in my Anatomy class too, are you?!" Seriously, the world was conspiring against me, along with my rapidly beating heart. I tried to take a deep breath, but I couldn't fill my lungs.

"Didn't notice me at all this week, huh?" People stopped to look at us as we walked down the hall. I'm sure their universe was getting tipped upside down too, to witness Emma Thomas walking down the hall with another student, who was also a guy – the same guy she made a scene with in the hall yesterday. Let the gossip begin.

It didn't take long to reach the classroom due to my escaping pace. I stopped outside of Anatomy and turned to face him. He peered down at me in anticipation.

"I get that you're new, and I must seem intriguing to you. But I assure you, I'm not that interesting. You really don't need to get to know me. I get good grades. I'm decent at sports, and I keep myself busy. I like my privacy. I like my space, and I like being left alone. That's it. You can get to know everyone else in this school who's dying to know you. I'm not. Sorry."

He grinned.

"And stop looking at me like I'm entertaining you. I'm not amused, so leave me alone." I rushed into the classroom. I thought I would feel better, relieved – but I didn't. Instead, I felt defeated.

I had no idea where Even sat during Anatomy, but it wasn't next to me. Actually, no one was sitting next to me. The seat where Karen Stewart usually sat at my table was empty. Karen was always lost during the lessons and constantly asked me questions to try to keep up. Today, I finally had the silence I kept pushing everyone away to get, but it wasn't comforting.

By the time the bell rang at the end of the day, I was over it. Knowing I was staying over at Sara's and didn't have to return home helped – as did not seeing Evan again.

"Hi!" Sara greeted me as we gathered our books from our lockers. "I feel like I haven't seen you at all today. How are you? You didn't get to tell me…"

"Don't mention it. Later, okay? I'm finally feeling better and just want to have fun tonight, alright?" I pleaded.

"Come on, Em. Don't do this to me. I heard you and Evan walked together to Anatomy. You *have to* tell me what's going on."

I hesitated, not wanting to say anything where we could be overheard. I scanned the halls, stalling to make sure I wasn't going to add to the already circulating gossip.

"He keeps trying to talk to me," I explained to Sara. I thought this might be enough, but Sara shrugged her shoulders, waiting for me to continue.

"You were right yesterday. He told me he thinks I'm *interesting*, whatever that means. Sara, he's in all of my classes, or at least it feels like it. I can't get away from him – he's always *right there*.

"I finally told him that I wasn't interesting and to leave me alone. That's what the walk to Anatomy was about. I don't get this guy."

"Em, he's interested in you. Why is that so bad?" Sara asked, genuinely perplexed. I was surprised she didn't understand the problem.

"Sara, I can't have anyone interested in me. You're my only friend for a reason." Her eyes lowered, beginning to understand my dilemma.

"I can't go out. I don't go to the movies. Tonight will be the first and probably only party I'll ever go to. I don't want to have to lie. And if anyone ever got close enough to touch me…" I couldn't finish the sentence. The thought of being afraid to be touched because I might cringe in pain made me shudder.

I wished I didn't have to be so convincing, but until I said it, Sara hadn't put it together. For just a moment, she saw the world through my eyes, and her sorrowed expression made my chest tighten.

"I'm so sorry," she whispered. "I should've realized. So, I guess you shouldn't talk to him."

"It's okay," I assured her with a tight smile. "I have six hundred seventy-two days left and then anyone can find me interesting."

She smiled back but not as big as usual.

The pity in Sara's evasive eyes reflected the patheticness of my life, it was hard to take. It was harder to escape – literally.

I couldn't remember a time when my life wasn't a disaster. I had images of a smiling child stored in shoe boxes, but my father was usually included in the pictures. When he was taken away, I was left with a mother who didn't know how to be one. So, I did everything I could to get by with as little parental interaction as possible. If I was perfect, then there wasn't anything to regret, or distract her from the replacements she sorted through, who would never live up to my father.

I was still too much – a burden. I hoped my academic drive would help my aunt and uncle accept me as an addition to their family. Unfortunately, the reception never warmed beyond the frigid steps when I crossed the threshold four winters ago. Guilt opened the door that night, and I couldn't be perfect enough to earn their forgiveness for what they never wanted. So, I've mastered evasion and over-achievement. Neither as deftly as I'd prefer, since Carol was right there to brand me with my lack of

worth at every opportunity.

4. CHANGE

SARA WAS QUIET WHEN WE DROVE AWAY FROM SCHOOL. I KNEW SHE was thinking, and hoped that it had nothing to do with me. Of course it did.

"There's a way around it, you know."

I sighed, afraid to encourage this train of thought.

"You don't have to cut yourself off from everyone to get through high school," she continued. "We just have to anticipate the questions and have answers ready. There are so many guys who would love to ask you out, but have no idea how to approach you. Em, we can figure this out."

"Sara, you're not making any sense. Besides the obvious—I can't go out."

"What's the obvious?"

"Honestly, who do you know who's interested in me? Be specific."

"Evan already told you he found you interesting," she said with a grin. "Let's start with him."

"Let's not," I groaned.

"Oh! Did you hear that Haley Spencer asked him to homecoming?" she exclaimed.

"Of course I didn't. You're my source of gossip, remember?" Something in my chest twisted. "Isn't homecoming a month away—and she's a senior – what's that about?"

Sara examined me with narrowed eyes. "Honestly? It's only *three* weeks away. Anyway, I heard he turned her down. I told you the senior girls were looking at him too. But Emma, he's into *you*."

"Sara, let's put this into perspective," I corrected. "I amuse him. He thinks I'm *interesting*. He didn't ask me on a date. He just probably thinks I'm a freak or something."

"Well, you are," Sara said with a playful smile. "Who else can live with pure evil while still maintaining a 4.0, play three varsity sports, be in what seems like every club and, to top it all off, be scouted by four colleges. That is pretty freakish."

Before I could respond, she continued, "Okay, let's just say we don't know his motives. He already knows you're a private person. It sounds like you made that perfectly clear. Why can't you give him what he wants and just talk to him? He's either genuinely interested and will ask you out, and we'll deal with that when it happens. Or he ends up becoming a friend, which isn't a bad thing. You have nothing to lose. Come on, the worst thing to happen is he loses interest, and everything's back to the way it was before he moved here."

She was so compelling. Besides, talking to him could get him to leave me alone, especially once he realizes there's not much to know – which will be the best thing that could happen, not the worst.

"Fine, I'll talk to him. So what's the story? And I don't want to lie." I figured she'd already concocted something during her silence.

"No lying, sort of. You just leave most of it out, so it's omission," she said smugly, confirming my suspicion. "You tell him you were adopted by your aunt and uncle after your father died and your mother became ill. That's pretty accurate. You can tell him anything you want about Leyla and Jack since that won't affect anything. Explain that your aunt and uncle are very busy with work and the kids, and that will hopefully be reason enough why they don't go to your games."

"He's definitely going to want to know why I'm your only friend and why you don't talk to anyone."

"He's already asked that," I admitted. "I didn't answer him."

"Well, tell him you and I became friends when you first moved here. That's true." She hesitated for a moment to think about the second part of the question. "Say that you're the first in your family to go to college – which is technically true—and that you have a lot of pressure on you to get a scholarship."

"That's not bad, but why don't I have more friends?" I challenged.

32

"How about, your aunt and uncle are very overprotective, and have no idea how to raise a teenager so they tend to be strict. Then you can admit that because you're so involved in school activities and sports, and with the early curfew, you don't get to go out much. That should work.

"Besides, that'll be like one conversation, and then you can talk about anything else. Almost all truthfully – you know, music, sports, college. You may have a hard time with pop culture though, but I can bring you magazines so you can catch up during the rides to school if you want."

I laughed. "Why is this so important to you?"

"I don't know," she paused, considering the answer. "These past two days, I've seen a fire in your eyes that I never have before. Granted, it's mostly anger and frustration, but it's still emotion. You keep everything locked up so tight—I'm afraid someday you're going to explode.

"This guy's found a way to get to you unlike anyone else. You're different, and I like it. I don't like seeing you upset, but I like seeing you *feeling* something. I know you put your guard down a little with me, but you refuse to show me the hard stuff. You never get angry or scared, or let me know when you're hurt. You don't want me to see you that way, but I know you have to feel it, especially with everything Carol puts you through.

"In the past two days, you've been angry, frustrated and humiliated. I was actually relieved that it didn't turn you into dust or a mass murderer. So if it takes this guy to annoy you to let some of it out, then I want you to keep talking to him. Sound crazy?"

"It does actually," I said. She scowled, not pleased with my honesty. "But I understand what you're saying."

After we pulled into her driveway, she shut off the car and turned toward me.

"What if I like him – that would be horrible. You're the only one who knows my secrets and I can't risk letting anyone else in right now. Not while I'm still living with them. It's too complicated." I took a deep breath before continuing, "But I'll try to talk to him." This caused a smile to spread on Sara's face.

"Besides, he'll probably continue to frustrate me, and I'll end up strangling him. If I murder him, you're my accomplice for encouraging it."

"Do you promise to tell me everything?" Sara asked, glowing.

33

"Of course!" I replied with a grin as I rolled my eyes. "If I don't tell you, then it's like it never happened. And besides, who's going to help me bury his body when I bludgeon him for patronizing me?"

She laughed and hugged me again. Feeling my body tense, she pulled back. "Sorry."

I followed Sara into her enormous house. Her family lived in a newer home compared to the historic Colonials and Victorians in the center of town. The development used to be farmland at one point, and was now broken up into expansive lots to showcase huge homes.

I could never get used to Sara's set up as we neared the top of the stairs. Sara was an only child, so she had a lot of room to herself in the three story house—actually, she had the entire third floor. The bathroom was larger than my entire bedroom, with its granite double sinks, Jacuzzi tub and separate shower. To the right of the landing, it opened into a game room with white walls leading up to the cathedral ceilings, accented by a hot pink racing stripe around the perimeter, and black electric guitars mounted on the walls.

There was a plush white couch with a matching recliner and love seat in front of a home theatre system that included a giant flat-screen mounted to the wall on the far side of the room. It was hooked up to several gaming systems that were set on a console beneath it.

Behind the couch was a reading area with built-in bookshelves that extended to the ceiling, with a sliding ladder attached to reach the higher shelves. Oversized pillows lined the floor beneath the bookcases, creating the perfect place to get lost in the pages. In the corner, opposite of the library, were air hockey and foosball tables.

Sara touched the screen of the built in music dock on one of the walls, releasing an Indie artist declaring what she expected from a guy. The rhythmic guitar strums filled the entire floor through the inset speakers in the ceiling. I followed Sara into her bedroom on the other side of the stairs.

"Are you ready to be pampered?" Sara asked, jumping onto one of her two queen-sized beds adorned with pink and orange pillows.

"Sure," I answered, hesitantly walking past the door that opened into her office with its walls covered with pictures of friends, record covers and celebrities torn from magazines with a clean glass desktop displaying Sara's Mac and printer, furnished with a bright pink chair. The room was small, but still large enough to squeeze in a full-sized, black vinyl couch. I sat down on the identical bed next to Sara's.

"I have the perfect sweater for you to wear with the best pair of jeans," she declared, bouncing off the other side of the bed and entering her walk-in closet.

This room—and I say room, not closet—was as large as my bedroom with two long walls lined with shelves and bars storing folded and hung clothes. At the end of the closet were racks of shoes in every color and style. Visiting Sara was like taking a break from reality – everyone's reality.

"Sara, you're five ten – there's no way I'm going to fit into your jeans," I argued.

"You're not that much shorter than me," she retorted.

"You have a good three inches on me. Besides, I brought a pair of jeans."

She paused, trying to decide if my jeans were acceptable.

"Okay. You can take a shower up here, and I'll use my parents' bathroom," she instructed handing me a scooped neck white shirt, paired with a light pink cashmere sweater with a square neckline.

"Two shirts?" I inquired.

"Well, it's supposed to be cold tonight and you can't wear a jacket that will hide the sweater, so… layers," she explained simply.

I raised my eyebrows and slowly nodded my head. It was obvious that she was loving this, and my lack of fashion savvy was not going to keep her from treating me like a life-sized Barbie doll. I couldn't imagine what else she had in store, or maybe I didn't want to.

"Listen," she said, trying to put me at ease. "I know you never make a big deal over clothes or any of that, but it's because you can't, not because you don't want to. I know they don't let you shop, so let me do this for one night, okay?"

Of course she knew that I appreciated the latest trends, as we often flipped through the fashion magazines together during lunch. But I was only allowed to go shopping twice a year – at the beginning of the school year and again in the spring. I had to get the most out of my bi-annual clothing stipends and buy items that could easily mix and match, so it wasn't obvious when I rotated them every few weeks. This practicality didn't allow me to shop in the trendy stores in the mall or the boutiques in the city like most of my classmates. It meant going to the discount chains in the plazas. I never let it mean that much to me—it wasn't worth it.

However, to have access to Sara McKinley's wardrobe for one night would be any girl's dream, so I wasn't about to refuse it. I knew she had clothes in that closet that still had tags on them. I took the tops, grabbed my tote and headed to the bathroom. Sara ran out of her room before I closed the door.

"Oh, I have this lotion I bought last week that I think you'd like. I was going to save it for a Christmas gift, but you should use it tonight," she offered, handing me a bottle of lotion with pink flowers drawn on the label.

"Thanks," I said, taking the bottle before I closed the door. It was great to take a long, hot shower without fear of *the knock* on the door, signaling the end of my allotted five minutes. It gave me time to think about the past couple of days and how different today felt. I was actually looking forward to the game, despite how awkward it was going to be. If I could get through the game, then I should be able to get through the party. I shut off the water with a new conviction – how long it would last was another story.

I flipped the top of the bottle and took in the soft floral scent. After dressing, I opened the door to find Sara on the stairs, with a towel wrapped around her head. She wore a flattering light blue angora sweater. Sara had no problem with tops that hugged her modelesque body. Sara looked amazing, even with the towel on her head. Conversely, I tugged and pulled at the pink sweater that felt like a second layer of skin, despite the layer beneath.

"Oh. That sweater looks great. You should wear more clothes that fit you like that instead of hiding your figure." I dismissed her with a shrug. She smiled before asking, "Are you ready for the next step?"

We were interrupted when her mom called up that the pizza was here.

"We'll eat and then finish getting ready," Sara decided, and turned to descend the stairs.

"I heard you scored three goals yesterday," Anna said from the refrigerator where she was pouring us glasses of diet soda. "Sara also told me about the scouts. You must be so excited, Emma."

"I am," I replied with a small smile. I was horrible at carrying on a conversation with my peers, forget about trying to say something worthwhile to an adult. The only adults I spoke to on a regular basis were my teachers, my coach, and my aunt and uncle. I only discussed my assignments with my teachers; coach was all about soccer—so that was easy. George hardly said a word, or maybe he couldn't get a word

36

in over Carol's rambling about how difficult it was to be her. Then of course the interactions I had with Carol were one-sided, usually reprimands about how useless and pathetic I was. So I didn't have a lot of practice. Anna recognized my conversational ineptitude, so she didn't push.

"Congratulations," she added walking towards the stairs. She paused to tell Sara, "I'm going upstairs to change for dinner. Your dad and I are going out to eat with the Richardson's and we've invited the Mathews to come along since they're new in town."

"Okay, mom," Sara said only half listening. My heart stopped when she said their name.

"Your parents are going to dinner with Evan's parents?" I whispered in disbelief.

Sara shrugged, "My parents have to know everyone in town. You know, they're like Weslyn's unofficial welcoming committee. My father is the ultimate politician."

Then she added with a grin, "Do you want me to get some dirt on Evan and his family for you?"

"Sara!" I exclaimed in shock. "Of course not. I'm really not that interested in him. I'm just going to talk to him so he'll leave me alone."

"Sure," she said with a knowing smile. I tried to ignore her and took a bite of the pizza slice.

"What's next?" I asked, needing to not talk about Evan any more.

"I was hoping you'd let me cut your hair," she said with a cautious smile. My hair was all one length, hanging past the middle of my back. There was no way I could get it cut every eight weeks or whatever was needed to maintain a style, so I kept it simple and trimmed it myself a few times a year. I usually wore it up out of my face in a clip or ponytail – again, simple.

"What do you want to do?"

"Nothing crazy," she reassured me. "Just shorten it."

"Whatever you want to do is fine with me."

"Really?! This is going to be so great!" she exclaimed, practically jumping off the stool and dragging me back up the stairs.

She opened the middle drawer of her vanity that displayed every shade of lipstick and nail polish on the market, and took out a comb and pair of professional shears. She invited me to sit as she laid a towel on the floor to capture the clippings, and attaching another around my shoulders. "No one's going to recognize you tonight."

That wouldn't be a bad thing.

Sara drew the comb through my hair and clipped portions of it up. I felt the weight begin to fall and decided it was best to keep my eyes shut and let her concentrate – or to keep me from panicking as more hair fell to the floor. Sara sung along with the music as she combed, clipped, and cut. Before I knew it, she plugged in the hair dryer and ran it over a round brush as she styled my hair.

"Keep your eyes closed," Sara instructed as she spread eye shadow along my lids with her cool fingers.

"Sara, please don't make me look ridiculous," I pleaded.

"I'm barely putting any on. I promise." The bristles of a brush streaked across my cheeks. "What do you think? Em, open your eyes!" she demanded impatiently.

I slowly opened my eyes to view the transformation. My dark brown hair gently rested on my shoulders, and layers of bangs softened my heart shaped face. I found myself smiling.

"I like it," I admitted. She hadn't put much make-up on, to my relief—just a slight shimmer on my lids and hint of pink to my cheeks, which wouldn't be needed if I was anywhere near Evan.

"Here," Sara said handing me a tube of lip gloss and mascara. "I thought it would be easier if you put these on yourself. I'm going to get ready in the bathroom, I'll be right back."

While Sara was drying and styling her hair, I sat on one of the beds and flipped through the latest women's magazine with articles on how to be more aggressive and the fastest way to lose ten pounds. When she glided back into the room, she radiated with loose curls of shiny red hair and just enough makeup to show off her blue eyes and pouty red lips. It deflated me a little.

"What's wrong?" Sara asked, reacting to my sunken shoulders.

"Are you sure you want me to go with you? I don't want it to be awkward for you having me tagging along when I know everyone will want to talk to you."

She scowled and threw a pillow at me. "Shut up. Of course I want you to go with me. Why should this be any different than any other day? If people talk to me, and I want to talk to them, I will. It's never bothered you before."

I looked at the floor, recognizing my nerves were getting the better of me – and it really had nothing to do with Sara's popularity. "You're right. Sorry, I'm just getting a little paranoid about going."

"We'll have fun, I promise." Sara flashed the whites of her teeth from between her shiny red lips. She went back into her closet and threw something out in my direction. "This white scarf goes perfectly with that sweater, and it will keep you warm, so you won't miss not having a jacket."

"Thanks." I grabbed the fuzzy scarf and wrapped it around my neck as I stood in front of the mirror. Sara was right—I did look different.

"This is going to be the best night," Sara reassured me when we got into her car to drive to the school. She was so excited she could barely contain her energy, which made me smile. I made an effort to let go of the anxiety that'd been building. I could do this. I could be social. Okay, let's not go that far. I would not be completely pathetic – that sounded better. Who was I kidding?

5. FADING

WHEN WE PULLED IN, THE PARKING LOT WAS FILLING WITH CARS, AND spectators were making their way to the ticket booth in a steady drove. A jolt of panic rushed through my body. I knew I was being ridiculous—this was only a high school football game—but I might as well have been walking to school naked. Sara jumped out of the car and yelled to a group of girls who were lost in a giggling conversation while heading toward the stadium.

"Sara!" they screamed in unison and ran to her, receiving her with hugs and gleeful babble. I followed behind her, suddenly feeling overly exposed in the fitted sweater—the fashionable scarf doing little to conceal the low neckline.

"Emma?!" Jill Patterson exclaimed in shock. Everyone turned to gawk at me. The fire ignited in my cheeks. I knew the artificial color would be unnecessary.

I forced a smile with my lips pressed together and waved casually.

"Wow, you look great," another girl declared in disbelief. The rest of the girls offered similar gushing compliments.

"Thanks," I mumbled, wishing I was invisible again.

Sara linked her arm through mine and led us to the ticket booth with a prideful smile. I took another deep breath and prepared myself for whatever the night presented. Unfortunately, there were many more reactions of astonishment and gawking

There was a lot of stares, whispers, and comments about my presence and transformation, but not a lot of conversation. It was evident no one knew what to say to me any more than I knew what to say to them. So I sunk into the metal bleachers and engrossed myself in the football game. Sara cheered for Jason and watched as much as she was allowed. She was often drawn away by just about everyone passing by, including some of the parents who were there to support the local high school football team or their son who was on the field—or bench. I couldn't get over how many people she knew and how effortlessly she'd come up with a witty remark or a kind sentiment. I should've taken notes.

During the third quarter, I decided to get a hot chocolate while Sara walked off toward the school with Jill and Casey to use the restroom, talking and giggling about something. While I waited in line, I scuffed the ground with my foot, lost in the booming voice of the announcer calling the last play as Weslyn continued to move the ball down the field.

"Not a bad game, huh?" His voice carried through the cheering crowd and the deep voice of the announcer. I turned to find Evan behind me, holding his camera.

"No, it's a pretty good game," I replied, struggling to find my voice. The sweater suddenly felt stifling as my cheeks set aglow once again, ignited by the frenzied beating in my chest. "Are you covering the game for the paper?" As soon as I said it, I knew it was a dumb thing to say. Of course he was covering the game—I assigned him the coverage!

"Yeah," he said holding up his camera, dismissing my ignorance. "I thought I heard you didn't go to the games?"

"I'm staying over Sara's tonight," I answered, thinking that would be enough of an explanation for him as it was for everyone else. But he appeared confused. I paused to recall the answer Sara had prepared.

"I'm usually so busy with school and everything that I don't get out much. It worked out that I could tonight."

The line continued to move forward, I stepped up. Evan followed.

"Oh," he replied. I could tell he still wasn't satisfied with my answer. "Are you and Sara going to the party after the game?"

"I think so," I said tentatively. "Are you?"

"Yeah. I'm supposed to follow some of the guys from the soccer team over there."

I nodded, not knowing what else to say. I turned back toward the counter, thinking this would give him the opportunity to escape and go back to taking pictures of the game. I remained facing forward, not looking back to see if he'd walked away. I ordered a hot chocolate and turned to find him still waiting for me.

"Do you want to walk around with me while I take a few more pictures?" My heart stopped again. I wished it would decide if it was going to pound out of my chest or fall out. The stopping and starting was getting to be a bit much.

"Sure," I heard my mouth say, before my brain registered what I'd agreed to do. He smiled, and my heart took off beating at its exhaustive pace again.

"So, you've decided to talk to me," Evan observed, looking at the ground as he walked next to me.

"I shouldn't. But, it's only a matter of time before you see that I'm not that interesting, and you'll let me fade into the background like everyone else."

He laughed and studied me, uncertain if I was serious. I was bewildered by his reaction.

He drew his eyebrows together with a smile and said, "I actually think you've become more interesting now that you've decided to talk to me, whether you *should* or not." I groaned. He smiled bigger and added, "Besides, I don't think it's possible for you to fade. Well, at least not in that sweater."

All of the blood in my body rushed to my face. "It's Sara's sweater," I confessed, looking at the ground to conceal the drastic color change.

"I like it," he admitted. "It's a good color on you." Maybe talking to him wasn't such a good idea after all. This was way more than I bargained for. What was I supposed to do with a comment like that? I took a sip of my hot chocolate, and sucked air between my teeth as the scalding liquid soaked into my tongue.

"Too hot?" he observed.

"Yeah – I don't think I'll be able to taste anything for a week."

He smiled again. I decided my heart had been tortured enough by his smile and stared back at the ground.

"I have a bottle of water in my bag, by the team's bench, if you want."

"No, that's okay, thanks. The damage is done." Before I knew it, we had circled back around and were walking in front of the bleachers where the cheerleaders encouraged the crowd to spell "Weslyn". I glanced up into the stands to locate Sara. She waved to me and pointed to Evan with her mouth open in disbelief. I shrugged in return, turning away before he noticed.

"Have you met many people yet?" I asked, trying to sound casual. It occurred to me that maybe he kept harassing me because he didn't know anyone else. Why he chose me was another mystery.

"Actually, I have," he answered sincerely, to my dismay. "It helps to be on the soccer team and involved with the paper. It gives me an excuse to talk to people. Someone's always eager to fill me in on who's who. That's how I learned more about you – which was harder than I thought it was going to be."

Before I could question what he found out, he continued with, "So you're name's actually Emily, huh?"

I nodded with a slight shrug.

"Then how come everyone calls you Emma?"

It had been awhile since anyone needed this explanation, but I found myself being more honest than I had with the others. "My dad used to call me Emma."

And I left it at that, and so did he.

We'd passed the bleachers and were standing in their shadows along the track. The cheering and announcing drifted away with the quickening of my pulse as panic raced through my body. I needed to know what he'd found out about me but was afraid to know at the same.

Unable to stop myself, I finally asked, "What else could you have possibly learned about me?"

He smirked and replied, "Besides the obvious – your perfect GPA, involved in three varsity sports, and all of that?"

"Yes, besides that." I held my breath. No one besides Sara knew about my life, right? There was no way he could know. Then why was I so paranoid?

"Well, you intimidate most of the guys in the school, so you never get asked out. The girls think you're stuck up and that's why your only friend is the most popular girl in school. It's assumed that no one else is good enough for you." My eyes stretched wide as he continued. "Your teachers feel bad for you. They think that you put too much pressure on yourself to be perfect and are missing out on what high school's all about. And your coach thinks he's lucky to have you, and is confident the team's a shoe-in for state champions this year as long as you don't get injured."

43

He became serious, noticing the awed look on my face. "But you've only been here a week," I whispered. "People actually told you this?"

Evan paused in confusion before he asked, "You didn't know any of this?" I could only stare at him. "I figured the reason you keep to yourself was because you were so confident, and you didn't care what anyone thought of you. You really had no idea what they say about you?"

I shook my head. "Honestly, I never gave it much thought because it wasn't important to me. I just need to get through high school."

"Why?" he asked slowly.

It was the question I couldn't answer, and the reason I shouldn't talk to him. I was saved from having to lie when the crowd erupted as the announcer declared a touchdown for Weslyn. I looked up at the scoreboard to see Weslyn's numbers change to 28, as the visitor's remained 14. The clock held steady with less than two minutes remaining in the fourth quarter.

"I should go find Sara," I said. "I'll see you later." I walked off before he could respond. There was so much to take in, and I didn't know how to absorb it all.

I located Sara along the sidelines, behind the rope that separated the field from the track.

"There you are!" she exclaimed. "Did you see Jason run in that last touchdown?"

"I didn't have a good view," I confessed. She clapped and yelled for the defense to stop the ball.

Then she pulled me aside, away from the crowd. "First," she said intently, "you are going to repeat every word of the conversation you had with Evan before we go to sleep tonight. Everyone's been talking about you two. I think half the school already assumes you're dating." My mouth dropped open.

"I know, it's stupid," Sara huffed with a shrug. "No one's ever seen you talk to someone besides me so much before. So most of the girls hate you, and the guys don't get what's so great about him. It's actually kinda funny."

"Great," I grumbled, rolling my eyes.

"Anyway, after the game, I'm going to wait outside the locker room for Jason to ask him to go to the party. Will you wait with me?"

"Sure, but I'm not waiting by the locker room door. That's all you. I'll sit on the stairs, okay?

"Okay," her eyes sparkled. "I can't believe I'm doing this!"

"He's going to say yes," I assured her.

"I hope so."

The air horn blared to declare the end of the game. There was a final cheer from the home crowd, congratulating the team for their win. The guys celebrated with chest bumps, and shoulder pad punches as they headed to the locker room.

Sara and I lingered while the crowd filed out through the gates. A few people asked if they'd see us at the party, to which Sara confirmed emphatically. Sara began silently wringing her hands as we got closer to the locker room. It was almost entertaining to see her this nervous. I'd never seen her so uncertain before.

"Wish me luck."

"I'll be right here," I promised, climbing the steps to observe from above.

Sara paced back and forth in front of the open double doors. Every so often she glanced up at me anxiously, and I'd return an encouraging smile. Before long, the guys started coming out of the locker room, showered, dressed, and carrying their gear bags over their shoulders. Most of them greeted Sara as they exited. It was evident a few of the guys hoped she was waiting for them, only to be disappointed when she'd respond with a casual greeting.

Then the damp golden hair of Jason Stark walked through the doors. I held my breath in anticipation as Sara said, "Hi Jason." Her voice didn't project its signature confidence, but her smile made up for it.

"Hi Sara," he responded. She'd definitely taken him by surprise. I listened intently.

A second passed—he was about to walk away when she finally asked, "Are you going to Scott's party?"

He was caught off-guard again. "Um, I don't know. I didn't drive, and I think Kyle wanted to go home."

"I could drive you if you want to go," Sara blurted. I gasped. What was she thinking? She only had two seats in her car. She glanced up at me quickly and cringed in apology.

"Ah, I guess I could do that," he agreed slowly. "You don't mind?"

"No," she answered casually. "I think you should celebrate your win."

"Okay, let me find Kyle to let him know. I'll meet you back here in a minute." When he walked into the locker room, Sara looked up at me, jumping up and down, and opened her mouth to release a silent scream. I laughed.

"It sounds like you'll need a ride to the party," the confidently charming voice concluded from the bottom of the stairs. Startled, I whipped around to discover Evan looking up at me.

"Sorry. I didn't mean to scare you."

"How do you do that?" I shot back.

"What?"

"Appear out of nowhere. I don't even hear you coming, and then all of a sudden, there you are," I accused.

"I guess you just don't pay attention. I think you're too busy attempting to fade." He chuckled. I scowled back in annoyance. "Well, do you want a ride to the party? Unless, you're going to sit on Jason Stark's lap?"

"You saw that? Do you usually go around eavesdropping?"

"I was taking victory shots after the game for the story and was heading to the locker room to get the rest of my things. I happened to notice they were having a moment, and waited here until it was over," he defended. "Besides, it looks like you're the one spying from up there."

"I'm being supportive," I snapped.

"Sure." He laughed. I clenched my jaw, trying to contain my aggravation.

"Well, do you want a ride?" Evan persisted.

"Fine," I said through my teeth. This only fueled his laughter before he walked toward the locker room. Why did he find me so funny? It annoyed the hell out of me. Then why was I driving to the party with him? Especially after hearing the latest gossip. If I showed up with him, it was only going to make it worse.

What did it really matter at this point? According to Evan, I wasn't well liked by just about everyone – so who cared what they said if I pulled up with Evan? But I did care. Not being liked was so much worse than being invisible. I took a deep breath and blew it away before it could hurt. I didn't need to know what people thought about me.

Before I could think too much more about it, Sara ran up the stairs. "Em, I am so sorry. It came out before I had time to think about it."

I could see Jason waiting for her by the locker room.

46

"It's okay. Evan's giving me a ride," I assured her.

"Evan? Really?" She narrowed her eyes and examined me.

"Don't worry, I'll see you there. Okay?" I forced a supportive smile to put her at ease.

"Okay," she said, still hesitating.

"Really. Go. I'll be right behind you." Sara gave me a quick excited hug and skipped back down the stairs to Jason. I watched them walk off toward her car, already in conversation.

"Ready?" Evan asked from the bottom of the stairs. I jumped again. "You honestly didn't see me coming from the locker room?"

"I guess I wasn't looking for you," I bit back.

"Let's go." He held out his hand, inviting me to take it. I creased my forehead in disbelief and walked past him. My rejection didn't seem to faze him as he walked alongside me to the parking lot. Nothing about Evan made sense. But for some reason, I kept finding myself with him.

He approached a black BMW sports car. I never really paid attention to the cars in the lot. Most of the residents in town could afford luxury cars to complement their ginormous houses — so of course their kids also drove cars to reflect their parents' success. Diversity in Weslyn came down to what you drove, not your ethnicity. So, I was a minority, especially since I didn't have a car. Forget that, I didn't even have a license.

Evan opened the passenger door for me, making me pause before I entered—not accustomed to the chivalrous gesture.

"Do you know where we're going?" he asked as he closed his door.

"No, don't you?"

He laughed. "I just moved here. I don't know where anyone lives. I thought you would at least know that much." I didn't respond.

Evan rolled down his window and hollered to a couple of guys he recognized, "Dave, you going to Scott's?" I couldn't hear the answer. "Do you mind if I follow you?"

Evan started the car and drove around to get behind the silver Land Rover.

"I didn't ruin your night, did I?"

"No," I answered casually, removing the scarf from around my neck. "But if you don't mind, I'd rather not talk about what other people think of me anymore, okay?"

"Never again," he promised. "So what are the parties like in Weslyn?"

I snickered. "Are you seriously asking me?"

"Okay," he said slowly. "Well, I guess we'll both find out tonight, won't we?" I didn't answer.

"If you want to do something else, I'm up for anything," he offered. I looked over at him, my lungs paralyzed.

"No, I want to go," I lied, almost choking on my words. "Besides, I'm meeting Sara there, remember?"

The Land Rover pulled away from the school, and we started down unfamiliar back roads. Evan turned on the radio. I wasn't expecting to recognize the voice of a female singer bellowing about how life sucked to the strums of a heavy guitar. He turned it down so he could talk. What else could he possibly have to say to me?

"Where did you live before you moved here?"

I hesitated to decide if I could tell him without backing myself into a corner.

"A small town outside of Boston," I replied.

"So you've always lived in New England?"

"Yup," I answered. "Where in California are you from?"

"San Francisco."

"Have you lived anywhere else besides here and San Francisco?"

Evan let out a short laugh. "We've moved just about every year since I can remember. My dad's a lawyer for a financial conglomerate, so his job takes him wherever he needs to be. I've lived in New York, different parts of California, Dallas, Miami, and even in several countries in Europe for a few years."

"Does it bother you?" I asked, relieved to be talking about him instead of me.

"It didn't used to. When I was younger, I'd get excited to go somewhere new. It didn't bother me when I left my friends behind because I was convinced that I'd see them again, eventually.

"Now that I'm in high school, it's not as easy. I made some decent friends when we moved to San Francisco two years ago, so it was harder to leave. Also, I don't want to keep fighting for a position on the sports teams. My parents offered to let me stay there to finish, but I decided to give Connecticut a chance. I can visit my friends during the breaks. If I don't like it here, I'll move back."

"By yourself?" I asked in amazement.

He smiled at my reaction. "I'm pretty much by myself as it is anyway. My father works all the time, and my mother is on every fundraising committee from here to San Diego, so she travels a lot."

"I'm sure Weslyn doesn't even compare to San Francisco. I'd choose California in a second."

"Weslyn's... interesting." He looked over at me with his infamous grin. I was glad it was dark so he couldn't see my scarlet cheeks. I looked out the window, still having no idea where we were.

"I hope you're paying attention to where we're going, because you have to figure out how to get yourself home," I warned.

"What, I'm not driving you back to Sara's?"

I wasn't sure if he was serious.

"This isn't a date," I blurted, knowing I shouldn't have said it as soon as it came out of my mouth.

"I know," he said, almost too quickly—instantly making me regret saying it. "I figured Sara would drive Jason home."

"Oh," I whispered. I felt like an idiot.

"I can offer to drive Jason so you and Sara can leave together," he suggested. "That may be easier for everyone."

We were quiet as we followed the Land Rover down a long driveway lined with cars, or it could have been a private road for as long as it was. Evan pulled behind the Land Rover and shut off the car.

"If this is going to be weird for you, I can go in by myself so no one knows we came here together," he offered. I must've really offended him.

"No, it's okay," I said softly. "I shouldn't have said that about it not being a date. I haven't been as filtered as I usually am, especially when I'm around you for some reason."

"I've noticed," Evan teased. "I never quite know how you're going to react. It's one of the things that makes you so interesting." His flawless smile reflected in the soft light of the driveway's lanterns.

"Let's get this over with," I said under my breath as I opened the car door.

"Do you really want to do this?" Evan asked as we approached the house.

I took a deep breath and replied, "Yes, it'll be fun." I forced a smile. It wasn't convincing, but he didn't call me out on it.

6. DIFFERENT PLANET

As we neared the front steps, we spotted Sara and Jason sitting off to the side, along the stone wall. They were deep in conversation with red cups in their hands, oblivious to the party happening inside.

"Hey, Sara," I said as I walked over, breaking her entranced attention.

"Emma, I was waiting for you!" she exclaimed as she jumped up from the wall and went to hug me, but restrained herself when she saw my body tense for the embrace.

Sensing Sara wasn't quite ready to give up her moment with Jason, I declared, "We're going in. Find me inside later."

"Okay." She replied with a beaming smile that could only mean that I wasn't going to see her for awhile.

I was so wrapped up in my anxiety that I didn't realize Evan had grabbed my hand upon entering the loud crowded space—not until he was leading me through the entanglement of bodies. I didn't pull it away as we squeezed through the bodies, in fear that I would be stranded if I let go. Wide-eyes followed me through the crowd—evidently, not everyone who was here was at the football game or had received the circulating texts.

The house was the typical huge estate that belonged in Weslyn, with an open floor plan that was conducive to throwing a large party. There were only two rooms in the front of the house that were encased with walls—the formal dining room, and another room with a large wooden door, which appeared to be locked.

We squeezed through to the back of the house where we found the kitchen. The island in the kitchen was lined with different colored liquor bottles and soda, ending with a large stack of red plastic cups next to a tap handle.

"Want something to drink?" Evan yelled, still holding my hand.

"Diet whatever's fine," I yelled back.

He left me standing on one side of the bar to get our drinks at the other end, instantly consumed by the crowd within the few feet it took to reach the sodas.

"Holy shit! Emma Thomas?!" I heard someone yell from across the room. I froze, afraid to look. His exclamation caught the attention of a few other people; they evidently were amongst the few who hadn't heard that I was at the party since they couldn't stop staring at me. I spotted a guy from my Chemistry class as he fought his way through the crowd, parting the bodies with his red cup.

"Hi, Ryan."

"I can't believe you're here!" he exclaimed, throwing his arms around me in a tight embrace with alcohol rolling off his breath. Great, he was drunk. I tensed, unable to react to his breach of my personal space until he finally let go.

"Wow, this is so great," he said with a ridiculous smile on his face. "I was hoping to see you tonight. I heard you were at the game. Do you want a drink?"

"Hey, Ryan." I heard Evan say from behind me. I turned toward him with a panicked expression, but he didn't pick up on it. Instead he handed me one of the cups he was holding.

"Evan!" Ryan hollered, in a volume too loud for how close we were standing to him. He put his arm around me and zealously pulled me toward him, making me spill my drink – he was oblivious. "Evan, you know Emma Thomas, right? She is the coolest person." I gave Evan my wide eyed look of despair—he raised his eyebrows, finally getting it.

"Yes, Ryan, I know Emma," he said, grabbing my hand, and pulling me carefully away from Ryan. "We actually came here together."

Ryan appeared confused and then shocked as he released me. "You did? Oh, man, I am so sorry. I had no idea."

"It's okay," Evan assured him. "We're going outside. We'll see you later." Evan turned toward the sliding doors that led to the deck.

It was a little less crowded and definitely quieter, leaving the music behind in the house. We found an empty section of railing and leaned our backs against it, watching the craziness inside.

"I'm sorry about that," Evan finally said, leaning on his forearm to face me. "I had no idea why you'd given me that look. I didn't know Ryan liked you."

"Neither did I," I confessed quietly. "Thanks for getting me out of there. I'm way out of my comfort zone with all of these people."

"Really?" Evan shot me a teasing smile. "I don't think I noticed when you could barely force yourself through the front door."

"Okay, so I'm here for Sara," I admitted with a sigh. "She's wanted to ask Jason Stark out since the beginning of the year, and this was the perfect opportunity. I'm here for moral support."

"It looks like Sara's doing just fine without you." Evan smirked. "I think you're the one needing the support."

I scowled up at him with a mocking smile. "Thanks a lot."

"Mathews!" a male voice yelled from the door exiting the house.

"Hi, Jake." Evan greeted the voice with a shake of his hand.

"It's good to see you," Jake stated. "No way, is that Emma Thomas?" I smiled awkwardly and nodded.

"Wait, did you come here together?" he asked, looking at Evan with a sly grin.

"I brought her here to meet up with Sara," Evan explained.

"Wow, I can't believe you're here." Jake shook his head while looking me over. "Can I get you something to drink?"

I raised my cup. "Thanks, I'm all set."

"Maybe I'll see you inside, and I can refill it for you," he said, flashing his teeth. I froze, trying to understand what was going on. I swore I was on a different planet. And on this planet, people noticed me, and some noticed me too much. I desperately wanted to be on the other side of the locked door of the room at the front of the house.

"Did you guys see the fire pit they have around the side of the house?"

"No," Evan replied.

"It's pretty cool, you should check it out," Jake encouraged. "I'll see you later." He winked at me before he turned away. I stood there, stunned.

"Did he really just wink at me?" I asked, completely astounded.

"I think he did," Evan confirmed with a small laugh.

"You're enjoying this, aren't you?" I suddenly realized. "I'm so glad I'm finding more ways to entertain you. This is horrifying for me. I don't think you quite get that."

Evan looked at my distraught face, straightening out his smile. "I'm sorry, you're right. I can tell you're not enjoying this. Let's go check out the fire pit; it's probably less crowded."

"Evan, you don't have to stay with me. You should go in the house and meet people. It looks like the entire junior and senior classes are here. I'll be fine." I tried to assure him with one of my forced smiles. He looked at me doubtingly. I really did have to work on faking it, didn't I?

"How about this—I'll walk down to the fire pit with you, and then I'll make a round inside the house before coming back to check on you?"

"Okay," I agreed reluctantly. As much as I hated the thought of being alone at this party, I wasn't going to ruin Evan's night by making him feel obligated to babysit me. I was used to being invisible, and I could sink into the shadows again – even on this planet.

The deck became more crowded as we moved toward the stairs that led to the backyard. Evan grabbed my hand to lead me through.

"Evan?!" an excited female voice exclaimed. Although he was still holding my hand, we were cut off by a person in-between us, so I couldn't see the owner of the overly excited voice. "I've been looking for you."

I squeezed through in time to find Halcy Spencer with her arms flung around Evan's neck, pulling him into her well-developed body. One hand was holding me and the other was holding his cup, so the embrace was not returned. An unwelcome heat turned in my stomach. I quickly shook off the insecurity and attempted to release his hand—but he held on tighter and pulled me closer.

Haley stepped back, keeping her hands on the back of his neck. "We were just going inside to get another drink. Join us." Her eyes met mine, then traced along my arm. Her eyes tightened when she realized that my hand ended in his.

"Oh," she said, quickly dropping her hands from his neck. "I didn't know you were here with someone." She eyed me up and down cynically.

"Sorry, Haley," Evan said sympathetically, "we were just heading down to the fire pit." He pulled me a little closer, wrapping his arm around me. My breathing stopped as I remained immobilized by his side.

"I guess I'll see you later then," Haley almost sulked. She flipped back her hair before strutting into the house, followed by the two aghast girls who'd been standing next to her.

Evan turned to face me, his hand still on my back, drawing me in so we could talk as people squeezed by us. It remained difficult to breathe while looking up at him, with my heart continuing to pound through my sweater.

"Still want to go to the fire pit?"

I nodded with wide eyes.

As he turned to head down the stairs, I missed his hand, and we were separated. In that brief second, I was aggressively pulled in the opposite direction, with the exclamation, "Emma Thomas! I heard you were here." The tug dragged me right into the large frame of Scott Kirkland.

"I can't believe you came to my party. This is the best night ever," he declared in slurred speech. Perfect—he wasn't just drunk, he was obliterated.

"Thanks for having me, Scott." I tried to step back from his strangling embrace. "It's a great party."

He peered down at me with his half closed eyes and breathed heavily in my face. "Would you go out with me?"

"Um... that's really nice of you." I struggled to find the words while pushing him away with a little more force. "But..." The panic rose in my stomach and spread into my chest. I started breathing faster as I remained trapped against him. I needed to get away from him, but he didn't show any signs of releasing me.

"Hey, Scott," Evan greeted Scott with an overly emphatic pat on the back. "This is a great party."

"Thanks, Evan," he slurred. "Evan, this is Emma Thomas." Scott captured me against his body with one arm. I had no idea he was so big, or strong, for that matter. I almost fit entirely under his arm. I looked up at Evan in despair, trying to squirm away—I wasn't making much headway.

"Yeah, I know," Evan began.

"Emma and I are going to go to homecoming together," Scott declared, interrupting Evan. "Right, Emma?"

I was finally able to back my way out from under his arm. My face was bright red, and my hair clung to my cheeks. He lifted his arm in confusion, searching for me.

Evan took my shaking hand and gently guided me next to him. I tried to regain my breath, overcome with the sudden need to sit down.

"Emma, I think Sara's looking for you." Evan scanned my face in concern. "Scott, we'll be right back."

Before Scott could respond, Evan held my hand tightly and led me down the stairs. My knees buckled slightly, but I recovered and kept my feet moving beneath me. We went around the corner, and I collapsed on the stone wall under the deck.

Evan crouched in front of me and looked up, trying to meet my eyes. "Are you okay? That was crazy. I'm sorry I lost you."

I took a deep breath and tried to will my hands to stop shaking. I couldn't understand why I was so worked up. Evan gingerly took my hands in his and looked at me intently, trying to get me to focus on him. I stared straight ahead, desperately needing to pull myself together. I barely noticed he was there.

There was something about the crowd, the smell of liquor rolling in the air swirled with cigarette smoke that transported me to another place—a place I could barely remember, but I had a feeling I didn't want to return. There was no space amongst the bodies. No space to breathe or move without being touched and jostled. The confinement and groping created a storm that erupted before I knew how to contain it. I shivered, not wanting to remember what was beginning to stir.

"Emma, look at me," he soothed. "Are you okay?"

I found his blue eyes and began to focus. My face became hot when I realized what I must have looked like to him. I tried to stand up, and he backed up to give me space, but my legs weren't as ready as my mind. I wobbled—he caught me by my elbows and pulled me into him to steady me.

I felt his breath against my face when he peered down to examine me. "Maybe you should sit down again." But he didn't move to let me go.

My pulse quickened with the warmth of his body against me as my hands rested on the hard curves of his chest. I looked up at him, but he was too close. I panicked and backed away. He let me go easily.

We stood still for a second, until I finally said without looking up at him, "I'm fine, really." I was mortified as my quivering body betrayed me. I must have appeared so pathetic.

"This was probably not the best first party for you," Evan said gently. "Maybe you should try something with about ten people before you jump to a hundred."

I pressed my lips into a smile and shrugged. He offered a warm smile in return.

"Do you want to leave?"

"No, you stay," I encouraged, determined to regain my composure. "I'm fine. I'm going to sit by the fire."

We continued to walk around the corner, where a cut stone patio lay next to the dark silhouette of trees along the perimeter of the property. In the center sat a stone wall encasing a blazing fire. There were two dozen chairs around the fire, but only half were occupied. I sat down in a chair on the opposite side of the small group, who were talking and giggling in low voices.

"Evan," I pleaded, "go have fun. I'll wait here for Sara. Thank you for bailing me out tonight, but I can take care of myself. I swear." His delving eyes tried to read my face, making me wish I could disappear and erase the whole night. I stared into the fire, unable to bare his silent inquisition.

"I'll be right back," he assured me. "I'll find Sara and get us something to drink, okay?" The careful tone of his voice fueled my embarrassment. I still couldn't look at him as he walked toward the house. I couldn't believe I let him see me like this, unable to fend for myself. I fumed in disgust at my vulnerability. I didn't want Evan to think I needed protecting. I pulled back my torment and let the numb blanket envelop me, pushing away the stirred memories, the noise of the crowd, and the trembling that still lay beneath the surface. I stared at the flames licking at the darkness and everything was lost as I sank deeper into nothingness.

"You know it's raining, right?" Evan asked from the seat next to me. I looked around, snapping back from my empty place. I was the only one sitting in front of the dwindling flames. A steady, cold rain pasted my hair to my face, causing me to shiver. Evan stared at the few defiant flames that remained, ignoring the rain while holding his black camera case.

"Are you going to stop talking to me?" Evan asked quietly.

A smile spread across my face, turning my head toward him. "No." I started to laugh.

"What?!" he asked, surprised by my reaction. A half-smile crept across his face as he tried to get the joke.

"I get accosted by a drunken bear and completely freak out, humiliating myself, and you're afraid I'm not going to talk to *you*?!" I laughed again.

Evan smiled lightly, still not getting the humor in my explanation.

"Why were you humiliated?" Serious once again.

I shrugged—hugging my knees into my chest, trying to suppress the shivering. I wasn't sure if I wanted to explain my vulnerability to him. He waited patiently for me to find the words. I took a deep breath.

"I saw the way you looked at me, and I know how I must have come across, reacting like that." I looked down. "I hate that you keep seeing me at my worst. This really isn't me."

"Emma!" Sara hollered from under the deck before Evan could answer. "You're crazy. Get out of the rain!"

I suddenly realized I was wearing Sara's cashmere sweater and jumped up to join her.

"Sara, I am so sorry. I completely forgot I had your sweater on."

"I don't care about the sweater," she replied. "What are you guys doing out there? You must be freezing." Evan joined us under the deck.

"Getting some fresh air," Evan answered with a smile. He was rubbing his arms, registering the cold.

"You're a bad influence on her," Sara scowled at Evan, which turned into a smile. She wasn't good at being mad—probably as bad at it as I was at delivering my forced smiles.

"Ready to go?" she asked me.

"Where's Jason?" I asked, not sure if I should be concerned.

"He rode home with one of the football players," she explained with a twinkle in her eye. I knew I was going to get a good story in the car.

"Let's walk around the house," I suggested. "I'd rather not go back inside."

We ran to Sara's car, trying to avoid being in the rain as much as we could. When we got in, Sara started the engine and turned on the heat full blast. Evan leaned against my door, remaining in the rain while waiting for me to roll down the window.

He bent down to peer in through the opening. The water ran down his artistically structured face, dripping off the tip of his nose over his shivering blue lips. My breath escaped me as I took in his steel blue eyes.

"Can I call you tomorrow?"

"You can't actually," I grimaced. He looked confused. "It's complicated. I don't exactly have phone privileges." I hated to say it out loud, but I didn't want him to think I was rejecting him.

The questioning look didn't quite leave his eyes, but he tried to respond understandingly, "Okay, then I'll see you Monday."

"Yeah, Monday."

He lingered a second too long, and I couldn't breathe again.

"Good night," I finally exhaled. "Get out of the rain before you freeze to death." He stood up and casually raised his hand to wave as I rolled up the window. He ran back into the house.

"No way! Was he going to kiss you?" Sara shrieked, breaking my lingering stare. "Emma, I swear if I wasn't in the car, he would have kissed you."

"No, he wouldn't have," I dismissed her. My heart collapsed at the thought of Evan leaning in just a little closer. I shook it off.

"You need to share details," she demanded as we pulled onto the road.

"You first," I insisted.

Sara didn't hesitate. The entire ride home, she gushed about her time with Jason.

It was dark inside her house when we walked in.

"I think we beat my parents home."

"What time is it?" I asked, having no idea how much time had passed since we left the house earlier in the evening.

"Eleven thirty."

It was earlier than I thought. That meant I was only at the party for a little over an hour. It seemed so much longer. But now that I looked back at it, I didn't really do much. Evan and I didn't have a real conversation the whole time we were there. I was too busy trying to avoid being grappled by drunken idiots.

I got ready for bed and scrubbed at the remaining make-up that the rain hadn't already washed away. If I were caught wearing makeup, I would probably need it to hide what Carol would do to me if she saw any traces of it.

Last year, Sara had given me a few samples of lipsticks she didn't want. I tried them on, but ended up wiping the colors off with a tissue. When I returned from practice that evening, Carol confronted me with the tissues removed from the bathroom trash with accusations that I was trying to sneak around wearing make-up behind her back after she had already told me it wasn't allowed. She called me a whore and other derogatory names as she squeezed my cheeks together so tightly in her hand that my teeth ground into the soft tissue until they bled.

So I'd rather have raw skin from scrubbing off the evidence than to face a second round over the make-up issue.

As we lay in the dark, Sara insisted, "You have to tell me what happened with you and Evan tonight."

I had hoped that Sara would be so lost in her night with Jason that she'd forget all about me, and we could avoid this conversation. No such luck.

I stared into the darkness above me, not certain where to begin.

"I talked to him," I confessed. I was quiet for a moment.

"Please don't make me drag this out of you."

"I found out he's from San Francisco and that he may move back if he doesn't like it here." I added, "I can only hope."

"What do you mean?" She sounded confused. "It looked like you guys really connected from where I was sitting—you know, his almost kissing you." My cheeks warmed at the mention of the close proximity of his face to mine when we said good night.

"Sara, I can't do this," my voice grew stronger. "I barely talked to him. He spent most of the night rescuing me from drunken hormonal gorillas. It was pretty pathetic.

"I don't want to like him. I don't want there to be anymore moments where he may kiss me. I need to stay away from him."

"I am so confused," Sara confessed. "I thought we had a plan. And who was hitting on you? Now I feel bad that *I* wasn't there."

"Don't," I said with an edge to my voice. "That's just it. I don't want to be protected or looked after. I should be so much stronger than to need you or Evan Mathews to stand up for me. I don't know how I'm going to be able to look at him on Monday."

"That's not what I meant," Sara said quietly. I heard the hurt in her voice. "I know you don't want me protecting you, you've made that clear way before tonight. But I feel bad because I knew how hard tonight was going to be for you, and from the sounds of it, it was pretty horrible. I should've been there as your friend, that's all."

"But it shouldn't be horrible, Sara. It was just a stupid party, and I freaked. I could barely function." I sighed in frustration. I was glad it was dark so she couldn't see the tears welling in my eyes. I clenched my jaw and swallowed the lump in my throat. I took a calming breath to be rid of the dizzying emotion, while wiping my cheeks dry. Safe again, I turned away from Sara.

"I'm sorry, Sara," I said softly. "It's been a long day, and I'm being ridiculous. We have to get up early so I can get home to do my chores. Let's just get some sleep, okay?"

"Okay," she whispered.

I was afraid that sleep wouldn't come easily, but with all that my psyche had fought throughout the day, I was exhausted.

7. REPERCUSSIONS

IT TOOK ME A FEW BLINKS TO REMEMBER WHERE I WAS WHEN I WOKE up in the queen bed, with the sunlight beaming behind the shaded skylights. I rolled over to find Sara in the bed across from me, still asleep with the down comforter pulled up around her. She groaned as the alarm beeped to wake us so that I could get home in time to do my weekend chores.

She grumbled, flopping her hand down on the snooze button. She revealed her blue eyes reluctantly, peering over at me with her head still on her pillow. "Hey."

"Sorry you have to get up so early," I offered, with my head propped up by my elbow.

"I know how it is," she replied with stretched arms above her head. "Em, I'm really sorry I bailed on you last night."

I shrugged, not wanting to think about it. "It's not like I'll be going to another party any time soon."

"True. So, Evan, huh? This is really happening, isn't it?" Sara ran her fingers through her long hair as she sat up in the bed, propping a pillow behind her.

"Not really," I contradicted. "I mean, I'm talking to him, or was. Who knows what he'll think of me after last night."

"I'm pretty sure he's still interested. Please don't give up on him. I don't know all that happened last night, but I still think he's good for you. Give him a chance. Try to be friends, or at least use him as an emotional punching bag. He seems to be able to handle the backlashes

61

that you can't unleash on anyone else." She said it like being reprimanded by me was a privilege. She studied my face with a soft smile to make sure I understood.

I returned a half smile, trying to digest her words.

Knowing I wasn't going to say anything, she flipped back the covers and swung her feet to the floor. "Well let's get you back to hell before the devil realizes you're not home." It would have been funny, except that it was too close to the truth for me to laugh.

When I walked in the back door, the house was strangely quiet. With George's truck missing from the driveway, I guessed he and the kids were getting the Saturday morning donuts and coffee. That meant she was here, somewhere—my stomach dropped. I focused on getting to my room without having to see her.

Just outside my door, I was abruptly stopped in my tracks with a sharp pain shrieking through my head. I winced as her claw dug deeper into the fistful of my hair, tugging my head back so that my neck snapped awkwardly, forced to face the ceiling. She hissed in my ear, "Did you think I wouldn't find out that you went out last night? What did you do, screw the entire football team?"

With an unexpected amount of force, she thrust my head forward without giving me a second to resist. The front of my skull collided with the doorframe. A thunderous bolt shot through my head as the hall blurred around me. Black dots filled my eyes as I attempted to focus. Before I could find center, her vise grip tore the hair from my scalp and drove my head into the hard wood again. The corner of the frame connected with the left side of my forehead. The stinging burn above my eye gave way to a flow of warmth that ran down my cheek.

"I regret every second you're in my house," Carol growled with contempt. "You're a worthless pathetic tramp, and if it wasn't for your uncle, I would have shut the door in your face when your drunken mother abandoned you. It says a lot when *she* can't even stand you." I slid down the wall, collapsing on the floor with my bags by my side. Something landed on my knees. I made out my navy blue soccer jersey from Thursday's game crumpled on my lap.

"Clean yourself up before they see you, and get rid of the stench in the basement. You'd better be done with your chores and out of my sight by the time I get back from grocery shopping," she threatened before disappearing.

I heard the truck pull into the driveway and the doors closing, followed by the excited voices nearing the back door. I didn't want them to see me either, so I clumsily tossed my bags through the open door of my room and pushed myself to my feet. I stumbled into the bathroom with the support of the wall, as I heard Leyla announce, "Mom, we have donuts!"

I pressed the shirt against the left side of my head, trying to stop the bleeding as the cut pulsed under my hand. My head pounded as I tried to regain control of my balance. The sensation that I was about to lose consciousness seized me. I gripped the sink, fighting to focus, as I took deep even breaths. A minute passed before I was able to stand up straight. The dizziness subsided but the claw of pain dug into my head.

I slowly let up pressure. The side of my face was covered with blood that ran down my neck, seeping into the collar of my turtleneck. I couldn't quite tell where the opening was. I took a few tissues and exchanged them with the shirt so I could run the shirt under cold water.

I wiped the drying blood from my face with the damp jersey and revealed the small incision above my left eyebrow. It wasn't very big, but it didn't want to stop bleeding. I applied more pressure with the shirt as I searched in the medicine cabinet for bandages. I pulled out two butterfly bandages and applied them to the gash, pulling the sides together so it could heal—hopefully leaving a minimal scar.

In the center of my forehead, along my hair line, was a large lump that was already turning purple. I couldn't bring myself to touch it – the unwavering pain was making my eyes water. I knew I needed to put ice on it but couldn't figure out how to do that without being seen.

I leaned against the wall across from the mirror and closed my eyes. I couldn't hold back the tears that rolled down my cheeks. I struggled to maintain a steady breath so I wouldn't cave in to the full out cry that the lump in my throat yearned for. The images of what happened flashed through my head. I didn't hear her come up behind me. She was obviously waiting for me.

As much I tried to be invisible, she was inescapable and her wrath was crushing. I wanted nothing more than to destroy her as I stared into the mirror at my seeping eyes, aglow with fury.

I looked down at the bloody jersey in my hand. Her blitz attack had nothing to do with the football game, or my dirty laundry; it had everything to do with me. I knew all I had to do was make one phone call, or walk into the school psychologist's office and utter one sentence, and this would all be over.

63

That's when I heard the squeal of laughter in the kitchen from Leyla, accompanied by a chuckle from Jack as she said something to make them laugh. It would be over for them too, but in a way that would damage them forever. I couldn't ruin their lives. Carol and George truly loved them, and I wouldn't take them from their parents. I swallowed hard, determined to compose myself, but the tears refused to stop.

I opened the cabinets under the sink and pulled out the cleaning supplies; with my lips quivering and hands shaking, I scrubbed the tub, swallowing against the sobs. The built up pressure from keeping the cries contained infuriated the pain in my head. My whole body ached.

I was back to my numb, emotionless state by the time I finished cleaning the sink. I blankly stared at the water running down the drain, rinsing away the chemicals and blood. My raging thoughts were quiet.

"I'll be back in a couple of hours," I heard Carol announce, closing the door behind her. The kids were watching TV in the living room. I couldn't hear George.

I looked at myself in the mirror and mindlessly wiped the remaining dried blood from around the bandages before I opened the bathroom door. I stepped into the hall to retrieve the broom and mop from the hall closet when George rounded the corner. He stopped and his eyes widened. But his shocked expression quickly dissolved.

"Bump your head?" he asked casually.

"That's what I get for walking while reading," I droned, knowing he would convince himself of anything except for the truth.

"You should put some ice on it," he recommended.

"Mmm," I agreed and walked back into the bathroom to complete my task.

After my chores were completed, I returned to my room to find a bag of ice waiting for me on my desk.

I gently put the bag of ice on the lump and watched Jack and Leyla chase after George in the backyard through my window – sworn to silence in my hell.

I awoke in a panic around midnight. I stayed pressed to my pillow, my eyes fervently searching the room. I was breathing heavily; my shirt was damp with sweat. I tried to detach myself from the nightmare that had awoken me. It was hard to push away the urgency of the dream that had me pinned beneath the water, drowning. I took in a deep breath, confirming that I was still alive as the air passed easily through my lungs. They weren't burning for oxygen as they had been in my dream. I had a hard time falling asleep after that. Sleep finally found me just before the sun rose.

I was awoken by a hard knock on the door. "Are you going to sleep all day?" the voice barked from the other side.

"I'm up," I mustered in a rasp, hoping she wouldn't come in. I looked at the digital clock next to my bed that read *8:30*. I knew I had to take a shower before nine o'clock or do without. I slowly sat up with the throbbing pain, a reminder of my living nightmare. I needed to find a way to ice it again so the lump would be gone by the time I went to school tomorrow. I knew there was nothing I could do about the dark purple bruise. Thankfully the area around the cut wasn't bruised. Sara's new hairstyle was going to come in handy with covering up most of it.

I gathered my clothes together and slipped into the bathroom without being seen. Washing my hair was more painful than I anticipated. I hadn't realized how sore the back of my head was from her iron grip of my hair. I felt blood scabbed over where some of the hair had been forcefully removed. I was so focused on the contusion that the back of my head didn't register until now. I gingerly used my fingertips to rub the shampoo into the front of my hair, but it still felt like a form of torture. I turned off the water before *the knock* and proceeded to dry off and get dressed. After gently drying my hair with a towel, I discovered that brushing my hair was worse than washing it. Tears filled my eyes with each stroke of the brush. There was no way I was going to be able to blow it dry. Reluctantly, I made the decision not to wash my hair the next day despite how atrocious I knew it would look after sleeping on it. I wasn't willing to go through the pain again.

"Does she know about this afternoon?" I heard Carol ask George from the kitchen as I sat at my desk engrossed in my Trigonometry homework.

"Yeah, I told her yesterday," he replied. "She's going to the library and will be back for dinner."

"And you believe she's going to the library?" she asked doubtingly.

"Why wouldn't she?" he questioned.

I didn't hear a response from Carol.

"I'll be back around one," she finally said. Then the back door opened and closed.

"Want to go outside and play with Emma?" George asked the kids.

65

"Yeah," they screamed in unison.

"Emma," George bellowed through the closed door, "do you mind taking the kids outside?"

"Be right there." I grabbed my fleece jacket and was greeted warmly by jumping, cheering kids.

The rest of my day was actually fairly pleasant. I kicked the soccer ball around in the postage stamp backyard with Leyla and Jack. George and Carols' house was modest, puny compared to Sara's. The section of town we lived in was typical middle America, but compared to the Pleasantville of the rest of Weslyn, it might as well have been the other side of the tracks.

I rode my bike to the library while George and Carol took the kids to the movies. I spent the remainder of the afternoon hidden in the stacks completing my assignments or in the computer room typing my English paper. I avoided human interaction at all cost, fearful of the reaction I'd receive at the sight of me. I finished with a few minutes to spare before I had to start home, so I called Sara on the pay phone.

"Hi!" she exclaimed, a little too overzealous for someone I had just seen the day before. "How are you calling me?"

"I'm at the library, on the pay phone."

"Oh! I'll be right there."

"No," I blurted before she could hang up the phone. "I'm leaving in a minute, but I wanted to prepare you for when you pick me up tomorrow."

"What happened?" Sara asked with concern, almost panic.

"I'm okay," I calmly assured her, trying to downplay her reaction. "I *fell* and hit my head, so I have a bandage and a little bruise. It's really no big deal."

"Emma! What did she do to you?!" Sara yelled with a mix of fear and anger in her voice.

"Nothing, Sara," I corrected. "I *fell*."

"Sure you did," she said quietly. "Are you really okay?"

"Yeah, I'm okay. I have to go, but I'll see you in the morning."

"Okay," Sara replied reluctantly, before I hung up the phone.

8. BAD LUCK

I WOKE UP TO THE SAME ROUTINE AS ANY OTHER MORNING, UNTIL I looked in the mirror – reminded that there was nothing routine about my life. I took in my nightmare of a hairstyle and knew there was no way I could get away with not washing and drying it. I was already going to draw attention—I didn't need to look like I'd slept on the streets as well.

My head still throbbed but the golf ball had significantly reduced to being almost flush with my forehead. I was able to tolerate showering and brushing my hair, and my eyes only watered slightly when I dried it. Maybe I would be able to survive today after all.

Then I saw Sara's dropped jaw when I slid into the car. Sara didn't say anything to me, and I couldn't read her expression with her oversized sunglasses covering most of her face. She handed me a bottle of water and aspirin. Then again, maybe today was going to be one of the longest days of my life.

"Thank you," I said as I dumped a couple pills in my hand and swallowed them down with several large gulps of water. I tried to act natural, despite the tension.

She barely glanced at me. I flipped the visor down to examine my cover-up in the mirror, trying to figure out what was making her so withdrawn. My bangs were swept across my forehead to conceal my bruise, and the bandages were barely noticeable under the fan of hair.

"Okay," I demanded. "Why aren't you talking or looking at me?"

"Emma," she breathed in exasperation, "look at you!"

"What?" I defended, glancing back up at the mirror. "I think I did a pretty good job of covering it up."

"That's what I mean." Her voice was shaky. It sounded like she was going to cry. "You should never have to cover anything up. I know you won't tell me what happened, but I know you didn't *fall*. Will you at least tell me what it was about?"

"What does it matter?" My voice was small, not anticipating the strength of her reaction. I wasn't expecting her to act like nothing happened, but I didn't want her to cry.

"It matters to me," she choked. I watched her blot her eyes with a tissue under her glasses.

"Sara, please don't cry," I pleaded. "I'm okay, I swear."

"How can you be okay with this? You aren't even angry."

"I've had the weekend to get past it," I admitted. "Besides, I don't want to be angry. I don't want to let her get to me. I'm not okay with this," I said pointing to my head, "but what other choice do I have? I'll deal with it. So please don't cry. You're making me feel horrible."

"Sorry," she murmured.

We pulled into the parking lot, and she slid off her glasses, blotting her eyes while looking in the rearview mirror.

"I'm okay," she breathed, trying to produce a smile.

"How bad does it look? Be honest."

"You actually did a decent job hiding it," she admitted. "I'm having a hard time because I know the truth." And then again, she didn't know the half of it.

"If anyone says anything, because I know they will, tell them I slipped on the wet floor and hit my head on the coffee table." She rolled her eyes at my lie.

"What, do you have a better one?" I countered.

"No," she sighed. "Keep the aspirin. I know you'll need them."

"Ready?" I asked tentatively. I didn't like seeing Sara upset, especially over me. The anger and sadness were in complete contrast to her personality. It was uncomfortable to witness.

She released a heavy breath and nodded.

I received a few questions about my injury from some of my soccer teammates and other brave gossipers, but most people just stared. I should've been used to the stares after Friday's disaster. I wished I invisible once again—or at least ignorant of the gossip that was always happening around me.

I found my way to English class without having to explain my *fall* to more than two or three more people. I sat in my usual seat, pulling out my paper to pass in.

"Does it still hurt?" Evan asked from the chair next to mine. At that time, Brenda Pierce approached the seat she'd been sitting in since the first day of class and scowled to see it occupied. He smiled politely and shrugged.

"Well, there's one person who's not going to like you," I said wryly, trying to avoid the question.

"She'll get over it," Evan stated with little interest. "So, do you still have a headache?"

I drew my eyebrows together and reluctantly admitted, "I took some aspirin this morning. So, it's better, as long as I don't turn my head too quickly."

"That's good," he said casually. Everyone else had asked what happened; no one bothered with how I was feeling—until Evan.

"How was the rest of your weekend?" Evan whispered.

"Okay," I answered without looking over at him.

Ms. Abbott began with the class discussion, handing out our newest reading assignment after we passed in our papers. She also handed us a short story which she allowed us to begin reading in class after she'd given us our writing assignment.

"Are we talking, or not?" Evan whispered when Ms. Abbott stepped out of the room.

"We are," I glanced at him, confused. "Why?"

"I can never figure you out. I want to make sure I'm on the same page today."

"I'm not much of a talker," I confessed, turning back to our assigned reading.

"I know." His answer drew my attention—he had that amused grin spread across his lips.

I wasn't in the mood to inquire about his antagonizing grin and didn't give him another glance for the remainder of class. I wasn't allowing myself to be dragged into the mystery that was Evan Mathews, not today. I just wanted to get through the day with as little attention paid to me as possible. I wished it could have been that easy.

Evan escorted me to Ms. Mier's Art class. He didn't try to talk to me. But he'd inspect me with a concerned flip of his eyes every so often as I walked blankly through the halls, not looking at him or anyone else. I had to sever my emotional cord to escape the anger and shame that silently slithered through my head, disconnecting myself from the stares and whispers that followed me down the hall.

"Today you are going to take a walk around the school property and snap pictures of scenes that inspire you for the calendar entry next month," Ms. Mier announced. "The final pieces will be displayed along the wall of the main entrance where the students and faculty can view them. A vote will decide the twelve pieces to make the calendar. The artistic creation that has the most votes will also be the cover of the calendar. Does anyone have any questions?"

The class was silent. Ms. Mier asked a couple of students to pass out the cameras from the storage cabinet.

"Are you submitting an entry?" I asked Evan, who was standing behind me with his own camera in his hands. I glanced back to catch him raise his eyebrows, surprised to hear my voice.

"I'll submit a photograph."

"Please meet back in the class in forty minutes to return the cameras," Ms. Mier instructed.

The class emptied into the halls, heading toward the stairs that led to the back of the school. I opted to take the side stairs that let out at the football field and tennis courts.

"Do you mind if I come with you?" Evan asked from the top of the stairs. I looked up at him from the middle of my descent and shrugged with indifference. Evan followed me in silence.

When we exited, the cool air blew against my face. The refreshing breeze sent a chill through me, waking me from my stupor. I observed the brilliant colors of the foliage and proceeded toward the football field.

"Did your parents say anything when you came home soaked the other night?"

"They weren't around," he replied dismissively.

"Does that bother you – not having them around?" I asked the question without thinking, not expecting an honest answer since it really was none of my business.

But he responded. "I've learned to cope. It was easier when my brother was still here."

"You live with your aunt and uncle, right?" he countered.

"Yup." I bent over to take a picture of the field through the fence, twisting the lens of the camera so it produced a blur of color. I stood up and continued toward the wooded area behind the bleachers.

"Not easy?" Evan stated casually, like he already knew the answer.

"No, not easy," I agreed. I wasn't finding the need to lie—yet. We were walking a delicate line of disclosure, without revealing too much.

"Tight reins?" Another question that sounded more like a statement.

"Definitely," I answered, still taking unfocused pictures of the green foliage mixed with hints of red and orange. "And you don't have any reins."

"I guess not."

The wind blew my hair from my face, and Evan winced. My cheeks reddened, realizing he hadn't noticed the bruise on my head until now.

"Prone to bad luck?" he asked, nodding to my head.

"Depends on where I am," I answered without answering. I tried to brush my hair back across my forehead with my fingers, concealing the purple reminder of my bad luck.

"How many brothers and sisters do you have?" I inquired, switching the focus back on him.

"Just the one brother, Jared. He's a freshman at Cornell. And you?"

"No brothers or sisters – just my two younger cousins. Is he anything like you?"

"Nothing. He's quiet, more musically inclined than athletically, and is really easy going."

I smiled at the comparison. Evan smiled back, and my heart woke up from its two day slumber.

"Where are you considering going for college?"

"Several schools in California mainly, along with a few others in the New York, Jersey area. I'd love to get into Stanford if they'll have me."

"I heard they were here watching your game Thursday."

I nodded, now focusing the camera on the ground brush and zooming in to capture the details of the fallen leaves.

"Where are you looking?"

"Cornell, obviously, but I have friends going to different schools in California, so I may head back. I have time to figure it out."

We continued our delicately balanced conversation until it was time to return to the classroom.

"You have a night game on Friday, right?" he confirmed as we climbed the stairs.

"Yes."

"What are you doing after school, before the game?"

"Probably staying at school and doing homework or whatever."

"Do you want to get something to eat?" he asked, hesitating on the landing before opening the double doors leading to the hall. I stopped, and so did my heart.

"And yes, this would be a date, so that we're clear," he stated with a smirk. I stopped breathing too.

"Okay," I breathed, still unable to move. Did I really just agree to go on a date?!

"Great," he said, producing a brilliant smile that caused my heart to catapult to life at such a frantic pace that it left me lightheaded. "I'll see you in Trig." He continued down the hall past the Art room.

I returned my camera to the supply closet and walked in a daze to my locker.

"What is that grin for?" I heard Sara ask from what sounded like a mile away. I brought her into focus, not realizing that I'd been grinning.

"I'll tell you later." The grin turned into a smile.

"I hate it when you say that," she groaned, but knew she didn't have time to interrogate me in between classes. I grabbed my books and headed to Chemistry.

Class went by so slow. I took notes automatically and worked on the lab assignment with my chemistry partner. I kept looking at the clock to find that only five minutes had crept by. Finally, the bell rang.

"I hope you feel better," my chem. partner offered. My forehead crumpled. "You seemed kind of out of it today." I grinned, which only made her more confused.

When I arrived at my locker, Evan was waiting for me.

"Sorry, decided not to wait for you in class," he explained with a grin.

Sara walked up to her locker. "Hi Evan." She gave me a suspicious look from behind his back. I looked into my locker, pressing my lips together to fight the urge to smile.

"Can you tell me what you're allowed to do?" Evan asked as he walked alongside me.

"Not much," I answered seriously, my grin deflating.

"But you can do anything that involves school, right?" he confirmed, trying to put the pieces together.

"Pretty much. As long as I have a ride and am home before ten o'clock."

"Would they know if you weren't doing the school thing that you said you were doing but still followed the ten o'clock rule?"

I sunk onto my seat with my stomach in my chest. I could guess where he was going, and it was a place I was too afraid to even consider.

"I don't know. Why?" I tightened my eyes to try to read his thoughts.

"Just wondering," he said, still thinking. My attention was snapped to the front of the room when we were requested to pass our homework forward.

"Have you ever purposely done something you knew you weren't supposed to do?" Evan continued with the inquisition on our way to Anatomy.

"Like what?" Again, not liking this line of questioning.

"Like sneaking out of the house, or saying you're at the library but go to the movies instead?" I looked at him with wide eyes. I swallowed the lump lodged in my throat at the thought of it.

"I guess not," he concluded by my speechlessness, and probably audible gulping.

"What are you thinking?" I finally asked.

"I'm just trying to figure this out."

"What out?"

"Us," he said as he entered the classroom and took his usual seat.

I stumbled to my seat, not breathing again. He was so confusing. I wished I had warnings when he was going to say things like that.

"Mr. Mathews," Mr. Hodges declared, "would you please join Ms. Thomas at her table. It appears her partner is no longer in this class, and there is no point in having two single tables, especially when we have our dissection labs."

Upon hearing this announcement, I stared down at the black surface of the table to conceal the blood that was rushing to my face.

Evan sat next to me and said, "Hi," like he was introducing himself to me for the first time.

I released a blushing smile and quietly replied, "Hi."

After Mr. Hodges began his lecture on the bones in the hand, I scribbled on a blank piece of paper, *Are you already assuming there's an us?*

Evan wrote in response, NOT YET.

I still didn't understand what that meant and drew my eyebrows together, so he wrote, I'M GETTING READY FOR WHEN THERE IS.

My heart felt heavy, like it just fainted. There was a huge grin on Evan's face. I wasn't as amused. His questions and comments were making me dizzy. I tucked the paper in the back of my folder and stared at my notes, trying to conceal my bright red cheeks with my hair.

"See you later," Evan said after class as he walked away. I was left looking after him, baffled. I knew there was a motive behind his line of questioning and the insane statements that followed, but I was so lost.

Sara was waiting for me, leaning against our lockers when I arrived. I opened my locker to return my books without saying anything. I knew what she was expecting.

"Do not do this to me," she demanded impatiently.

"How was your date with Jason this weekend?" I attempted to redirect her attention.

"Not this time you don't," she scolded, still way too serious for Sara. "We'll get to me later—talk."

I paused, trying to digest what I was about to tell her.

"We're going on a date after school on Friday, before our soccer game. We're getting something to eat," I confided. I wasn't sure what else to say.

"Wow," she responded with a smile that made me flush with color once again. "That's really great. I really like this, Em. I have a good feeling about him."

"I'm glad *you* think so."

She flashed her eyes toward me, not understanding my reaction.

"I still don't get him, Sara," I admitted with a heavy sigh as we tread down the stairs toward the cafeteria. "He asks these questions and makes these cryptic remarks. I feel like I'm trying to read between the lines, but I'm still coming up blank. And then when I have an opportunity to ask him what he means, he disappears."

"I know he's been collecting his surveys from people and has a couple more interviews for the article that's due tomorrow. He's interviewing me at the beginning of Journalism class. Maybe that's where he keeps disappearing to."

"I'm not really worried about where he's going," I corrected, knowing she was trying to put me at ease. "The timing of when he leaves is always after he makes some remark or asks a question that I need him to explain. That's what's driving me crazy."

"Like what?" she inquired.

"I don't even know where to start."

"Do you like him?" We pulled the chairs back at our table in the back corner of the caf.

"I'm still trying to figure him out. But I'm getting used to being with him in class and walking down the halls together. I don't have the urge to push him away like I did before. So maybe he's wearing me down."

"Or maybe you like him," Sara countered with a devious smirk.

Before I could answer, Jason approached our table with a tray of food.

"Hey Sara," he greeted, hesitating before sitting next to her.

"Hello Jason," she beamed, shifting in her chair to face him. I suddenly felt like I was witnessing something that wasn't meant for a third pair of eyes.

"I'm going to get something to eat," I announced to ears that were deaf to my voice.

On my way back to the table with my lunch, I caught Sara and Jason smiling absurdly at each other. I hoped I didn't look at Evan that way. I'd feel like an idiot if that's what everyone saw whenever he was around me—although it looked nauseatingly adorable between Jason and Sara. The ogling was enough to deter me from returning to the table, so I went to the Journalism room instead to get a head start on my article.

Since the class was in the computer lab, no one came into the room, besides Ms. Holt, who grabbed some things from her desk and checked on my progress. She didn't have a class after Journalism, so I stayed during study as well. I buried myself in my homework to avoid thinking about Sara's reaction that morning or Evan's persistent interest. But my mind drifted towards those unavoidable thoughts anyway.

I was overwhelmed by the whirlwind that had forced its way in, turning everything upside down in such a short amount of time. I was losing control, and it was making me panic. I was having a hard time staying focused on what had always come so naturally before. The end was within sight, and I couldn't jeopardize everything and let it all slip away now.

So, if I was going to make it to college (in one piece), I had to avoid these panic-inducing situations, like the party—or anything else that distracted me for that matter. That included... dating. My heart sank in my chest at this realization. But I knew it was what I had to do – I had too much to lose.

"There you are," Evan declared as he entered the room. "I was wondering where you've been."

"Hi," I responded, looking down at the keyboard.

"It's definitely quieter in here," he observed, then noticed my avoidance. "What's going on?"

"I can't go on a date with you," I blurted in a rush. "I need to stay focused on school and my responsibilities. I can't afford distractions. I'm sorry."

"I'm a distraction?" he asked in bewilderment.

"Well... yes, you are. The fact that I think about you at all is a distraction, and I can't commit myself to any more extra curriculars." That came out way worse than it did in my head.

"Are you comparing our date to Art club?" I couldn't tell if he found it insulting or amusing.

"No." I sighed in frustration. "Evan, I'm not good at this. I've honestly never been on a date in my life, and I'm just not ready. I said it. Is that good enough for you?" My faced turned crimson with the spontaneous confession. I continued to reveal too much to him, and that was a part of the control I needed back. There was too much he couldn't know, and I couldn't keep slipping up.

He tried poorly to suppress his signature grin. I grunted in annoyance and threw a paperback book at him from atop my pile.

"I always bring out the best in you, don't I?" He released a short laugh as he avoided my throw. "Okay, no date. But we can still hang out, right?"

"As long as you promise not to ask me on a date, mention *us* as if we were an entity, and no comments about sweaters," I insisted. I realized my demands were ridiculous and didn't make much sense, but it was what my insubordinate heart would need to survive a friendship with Evan Mathews.

"Okay, I think," he agreed in confusion, nodding slowly. "But you're still talking to me, and I can sit next to you in class and even walk with you in the halls, right?"

"Sure," I replied after hesitating.

"Can we hang out outside of school?" he pushed.

"When would we possibly do something after school?"

"Friday – no date, I promise. But you can come over after school, and we can hang out before the game," he offered. "We can even do homework if you prefer."

I examined him with narrowed eyes, trying to decide if he was serious. More importantly I needed to decide if I could handle the offer – a small voice was screaming at me to say no, but I didn't listen.

"Alright," I conceded. "But just as friends."

"I can do that," he replied with a smirk, "for now."

"Evan!"

"Just kidding," he said as he held up his hands in defense. "I can be just friends with you—no problem."

The bell rang, declaring the end of the day, and the halls started to fill with the voices and footsteps of students anxious to leave.

"Good luck in your game today," I said, gathering my books together.

"Thanks," he replied. "I'll see you tomorrow in English?"

"I'll be there."

He smiled as he walked away.

I remained in the seat, absorbing the results of my attempt to put my life back in order. It didn't go exactly as I planned. I was supposed to cut him out completely, and a part of me was furious that I hadn't. I knew I was taking a big risk involving someone else in my life. I tried to convince myself that I could be friends with him, not allowing him to get too close, while still remaining focused on school. But I wasn't as confident as I should have been.

I fell back into my routine for the remainder of the day. My head hurt from running around during soccer practice, but I got through it.

Sara was gushing about Jason and her date, so I was convinced that she was over the emotional trauma from earlier that morning.

Actually, the rest of the week fell into a familiar pattern as well. The only difference was that most of my classes, along with my journeys to them, included Evan. He respected my reserved disposition, keeping conversation within the boundaries of school topics. I continued breathing and my heart kept beating, although at times it still acted insane and sped up at the sight of one of his mesmerizing smiles, or when he'd look into my eyes a little too long. But even that I could push in the pocket of acceptance. I had my safe place back, and that helped when I had to cross the threshold of instability at home.

I avoided Carol as much as possible, although her slicing tongue always found an insult to carve into me every time she saw me. I had an away game on Tuesday and worked on the newspaper layout on Wednesday, so I was able to stay away until after dinner. On Wednesday night, I even felt brave enough to sneak into the fridge at two o'clock in the morning to take a filet of cold breaded chicken and a granola bar back to my room to quiet my rebelling stomach. I was back to focusing on surviving the next five hundred and sixty- seven days however I could.

9. NOT A DATE

THE GREY MISTING SKIES DID LITTLE TO QUASH MY EXCITEMENT FOR the night game when I left for school Friday morning. It was also the day I was spending the afternoon with Evan. The thought of being alone with him shot a current of thrilling terror throughout my body. What a strange contradiction of emotions, feeling exhilarated and terrified at the same time.

I double checked the calendar on my way out to make certain my game was written on it. If it wasn't on the calendar with plenty of notice, then I wasn't allowed to do it. That included going to the library, which I marked for every Sunday afternoon. I was surprised I didn't have a tracking device inserted into the heel of my foot – but that would mean they'd have to spend money on me, and that was laughable.

"Good morning," I almost sung when I entered the car.

"Good morning," Sara replied, looking at my curiously. She began to say something, then thought better of it, and kept quiet. Instead, she turned up the radio and we drove off to the drum beats, guitar riffs and angst of a singer bellowing about being misunderstood. I let the music soak in with a grin on my face.

"Are you still going to Evan's after school?" Sara asked, turning down the music.

"As far as I know," I replied, trying to sound casual, like it wasn't the only thing I could think about.

"Then I'll see you at the game tonight."

"I'll see you in study, right?"

"I have a note from my parents allowing me to get out early. I'm going to Jill's house for the afternoon. You could probably get out early too if you wanted. The study period teachers don't always expect you there since you work on the paper or whatever."

The thought of breaking the rules and leaving school early without permission made my stomach turn. Or perhaps it was the thought of spending an additional hour with Evan.

Sara eyed my distressed expression. "It was just a suggestion; you don't have to do it."

"I'll think about it," I muttered. Another surge of thrilling terror flashed through my body with a shiver.

"I expect details," Sara blurted over her shoulder upon exiting homeroom. She was about to continue to class when she took notice of the dazed look on my face and stopped. "Are you nervous?"

"I'm pretty freaked," I whispered, oblivious to the buzz of bodies passing us.

"You have nothing to worry about. You made it clear you just want to be friends. But if you're really that afraid to be alone with him, I could give you an excuse to bail."

"No, I want to hang out with him. It's just something I've never done before, and I'm not sure what to expect. It's not like hanging out with you."

"Why don't you pretend that it is?" Sara gave me an encouraging smile. "Details," she repeated as she walked toward the stairs.

Evan was seated in English when I slipped into the desk next to him.

"Hi," he said, his mouth twitching, trying not to smile.

"Hey," I returned, without looking over at him.

"Do you want to skip study period and get out of school early?" My heart stopped as a million excuses not to leave ran through my head.

"Sure," I heard my mouth say, glancing at him quickly. Panic overtook my body, having never broken the rules before. I fumbled with my notebook and pulled out the completed assignment to pass in. I thought I noticed Evan smiling out of the corner of my eye, but I stared intently at my notes.

"You're quieter than usual today," he observed as we gathered our books to leave when the bell rang.

"Distracted by the back to back tests later," I lied, not truly concerned about the Trigonometry and Anatomy tests awaiting us. I'd studied the test material and was pretty confident that I knew it inside and out. Why couldn't I be as confident about everything else?

"I wouldn't have expected you to be nervous." He knew me better than I wanted to admit.

"It was a lot to study. You're not worried?" I asked, trying to deflect the attention from me.

"Why should I be? I've studied; there's nothing else I can do." Great, he was confident in school *and* everything else. "I'll see you in Trig." He walked down the hall as I headed to the stairs. History, Chemistry and my two tests distracted me enough to keep from completely obsessing about the end of the day and being alone with Evan – until it was unavoidable.

"How'd you do?" Evan asked as we walked out of Anatomy.

"I think I knew what I was doing," I admitted. "And you?"

"I got through it," he said with a shrug.

I noticed he was walking with me instead of going in the opposite direction as he usually did.

"Where are you going?"

"To your locker," he stated bluntly.

"Why?" I asked, not catching on.

"What? You don't want to have lunch with me?" His tone sounded almost offended, but then again, I knew him better than that and dismissed the possibility.

"You never have lunch with me, I don't get it."

"There's a first for everything. Sara left to go to Jill's, so I thought you could use the company."

"That's right," I remembered. "I'm actually not that hungry. I was going to pick up something small and get started in the Art room."

"Would you prefer to be alone?"

"Doesn't matter to me; do what you want." I shrugged, attempting to sound disinterested.

"That's not possible," he responded casually. I narrowed my eyes, trying to read between the lines of his comment. Before I could demand an explanation, he asked, "Will you ignore me if I have lunch with you in the Art room?"

"I don't have to." How was I possibly going to survive the afternoon with him? Maybe I should make up an excuse and stay at school instead. My heart skipped at the thought of bailing. I could be

81

friends with him—I just had to keep reminding myself that's what I wanted.

I placed my books in my locker, and Evan slipped his books on the top shelf as well. My mouth dropped in disbelief.

"What?!" he defended. "We're leaving together after Art. I'll take them out. I promise." We walked in silence to the cafeteria.

Before we entered, he said quietly, "You know that the latest rumor is that you and I are dating, right?" I stopped to stare at him with wide eyes, my arms crossed.

"It's just a rumor!" he said with his hands in the air and a half smile that made me fume.

"Do you really want me to come over today?" I snapped.

"Of course," he answered eagerly.

"Then don't share things like that with me. Remember, I don't want to know what people are saying about me?"

"I didn't realize our friendship had rules," he replied, grinning.

"I'll be sure to point them out when you don't follow them. Try to keep up." I was hoping to sound severe, but he continued grinning at my reprimand. I huffed and walked into the cafeteria at an exaggerated pace.

"Are you this strict with all of your other friends?" he inquired with a chuckle while keeping up with me.

"Sara is my only other friend and she plays by the rules. She doesn't need lessons." I glared at him so he'd take me seriously. I knew he didn't since he still seemed more entertained than offended.

"All you're getting is a granola bar and an apple?" He nodded toward the food in my hands as we made our way through the lunch line.

"I told you I wasn't very hungry. Besides, aren't we eating in a few hours?"

"Yeah but you're an athlete, and you have a game tonight—you need more sustenance than that." He almost sounded concerned.

"Fine," I caved and grabbed a banana. Evan eyed me disapprovingly, shaking his head.

"So much better," he commented with sarcasm.

I walked away, leaving him to catch up after he bought his lunch.

When we entered the Art room, he settled on the stool next to me to eat while I gathered my project that currently consisted of shades of green sweeping along the bottom of the predominantly blank canvas. I removed the picture of the early October foliage taped to the back and set it on the table next to me.

"Are you having a hard time liking me?"

I figured he was messing with me until I turned on my stool to find that he was seriously concerned about the answer.

"I'm not having a hard time liking you," I assured him. "I don't understand you. You say things that don't make sense or could mean more than they do. I'm trying not to let you get to me—that's all." I turned back to my painting and began squirting different shades of green on the palette.

"But I get to you?" he confirmed, his signature grin creeping on his face. I rolled my eyes.

"Not if I can help it. But watching you enjoy my discomfort is always a great way to win me over," I retorted, flashing my eyes at him.

"Sorry," he said with an insincere smile.

"I'm sure you are," I huffed. I proceeded with mixing colors and applying them to the canvas in blotches and heavy strokes. I concentrated on painting while he sat behind me, silently watching. I was flustered by his presence and couldn't summon anything to say to lighten the awkwardness, so I kept my back to him.

"I think I'll go outside and work on my assignment," he finally announced. "I'll meet you at your locker after class."

"Okay," I answered without looking. After he left the room, I put down my brush and took a deep breath. He *was* getting to me, and my defensive retorts bothered me, despite how much they appeared to amuse him. I made the conscious decision to be friends with him – that I could handle it. So far, I was failing miserably – trying so hard to keep him at a distance that I was practically cruel. If I kept this up, he'd probably decide not to have anything to do with me at all – and I wouldn't blame him.

Evan was waiting for me at my locker after class as he promised.

"Hi," I said with a gentle smile, hoping he wasn't regretting inviting me over.

"Hi," he smiled back.

"Come back for more punishment?" I asked quietly, leaning against the locker to face him. I kept glancing at the ground, having a hard time looking him in the eye.

"I can handle it." He tilted his head down, forcing me to look at him. I reluctantly connected with his riveting blue eyes. "Besides, I'm getting used to your reactions, so they don't really bother me. You can actually be pretty funny." His lips relaxed into a vibrant smile.

"Great, here I am feeling horrible for how I've talked to you, and you think it's hilarious. I guess you bring out the best in me, don't you?" I smirked.

"That's why I'm here."

He reached over my head to grab his books out of my locker. His shirt brushed against my back, causing me to inhale quickly, unable to move. My heart began its ritualistic dance in my chest, sending a surge of blood to my cheeks. I slowly let out the captured breath when he backed away.

"I just have to get a few things from my locker before we go, okay?"

"Sure," I whispered, still distracted.

The halls were vacant when we walked to Evan's locker so he could stuff a few books into his backpack. I was relieved not to have witnesses when we left together. I really didn't want to fuel the gossip – or get caught skipping class, even if it was just study period.

I looked around nervously, expecting a voice to stop us and ask where we were going when we exited the school. But we were never stopped. We didn't say anything as we walked to his car through the thick mist of the persisting grey skies. Evan held the car door open for me again—the gesture still caught me off guard. I slipped into the car, and he closed the door behind me.

"This should be an interesting game in the mud tonight, huh?" he noted as he started the car.

"It slows the game down," I admitted, "but I actually like sliding in the mud."

"I know what you mean."

I relaxed into the leather seat as we talked the entire ride to his house. My guarded tension was finally melting away when we pulled into his driveway.

Evan lived in one of the historic homes in the center of town. The extended driveway pulled the white farmhouse with black shutters away from the road, revealing a perfectly manicured front lawn with a large maple tree that was turning a magnificent red. The house was wrapped with a wide porch, accented with white rocking chairs and a hammock—it was a three dimensional Norman Rockwell painting. At the end of the driveway, behind the house, was a two story barn that had been converted into a garage. Beyond the barn was an expansive field surrounded by trees, without a neighboring house in sight.

We entered through the door on the side of the porch that led into the kitchen. The house may have been historic, but the kitchen had every modern amenity available. It was a large room with a shared dining area. The space still held the rustic charm of the farmhouse, with exposed beams and wood framed walls, stained a warm brown.

"Do you want something to drink? I have soda, water, juice and iced tea," Evan presented, attempting to be hospitable after placing his backpack on a chair. The peninsula separated the cooking space from the dining area that recessed into the floor, with three long steps leading to a large dark wood dining table.

"Iced tea would be great." I sat in a chair along the peninsula while he filled two glasses with iced tea from a glass pitcher he removed from the refrigerator.

"I like how you set up the newspaper," he said, handing me a glass from the other side of the counter. "The paper at my other school was rougher looking since the printing was done in-house. It was more of a flyer than a newspaper. The *Weslyn High Times* actually resembles a newspaper."

"Thanks. Have you received any comments about your article – you know, since it made the first page?"

"Yeah, I have," he admitted with a grin – knowing that was the only acknowledgement he was going to receive from me that it was a well written article. "Mostly questions about my sources, trying to pair up an insecurity with a person. It's kind of annoying, but I should've expected it."

After a moment, he added, "I never did get to interview you. I thought it would be a conflict of interest."

"I don't think I would have let you interview me," I replied. "But if I had, what would you've asked?" As soon as I said it, I regretted it. What was I thinking putting myself out there? Telling Evan my physical insecurities was not on the top of my list.

"Name one part of your body you're insecure about and how you would change it?" His expression was calm and attentive. His demeanor was unexpected. I thought this topic would definitely have evoked one of his wide smiles.

I hesitated.

"Okay, I'll tell you mine first if that'll help," he offered, still serious.

"You're insecure about your body?" I scoffed.

"I hate the size of my feet. They're huge," he confessed.

"You're feet? What size are they?"

"Fourteen and the average size is ten. It's not easy finding shoes I like that fit." Oddly enough, he remained genuine.

"I can honestly say I've never noticed, maybe because you're tall. Or maybe because your feet are not what most people look at." I realized, with a blush, that I shouldn't have made a comment that he could misinterpret.

"Really?" he grinned, confirming my fear.

"You know what I mean," I retorted, my whole face reddening.

"What's yours?" he prodded.

"My lips," I admitted cautiously. "I've always wanted them to be smaller. I've even practiced tucking them in in front of the mirror," revealing more than I intended, as usual.

"Really? I love your full lips," he said without hesitating. "They're perfect k-"

"Don't say it," I shot back at him, turning redder by the second.

"Why?" he questioned with a crease between his brows.

"Do you want to be friends with me?"

"Yes," he answered quickly.

"Then you can't say things like that. It's one of the lines you don't cross. Remember the rules I set if we're going to be friends? You are not playing by the rules," I explained firmly, hoping this time he'd take me seriously.

"What if I don't want to be friends with you?" he challenged, grinning again, staring directly into my eyes. Obviously taking me seriously was an impossibility for Evan.

Despite not being able to breathe, I connected with his taunting gaze and refused to look away. "Then we won't be friends," I said flatly.

"What if I want to be more than friends?" He grinned wider, leaning his forearms on the counter, shortening the distance between us.

"Then we won't be anything at all." Along with not being able to breathe, my heart stopped, making it harder to keep up my defiant stare when he leaned in closer; but I was determined not to back down.

"Okay, then friends we are," he declared, suddenly standing up straight, taking a gulp of iced tea. "Can you play pool?" I couldn't say anything for a few seconds—my head was spinning as I tried to reel my heart back from across the counter.

"I've never tried," I floundered.

I took a deep breath to clear my head before I stood up. Evan was waiting for me patiently, holding the door open for me to follow him.

We entered the large white barn through the side door into a space that could easily fit two cars. There was a door to the right of the stairs that led to another area, unrevealed.

Hung on the opposite wall were shelves displaying tools and other typical garage items. But what caught my eye was the extensive amount of recreational equipment stored beneath the stairs. There were snow shoes, skis, two surf boards, a couple of wake boards and everything in-between. There were bins of basketballs, soccer balls, volleyballs – it looked like a sporting goods store.

"Can't say you're bored," I commented as we climbed the stairs. He let out a short laugh.

I followed him into a full rec room. Along the far wall was a dark wooden bar with a flat stone top, fully stocked and furnished with complementary wooden stools. There was an oversized, dark brown leather couch and recliner set in front of a large flat-screened television suspended on the wall to the left. Abandoned on the floor were several video game components and corresponding gear. I wondered if all of the wealthy kids at Weslyn High had similar set ups to Sara and Evan.

A pool table, lit by suspended chrome canisters, stood on one side of the room with plenty of space to maneuver a pool stick without bumping into a wall. A dart board hung on the wall to the right of the door, and to the left were two foosball tables. There was a closed door behind the tables. The walls' deep red paint and the barn's exposed wooden beams along the pitched ceiling, created a masculine tone that was finished with framed rock concert posters, showcasing a variety of bands over a span of a few decades.

"This is my mom's way of trying to get my brother to come home more," Evan explained as he crossed the room toward the bar. "So, this room is more for my brother than me. My stuff is in the other room." He nodded toward the closed door behind the foosball tables.

Music erupted through the strategically placed speakers when Evan turned it on from behind the bar. He lowered the volume so that we could hear each other.

"I've never heard this band before," I noted, listening to the rock band with the reggae influence. "I like it."

"I saw them at a concert in San Francisco and really liked them. If you give me your iPod, I can download them for you."

"Sure."

"Darts first?" he suggested, heading to the corner where the dart board hung. I sat on one of the stools dispersed along the dark wooden bar running the length of the wall while he pulled the darts from the board.

"I think I've only played darts once before, and I sucked," I warned. He handed me three darts with silver metallic wings while keeping the darts with the black metallic wings. He stood behind the black line painted on the dark hardwood floor and threw each dart with ease. I watched them penetrate the pie and rectangular shapes. He made it look so simple, but I wasn't convinced.

"We'll warm up first and then go from there." I approached the line and he demonstrated how to hold the dart for the best control. I attempted to duplicate his example. "Getting used to the weight of the dart is the hardest part in order to determine the angle and speed you want to throw it. Then aim, and toss with a quick, steady hand." He threw the dart firmly, and it stuck easily into its intended target.

"You may not want to be anywhere around me when I attempt this," I advised cautiously. He smiled and sat on a stool, giving me my space. My first shot was weak. I missed the dartboard completely. The dart landed low, and stuck to a black board that covered the length of the wall behind the circle.

"Oops, sorry," I said, scrunching my face. This was going to be a long game, especially if I couldn't even make the board.

"That's what the black board's for. You're not the first, and won't be the last, to miss," Evan assured me. "We won't play an actual game until you feel comfortable. Try it again." I threw the last dart with a little more force and it hit the number 20, not in the points area, but the actual number.

"Well, at least I hit the board," I stated optimistically. Evan smiled and retrieved the darts.

We threw three more rounds until I was consistently hitting within the colored ring. I wasn't exactly hitting the areas I was aiming for, but I was getting closer. With all of my near misses and extreme misses, I wasn't embarrassed or self conscious for my lack of dart experience.

Evan made it easy with his patience and advice. I was actually enjoying myself.

We played a round of cricket. I made Evan take two steps back from the line, in attempt to make it slightly more even. He still won – it wasn't even close. During the game, we talked about sports and what we've tried, or in my case, never tried.

"So you're great at everything, huh?" I confirmed, after he shared surfing and kite boarding experiences he'd had in different parts of the world.

"No, I'll try just about anything," he corrected, "but I'm only really good at a few things. My brother's better at pool and darts than I am. I'm decent at soccer, but I'm not the best player—the same with basketball. I think I'm best at baseball. I have a consistent swing and pretty good reaction time at short stop.

"I bet if you were exposed to more experiences, you'd find you're better than I am at most of them. You're definitely a better soccer player. I haven't seen you play basketball, but I heard you have an impressive outside shot." The heat made itself known across my cheeks as he spoke of my athletic abilities.

"I love soccer, I really like basketball, and I run track just for something to do in the spring. Since I play a sport, I don't have to take Gym, so I haven't attempted anything else for a long time. I'm not sure how I'd do."

"Do you want to find out?"

"What are you thinking?" I asked cautiously.

"Tomorrow, I'll meet you at the library and then we'll go from there." My stomach twisted at the thought of lying. "Or maybe not," he corrected after observing my pale face.

"I can't tomorrow," I said quietly, but before I realized what I was about to say, I finished with, "but I could on Sunday." Evan's eyes lit up. My heart leapt into its high speed patter.

"Really?" he asked, not convinced.

"Sure," I confirmed with a smile. "What did you have in mind?"

"Batting cages?"

"Why not," I replied with a shrug.

"Noon?"

"Noonish."

"Great," he stated with a full-fledged smile that left me lightheaded with the rush of blood to my face. "Ready to eat? You must be after that sad lunch."

"I could eat," I stated casually, ignoring his antagonizing remark as he turned off the music.

I watched from a stool at the peninsula while he pulled items from the refrigerator and cabinets and started cutting up celery, mushrooms, chicken and pineapple.

"What are you making?" I asked, not anticipating the huge production. I'd expected something from the typical food groups of pizza and subs.

"Chicken and pineapple stir fry," he replied. "Sorry, I didn't ask you if you were a picky eater. Is this okay?"

"Sure," I said slowly. "You cook?" I didn't know why I was so surprised. I should be used to the unpredictability of Evan Mathews, but I still couldn't help but follow the production in amazement as he measured, mixed and chopped with ease.

"I have to fend for myself a lot, so yeah, I cook," he explained without looking at me. "You don't, I take it?"

"Not since eighth grade Home Ec."

"Huh, that actually surprises me." He didn't say anything more, and I wasn't about to try to explain the rules of Carol and George's kitchen.

"Can I ask you something?" I blurted without really thinking through what I was about to say. This was becoming a habit that was causing my heart and head more distress than I could handle. Whenever I was with Evan I found myself revealing, asking, and agreeing to things that were sending my brain into shock.

"Go for it." Evan stopped what he was doing to lean his back against the counter, still holding the knife in his hand.

"Do you always get what you want?" He looked at me with uncertainty, so I attempted to clarify, "I mean, are you as forward with everyone as you are with me?"

He chuckled, not the answer I was looking for.

Evan paused long enough to make me wish I hadn't asked the question. He smiled before he replied, "No. Normal girls wouldn't be able to handle it. They tend to respond better to subtlety and flirting. I know that whatever I say to any other girl would be passed on to her friends and eventually to the rest of the school, so direct doesn't work in most situations. But this is not most situations, and you are far from any other girl." He turned to continue his preparation.

His answer left me baffled. If this was direct, then I would hate to be a normal girl, because I had no idea what he meant by half of what he just said. I decided not to even attempt to understand it—fearing it would only make me more confused.

"Okay," he said, still with his back to me as he dumped the contents of the cutting board in the wok on the stove, "I have a question for you." Now look what I started—I sighed and braced myself.

"How come you've never been on a date?" Evan turned to look at me, anticipating my answer.

"Why would I?" was the first thing that came out of my mouth.

He laughed and went back to tossing the contents of the wok. "I wasn't expecting that," he said with a smile. I shrugged, fiddling with a string on my sweater. I had to change the subject, but I was coming up blank.

"Have you ever been kissed?" he asked suddenly. My face flashed with the familiar warmth as my mouth dropped open.

"Well, that was *definitely* direct," I accused. "And I don't think I'm going to answer that question."

"You have," he concluded, glancing back at me with a smirk. "Good to know."

"Let's change the subject," I pushed as the heat on my face spread to my ears. "Where was your favorite place to live?"

He didn't respond.

"Evan?"

"What? Sorry, I didn't hear the question," he confessed, absently pushing around the ingredients sizzling in the wok. "I was trying to figure out if I know who the guy is. But if it was someone from school, I'm sure I would have found out by now. Is he in college?" He leaned against the counter to examine me, trying to pluck the answer from the mortified expression on my face.

"You're forgetting the line," I reminded him with wide eyes.

"What? This isn't about you and me," he defended. "I thought friends shared this kind of stuff. I'll tell you who my first kiss was if that will make you feel better."

"No, not really," I stated emphatically. "I'm not interested, and I'm not going to answer your question about my private experiences. We're not that good of friends."

91

"But you have been kissed—I was right, wasn't I?"

"So," I gaped. "What does it matter if I've been kissed?"

"But you've never been on a date," he mused, like it was a mystery he was attempting to solve. If he thought that the answer was going to reveal something surprising, he was definitely going to be disappointed. He set two filled plates on the counter.

"This is really good," I said after taking a bite, anxious to change the subject. But I wasn't being dishonest, the stir fry *was* good. I wasn't sure I liked continuing to find things about Evan that impressed me.

"Thanks," he said inattentively, still thinking about my responses.

"Can we please move past this?" I pleaded.

"Sure, but you'll tell me eventually," he said confidently.

"I don't understand why you want to know." I realized, after I spoke, that I was feeding into the same topic I was trying so hard to get away from.

"I'm still trying to figure you out."

"There's nothing to figure out. I'm not that interesting." Evan didn't respond. He looked down with his mischievous grin and pierced a piece of chicken with his fork.

As we ate, I was finally able to redirect the conversation toward different places he's lived. He described each country or city and what he liked and didn't like about it. I breathed easier, having escaped the ever revealing inquiry about my personal life. I helped with the dishes while we continued talking about a skiing trip he went on with his brother in Switzerland a couple of winters ago. I was extremely enthralled with his travel stories and the many experiences he's had in only seventeen years. Especially since my sheltered life within the confines of New England had little experience to compare it to.

"Do you have your license?" Evan asked as we sat back at the counter.

"No, I don't have my permit yet," I admitted.

"How old are you?"

"Sixteen."

"You're sixteen?" He seemed surprised.

"Oh, something you didn't know about me?" I taunted. "I skipped a grade early in elementary school. My birthday's in June, but I've been too busy to get my permit and take classes."

This, of course, was a complete lie. In order to get my permit, my guardian was required to take two hours of parent classes—that was never going to happen. Carol and George weren't burdened with having to drive me from place to place—so why would they care if I had my license? Besides, what good was a license if I couldn't afford a car?

"Do you know how to drive?"

"Sara's tried to teach me the basics in empty parking lots. She wants to take me on the road, but I'd die if anything happened to her car. If we ever got caught and she lost her license, it would suck for both of us."

"Does she have an automatic or manual?"

"Automatic."

"I'm surprised that her car's an automatic. Want to learn to drive a stick?"

"Not today," I replied bluntly.

"A library day," he determined with a grin.

"Maybe," I said hesitantly. How many of these library days was he planning? The thought of getting caught made my stomach hurt. It was bad enough I had agreed to go to the batting cages on Sunday. There was no way I could risk more excursions.

"Do you want to give me your iPod and I'll download that band for you?"

"It'll be hard to be without it for the weekend or actually even for the game today." I reached in my backpack trying to decide if I should give it to him.

"You can borrow mine," he offered without hesitating. Trading personal property already? This simple gesture felt so much bigger than just exchanging music. Or perhaps I was reading too much into it. *Relax*. It was just music.

"Okay." I handed him my lime green player in exchange for his black one. It may have been just music, but my heart was pounding so hard it might as well have been a ring.

"I should get ready for the game. Can you show me where the bathroom is so I can change?"

"Sure."

I followed him into a soft yellow room that was elegantly furnished with a Victorian style couch and chair set, upholstered with light blue velvet and framed with hand carved white wood. A small, but stunning, crystal chandelier was suspended above the hand crafted coffee table. I looked across at the picture window, which allowed a full view of the front yard. The room opened up into a receiving area at the main entrance with a small table set against the wall, where a colorful arrangement of flowers was set next to a picture of four people, who I presumed to be the Mathews family.

"The light switch is inside on the right," Evan explained when we stopped at a door along the long hallway, leading away from the elegant sitting room. "I'll be in the kitchen."

"Thanks," I replied, before closing the door.

10. NIGHT GAME

WHEN WE PULLED INTO THE PARKING LOT AT THE SCHOOL, I ASSUMED Evan would drop me off and come back later for the varsity game. The junior varsity team didn't draw many spectators besides their parents and the varsity team. But he shut off the car and proceeded to get out.

"You're staying?" I asked, grabbing my bags from his car.

"Is that okay?"

"Sure," I replied. "There aren't a lot of people here, but it's up to you."

"Can I sit with you and Sara?"

"We usually sit with the team, but I don't see why you can't. I have to warn you, I listen to music to block everyone out so that I can get focused. I'm not going to talk to you."

"That's fine. I'll find something good for you to listen to." He took the iPod from my hands and started scrolling through the music selections.

"Hey Sara," I called to her when we neared the first row of the bleachers. She hadn't noticed us approaching with her attention on the game and talking to one of the girls.

"Hi," she exclaimed excitedly when she caught sight of me. "How did – " Then she noticed Evan, and her question turned into a smile that lingered a little too long. I knew she had a thousand questions about my afternoon, so I was relieved that Evan was here, allowing me to avoid them until the drive home. "Hi Evan," she greeted him warmly.

Evan sat next to Sara so that they could talk, and I zoned them out while listening to my—well Evan's—music. He'd selected a band I was familiar with, allowing me to get lost in the high energy beats while I silently watched the game on the field. I didn't look over at Evan or Sara and kept the volume up so I couldn't hear them.

The bleachers started to fill in with the remaining members of the varsity team as the first half of the game came to an end. They'd acknowledge me with a wave, and I'd nod back in recognition. My teammates were familiar with my ritual and didn't bother trying to interact.

Every so often, Evan would reach into my jacket pocket and pull out the iPod to find another selection of songs. When his hand first entered my pocket, my heart stopped – actually, so did my breathing. Once I realized what he was doing, I continued to ignore him and watched the movement in front of me.

The junior varsity teams were having difficulty moving the ball due to the saturated field and the divots created by the football game. Grass flew, cleats were caught in the grass, and bodies slid in the mud. The mist had ended by the end of the first half, but the damage was done.

When the JV game concluded with the Weslyn girls losing, two to one, the varsity players gathered on the track to prepare for the warm up laps. While we ran our warm up laps, the bleachers continued to fill in with spectators. I didn't check the stands to see how big of a turn out the cool damp night had collected—it had nothing to do with the game.

When the whistle blew to begin the game, I was entranced. My mind was clear of every thought other than where the ball was, where it was going, and who was going to be there to receive it. The ball did not go anywhere very fast. There were a lot of missed kicks, sliding attempts to dribble or pass the ball, along with times when the ball was left spinning in place. By half time, there wasn't a score, but everyone was covered in mud.

The second half started the same as the first. After a time, it became evident that the best way to move the ball was to get some air under it. There were a lot of collisions when fighting for position to receive the soaring ball. It developed into more of a physical game than a ball controlling game, with plenty of yellow card warnings as a result.

With approximately five minutes left in the game, Weslyn had control of the ball. Our sweeper booted the ball from the top of the keeper's box to about mid-field, where the mid-fielder gained possession. She dribbled a few yards, avoiding the defender, before she sent it further up-field to Lauren. Without hesitating, Lauren sent the ball up the sideline to Sara. The sidelines weren't as muddy and treacherous as the center of the field, so Sara continued the ball along the painted white line. She drew a defender, who came at her with a sliding tackle. Before Sara slipped off her feet, landing on the attacker, she sent the ball sailing across the center of the field.

I was a few yards inside the keeper's box, with the sweeper coming towards me, eyeing the ball that was floating right to me, but was waist high. Without considering the success of it, I crouched down and forced the balls of my feet into the field and pushed back up with everything I had, propelling myself in the air. I leaned to my left, concentrating on the ball, and swung my right foot in attempt to make contact. I wasn't aware of where the sweeper was, but I hoped I had sent the ball around her, towards the goal. After connecting with the ball, my shoulder collided with the wet surface, followed by my hip as the mud splashed on my face. I grunted in response to the contact, still focused on locating the ball. I couldn't see anything through the sweeper's feet while I lay on the ground. I lifted my head to hear the ref's whistle declaring the goal, just as I found it resting in the back of the net.

Sara pulled me off the ground, screaming. She embraced me while jumping excitedly. I was greeted with additional cheers and jumping. I raised my arms in the air in celebration of the score as I ran back to mid-field to prepare for the kick off. I was soaring, filled with the rush I sought from the game. The remaining time ran down without another goal.

At the sound of the long whistle concluding the game, the team ran out to the center of the field, hollering and jumping in celebration. When I looked around, I realized there was more than just our team on the field, as many of the spectators had come down from the stands to congratulate us. I received pats on the back from people I recognized and many that I didn't. It was a whirlwind of faces, cheers and hands. I was coming down from the high and decided I needed to remove myself from the chaos.

I told Sara I'd meet her in the locker room. She promised she'd be right behind me. I slipped away from the crowd and jogged to the school. As I approached the stairs, I saw a tall silhouette leaning against the building.

"Congratulations," the smooth voice said from the dark shadows.

"Thanks," I replied, slowing to a walk as I approached the figure. Evan stood with his hands in his pockets, waiting for me.

"That was an impressive goal."

I smiled, accepting the recognition, while my cheeks warmed.

"Do you want me to wait here for you while you change?" I stopped, not prepared for the question.

"You don't have to wait," I said slowly.

"I was hoping to drive you home." My stomach fell at the thought of him pulling up to my house. I didn't anticipate Carol and George waiting to greet me, but I knew she didn't sleep until I was locked within the house. The last thing I wanted was for her to look out of her bedroom window to see Evan's sleek black car letting me out. It would be a morning I'd never live down.

"Thanks," I replied sincerely, "but I haven't seen Sara all day. I promised to ride home with her."

"Okay." He sounded disappointed, which kinda surprised me.

After a second, I awkwardly added, "I had a good time today. Thank you for dinner."

"Me too," he agreed, without the awkwardness. "I'll see you on Sunday then?"

"Yeah."

Evan flashed a quick grin before walking back toward the field. He met up with a few guys from the soccer team and was immediately conversing. By this time, Sara was jogging toward me—her mud blotched face unable to conceal her enormous white smile. She greeted me with an enthusiastic tight hug.

"I loved that game!" she exclaimed.

"Yeah," I exhaled. "Sara, I ... can't ... breathe."

"Sorry," she said, releasing me. "But that game was fuckin' awesome." She was bouncing in her skin and could barely stand still.

"Yeah, it was," I agreed, but my energy was nowhere near the level of Sara's. "Let's get changed. I'm tired and am ready to crash."

"Don't think I'm letting you get out of my car without providing details," she added. I groaned. "You two looked really comfortable sitting next to each other tonight. Are you sure you're still *just friends*?"

"Sara," I stressed, my voice raising an octave higher than normal, "I didn't even talk to him the whole time he sat next to us." She laughed, and I realized she was playing with me. I shook my head with an accepting smirk. "You're such a jerk."

After showering, Sara drove me home, and I provided her with the details she sought regarding my afternoon with Evan. I even told her about his confusing comments, and to my dismay, Sara laughed.

Then she proceeded to catch me up on her situation with Jason. Sara was still enthralled with him, which was good to hear, but seemed flustered that he'd barely kissed her. Sara wasn't exactly shy when it came to getting *to know* guys. I was hoping she'd finally found a guy that respected her, but instead she was wondering what she was doing wrong.

We pulled up in front of my house. I looked out the car window at the grey Cape. The dark windows didn't reveal any movement inside. I took a deep breath and said goodnight to Sara before exiting the car.

I dragged my feet along the unlit driveway to the back of the house. When I turned the handle of the back door, I was met with resistance—it didn't move. The door was locked. My stomach dropped.

Sara had already driven away. There was no way I was going to knock, since they made the conscious decision to lock the door, knowing I wasn't home. My mind raced to try to think of what I possibly could have done wrong to get locked out of the house. My pulse quickened, wondering how much trouble I was in, fearing the worst.

I cupped my hands to the glass to look inside. My reflection shielded me from seeing into the kitchen. Then the reflection smirked and the eyes squinted into a glare. I jumped back, realizing I was staring at *her*. I remained frozen, not sure what to do next, waiting for her to make a move. But the darkness remained still.

A light illuminated the kitchen. I expected to find Carol glowering at me, but the kitchen was empty until George appeared from the dining room where he'd turned on the light. I scrunched my eyes in confusion – questioning if I had really seen Carol. George opened the door with his lips pressed in a tight scowl.

"You're supposed to be home before ten o'clock," he reprimanded.

"I had a game tonight," I said softly, confused by his reaction.

"That doesn't matter. Your curfew is ten o'clock. If you can't get home in time, then maybe you shouldn't participate in the night games." His voice was unsympathetic, and his eyes were hard. I knew there was no point in arguing. If I did, he could take soccer away altogether, and I wouldn't risk that.

"Okay," I whispered. I slipped by him and went to my room without another word.

"I would have left you in the cold," hissed through the dark as I passed the living room. I took in a quick startled breath. I continued to my room, quickly closing the door behind me, fearing what awaited me in the dark if I paused to look.

11. THE LIBRARY

I WAS BENT OVER, WITH MY HEAD IN THE REFRIGERATOR, WIPING THE back wall when the air expelled from my lungs and I gasped in pain. I groaned, the force knocking me to the floor. I collapsed onto my side, cradling my stomach. My eyes filled with tears as I tried to gulp in air.

I pulled myself into a ball, not sure if another blow would follow. Carol stood over me with Jack's aluminum baseball bat in her hand. She glared at me with a tight smirk as I tried to shrink against the refrigerator.

"You are not important. Nothing you do is important. Don't think that you will ever amount to anything more than the whore that you are." She walked away.

My quick gasps slowed as the air came back in easy breaths. Shaking, I pushed myself off the floor and wiped the tears from my face. I winced when I stood, holding my stomach. Without thought, I replaced the contents of the refrigerator before walking to the bathroom.

Wet, red eyes stared back from the mirror. I blankly studied the pale image. Exhaling slowly, I tried to control my shaking limbs. The cold water soothed my distraught face as I gathered water from the faucet. I crushed the anger that was beginning to boil and filled my lungs with another soothing breath. I closed my eyes and reminded myself that I wasn't going to live here forever before returning to the kitchen to complete my chores.

I breathed in sharply when I sat up in bed the next morning, my hand reaching for my sore stomach, feeling like I'd executed a thousand crunches. Despite the misery of my condition, I was still going to the library. There was no way I was staying in this house all day.

George and Carol didn't think twice about allowing me to go. I was sure they wanted me out of the house as much as I wanted to leave it. I promised I'd be back in time for dinner at six. When I started out, the need to contract my tender muscles was excruciating. I pushed through the discomfort, eventually able to block it out completely – a coping skill I'd mastered over the years.

My heart fluttered faster than the effort needed to pedal the bike when I neared the library. My mouth crept into a smile at the thought of seeing Evan. I knew I should have been paranoid about being caught, but after last night, I knew there was going to be pain whether I did anything wrong or not – so maybe I should do something to actually deserve it. I locked my bike at the rack in the front of the building and leapt up the stairs. Before I entered, I discovered him propped against the stone exterior.

"Hi," he said with a grin on his face.

"Hi," I replied, my heart shifting into a higher gear. Seeing him standing there waiting for me only confirmed that this was worth the risk.

"Ready to hit some balls?"

"I'm ready for anything," I declared, following him down the stairs to his car.

"Anything, huh?" he confirmed with a smirk, opening the car door for me.

I hesitated and looked up at him before I crouched to enter the car, "Yeah, anything." The smile spread wider across my face.

His blue eyes sparkled as he returned the smile, having no idea what I really meant.

"Ok," he said emphatically and closed the door behind me.

"How was your Saturday?" he asked as we drove away from the library.

"Uneventful. How was yours?"

"I went to New York for one of my mother's charity dinners. So it was uneventful too."

"Sounds it," I said sarcastically. He grinned.

When we arrived at the recreation center, the distinct crack of aluminum bats making contact carried across the parking lot. There were also the low thuds of clubs connecting with golf balls coming from a different direction.

"Are you cold?" Evan asked.

"No, it's really nice out today," I responded, not knowing why he'd asked.

"I thought you shivered."

"I'm fine," I replied dismissively, not realizing my body had reacted to the sound of the bats smashing their targets.

We walked toward the office to gather our helmets and bats.

"Have you ever swung a bat?" Evan asked, stopping near the slow pitch softball cages.

"Maybe in elementary school," I confessed.

"Let me show you first, and then you can give it a try." Evan continued to the medium pitch baseball section. "I'll start here so I can talk while I demonstrate what to do, then we'll move to slow pitch softball for you."

"I'd like to stick with baseball actually."

"That's fine," he agreed. "Can you hold this for me?" Evan took off his jacket and handed it to me. I couldn't help but take in the subtle clean scent as I folded it over my arm. My heart hummed into action as I inhaled deeply.

Before he inserted the coins to begin, Evan stood in the hitting stance. He explained his position and grip while demonstrating a swing. I listened as best as I could but kept getting lost in the fit of his shirt along his chest and back. The lines revealed the lean muscles concealed beneath. I shook off my daze and forced myself to concentrate on his words. He paid the machine, and it started sending baseballs flying at him.

Evan made contact with most of the mechanical pitches. I watched as they arced across the net to the back of the enclosed space. He would occasionally miss when he was providing instructions on how to follow through with a steady swing, noting the importance of keeping an eye on the ball. The balls were hurled toward him at a blurring speed. I didn't know how he could see the ball—forget about keep his eye on it.

When his turn was over, we walked over to the slow pitch baseball cage. Evan entered the cage with me to get me set up. I stood in what was my impression of the hitting stance. Evan stood behind me and placed his hands on my hips to adjust my angle. He wrapped his arms around my shoulders and grabbed hold of the bat, covering my hands. I tried to listen to what he said, but all I could hear was my heart thumping in my chest as his breath tickled my neck. He instructed me to keep my elbow up as he eased me into a slow swing with the warmth of his chest pressed against my back. I was entranced by his clean, almost sweet, scent.

"Ready?" he asked, backing away.

"Sure," I replied in a daze, not realizing he had finished his instructions.

"I'll stand in the corner so I can correct your swing."

"Are you sure that'll be safe? I would hate to knock you out." He laughed and assured me he'd be fine. Then he pressed the button to begin the pitches. The first few whizzed by me before I had time to react.

"I thought this was supposed to be slow pitch," I accused.

"Just concentrate on the ball," Evan instructed patiently. I watched the next ball fling at me and swung. I connected with a piece of it, flipping it in the air right in front of me. The twisting motion ignited a fire in my tender stomach muscles. I kept my face blank, determined not to let the soreness get to me.

"That's it," he encouraged. After a few more swings and misses, and a few weak connections, Evan adjusted my swing with some advice. He put in more money for another round of pitches. This time, he stepped out of the cage and sat on the bench.

I improved with each pitch, finding my rhythm. Soon I was sending the balls through the air, not covering the distance Evan had, but at least I was hitting them.

"Much better," he praised. I enjoyed the release, feeling my tension and pain slip away each time the ball made contact with the bat.

"That was great," Evan commended while we walked to the fast pitch baseball cages. "You picked it up fast, but I knew you would." I didn't say anything.

After a few more rounds each, Evan asked if I wanted to get a burger from the small restaurant that extended from the office.

"What do you want to learn to do next weekend?" Evan questioned as he set a tray of food on the table. "Golf?"

"I really have no interest in golf," I admitted. "And I'm not sure we should make plans for next weekend yet."

"If we are able to do something, what do you want to do?" he pressed, but then his eyes lit up. "I know the perfect thing we can do." A devious smile spread across his face as he thought about it.

"What?" I asked cautiously.

"I'm not going to tell you, but you'll love it." I narrowed my eyes, taking in his smug expression.

"Oh, I have your iPod in the car. You have an interesting selection of music. If I'd looked through the playlists without knowing who it belonged to, I would have assumed it was a guy's. Well, accept for that one playlist."

"That one's good for when I can't fall asleep," I defended quickly, my cheeks flashing with heat.

"It's very –," Evan hesitated, searching for the right word.

"Soothing," I interrupted.

"Sure," he laughed. "It definitely sets a mood, let's put it that way." The color continued to spread across my face.

When we were in the car driving back to the library, Evan asked one of the questions I had been bracing for. "Why do you live with your aunt and uncle?" My heart skipped a beat, but I knew that avoiding the question would only make him more curious.

"George is my father's brother," I began. "My father died in a car accident when I was seven, so George and his wife, Carol, took me in."

"What about your mother?" I knew that the questions weren't meant to be invasive, but they brought me crashing back from our escape at the baseball cages to a reality that was inescapable.

So, I inhaled deeply and answered each question with a truthful brevity that flowed out of my lips like I was reciting it from a newspaper. No connection, no emotion – truth at its simplest.

"She became ill after my father died and wasn't fit to care for me anymore."

"I'm sorry to hear that," Evan replied genuinely. I forced my lips into a pressed smile, letting his sympathy roll off me. It didn't feel warranted and made me uneasy.

I had accepted long ago that the death of my father and fall of my mother were part of my life—I was unable to give in to the grieving. I refused to feel sorry for myself or receive pity for my circumstances. Besides, I had to focus on the present – which included surviving the wrath of Carol—so I couldn't afford to live in the past. My future was the only thing that mattered now.

"So you have a game tomorrow?" I asked, trying to sound unaffected but needing desperately to change the subject. We continued to talk about the last two weeks of the soccer season until we pulled up alongside the library.

"See you tomorrow," I said casually, getting out of the car.

"Bye," he replied before I shut the door.

I rode home, arriving in plenty of time for the grilled cheese and soup that was served for dinner. I was able to hold on to the day with Evan for a little while longer, letting it replay in my head when I sat down to dinner, keeping me oblivious to the stares I received when I took a second helping of soup. I think I was even grinning.

12. BAD INFLUENCE

THE NEXT TWO WEEKS GLIDED BY WITH THE SAME AMOUNT OF carefree ease. Evan became part of my routine, accepting all that came along with it – and finding ways to add to it as well.

Remembering my ten o'clock curfew and taking advantage of my after school activities, Evan easily convinced Sara and I to come over to his house one night after completing the layout of the newspaper with hours to spare before my deadline. Jason met us there, and the four of us attempted to play pool. I should say Sara and I attempted, Evan and Jason were pretty decent. I laughed as Sara made fun of her miscalculated shots, and she teased me for not being able to draw a straight line when I'd hit the cue ball in an unintended direction. Still smiling, I walked in the door before ten o'clock. I was oblivious to Carol and George's presence, consumed by the playback of the day in my head.

Not getting caught empowered me; making it easier to concede each time Evan came up with something else for us to do. I should've remembered I wasn't the luckiest person in the world, but the thrill of getting away with it was too addicting.

One of the nights, Sara watched in rolling laughter as Evan taught me to drive his car in the parking lot of the high school. It was late enough so no one was there, and the parking lot was on the side of the school, not easily seen from the main road since it was lined with trees. I suppose if I had witnessed the car jerking and stalling and heard me yelling in exasperation, I would have been laughing too. Evan was patiently determined, and after what felt like a whiplashing eternity, I drove his car around the parking lot, shifting from first to second. He tried to convince me to take it on the road to get used to shifting, but I refused.

That Sunday, I met him at the library again. I told my aunt and uncle I had a huge History project to work on so that I could meet Evan earlier, and we'd have more time together. He'd warned me to dress warmly when we left school on Friday. I was glad I did when he pulled into the state park a few towns west of Weslyn.

Evan guided me along a dirt trail, through the leaf encrusted woods, with the cool crisp air sweeping across our faces. The warm layers became unnecessary after my blood started pumping, wielding some effort to climb the loose terrain as we progressed further into the woods. I removed my gloves and wrapped my outer layer around my waist, leaving on my fleece.

We didn't talk much as we walked. The quiet was comfortable, and I was relieved to be away from Weslyn and enraptured by the serene setting with the chirping of the birds and the light breeze rustling the leaves. I absorbed the colorful wilderness while following Evan's navy backpack, allowing a grin to rest on my face.

Evan stopped at the base of a tall rock structure, which was virtually flat along its vertical line, accented by subtle curves and indentations. It appeared to be about a hundred feet tall inset in the earth, so only the one side was exposed.

"Ready?" he asked, looking up. I stopped and took in his line of sight, eyeing the large structure.

"Am I ready for what?" I asked tentatively.

"We're going to rappel down the face of this rock," he answered, smiling back at me. "It's really not that big, don't worry."

"We're going to do what?!"

"You'll love it, I promise." My reaction did little to deter his huge smile. "I was here yesterday scoping it out. There's a path around to the left that brings us to the top."

He took in my frozen stature and added, "You trust me, right?"

I looked at him and shook my head. "Not anymore."

He laughed. "Come on." He hiked along the path that traced the massive structure. To my dismay, my legs followed.

When we climbed to the top, the distance looking down appeared twice as far as it did when I viewed it from the bottom. My stomach rolled, but instead of becoming overtaken by panic, I was unexpectedly struck with a surge of adrenaline.

"Here's to falling to my death," I thought to myself. I joined Evan in the center of the flattened area where he was laying out the equipment.

"Ready yet?" he asked, grinning at me.

I took in a lung full of air and released it slowly through my puckered lips. "Sure."

Before I could change my mind, Evan had me slip my legs through the holes of the harness and fastened it securely. He proceeded to explain the rope system and where I should place my hands and how to release it to let myself down. I listened carefully, knowing if I didn't pay attention, I would never be listening to anything again – even with Evan's promise that he'd spot me the entire time and I had nothing to fear. Easy for him to say.

Once the rope was anchored to a sturdy tree and the figure eight was clipped to me, Evan returned to the base where he held the dropped rope to assure that I didn't fall – or to get the best view when I plummeted to my death. I backed up to the edge of the rock. The first step was the hardest, especially leaning back into a position that defied gravity. The adrenaline pushed me over the edge, and I was planted on the side of the rock, staring straight up through the treetops toward the sky. I remained still, trying to fight the urge to lean upright.

Evan hollered instructions from below to correct my angle and the positioning of my feet. I tentatively fed the rope with my right hand as my feet slowly crept down. After I got used to the release and footing, my stuttered steps progressed into small hops, until my feet found the safety of the ground. It didn't take as long as I imagined, but I still felt exhilarated to be standing on my own – upright.

"What did you think?" Evan asked with a grin.

"I liked it," I surrendered, grinning back.

"I knew you would." I rolled my eyes as he unclipped the rope from my harness.

We rappelled a couple more times, and I felt more comfortable with each attempt. Evan chose to go face-first his last time, which was difficult to watch. The speed with which he ran down the rock caught my breath.

"Show off," I mumbled as he landed with ease on the bed of fallen leaves.

"Don't worry, you'll be looking for the next rush too after you get used to it."

"I don't think I'll ever want to do that."

"I think I found the perfect place for you to try to drive my car. The road that almost never has cars on it," Evan declared on our way back down to the car. "We can go out after you work on the paper on Tuesday."

"You really think that I should be driving on the road for the first time in the dark?"

"You're right," he agreed. "Let's go out while it's still light after soccer practice. Then we'll go back to the school so you can work on the paper."

"We'll see," I said, without committing.

"Do you think you'll be able to go to the homecoming game on Friday night?"

"No," I said without even thinking twice.

"So no dance on Saturday night either, huh?"

I let out a laugh in response.

"Are you going to the homecoming dance?" I asked, not sure why I wanted to know.

"Don't think so."

"Why not?" I encouraged, but oddly filled with a sense of relief. "You can't tell me you couldn't find anyone to go with."

"Emma, you and I are dating, remember?" he taunted, his mouth pushing into a slow grin.

"Shut up," I snapped back. "You can't tell me people still think that? Haven't you told them we're not?"

"I haven't said anything either way."

"That's stupid." I stopped to look at him. "Why would you want everyone assuming something that isn't true?"

"Why should I care?"

"So you can ask someone you're interested in to go to the dance with you," I replied, not expecting his lack of concern.

"I just did."

"You did not just ask me to the dance." I crossed my arms across my chest in defiance. He smirked and shrugged. I turned and kept walking along the path.

"Whatever happened with Haley?" I questioned, changing the focus. "She's nominated for homecoming queen."

"Seriously?" he scoffed. "Have you ever tried having a conversation with her?"

"I don't think she even knows my name."

"I think she does now," he teased. "You know, now that we're dating."

"Evan! Knock it off," I huffed. He laughed.

"Honestly," he admitted, "I haven't been here that long, and the thought of going to the dance doesn't appeal to me. I'm not that into anyone else." My heart stammered at the last word, but my mind dismissed it before I could think too much about it.

"Is there a way you could stay over Sara's after your game on Saturday? That way you and I could hang out and watch movies or something."

"That's probably unlikely. My aunt works for the school system, in their administrations building. She'll know that it's the homecoming dance and will doubt that Sara would give up the dance to hang out with me."

"Why doesn't she like you?" A spasm shot through my chest, realizing I'd revealed too much.

I must have been silent for too long because Evan added, "Sorry. I don't get it, but you don't have to explain." We walked without speaking the remaining distance to the car. I searched for a way to recover.

What was I supposed to say? *No Evan, she doesn't "not like me", she despises me. She lets me know it every opportunity she can because I invaded her life, and she wants me out. But her marriage to my father's brother keeps me in her house, so it's her mission to make every second of my life torturously miserable.*

I knew those words would never leave my lips, so while Evan loaded the backpacks into the trunk, I leaned my back against the car and blurted, "It wasn't easy to be an instant mother of a twelve year-old. I'm sure she's just being way too overprotective, not wanting me to get into trouble."

Evan let my words sink in for a moment before responding. "Does she even know you?" he challenged. "You're not the type of person to hang out with the wrong crowd. You're the perfect student, a talented athlete, and the most responsible person I've ever met." He almost sounded angry.

111

I turned to look at him, confused by his fervent reaction.

"I don't understand why they can't see who you really are and allow you to live a little. You know—go to football games, dances or even on a date." He was speaking louder, more agitated as he completed his thoughts.

"No, you don't understand," I said quietly, but firmly, taking in his agitation. His reaction bothered me. He shouldn't care if they knew me or not. He was just supposed to accept my answers and let it go. "I think I should get back to the library." I turned, leaving him looking after me as I entered the car.

Evan slipped quietly onto the driver's seat and hesitated before starting the car.

"Emma, I'm sorry." I looked out the window, not ready to face him. "You're right, I don't know. If it's none of my business, then I promise not to bring it up again. I didn't mean to make you upset." His voice was quiet and pleading. I heard his sincerity through my defenses.

"It *is* none of your business," I confirmed quietly, still not looking at him. He started the car, and we drove away in silence. "And I'm not mad at you." I looked over at him with a soft smile to convince him I wasn't – he smiled back. My cheeks flooded instantly with heat.

"Do you think you and Sara could get out of watching the JV game to get pizza or something on Wednesday?" I smiled, recognizing he wasn't ready to give up trying to stretch my boundaries.

"I think so."

Evan and I continued as if the conversation never happened. He didn't talk about my lack of freedom, and I didn't push him away. We had our driving lesson on Tuesday and pizza with Sara and Jason on Wednesday. My world revolved in a fairly predictable rotation, despite Evan's impulsive persistence – determined to be a bad influence. Miraculously, I was still able to avoid Carol for the most part. Each day, I found it easier to smile.

To top it all off, the soccer team was locked in as the division champions. We had one game left of the regular season before the state championship playoffs. Coach Peña revealed he'd been taping my games to send highlights to college recruiters. I didn't realize he'd been doing this, but the knowledge that more schools were interested made me believe that escape was actually possible. He even warned that more scouts may be attending the first round of the playoffs. For the first time, my life felt livable.

13. REPLACED

"YOU'VE CHANGED," SARA OBSERVED WHEN WE DROVE HOME ON Friday.

"What are you talking about?"

"It's not bad," she said quickly. "I think it's Evan – he's made you... happier. I like seeing you like this." I absorbed her words with my eyes scrunched. She continued, ignoring my reaction. "Why aren't you dating him yet?"

"Are you done?" I asked dubiously.

"What?!"

"Sara, I cannot date anyone, forget about Evan Mathews," I declared. "And despite your assumptions, he really doesn't want to date me."

"Em, you're seriously blind. Why *wouldn't* he want to date you? He spends just about every second that he can with you."

"We're friends," I stressed.

"Whatever you have to say to convince yourself," Sara said, shaking her head. "But did you know that he's been asked out by several girls and won't even give them the time of day?"

I shrugged, but a smirk crept on my face in hearing this. Sara eyed me with a small shake of her head as she pulled up in front of my house.

"I'll pick you up at two o'clock tomorrow," Sara said as I got out of the car.

"Have fun at the game tonight," I told her, leaning in the car. "All the nominees get announced onto the field at half time, right?" She rolled her eyes at the thought of being paraded in front of the spectators. I laughed and closed the door.

⊶⊷

I practically hummed through my chores the next morning. I was looking forward to getting out of the house for the last game before the playoffs and the ice cream Evan, Sara and I were going to try to sneak in on the way home. After replacing the trash bag in the kitchen, I turned to go back to my room to find Carol blocking my path.

"What are you up to?" she demanded.

"I don't understand," I said slowly, recognizing the fire in her eyes. My body tensed, evaluating her stance and checking to see if she was holding anything in her hands. Her hands were empty and set firmly on her hips.

"Are you fucking someone?" she accused with disgust. My jaw dropped open. "I don't know what you're up to, but you don't seem to care about anyone other than yourself—even more than usual. When I figure it out, you'll wish you never treated me with such disrespect."

Confusion swirled with anxiety as the tension continued to build. I couldn't find the words to provide her with the proper answer to her illogical accusations.

"Maybe you should be spending more time at home, so I know what you're up to."

"I'm sorry," I blurted, not knowing what else to say. I was terrified by the thought of being confined within these walls any longer than I was already sentenced, and it was the first thing that came out of my mouth. My head rocked to the right as her closed fist collided with my jaw. My hand instinctively covered where she made contact as my eyes watered from the force of the blow.

A sharp breath inhaled, but not from me, followed by whimpers. I looked toward the small sounds and found Jack and Leyla standing with big eyes in the dining room. Leyla was crying, her sobs muffled by her small hand that hung from her mouth. Big tears soaked her soft, round cheeks. Jack was silent, but his wide shocked eyes were more painful than Leyla's uncontrollable sobs. My heart broke as I stepped to comfort them. Carol grabbed my arm, stopping me.

"Look what you've done," she growled, glaring at me with her cold hateful eyes. "Get out of my sight." I allowed the heart wrenching

114

image of Leyla and Jack's terrified faces to brand me before retreating to my room.

I threw myself on my bed and cried into my pillow. My heart ached as their image continued to burn in my head. They were never supposed to see. It was never supposed to touch them. I couldn't contain my spasms as I cried harder, stifling my moans with my pillow. I was supposed to protect them from this. The guilt consumed me until I couldn't cry anymore and sunk into a draining sleep.

My body tensed with a streak of pain across the back of my legs. I shook out of my slumber, not certain if I'd dreamt it. The second lash against my bare skin confirmed my waking nightmare.

"You selfish cunt." I recognized the words through clenched teeth.

I pulled my legs into me, covering my head with my hands, leaving my back exposed. With each rageful swing, my body recoiled, receiving the sharp burning lashes with a jaw tightened grunt.

"How could you hurt them like that?" she demanded, with a fury that made her almost unintelligible. "I knew I should never have let you set foot in my home—you've destroyed everything." Her hatred streaked across my back as she swung wildly. I could barely breathe. I clenched my teeth harder, tensing with each strike, unable to escape.

"You fucking worthless piece of shit. You should never have been born." She continued with her expletives, inaudible to my ears. I remained in my protective ball, shutting her off, and blocking out the fire emblazoning my flesh – searching for an escape. I retreated deeper until I was no longer in the room with her, blocking out the pain and rage and the tears dripping off my nose.

"I don't want to see you for the rest of the day," she grunted in exhaustion, leaving my room.

I remained still for another minute, listening to my erratic pulse thumping in my ears and my breath quivering with each inhale. I slowly unwrapped myself, my back an inferno. I turned to sit on the edge of my bed, looking down at my trembling hands, embossed with red streaks.

I leaned forward, my forearms on my thighs, forcing the air to pass through my lungs at a slow even pace. That's when I noticed the thin leather belt coiled on the floor. Anger overtook me, slithering around my heart. I continued to breathe deeply through my nose with a clenched jaw. I was consumed by loathing, allowing the venom to pump fervently through my veins. I didn't have the strength to push it away. Instead, I let it rest under my skin and feed my weary muscles. I stood to prepare for my game.

I slid gingerly into Sara's car, sitting up straight to avoid contact with the seat.

"Hi," she began with a smile, and stopped short – her smile instantly fading. I knew what I looked like, and her eyes reflected back the same image I had seen in my mirror. My face was pale, contrasting with the dark circles under my withdrawn, vacant eyes. I kept my lips pressed together, afraid of being betrayed by a gasp of pain. I couldn't look at her, but I didn't try to be anything different than the person she stared at in horror.

She slowly pulled away, unable to say anything. We drove in silence for a moment until she finally demanded, "I need you to tell me what happened." I kept my eyes directed toward the side window, without seeing the passing scenery.

"Emma, please." I could hear the desperation in her voice.

"It's nothing, Sara," I said flatly, still unwilling to look at her.

We arrived at the school without saying another word. Absently, I walked to the field, not noticing Sara walking beside me until a few girls greeted us. As we approached the field, I pulled the hood of my sweatshirt over my head, focusing on the ground, ignoring everyone around me. The varsity game was the only game being played, so as soon as the other team arrived, we gathered for our pre-game warm-ups.

The first half of the game was an agonizing blur. I couldn't focus, and my legs failed me when I sprinted to a pass. I ended up quickly passing the ball off or was unable to intercept it at all. At half time, Coach Peña pulled me aside.

"Are you okay?" he asked, the concern reflecting in his eyes. "You seem stiff out there. Are you hurt?"

"I think I moved wrong and pulled something in my back," I lied, looking down.

"Do you want the trainer to look at it?"

"No." The urgent words came out too quickly; shock flashed across his eyes. "I'll be fine, really," I pleaded.

"Okay." He paused. "I'll sit you out the second half, so you don't push it. I can't afford to have you injured for the quarter finals on Friday." I nodded.

We returned to the team that was gathered around the bench. To everyone's surprise, Coach Peña told Katie Brennan she was starting the second half in my place. I sat with my hood over my head and my hands in my pocket, avoiding the questioning stares.

When the final whistle blew, I rushed to the locker room before anyone knew I was gone. I knew I'd have the locker room to myself since everyone usually went home to shower and change. It was a quick shower with the warm water burning my inflamed skin, making it difficult to breathe. I was getting dressed with my back to the door when I heard footsteps behind me. I should have pulled the curtain shut behind me, but it didn't matter now.

I didn't turn around and the person behind me didn't say anything. I delicately pulled the turtleneck over my head, covering my marks of disgrace. Unable to avoid the confrontation any longer, I turned to face Sara. She was sitting on the bench across from me with tears running down her cheeks and her jaw tensed. She looked... broken.

"I can't," she began, but choked on the words. Sara stopped to breathe it away before uttering, "I can't do this anymore." I could only stare at her, watching her crumble. A wall encased me, separating me so I wouldn't break with her. "I can't ignore it; I can't pretend that I don't see what she's doing to you."

Sara's shoulders sunk as she slowly lifted her head, revealing the tears streaming down her cheeks. "Emma, you have to tell someone." Her words sounded desperate and urgent. "If you don't, then I will."

"No, you won't," I snapped. My tone was coated with ice that made Sara wince.

"What do you mean?" she demanded, even more passionately. "Did you see your back? The blood was seeping through your shirt during the game. Emma, I'm afraid some morning when I pull up to get you, you won't come out. I care about you, and I can't watch her do this to you."

"Then don't," I stated coldly. I was disconnected from my thoughts, and the words dug into Sara like daggers. She recoiled with each jab. This was a confrontation I never saw coming, and my defenses were heightened, not willing to let her jeopardize everything I'd sacrificed to protect Leyla and Jack.

"You won't tell anyone about me, and I won't tell anyone about how you fuck every other guy that gives you the time of day."

Sara's eyes widened filled with pain; the mortal blow had been driven. "You're not the only one who's good at keeping her mouth

117

shut. I know exactly who you are Sara, so don't think for one minute you know what's good for me."

"You bitch," she murmured, the shock settling into her shoulders as she practically disintegrated in front of me. "You fucking bitch." She couldn't look up at me, covering her face to conceal the cascade of tears.

"Stay out of my life. And keep your mouth shut." I took my possessed body and left her fighting to gain control of her breath after my verbal assault. I didn't look back. With my bag in hand, I walked away – not truly comprehending what I'd just done, and at that moment, I didn't really care.

Jason and Evan were waiting outside the building when I walked out of the school.

"Sorry about the loss," Evan said. Then he looked at me, taken aback, like he didn't recognize me.

"Can you drive me home?" I asked before he could say anything.

"Sure," he answered, deciding it was best not to ask the question that flashed across his eyes. Jason remained quiet as we left him waiting for Sara.

I gave him directions in a foreign flat tone when we drove out of the parking lot.

Unable to contain the question any longer, he asked, "What happened with Sara?"

I stared out the window, not wanting to think about what I'd done – letting the question dissipate into the air. He let my silence answer for me and kept driving.

"Do you want to talk about it?" he offered gently. I could feel him looking at me, but I kept staring out the window. I shook my head and held my hands together to conceal the shaking.

We pulled up to my house in tense silence. I got out of the car and shut the door before he could make me face my betrayal with another question.

Dazed, I walked up the driveway to the back door. I looked around, perplexed, when I found it locked. That's when I realized the driveway was empty. I was too entangled in my whirling emotions to care that I was locked out of the house. I sat on the top step of the deck and wrapped myself in my jacket against the cold October evening. I brought my knees up to my chest and collapsed my head in them, releasing my regret. I cried until the muscles in my chest hurt and my sobs were tearless.

When the anger washed away, I was left sad, defeated and alone. The darkness surrounded me while I waited for someone to come home. I shivered against the cold wind whipping against me. I had no idea how long I'd been sitting there, but I was startled from my hollowness when the headlights illuminated the driveway. Suddenly comprehending what this might mean, my stomach released a surge of paralyzing fear.

When George walked around the side of the house alone, I released the tension with a long breath.

"Carol and the kids are staying over at her mother's tonight," George stated as he unlocked the door. I followed him in silence. Before I could retreat to my cave, he added, "I don't know what happened between you two today, but I want you to take it easy on her."

The statement threw a shocked look across my face that I knew he saw.

"She's under a lot of stress at work, and she needs to be able to relax at home," he explained. "Do what you can to make it easy for her."

I stared at him for a second, before I whispered, "Okay." My stomach turned in disgust as I continued toward my room. He was never around to see what happened – he couldn't feel guilty for what he refused to see.

I entered the dark room, closing the door behind me—not bothering to turn on the light. I dropped my jacket on the floor and collapsed onto my bed, falling into a restless sleep.

I couldn't breathe. I grasped at my neck, trying to loosen the tightening cord as my feet were pulled off the bed. I couldn't see in the dark, but I could feel my body sway with each jerk of the thin rope. I tried to reach above me to find something to pull myself up on. The line was cutting into my neck, crushing my trachea. I became dizzy with the pressure building in my head and the screaming of my lungs, demanding the air that would never come.

119

14. HOLLOW

I WOKE UP GASPING, DRENCHED IN SWEAT. I SLOWLY ROLLED ON MY side, trying to orient myself as I sat on the edge of the bed, breathing heavily. My turtleneck was sticking to my enflamed back, and all I could feel was the burning. I slipped into the bathroom with the sound of the TV in the kitchen, where I'm sure George was drinking coffee and reading the paper.

I slowly peeled off my turtleneck, revealing the swollen red striations of different lengths sprawled across my back. Most of the marks were superficial, with a few scabbed over. The lashes were thin, but the swelling made them appear so much worse.

Pushing away the sorrow, I eased into the shower, wishing I could wash away the pain along with the sweat that still clung to me from my nightmare

I stayed in my room for the remainder of the day. I forced myself to focus on homework assignments I had yet to complete. It allowed the day to slip by, but my lack of concentration made the work twice as long to finish.

I heard Carol and the kids return in the early afternoon. I stayed out of sight until I was startled by the door opening and found Carol standing in its frame.

"They need to know you're okay, so be happy to see them," she said coldly. "Come eat."

After allowing the paralysis to wear off, I walked to the dining room.

"Emma!" Leyla greeted me with a huge hug. I didn't flinch against the stinging pain when I bent over to put my arms around her.

"Did you have fun at Nanna's?" I asked. Leyla responded with a jubilant recollection of her time at Janet's house.

My eyes caught Jack's and I smiled at him reassuringly. He cautiously examined my smile, determined it was genuine, and smiled back. I could see the light in his eyes again, and I smiled bigger.

"We went to the aquarium today," Jack announced, adding to Leyla's exclamations about sharks and starfish.

I sat in my seat and focused my attention on their stories while I ate the meal George had prepared. I didn't look at Carol or George throughout dinner. After everyone left the table, I performed what was expected of me. The entire time, I couldn't escape the empty feeling in the pit of my stomach. When I finally went to bed, I lay awake, thinking about what was going to happen in the morning. I tried to remember if I knew where the bus stop was, fearing Sara wasn't going to be waiting for me.

❧

Sara wasn't waiting for me. As happy as I was to see his car, it meant that I'd hurt Sara even more than I could have imagined, and that was crushing.

I opened the car door to Evan's warm smile. "Good morning."

"Good morning." I offered a small smile in return. "Thank you for picking me up. I really appreciate it." I was filled with his intoxicating clean scent upon entering the car. Not a bad way to start the morning.

"Not a problem," he returned casually. After a minute of driving, Evan finally said, "I was hoping to see you at the library yesterday. I had a great plan to cheer you up."

I bit my lip. "I am so sorry. I completely forgot. It wasn't the best weekend of my life."

"I understand," he replied. "You seem a little better today."

"I'm okay," I said quietly. Knowing Sara wasn't able to be in the same car with me meant that nothing about me was okay. My chest hurt with the thought that she might not forgive me.

"How was the game on Friday?" I asked, attempting to sound interested.

"Weslyn lost, but it was close."

"Did you end up going to the dance?"

"No, I met my brother and some of his friends in New York. We went to a bar to check out this local band." Then he continued to tell me about his night and that I'd have to look up the band to download a few songs. I tried to be attentive to his story, but I became more distracted the closer we got to school.

I'm not sure how much of what Evan said I heard, because I was snapped back to the confines of the car when he said, "I have to find a way to get you to New York."

"What?! No—there is no way I'm going to New York." Then I looked over at him and his lips were pressed into a devious half smile. "Nice. That's exactly what I need in the morning – a heart attack."

"I was just seeing if you were paying attention," he said, still smirking.

After a short silence, he consoled, "I promise it will get better." I knew he was promising something he knew nothing about, but I forced an appreciative smile anyway.

The halls seemed so long and crowded today – it felt like it took forever to reach my locker. My heart was thumping loudly when I rounded the corner, but it sank when I saw that there wasn't anyone at the locker next to mine. I gathered my books and slipped into homeroom without looking at anyone. I sat in the first available desk and waited for the daily announcements and attendance so I could begin my excruciatingly long day. I couldn't bring myself to look around the room to see if Sara was there.

I did see Sara as the day progressed. Her vibrant red hair was easy to spot amongst the other bodies occupying the halls. She was usually walking alongside Jill or Jason. So, I knew she was in school; however she chose to place herself in a space other than where I was. I watched her from a distance, wishing she would look at me and know how sorry I was. But I couldn't tell her since she wasn't there to listen.

Evan accompanied me to every class, even the ones he wasn't in with me. My heart would have been fluttering uncontrollably by his constant presence if it hadn't already sunk into my stomach. At first, he tried to pre-occupy me with superficial conversation about topics I couldn't recall even if I tried. Once he realized I wasn't listening and was just nodding politely, he stopped trying to distract me.

I was too consumed with my own remorse and misery to consider how he must have felt walking alongside a shell of a human being. I wasn't whole; the guilt was eating away at me – slowly devouring my insides.

When we left Journalism with Sara's presence still burning beside me, Evan said, "Let's get out of here." Was it the end of the day already? "You can't be here anymore. Let's get your things and we'll go to my house and hang out."

Registering what was happening, I asked, "Don't you have soccer practice?" I knew coach had given us the day off, planning to work us hard for the next three days before our game on Friday – but I was pretty sure the guys still had practice since their game was on Thursday.

"I told one of the guys to tell coach that I have a doctor's appointment."

I couldn't come up with a reason to reject his invitation. I followed him to my locker and threw books in my bag, not paying attention to whether I needed them or not. Then Evan led me to his locker where he grabbed his things.

I didn't remember driving to his house. The next moment I was aware of was when we slowed down to pull into his driveway. I looked around, dazed, wondering where my thoughts had taken me in the time it took us to drive here. Did Evan try to talk to me? Did I answer him?

"We're here," he announced. The way his voice cut through the air let me know we'd driven in silence, and perhaps I'd fallen asleep.

I took a deep breath and got out of the car. Before I took a step toward the house, I said, "Evan, I'm not sure you really want to hang out with me today."

He stopped on the steps of the porch. "Of course I do. Come on."

I wanted to force myself to put up a pleasant pretense so that his efforts to cheer me up wouldn't be completely lost. I searched within the shadows but couldn't find a persona that was remotely convincing. I decided to do my best not to be completely devastating.

Evan grabbed two bottles from the refrigerator and continued down the long hall which opened up into a brightly lit space containing a piano and a built-in bookcase. Besides some large planted trees, there wasn't anything else in the window encased room except for a set of winding wooden stairs that led to a landing overlooking the perimeter of the room.

I followed Evan up the stairs into a door off of the landing. The dark room was much smaller than Sara's, but still twice the size of mine – and with it's own bathroom. Overlapping images of athletes and musicians covered the wall behind his bed. A simple black desk with a rolling chair was set in the opposing corner – above it hung a board with pins securing snapshots of friends and creased concert tickets. The queen sized bed filled the center of the room with the headboard set against the wall. A tall bureau displayed a flat-screen television, and a closet ran along the same wall as the entrance. The bed and tower of drawers were stained a deep espresso, adding to the darkness of the space.

Evan set his backpack next to his desk and pushed a couple of buttons on his laptop. Music hummed through the speakers that were suspended in each corner of the room. The soothing acoustics and rhythmic melodies filled the bedroom.

"Sorry, I don't have anywhere to sit besides the bed," he said, offering me one of the bottles of soda he had in his hands.

I remained still inside the doorway. My heart found a rhythm from within the cave where it was held captive. Sit on his bed, really? I slowly walked over and sat on the edge of the bed, not ready to commit to putting my legs up.

Evan propped up one of his pillows against the headboard and sat next to me on the deep red comforter. I knew I had to move further onto his bed in order to face him. I pushed my shoes off and shuffled towards the foot of the bed, sitting opposite of him with my legs crossed beneath me.

"I don't like seeing you upset," he finally said.

"Sorry," was all I could find to say, looking down at my hands.

"I wish I could do something to make you feel better. Can you tell me what happened?" I shook my head. Silence followed for a minute as the comforting tunes continued in the background.

"Sara will talk to you again," Evan said as if it were a fact.

"I don't know if she will," I whispered. My chest ached thinking about why she may not. "I said some pretty terrible things." My eyes brimmed with tears that I tried to blink away.

Evan scooted toward me and placed his warm hand on my cheek, brushing away the escaped tear.

"She'll forgive you," he said lowly. He pulled me towards him and put his arms around me. I buried my head in his chest and released the seeping tears. After a time, I collected myself and pulled away.

"How is it you always see me at my best?" I asked, trying to smile, feeling emotionally exposed.

"It's not a bad thing."

I wasn't sure what he meant, but decided to leave it alone.

"Can I use your bathroom?"

"Sure."

I entered the small bathroom with the pedestal sink, toilet and glass enclosed shower, closing the door behind me. I rinsed the emotions away, splashing my face with cool water. I took in the light brown eyes looking back at me and urged myself to recover. After drying my face with a towel, I inhaled a calming breath before opening the door. It didn't hurt that the breath contained Evan's soothing scent.

Evan was sitting against the headboard again, flipping through channels on the flat-screen.

"Still haven't unpacked?" I asked, nodding toward the boxes marked "Evan's room" that remained unopened under the empty built-in bookcase, and another box beneath the only window.

"Getting there," he replied casually.

"How is it that the rest of your house looks like people have been here for years, and you can't finish putting away a few boxes?"

Evan let out a quick laugh.

"We have moving down to a science. My mother plans out in advance where everything is to be displayed, stored, and hung; then they hire the same moving company we've used for every move. They not only pack and move us, but then unpack us when they arrive. We walk in, and this is already done. The only thing they don't touch is my stuff."

"And..." I pushed for him to explain the reason for his taped boxes.

"Well... I haven't decided if I'm staying." Something shot through me – I couldn't tell what it was, but it felt a little like panic.

"Oh," I murmured.

"Do you want to watch a movie?"

"Sure." I walked around to the vacant side of the bed and propped the other pillow up to sit next to Evan.

He found an action movie he had saved in his digital movie library. I didn't last very long before my eyes became heavy. Being miserable was exhausting. I surrendered to their weight and drifted to sleep.

"Emma," Evan whispered in my ear. It took me a minute to comprehend that his voice was real. "Em, the movie's over." His voice sounded too close.

My eyes popped open. My head had slipped into the hollow of his shoulder, with his arm resting on the top of my pillow. I pushed myself up to sit on my own, still trying to blink the sleep from my eyes.

"Sorry. I didn't mean to sleep through the entire thing." I stretched my arms over my head, expecting to be sore or stiff – surprised to find that I wasn't.

"It's okay," he said with a laugh. "I think you drooled on my shirt though."

My mouth dropped open. "I did not."

"I'm just kidding." He laughed louder.

"You're such a jerk," I declared, throwing my pillow at his head.

Evan took the pillow and swung it back at me. I jumped up, standing on the bed, and grabbed the pillow from behind him. I swung it, connecting with his back. He tackled my legs out from under me, and I toppled on the bed, igniting my back. He proceeded to pelt me in the face with a pillow.

"That's cheating," I murmured from under the pillow, trying to dismiss my discomfort. "No tackling."

"You can tackle," he defended.

"Fine." I charged, pushing him onto his back with all my force and sat on his chest, pinning down his arms with my knees, connecting his face with the swing of a pillow.

"Uh, playing dirty," he grunted as he flipped me over, easily sliding his arms out from under my weight. He was poised over me with his hands on either side of my head, his body still, between my knees. He held himself above me, looking down with a smirk. I could feel his warm breath on my face, and the burning along my back disappeared. We both recognized at the same time the close proximity of our bodies and that neither of us was holding a pillow. I stopped breathing, looking up at him with wide eyes, watching his smirk slowly disappear.

"Want to play pool?" I asked, quickly rolling out from under him as he fell to his side. In a continuous motion, I stood and grabbed my shoes before leaving the room. Evan looked after me from his bed, still propped up on his side as I scurried down the stairs.

He sauntered into the kitchen with his cheeks flushed.

"Want a bottle of water?" he offered, casually opening the refrigerator.

"Sure," I said, unable to ignore the fire engulfing my back from the pillow fight. "Do you mind if we play darts instead?" I asked. While his back was turned, I washed down a few ibuprofen that I had stuffed in my pocket.

"Works for me," Evan commented, studying my face for a moment. I grinned before he saw the pain dart across my eyes. He grinned back and I followed him to the garage.

After a few rounds of practice, my thoughts drifted to the unpacked boxes in his room.

"I thought you liked it here?" I watched him hesitate before throwing a dart.

"What do you mean?"

"You said you didn't know if you were staying, and that's why you haven't unpacked."

Evan stopped before he threw the last dart, and turned to face me. "Are you worried you'd miss me if I left?" he asked with a wry grin.

I raised my eyebrows in disapproval – I refused to answer.

"I like it here," he finally said, after tossing his last dart. "Honestly, I've never completely unpacked anywhere. I still had unopened boxes after living in San Francisco for over two years."

"Why?"

"I don't know," he replied, stopping to think about it. "Maybe I was never completely convinced I was going to stay – and look, I was right. You didn't answer my question – would it bother you if I left?"

I shrugged, "I'd survive." I smiled, giving away my inability to be serious.

"Now you're the jerk," he said, smirking back. "Don't worry; I won't throw darts at you."

The rest of the afternoon passed with darts and foosball, allowing my back to cool to a simmer. Evan still won every game; but he appeared impressed when I didn't lose by much. I kept my sorrow at bay while in his company, thankful he helped me escape the rest of my day at school. It was so hard to be there with Sara, knowing she was so angry with me. But it was harder to go home.

My smile faded when I got into his car. Evan noticed my solemn transition, but he didn't say anything to distract me from my silence as I braced myself for the tension that still festered in my house.

"I'll see you tomorrow," he said softly, as I opened the car door. I nodded and then stopped to look at him.

"Thank you for today." I offered him a small smile. He lightly smiled back.

"Whose car was that?" Carol questioned as soon as I walked through the door.

"Sara's car is getting a tune up," I lied; a spasm of anxious nerves shot from my stomach through my chest, fearing she'd see right through it. I kept walking to my room without hesitating before I could find out.

∾

I was greeted with the same mixed feelings of seeing Evan's car when I walked down my driveway the next morning. The improbability of Sara forgiving me was sinking in. I was so very cruel; how could I blame her. Besides, why would she want to put up with my insane life anymore? I wasn't sure how I was still coping.

I knew I'd never be able to confide in Evan the way I did Sara. I was still struggling with allowing him to be as close as he was. I suppose I was selfish to think that Sara would always be there. We came from two completely different worlds, and the reality of these differences was unavoidable. It was only a matter of time.

Evan allowed me to grieve without much intervention. He escorted me through the bustle of the halls to each of my classes, and somehow, I got through the day. The teachers' incoherent lessons hummed in my ears. The minutes crept, and the hollowness grew. Sometime during the day, Evan disappeared too. I almost didn't notice until I rounded the corner to my locker and saw him standing in front of it with his back to me.

Evan was talking to someone. He seemed really upset. Then I saw the red hair shaking back and forth. My feet kept me moving forward against my will. I couldn't hear their voices, but her face looked so sad. Evan's hands were pleading.

Then I heard, "Sara, please tell me what happened. She's devastated, and I need to understand why."

"If she hasn't told you, then I can't."

Her eyes caught mine. I froze a few lockers away, unable to process what was happening. Sara closed her locker and rushed away. Evan slowly turned to acknowledge me. I examined him with narrowed eyes, trying to understand.

"Why did you do that?" I accused, horrified.

"If you only knew what I've seen for the past two days, you would have done the same thing."

I still didn't understand. His intrusion rocked me, and I needed to get away from him. I turned and dodged my way through the crowd, my books still clutched to my chest.

"Emma, wait," he pleaded, but he didn't come after me.

I ducked into the bathroom and found an empty stall. I pressed my back against the partition, remembering Sara's sad expression. I allowed the tears to burn down my cheeks while the scene replayed in my head. I didn't know why I wasn't relieved that she hadn't told anyone about my situation—maybe because I never thought she would.

As much as I wanted to, I couldn't be angry with Evan. I didn't like that he upset Sara, but I knew it wasn't his fault. He really had no idea what he was walking into. Could I continue to allow him to be a witness to my misery without an explanation? Knowing I wouldn't ever tell him what came between Sara and me and that I could never confide in him if something were to happen to me again, only left me with one answer. I needed to give him up. I struggled with the decision, but it was something I always knew I'd have to do.

15. RELENTLESS

"IT'S NICE TO SEE YOU USING SUCH VIBRANT COLORS," MS. MIER noted as she stood behind me, admiring my painting. "You have always used such deep colors in the past, still with extraordinary results, but this is refreshing. Whatever's changed, I like it."

Then she walked on to the next easel. I leaned back and looked at the nearly completed portrait of the fall foliage. Before Ms. Mier approached, I was thinking that the colors were too bright and unrealistic. The paint brush in my hand was coated with a burnt orange, to fade the fiery hues on the canvas. I set the brush down and stared at the colors again. They were blinding to my dull eyes.

I continued to stare at the blur of colors until Ms. Mier asked everyone to begin cleaning up. Startled by the sudden movement, I looked around and clumsily began gathering my supplies. I caught Evan standing in the back of the room, by the photography supplies, watching me with concern. I continued cleaning up my unused paints, ignoring him.

"Do you want to study for the Anatomy test with me?" Evan asked when we left the room.

"Uh... no, I can't," I stumbled. "I have to work on the paper."

"I can go with you."

"No, that's okay," I said quickly, barely giving him a glance. "I think I'd rather be alone."

"Okay," he said slowly and continued down the hall when I stopped at my locker.

I was forced to look after him, reminding myself that closing him out was the right thing to do. The right thing felt horrible—my eyes followed him until he rounded the corner. My heart ached, and for a second I reconsidered my decision, but I shook it off and opened my locker.

Soccer practice was not only hard physically but emotionally as well. Having to interact with Sara without connecting was torturous. When we weren't on the field, she remained as far away from me as she could. When we were on the field, she'd only pass to me when she didn't have any other choice.

"Lauren, would you be able to give me a ride home today?" I asked when we were standing on the sidelines during one of the drills.

"Sure," she answered without hesitation.

I kept walking alongside Lauren after practice, without looking at Evan as he waited for me by his car. I felt his eyes follow me to her car. I reminded myself again that it was for the best. But it didn't help.

"Thank you for doing this," I said to Lauren, ducking into her dark blue Volvo.

I had no idea what I was getting myself into when I asked Lauren to drive me home. She was very sweet, but she talked non-stop the entire drive. I heard about the homecoming dance and how Sara and Jason won homecoming king and queen, but neither had shown up. I tried to conceal my shock. She assumed I knew why they weren't there and tried to get me to confess. She obviously hadn't noticed Sara and I weren't talking. Why did she think she was driving me home? I played it off and said that I didn't know either.

Lauren went on about soccer and the upcoming game. She was obviously excited to make it to the championships as captain for her senior year. I was given the details of every college she applied to and how she was having a hard time deciding which she preferred. Did most girls talk this much? I tried to figure out how she breathed in-between each sentence. The topics blurred together like the scenery, and I was almost relieved when she stopped at my house, feeling exhausted after having listened to her.

"Thank you again, Lauren," I said as I opened the car door.

"If you want a ride home tomorrow, let me know. It was nice talking to you. I feel like we never get to really talk."

"I may take you up on that," I said reluctantly, knowing I'd rather walk then ask for another ride.

I tried to make it through the kitchen, but was stopped in my tracks by a stinging pain to my right arm. I winced and turned to find Carol with a metal serving spoon in her hand.

"Who the hell was that?" Carol demanded, obviously very agitated. I looked around and realized George wasn't here, and from her grip of the spoon, this could not be good for me.

"That was Lauren. She's one of the team captains," I tried to explain. I was too nervous that she'd see through my lie if I tried to explain why Sara didn't drive me, so I left it at that.

"You're pathetic. If you're begging for rides and embarrassing me, I will hurt you severely. Sara's finally seen you for who you are, huh?"

The mention of Sara's name stung worse than the red mark on my arm. I remained still, looking for any opportunity to back away to my room before this escalated.

That's when her eyes widened, and the metal spoon walloped the side of my head. I let out a moan and put my hand to my head, backing against the wall.

"You're fucking disgusting," she declared, the storm in her eyes brewing, making me fear what was to come. "How dare you come into my house smelling like that."

I looked down at my practice clothes and released a breath of defeat. I chose not to shower after practice today, so I wouldn't keep Lauren waiting. Wrong choice.

"Mom," Jack yelled from upstairs, distracting her. "Is Dad back with the pizza yet?"

She had to shake the fury from her brow before she replied in her best mother tone, "No honey, but he should be here soon. Why don't you and Leyla get washed up."

"Get out of my sight before I make you sleep outside," she snapped. I took advantage of the opportunity to rush to my room.

Upon shutting my door, I dropped my bags and rubbed the small bump on my head, relieved that's all I walked away with. I was starving but knew I'd have to suffer through it.

I tried to focus on my homework instead. I couldn't concentrate to save my life, staring at the words as they blurred in front of me. I only faintly recalled the lessons in class to coincide with the assignments, and my notes were a scribble of incoherent words. I jumped at the sound of the knock on the door at ten o'clock—signaling to turn off the lights.

I set the Trigonometry book at the bottom of my closet, and shut off the lights. I waited in bed until I heard two sets of footsteps ascend the stairs. I crept breathlessly out of bed and slipped into the closet, closing the door behind me. My closet was not very wide, which was fine since I didn't own a lot of clothes, but it was tall and deep. I had plenty of clearance to sit under my clothes without them touching the top of my head. There was a small door at the back of the closet that led into a crawl space where I stored the things that meant the most to me.

That minute space contained the only pictures I had of my parents and memories of a time that was almost too distant to remember. It was certainly a universe away from where I sat now in the confines of a closet. I also stored some of my favorite paintings and athletic awards, along with a small shoe box of letters that my mother sent to me after I'd moved in with George and Carol.

She wrote frequently at the beginning, about nothing of importance, just rambling on paper. After a while, the letters arrived further apart; until finally, they stopped coming altogether about a year and a half ago. I figured she was consumed with her life and couldn't bother with me. She had always been consumed with her life—that's why I was in this house and not hers.

I read by the pull-string light bulb suspended above the closet shelf. I referenced the textbook, trying to teach myself what I'd neglected to learn in class. By the time I crept out of my study space, it was after one o'clock in the morning. I collapsed on bed, never changing from my practice clothes. Sleep came quickly, but the dreams kept me twisting.

∞

I dragged myself to the bathroom and prepared for another day with little to look forward to, but got ready all the same. I intended to walk to the bus stop, but there he was—relentless. I was determined to keep walking, ignoring his shiny sports car.

As I walked past him, he stepped out of the car and pleaded, "Emma, don't do this."

My eyes widened in panic as I glanced from him to the picture window of the house. He saw my look of terror and glanced to the house as well.

"Then get in," he demanded. With an exasperated sigh, I stomped to his car and slid in. He closed his door and began driving away. I sat stiffly against the leather seat, with my arms crossed around my backpack and my lips pressed together, staring straight ahead.

"Are you sulking?"

Insulted, I glared at him. He produced his amused grin, agitating me more.

"You're seriously sulking," he concluded, almost laughing.

"Stop," I shot back, attempting to be serious. But the more I tried, the harder it was, and I felt my lips curl into a resisted smile. "I am not *sulking*."

Evan burst out laughing.

"Enough," I yelled, but found I was involuntarily smiling.

After he was able to stop laughing, he became too serious.

"Now you have to tell me what's going on. Why are you avoiding me?"

I remained quiet. I struggled for a rational explanation, so he would respect my decision to cut him out of my life. I couldn't come up with anything that would make sense to him. Everything I wanted to say would reveal too much. He waited patiently for my response.

"You're not Sara," I finally breathed.

"I don't want to be Sara," he replied in confusion. "I still don't understand."

"I don't know how to fit you in my world without hurting you too." The truth in my words revealed more than he'd ever know.

"Don't worry about hurting me," he replied calmly. "I like being a part of your world, and I understand that it's more complicated than you're willing to share with me. But I'll respect that, for now."

He pulled into the parking lot of a drugstore and put the car in park. Evan seemed nervous as he turned to speak to me. He released a quick breath before he spoke. My chest tightened, afraid to hear what he had to say.

"I don't do this." His hands gestured between us. My eyes narrowed, trying to interpret his meaning. He exhaled and looked out the windshield. "I don't stay, and I'm used to that. And I'm always prepared to leave – because I have to eventually."

He stopped again, frustrated with himself. I sat motionless, absolutely convinced I didn't want him to continue – but I couldn't bring myself to ask him to stop.

"I want to stay here," he finally declared. "It would bother me if I left. I mean, I've already unpacked."

Evan looked at me with a small, uncertain smile. We sat silently, looking at each other for an excruciatingly slow minute – he waited for me to say something. I broke his gaze, flashing my eyes around the car, searching for the right words. Disappointed, Evan looked away, his face turning a hue of red before he continued driving toward the school.

The tension was unbearable in the awkward silence. I was still struggling to say something that would make him give up on me; but every time I went to say it, the words were strangled in my throat. Finally, when he pulled into a parking spot and shut off the car, I looked over at him and said the only thing my heart would allow me to say.

"You should stay," I encouraged, as a smile crept across my face. Then I quickly added, "But you'll probably wish you hadn't when you finally realize I'm not all that interesting." His eyes sparkled and I watched the tension drain from his face.

As much as I knew it was the right thing to do, I couldn't continue to push him away. I searched for a logical reason to remain friends with him without finding one. It was a risk having him around, and he could never know the truth—but I wasn't ready to give him up.

"Did you really unpack?" I asked skeptically as we walked into the school.

"Actually I did – the other night after I got back from dropping you off. I think you guilted me into it."

I laughed. "So that's the secret to getting to you – guilt."

"There are other ways," he replied with his grin.

About to respond to his taunting, I stopped, realizing where we were. I searched to see if Sara was at her locker from the end of the hall. I let out a defeated sigh when I saw that she wasn't.

"How do I get her to listen to me?" I murmured, still staring down the hall.

"Maybe you have to make her," Evan answered before walking away toward his locker.

Crushed with the acceptance that this was going to be another day of avoidance, I slowly sauntered to my locker to prepare for class. I remained hollow, but I was beginning to accept the emptiness as a part of me.

I was able to listen in class and understand the lectures. I walked alongside Evan and heard his words, and even contributed to the conversation. But my eyes still searched for her in the halls, continuously disappointed when she was too far away, or if I didn't see her at all.

I tried to convince myself to give up on her and accept that I was alone in my truth. That's when it hit me – *the truth*. I stopped in the middle of the hall with Evan in mid-sentence. His words faded when he turned back to find me.

"Are you okay?" he asked hesitantly.

"I think I am." I said each word slowly, contemplating my epiphany—she *knew* the truth. Evan appeared worried. I turned my attention to him and grinned.

This did not change his look of concern, but he didn't say anything as we continued to Anatomy. Once class let out, I hurried into the hall, leaving Evan questioning my retreat. I almost ran to my locker, hoping I'd get there in time. I breathed an anxious sigh of relief when I found her still putting her books away in her locker. I moved to intercept her before she could walk away.

Spotting my approach, Sara attempted to escape in the opposite direction. Thankfully, she was alone. I followed after her and before she could exit through the doors leading to the stairs, I bellowed, "That wasn't me."

Sara stopped in her tracks when she heard my voice but didn't turn to face me. I caught up with her and stood behind her, close enough so my words wouldn't draw attention.

"I know I said some horrible things, Sara, and I will always be sorry for what I said," I offered in a rush before she could change her mind and keep walking. "But *you* know that wasn't me."

She turned apprehensively, without responding.

"Can we please talk?" I begged. She shrugged and pushed the door open. I followed her down the stairs and out the side door where she sat on the grass beside the school. She rested her arms on her bent knees, staring straight ahead without looking at me.

I slowly sat beside her and let my words float into the air, in hopes that she'd hear them.

"I'm so, so sorry for what I said to you. I wasn't myself, and I hope you know that. I was hurting, and angry, and unfortunately you were there to receive it. It wasn't right. But you know that person is not who I am."

Sara tilted her head to look over at me, so I knew she was starting to understand.

"I don't get angry. It feels horrible, and I can't stand to be like that. If I do... If I let her get to me, then she wins. She destroys me along with everything and everyone who's important to me.

"I let her get to me that day. I was consumed by it. I shouldn't have said what I did, but I also couldn't let you tell anyone. I know how easy it would be to end all of this, but I can't. It's not just my life I have to think about. Taking Leyla and Jack away from their parents would destroy them, and I can't be responsible for that. I'm strong enough to handle this. They're still kids, so I have to put up with it for a little while longer. Do you understand?"

Sara's eyes brimmed with tears. She looked away so she could wipe them.

"I know I don't have any right to ask you to be there for me. It's not the ideal friendship to be involved in, but I know I can get through this if you're there to help me. You're the only one who really knows me, and I trust you. I will never ask you to lie for me, and I will never make you be a part of anything you don't want to. But the thought that you may never talk to me again hurts worse than anything Carol could ever do to me. I don't want to lose you too."

My heart stammered at the honesty I spilled at her feet. I had never been this exposed, not even to Sara. I couldn't take back the words. I couldn't hide my vulnerability. I knew I meant what I said more than any bitter, hurtful word I spewed in the locker room, and I hoped the truth was enough.

I waited in tense silence. "You haven't lost me, Em," she finally whispered. "You're right, as much as I don't understand it—you're not an angry person. Sad and withdrawn, definitely—but not angry; even though you have every right to be." She paused.

"I knew you didn't mean what you said. The reason I haven't been able to face you is because *I* get so angry when I look at you." I was confused by her confession. "I *hate* this woman for hurting you. It makes me so angry I can hardly contain myself, and I don't like feeling angry either. But you're right – this is exactly what she wants – to isolate and destroy anything positive you have. We can't let that happen. I know you're strong enough to do it without me, but I'm not ready to quit being your friend either." Her eyes glistened as she offered me a soft smile.

I tried to blink away the wetness in my eyes. Sara stood up and opened her arms to hug me. I stood as well, and I let her without tensing.

She pulled away and smiled, wiping the tears from her cheeks again. "Let's get one thing straight," she said looking me in the eye with all seriousness, "if you ever call me a slut again, I will never speak to you. I know what I'm doing, so stay out of it. Got it?"

"Yes, I got it," I promised sincerely. "I am still really sorry about that."

"I know," she replied, grabbing my hand. "And I'm sorry I threatened to expose you. I understand why you're doing this. I hate it—I'm not going to lie. But I'm here for you, no matter what."

This time, I hugged her tightly. "Thanks."

16. THE PLAN

WE WALKED TO THE CAFETERIA TOGETHER. WHEN WE NEARED THE entrance, Sara said, "We have to come up with a plan."

"What kind of plan?"

"You deserve to be happy. I've noticed how much more relaxed you've been since Evan's been a bad influence. So, let's figure out a way for you to get into college, survive living with your aunt and uncle, and still have fun."

"That sounds impossible," I said, shaking my head.

"We'll be smart about it," she winked.

"You did not just wink at me."

"Shut up," she said, playfully shoving my arm. Thankfully not the arm with the fresh bruise.

When we were seated at the lunch table with our trays of food, Sara continued with her thoughts. It was obvious that she'd given this some attention before today.

"Okay, you and Evan have already started doing what I have in mind. You know, with pushing your "at school time", and going to the library. I think we can try to expand it to a Friday or Saturday night so you can stay over my house. It will definitely work the nights you have basketball games, but the game will take up most of the night and not give us much time to do anything else. I have to figure out an excuse that they'll buy to get you out of their house as much I can."

She was right—I was already stretching the little freedom I had when I claimed to be at school or the library. What was another night? Then I remembered Carol's suspicious interrogation, sending an icy chill down my spine as the doubt settled in. How was I going to get away with this?

"But Emma," Sara stated seriously, "if you ever get caught, I will not let her hurt you. I will tell my parents, or call the police, before I allow you to get hurt for my plan. Okay?" From the stern look upon her face, I knew she meant it.

"Okay," I whispered, knowing I'd never let it happen. "Sara, while we're talking about that – you have to trust me." I could tell she didn't quite understand. "I know what I can handle. Even though it's not right, it's the way things are until I can get out of their house. So you have to trust me when I don't tell you what happens sometimes, okay?"

Sara paused for a moment, absorbing my words. "Emma, always be honest with me." I connected with her penetrating eyes and nodded slightly – again knowing I wouldn't.

On our way back up to our lockers, Sara turned to me and asked eagerly, "Are you and Evan officially dating yet?"

I rolled my eyes. "That still will not happen."

"I don't understand why not," she teased.

Sara's smile got bigger when we found Evan waiting at my locker. He released a smile when he saw Sara walking with me.

"Hi Sara," he said, still smiling.

"Hi Evan," she greeted, smiling back.

"Ready for Journalism?" he asked. "Oh, Em, do you think you'll be able to finish with the paper during class and study period so that maybe we can do something after practice?"

"That's perfect," Sara interjected, before I could answer. "Let's go back to my house and get pizzas and hang out." She was thrilled to have an accomplice in *Operation: Free-Em*. She was almost jumping up and down.

Evan took in her over joyous response with pause, having no idea what Sara and I had been discussing during lunch.

"Sara's trying to come up with a plan to expose me to the world outside of school and my house, and you're just feeding into it," I explained.

"That's always been *my* plan," Evan admitted. Sara beamed.

"I hope I know what I'm getting myself into," I said with a sigh and a roll of my eyes.

"The chance to live a little," Sara offered, barely able to contain her enthusiasm.

"So *you* say," I grumbled. She laughed. I loved having her back.

After practice, Evan and Jason followed us to Sara's.

While we were in the car, I told Sara, "I'm so sorry you and Jason didn't go to homecoming. I can only assume it was my fault."

Sara scoffed, "Don't even worry about it. I really didn't want to go and Jason is so shy, he would've been mortified to have to wear the crown on stage." I still felt bad for being the reason she missed out on such a huge moment.

"How was the ride home with Lauren yesterday?" she asked, changing the subject.

"Exhausting," I sighed, which made Sara laugh. "I didn't realize anyone could talk so much or so fast."

"She's so nice, but yeah, she likes to go on and on about anything and everything."

Sara's house was dark when we pulled up.

"My parents went out to dinner *again*," she observed with a heavy breath.

The next few hours epitomized everything Sara wanted for me. We ate pizza, listened to music, played video games, and laughed. The laughter filled up the hollow hole, and my heart returned to its proper place in my chest, putting me back together again.

Not wanting to risk it, I decided it was best to leave around nine o'clock. Evan volunteered to drive me home. Sara hugged me good night and said she'd see me in the morning. Evan looked up from putting on his jacket when she said this.

"I liked picking you up," Evan admitted when we stepped outside. "Although you were less talkative than usual, I actually looked forward to seeing you first thing in the morning."

"Sorry. You'll have to be satisfied with seeing me in just about every class instead."

"It's good that you and Sara are okay," he said during the drive to my house. "How'd it happen?"

"I made her listen." He smiled at my response.

∞

The next week continued like the time without Sara was just a hiccup. Sara and I were inseparable again. Evan still walked me to class, but became absent during the second part of the day when I had lunch and study with Sara. I noticed the first couple of days and couldn't figure out why I was bothered by it.

We did things together as the three of us, and occasionally four when Jason joined after school. Coach let us watch the second half of the guys' quarter final game on Thursday, which they lost. Evan was crushed, but he recovered when I told him that I wasn't expected home until nine o'clock.

Weslyn won the soccer game that Friday with a score of four to three. I contributed two of the scores, which was fortunate since three scouts were in attendance. I was assured by Coach Peña that I played well and that I'd be hearing from them. I could only hope.

Sara joined Evan and me that Sunday for our library day. I think she was trying to make up for lost time, which made me happy. But I noticed the surprise on Evan's face when Sara pulled up behind his car. I don't know what Evan had initially planned, but once he saw Sara was joining us, he suggested we go back to his place to play pool.

Sara and I were a team and played against Evan. Of course, he still beat us. Despite his initial reaction, Evan didn't show any signs that he wasn't happy to have Sara there. While we played, Sara instigated a plan for the following weekend. She figured I'd be able to sleep over at her house on Friday for the championship game, assuming we won the semi-finals on Tuesday. I wasn't convinced since it was a five o'clock game and wouldn't warrant me having to stay out past my curfew.

Sara wanted to think of a way for me to stay Saturday as well, so we'd have Saturday and then Sunday day together. Evan glanced at me when she mentioned Sunday, but he didn't openly object. I let Sara go on with her pretend plans, because I knew it wasn't going to happen. The only day that had a chance was my usual library visit on Sunday.

Everything changed that night when George told me, "We're taking the kids skiing next weekend. Janet said you could stay with her."

My stomach dropped. Janet lived two towns away, and there was no way I would be able to play in the game on Friday, forget about go to the library on Sunday.

"The championship game is Friday night," I said urgently. Carol glared at me.

"Maybe you'll have to miss it," Carol snipped. "My mother is kind enough to let you stay with her; you should be more appreciative."

My chest tightened as the fire of nerves twisted in my stomach. This could not be happening.

"Can I ask Sara if I can stay with her instead?" I pleaded, looking directly at George, ignoring Carol.

"That would be okay," George agreed reluctantly. I could hear Carol take in a breath.

"I'll ask her tomorrow," I said, relieved.

"Why don't you let me call her parents tonight," Carol interjected. "I want to be sure this is really okay with them. I don't want them to feel obligated to say yes if *you* ask."

I still wasn't concerned since I knew Anna and Carl wouldn't care if I spent the weekend. They've made it more than clear every time I see them that I am welcome to stay whenever I'd like. I tried to look worried, and suppressed my smile – I had to appear miserable to stay under Carol's radar.

After dinner, Carol called and spoke with Anna. Of course Carol made a case for what an inconvenience I'd be for two nights, but to her dismay, Anna was pleased to have me. I knew Sara was going to be beyond excited to hear that we didn't have to come up with a lie for me to stay the weekend.

I wasn't wrong. When Sara pulled up the next morning, she was a burst of energy. I smiled at her enthusiastic greeting. She was already trying to decide how we were going to spend the weekend. She mentioned a party on Saturday night and dismissed it as soon as she saw the blood rush from my face.

"I know," Sara exclaimed while we walked down the hall. "Want to have a sleep over on Friday night with some of the girls from the team?"

"I don't mind that idea," I agreed, to her surprise.

Sara was satisfied with Friday night's plan, even though the details still needed to be worked out. That included making it to the championship game and winning.

Sara was still going on about the weekend when Evan met me outside of homeroom.

"Emma's staying over my house this weekend," Sara gloated, before disappearing down the hall.

"Really?" Evan mused as we walked to English.

"My aunt and uncle are taking the kids skiing in Maine for the weekend," I explained.

"Then what are we doing this weekend?"

"I think Friday night is going to be a girls' night. But I'm not sure about the rest of the weekend. You'll have to ask Sara. I think the planning's out of my hands."

I was so afraid the week was going to drag now that I had the weekend to look forward to, but thankfully, it sailed by.

Friday night's plans were sealed after we won the semi-final game on Tuesday. It was a close game, and we only just won, scoring two points to their one. Lauren tipped in the winning goal with less than a minute to play, perfecting her senior year.

Lauren decided to have the team over after the game on Friday, regardless of the outcome. Sara discretely invited five of the girls to sleep over at her place after. I was truly looking forward to the estrogen overload. I knew the girls on the team and didn't mind the idea of spending the night hanging out.

We still hadn't figured out what we were doing on Saturday—that was until Wednesday afternoon, when the decision was made by... me. I was standing at my locker getting my books for Chemistry when I was approached by Jake Masters—the same Jake who was friends with Evan, captain of the soccer team, and who *winked* at me at Scott Kirkland's party.

"Hey Emma," he said casually, like we spoke every day. "How are you doing?" He leaned against the locker next to mine, giving me his full attention.

"Good, Jake," I answered looking around, making sure he was really talking to me. "How are you?"

Ignoring my question, he continued.

"Listen, I'm having a party on Saturday night. It's not going to be big, only about twenty or so people who I really want to be there. And I really want *you* to be there. What do you think?"

Before I could process what he was asking, he added, "Oh, you can bring Sara or whoever with you if you want."

"Okay," I said, without realizing I was answering him.

"Great! Then I'll see you on Saturday," he winked and walked away, leaving me stunned. I stood there for a moment, glancing around, waiting for someone to tell me it was a joke. And, what was up with the *winking*?! Seriously, it was weird!

As we walked to Trig, I told Evan, "I know what we're doing Saturday night."

Evan sighed and asked, "Great, what has Sara planned now?"

"Actually," I corrected, "I told Jake Masters we'd go to his party." I expected to hear him laugh at the irony of me deciding to go to a party, but he was silent. I examined his pensive expression.

"What?"

"Jake asked *you* to go to his party?"

"Yeah, I was completely surprised and still haven't figured out why—but he did. So I kinda agreed."

Evan let out a short laugh. "You don't know why Jake asked you to the party? Does he know that you want to bring me with you?"

"He said I could bring whomever I wanted." I wasn't following along and didn't understand why Evan found this so intriguing.

"Okay, we're going to Jake Masters' party," he finally conceded. "Have you heard about his parties?"

"No. Why?" By the tone of his question, I wasn't sure I wanted to know.

"They tend to be pretty... exclusive," he explained. "I've been to one of them."

"Was it horrible?" I asked, when he didn't say more. I wanted to know what I was about to walk into.

"No," he said dismissively. Then he must have realized he was freaking me out and added, "It'll be fine. Don't worry."

Sara had a much more excited reaction than Evan when I told her. She had also heard about the handpicked guest list of Jake's parties and was thrilled to finally get to see what they were all about. I was surprised to learn she'd never been to one before. I told her to bring Jason, which I think she had already planned to.

When Friday arrived, I was a bundle of nerves. All I could think about was the game that night. The Weslyn girls' soccer team had always been pretty competitive in the division, but this was the first time in almost ten years that the team had made it to the finals.

My quiet anxiety was mirrored by Sara's exuberant anticipation. She was unable to contain her energy and kept fidgeting during the car ride to school. Trying to keep our minds off the game, Sara started to run through our plans for the weekend. I let her talk the entire drive, unable to focus on what she said enough to contribute.

When we arrived at school, we were greeted with homemade banners and flyers displayed along the halls, wishing the girls' soccer team luck in the championship game. Our lockers were decorated with

145

streamers and glittery letters with a message of encouragement along with our jersey numbers. Instead of groaning as I had at the sight of the glittery mess, Sara shrieked with excitement.

"I don't know how I'm going to get through the day," Sara exclaimed. "I can't wait for tonight!" I was trying to figure out how I was going to get through the day as well. It was hard to focus knowing the game was approaching, and the excited energy wasn't helping—it felt overwhelming and disorienting. I wanted to slip into an empty room, with music blaring in my ears, to gather myself.

Then it only got worse. During morning announcements, we were informed we'd be getting out of our last class early to assemble for a pep rally in the gymnasium for the soccer team. My mouth dropped as I heard Sara holler with enthusiasm, joined by the rest of the room.

"Looking forward to the game?" Evan asked while Ms. Abbott handed back our latest writing assignment.

"I think I'm going to throw up," I confessed and dropped my head onto my folded arms. Evan chuckled.

"Don't worry, you'll be great," he assured me.

"I wish everyone would treat this like every other game and stop acting so insane," I said, facing him with my head still resting on my arms.

"Not to add to your nausea, but I don't know if I can go to Jake's party tomorrow night."

"What?!" My head shot up. The exclamation came out a little too loud, turning a few heads. Ms. Abbott continued handing back papers, unfazed by my disruption.

Evan looked around and waited until no one was looking before he continued.

"My parents are making me go to dinner with them," he explained, annoyed. "It's being hosted by one of the partners, and we have to put on appearances. I don't have a choice, I'm sorry."

The thought of going to a party with just Jason and Sara did not appeal to me. I didn't want them to feel obligated to entertain me when I knew they'd want alone time. That would mean *I'd* have alone time, which terrified me.

That thought must have translated on my face because Evan said, "Don't worry. I'll see what I can do."

"It's okay," I said, trying not to sound as disappointed as I was. "I understand."

I had to survive History and Chemistry, not only with nausea from the approaching game, but also the building anxiety of going to Jake's party without Evan. I decided I needed to shake off the distraction of Jake's party and stay focused on the first hurdle – winning the game.

Evan met me outside of Chemistry with a mischievous grin on his face. I approached him cautiously.

"I'm afraid to know."

"I think I've figured out a way to help us both get through tomorrow night."

"How?" I asked, still afraid to hear his plan.

"You can come with me to the dinner – "

Before he could continue, I took in an audible gasp of air. He pressed his lips together at my reaction.

"It won't be that bad," he comforted. "It'll get you warmed up for the party. You can be my excuse to get out of staying the whole time, and then we can go to the party together." I wasn't sure what was more terrifying, going to a party practically alone or meeting Evan's parents and being surrounded by adults who'd expect intelligent, coherent conversation.

"Maybe I'll beg Sara to stay home and watch movies instead," I whispered, trying to breathe evenly.

"I knew it was a long shot," Evan said quietly, looking away. "I hate these dinners—having to pretend to be the perfect son to the perfect parents, while talking to pretentious people gloating about their accomplishments. I thought it might not be so miserable if you were there too."

I didn't say anything as we found our seats for class. Evan sat quietly next to me. I kept glancing over at him throughout class. He looked... sad. I didn't like seeing his drawn mouth and his slumped shoulders. It was obvious that this dinner was Scott's party for Evan. I didn't know how I would have gotten through that night if Evan hadn't been there.

I took a deep breath and swallowed my stomach, digesting what I was agreeing to do. I felt nauseous at the thought of meeting his parents, but my chest warmed when I looked at Evan, knowing I was doing the right thing.

"I'll do it," I said when the bell rang at the end of class.

"What?"

"I think that it's a good compromise." I tried to sound confident. "I'll go to dinner with you, and you go to the party with me." He examined me cautiously, making sure I was serious before he let the smile release on his face.

"You know I'm making out in the deal, right?"

"Whatever," I said dismissively. "I still owe you for Scott's party. But I have to warn you, I'm not great with small talk, so I may end up embarrassing you."

He laughed. "I don't think that's possible. Besides, you'll find you won't have to do too much talking. This crowd loves to talk about themselves, so all you have to do is stand there and nod politely. Don't worry; I won't leave you alone with any of them."

Just before we entered the Art room, Evan stopped to face me.

"Are you sure you want to do this?"

I pressed my mouth into the best fake smile I could and said, "Of course I do." When I saw the relief in his eyes, I found that I didn't need to fake it.

I told Sara the revised plan during lunch.

"No way," she gasped. "You're going to meet his parents?"

After thinking about it for a minute longer, she added, "You know I don't believe you when you say you're just friends. You have a thing for him, whether you're ready to admit it or not."

"Sara," I exclaimed with fiery cheeks, "you don't know what you're talking about!" I couldn't cool my face for the rest of lunch. It didn't help that Sara kept a stupid grin on her face the entire time, fueling the fire.

"You have to promise me that you'll keep your thoughts to yourself when we're around him," I begged.

"Em, I would never say anything about how you feel about him," she promised.

"How *you think* I feel about him," I corrected. But I couldn't argue my point beyond that.

I was so overwhelmed I could barely sit through Journalism class. With Sara's provoking smile on one side and Evan's heart stopping grin on the other, my head was spinning. I couldn't deny how I felt every time I was around Evan. But I'd convinced myself that being friends was what was best. I knew what was best, right?

I *couldn't* think of him as any more than a friend. I had too much to lose. Why did I let Sara get to me? I didn't have any serious feelings for him, right? There was no way...

I watched while Evan listened to Ms. Holt's review of the current assignments. I traced the profile of his straight nose with his distinct cheekbones, down to his chiseled jaw. His perfect lips were separated slightly as his steel blue eyes glanced from Ms. Holt down to his notebook, where he would occasionally jot down notes. I followed the tight muscles that extended down his neck, concealed under the blue sweater that hinted at the contours of his chest. I was breathing slowly, unable to redirect my eyes. My heart murmured softly in my chest, releasing a tingling that sent goose bumps along my arms.

Evan glanced at me, and I quickly turned my head, my cheeks warming. I knew he didn't know what I was thinking – I didn't know what I was thinking – but I didn't want him to catch me staring. Seriously, what was I thinking? I could not have feelings for Evan! What *was* going on?! My mind unraveled as images of our time together flashed through my head. I finally gave in to what I'd been trying to ignore for the past month. I took a gulp of air as I finally faced the truth – I was in love with Evan Mathews.

"Are you okay?" Sara whispered. "You look freaked."

"Ms. Holt," I interrupted with an unsteady voice. The whole class turned to look at me. "Uh, Sara and I have to leave now so we can get ready for the pep rally."

Before she could answer, I stood with my books in my arms, heading out the door. I turned when I got into the hallway, urging Sara to hurry up as she slowly gathered her things.

"What is wrong with you?" she demanded when we walked into the girls' bathroom. I checked the stalls before answering. Sara followed my actions with a worried stare.

"I *am* freaked," I admitted in a loud whisper. "Sara, I can't believe I like him."

"I'm not following," she replied with narrow eyes. "And why are you whispering?"

"You're right. I like Evan a lot more than a friend," I sighed.

"You are just now realizing this?" she almost laughed.

"Shut up, Sara," I snapped, still whispering. "This is horrible. I can't feel this way. And you can't tell me you don't understand why I'm so freaked."

She absorbed my desperate words and took a long breath.

"I know why *you* think you can't date him. But I think you're only hurting yourself more if you try to deny how you feel."

"Besides, how do I know he feels the same? I can't *tell him*. Then it would be so weird, and we wouldn't even be able to be friends."

Sara shook her head and grinned, "You are such an idiot. Of course he feels the same way. I can't believe how blind you are. Are you worried that if you dated him, she'd find out?"

"If she ever found out I was dating someone, I'd lose everything. She would never let me out of the house. And he can never find out what it's like for me! I can't do this."

"No, you can't do it," she agreed firmly. "I'm already going against everything my gut is telling me by keeping your secret. I'm not going to let you risk it more by pissing Carol off if she found out about Evan."

I wasn't expecting Sara to say this. I knew she was right, but my heart still sank.

"I don't want you to have to give him up, so we'll just have to figure out a way for you to remain friends – nothing more. Maybe you shouldn't spend time alone together."

"I have to this weekend," I huffed, now even more tormented by the thought of going to dinner with him. "But Sara, if I can't be alone with him, then I shouldn't be friends with him. You can't chaperone to make sure he doesn't stand too close. Just help me keep my head on straight, that'll be enough. If I can't handle it, then I can't be around him anymore. It's that simple."

"We can do this," she assured me, unable to contain her grin. "Although I've wished for forever that you guys would hook up."

"Sara, that's not helping," I snapped, no longer whispering.

"You're right, sorry," she said, still grinning.

17. UNEXPECTED VISIT

"DO WE REALLY HAVE TO GO TO THIS PEP RALLY?" I MOPED WHEN WE returned to our lockers to get our game jerseys.

"Of course we do," she exclaimed, amazed by my question. "Em, it will get us so pumped to have the whole school cheer for us before the game."

"Can I listen to my music, so I don't have to hear it?" She looked at me with her hands turned up in front of her, unable to process my deterrence to be a part of the excitement.

"Sara, I need to get focused on the game. I've been distracted all day with this Evan stuff. I can't be swooped up in the chaos of listening to everyone screaming."

"You are so strange," she determined with a shake of her head. "You cannot get away with listening to music during a pep rally. We have to run in as they announce us, and we sit together at the back of the gym where everyone can see us—so you will have to put up with the *chaos.*"

"Are you serious?" I almost yelled. "We get announced and have to sit in front of everyone?!"

"Don't you remember the football pep rally?"

"I didn't go."

Sara sighed. "Em, it will be fine. You have the half hour bus ride to get focused, and we aren't even leaving the school until three-thirty. So after the rally, we'll find an empty room where I promise not to talk to you. You can listen to music, do homework, or whatever ritual you need to do to get your head ready for the game. Okay?"

I sighed with a heavy nod.

The pep rally was worse than I imagined. The band played, the football cheerleaders cheered, there were a ton of balloons, and lots of screaming. The worst part was when they "announced" the team. Sara neglected to mention that we were announced individually, I thought we would run in together. I was mortified when I was introduced *last*. It only added to my humiliation when they noted I was the leading scorer in the state, causing the screams to escalate. I really didn't want to be there.

When it was eventually over, I hid from everyone in the Art room and worked on my Trigonometry homework while listening to the band Evan added to my playlist.

I remained quiet on the bus, drowning out the chants and cheers as we approached the school. I sunk further into my seat and closed my eyes.

I felt a hand on the knee that I had pressed against the seat in front of me. I opened my eyes to find Coach Peña sitting across from me, the bus was almost empty. I sat up and turned off the music.

"Ready?" he asked with a confident smile. "You can do this, you know."

"I know," I assured him.

"Let's go." He patted my leg and headed down the aisle to exit the bus. I followed behind him, turning the music back on.

More and more people flowed into the stadium as we settled into our pre-game warm-ups. The air was whirling with the voices and energy from the crowd and the players. I didn't look around; not wanting to see what was at stake. I shut out the cheers, the flashes from the cameras, and the announcements over the speakers. I breathed in the cold November air, settling my thoughts on what was about to take place. When I was oblivious to the distractions, I knew I was ready.

The game was better than I anticipated. It was aggressive, with bodies bumping and fighting for possession. It was fast, as the ball flew from foot to foot covering the length of the field and back again within a minute. It was hard, with each intercepted pass and blocked goal. It was still scoreless at half time.

The second half exploded with the same intensity as the first. Neither team wanted to be the one with the final loss. Midway through the second half, we were able to charge in tight around the goal. There was a lot of bumping and pushing as the ball shuffled amongst the feet. The sweeper attempted to clear the ball up the sidelines with a forceful kick that was blocked by Jill's braced body. The collision sent the ball arching back toward the middle of the field. Concentrating on the arc, I took a few hard strides forward, pushing my body into the air to make contact with the ball using my head. The side of my head connected with the ball, redirecting it towards the goal in a single motion. At the same time, my shoulder collided with a body pushing up against me. The hands of the goalie landed on my head a second too late. The ball was already moving towards the net where it bounced to the ground.

I fell to the ground with the goalie, knowing my timing was a fraction of a second faster than hers. This was confirmed when the whistle blew, announcing the goal. I heard the eruption from the crowd, something I had never noticed before. It was startling as I looked around to take in the lights and the flashes, right before Sara and Jill pulled me off the ground and embraced me, screaming in my ears.

Each team scored one more time, but we came out with the win. When the final whistle blew, the field was inundated with a rush of people yelling and cheering. I received hugs and pats from a blur of faces. I was too excited to be bothered by the invasion. I was still floating on adrenaline.

Evan pushed his way through to find me, his camera in his hand. Before I could react, he wrapped his arms around me, and pulled me to him.

"Congratulations," he said in my ear before letting me go. "You always find a way to make the most impossible goals. I think I have a decent picture of it."

"Thanks," I said, with a huge smile.

Before I could say anything more, I was attacked by more hands, hugs and shouts of congratulations. I lost sight of Evan in the crowd, but I kept searching for him. The crowd slowly eased up and after shaking hands with the other team, I made it back to the bench to gather my things.

The spectators steadily dissipated, filing through the gates toward the parking lot. Evan was somewhere among them. Sara waited for me in the middle of the field. As we approached the exit, I caught a glimpse of someone lingering on the other side. I kept my head down and continued toward the bus.

"Emily!" the figure yelled when I neared. I looked up and stopped abruptly. Sara hesitated a step ahead of me, following my frozen stare. Her eyes widened.

"I'll tell Coach you'll be a minute," she said quietly and left me alone.

"What are you doing here?" I asked, my voice not as strong as I wanted it to be.

"A friend dropped me off so I could see your game," my mother replied with a cautious smile. "Congratulations, I'm so proud of you."

Then a slight breeze allowed her signature sweet perfume to burn my nose. "You've been drinking," I murmured, crushed. She hadn't changed.

"I was nervous about seeing you, so I had a couple of drinks. No big deal."

I couldn't say anything. I couldn't move. My body quivered with nerves.

"I've been following you in the papers," she explained. "I had to see you. You look so great."

I stared back.

"What happened above your eye?" she asked, nodding toward the small scar above my left eye.

I shrugged, looking at the ground – afraid she'd see the emotion in my eyes that were starting to tear.

"I figured you didn't want to hear from me," she said sheepishly while playing with her hands, "especially since you haven't written back in so long."

"What are you talking about?" I asked in confusion.

"You haven't been getting my letters?"

I shook my head.

"I think about you all the time," she started.

"Don't," I interrupted, beginning to feel anger amongst the swirling emotions. "Don't say it. I can't hear it again. How much you love me but can't take care of me the way I deserve. Just... just don't because you have no idea what I deserve." She couldn't look up to meet my watering eyes.

Before she could defend her abandonment once again, a voice hollered, "Rachel, there you are. We've gotta go, babe."

I noticed a guy with a shaved head in a leather jacket and worn jeans approaching us.

"We can't be late," he stated impatiently, not giving me a second glance. My mother eyed me apologetically, but I knew I wasn't a choice—I never had been.

"I have to go," I said, nodding toward the bus, needing to escape the tension before I was smothered by it.

"Emily, this is Mark," she tried to introduce. He barely acknowledged me with a quick "Hey" as he grabbed her hand with an impatient tug.

I nodded my head, understanding exactly who he was. *He* was her choice.

"It was so great to..." she started as he led her in the direction of the running Charger in the parking lot. I turned my back to her and walked away without letting her finish.

The bus was filled with excitement and chatter—no one realized they were waiting on me. I tried to smile as I received praise from my teammates, making my way down the aisle to sit next to Sara.

"Do you want to sit next to the window?" she offered.

"Yeah," I replied, my voice shaky. I moved in as Sara scooted towards the aisle. I collapsed on the seat and rested my head against the cool glass, trying to fight back the tears. My hand shook as I wiped my eyes with the cuff of my sweatshirt. Sara grabbed my hand and gave it a gentle squeeze. We sat in silence while I stared out the window, trying to regain control.

"Your mom, huh?" she eventually confirmed. "She looks..."

"Nothing like me," I muttered, wanting there to be more than her light blue eyes and thin lips to differentiate us. "After four years, why did she have to choose one of the most important nights of my life to show up?"

"I don't know," she whispered. "If it's easier, we can pretend it never happened. I won't mention it, and you can forget it. We'll have a great time for the rest of the night."

"I'll try," I promised, pushing away my mother's depressing image.

"We'll take showers at the school and go straight to Lauren's," she explained, keeping me distracted. "Let's only stay for an hour or two before we head back to my house with the girls. We're going to have an amazing night." She smiled and squeezed my hand, then added, "But if you ever want to talk about her, after tonight, I'm here."

I nodded slightly, knowing that was highly unlikely. I washed my mother away in the shower – tucking her back in the dark place where I

155

kept her. And that's where she stayed... at least for the rest of the night.

After being at Lauren's for an hour, surrounded by hyped girls who talked even faster than usual, Sara nudged me that we should go. Five other girls joined us, following us to Sara's in their cars.

We listened to music, ate junk food and eventually the topic of boys came up. I knew it was inevitable, so I chose not to contribute until I was forced into the conversation.

"So, what's up with you and Evan?" Casey demanded.

"We're just friends," I said casually, hoping that would be enough for them to move on.

"Then what's wrong with you?" Veronica accused. "He's totally hot."

"We're just not interested in each other that way," I defended.

"You know that Haley Spencer pretty much hates you, right?" Jill added.

"What?" I asked incredulously.

"She's obsessed with Evan and thinks the only reason he won't go out with her is because of you," she explained. I laughed.

"Emma, are you serious?" Jaclyn accused. "You have to admit he's gorgeous, and smart, and athletic – "

"Basically perfect," Casey finished.

"No one's perfect," I rebutted.

"So, what's his flaw?" Casey demanded. I looked at Sara hoping she'd change the subject.

"He can be really annoying," I offered, knowing that wasn't going to be enough to satisfy them.

"I think you should date him," Jill said bluntly. "You two would be as perfect together as Sara and Jason." I turned red.

"Speaking of Jason," I finally saw a break, "Sara, what's he doing tonight?"

Sara intercepted the girls' attention and started talking about Jason's perfections. As Sara fed the girls' intrigue into what it's like to be with Jason Stark, I thought I heard something off in her enthusiasm. I couldn't figure it out, but there was something missing.

I let the buzz of voices continue without my participation. I settled back into the recliner, but I couldn't help thinking, what *was* going on between Evan and me?

18. ANOTHER DIMENSION

"WE'D BETTER HURRY," SARA SAID AS WE ENTERED THE DIMINISHING daylight through the doors of the movie theatre. "We only have two hours to get you ready."

"How long could it possibly take me to get ready?"

"Well, you have to take a shower, and make sure you shave. Oh, and I bought you more of that lotion."

"I still have lotion left from the first bottle. And why are you concerned if I shave?"

"Well, now you have more. I really like it on you. It's subtle and pretty."

"I like it too, thank you. But you didn't answer the shaving question." She was beginning to make me nervous.

"You're wearing a skirt," she revealed cautiously.

"Seriously?" I couldn't remember the last time I wore a skirt. When *was* the last time I wore a skirt? Then I tried to remember what my legs looked like. Did I have any bruises or scrapes on my knees from the game? "A skirt?"

"Em, you're going to look amazing." Then Sara quickly added, "But not too amazing. The last thing we need is for him to want to kiss you." She paused, looking me before sighing. "This is going to be harder than I thought."

"I don't think you have to worry about that," I assured her.

When we arrived back at her house, the grand production began. While I showered and shaved, Sara went through her closet, rifling through what seemed like everything she owned. She wouldn't let me see what she'd finally decided on until I was ready to get dressed.

Sara dried my hair and rolled it in hot curlers. I was panicked when I saw my head full of the white cylinders. Then my eyes popped at the sight of the ringlets dangling from my head after she unrolled them.

"Sara, you cannot let me go out like this," I pleaded.

"Don't worry, I'm not done," she promised.

She gathered my hair into a high ponytail, allowing my bangs to sweep across my forehead. I decided it was best not to look until she was done, so I closed my eyes as she teased, pinned and sprayed. I opened them to find a large, smooth bun on the back of my head. It looked more sophisticated than anything I could've imagined.

Sara handed me the softest pink sweater I'd ever seen. Once I was dressed, I stood in front of the full length mirror, admiring the boat neckline of the fitted sweater that subtly revealed the tops of my shoulders and the dark skirt that swayed above my knees – it was a classy vintage look, and I loved it. She attached a thin silver chain with a single diamond around my neck – the diamond sparkled as it settled into the hollow of my throat. Finally, she handed me a pair of black heels that were at least three inches high.

"Heels?" I grimaced, with images of falling on my face playing in my head.

"Yup."

"Sara, I'm going to kill myself," I pleaded. I'd never worn heels and knew this was not the night to be experimenting with my grace or balance.

"You'll be fine. Just take small steps."

I slowly hobbled around the room, my ankles threatening to give way with each step. We wobbled into the entertainment room so I'd have a larger catwalk. I delicately strolled the length of it several times before the doorbell rang.

"He's here?" I panicked. Sara laughed.

"It's not a date, remember?"

"You're right," I breathed.

"It's only dinner with his parents and a bunch of stuck-up old people." She laughed again.

"Emma, Sara," Anna yelled up the stairs, "Evan's here." My heart fluttered into my throat.

"Here." Sara handed me a long white wool coat that hung to the middle of my calves, along with a tote bag so I could change before the party.

"Thanks."

"Em, try to relax. You have nothing to worry about."

I took a deep breath and walked carefully down the stairs, trying not to fall. I hated heels already. They were too much work. Walking shouldn't be something I had to worry about. I had far too many other things to be concerned with, like how to not sound like an idiot in front of a room full of over-educated wealthy men.

Evan waited for me at the bottom of the stairs. I couldn't look up as he came into view, afraid that not looking at my feet would cause me to crumble to the bottom step. When I was finally able to look up, I noticed that his cheeks were flushed and he had a grin on his face that made my breath stop for a second.

"Hi," I greeted him.

"Hi," he smiled.

"Hey Evan," Sara said, leaping down the stairs. "How'd I do? Is she acceptable?" I widened my eyes, wanting to shoot her for asking him to comment on my appearance.

Evan laughed. "Yeah, she's *definitely* acceptable."

"You met my parents, Anna and Carl?"

"Yes, I did."

"Have a great time tonight, Emma," Anna said, giving me a gentle hug and kiss on the cheek. "You really do look beautiful."

"Thank you," I replied, blushing.

"I'll see you at Jake's. Evan, I have your cell number in case we get there before you," Sara stated.

"Ready?" Evan asked me.

"Sure." We said good-bye one more time and headed out the door.

Evan waited until we were in the car before he said, "You really do look beautiful."

"Thanks," I murmured.

"You're not comfortable, are you?"

"Not at all," I admitted with a small laugh. Evan laughed with me, releasing the tension.

"Well, I'll try not to torture you too long. Let's get this over with," he said, pulling out of Sara's driveway.

"I have to warn you, I suck in these shoes. I could fall and break something very expensive."

He laughed. "I'll be sure to keep you away from anything breakable."

"If there is any way I can sit the entire time that would be great."

"Let's see what we can do. But I'm afraid we'll be in a room without many options during the cocktail hour."

"The what?" I asked, confused and embarrassed that I had to ask.

"Sorry, I forgot that this is your first time. We're meeting my parents there. They'll wait for us and we'll all go in together."

"Your parents know I'm coming, right?" I was suddenly nervous that they might not be expecting me.

"Yes, they know you're coming. They may refer to you as my girlfriend when they introduce you to everyone. I keep trying to correct them, but..." He sighed. "Anyway, I'm sorry about that."

"It's okay," I whispered, feeling the fire on my face once again.

"So, Mr. Jacobs and his wife are hosting the party and they'll be greeting everyone at the door. I think it should only be about twenty people, so that shouldn't be bad." Only twenty people? That meant there were twenty names to forget and twenty hands to shake and exchange meaningless small talk with – not comforting.

Evan proceeded to give me a rundown of the flow of the evening and the expected etiquette.

"I'm hoping I'll be able to excuse us after dinner. I'll say that we have a show to go to or something. Just agree with whatever I say, okay?"

"Okay." This sounded way more complicated than just eating food and making mindless conversation. I knew I was getting a glimpse of Evan's world tonight, but I had no idea how much I didn't fit in.

"Thank you so much for doing this," he said glancing at me as he drove. "I'll seriously owe you after tonight."

"I think we'll be even."

"You may want to wait to say that until after we leave."

A few minutes later, Evan pulled out his cell phone. "Hi mom. We're just about there." He listened for a moment and responded, "Okay, I think I see you now. Sure, I'll follow you in."

On the side of the road, a large black Mercedes was pulled over. As we neared, Evan slowed down to let it merge in front of him. I knew it must be his parents. We followed them into a driveway that was guarded by two large stone pillars with corresponding ornate wrought iron gates that were swung open in expectation. We followed the long winding driveway, lined with antique wrought iron lanterns, until it opened up to reveal a spectacular white stone mansion.

The front of the house was dramatically up-lit, illuminating its grandeur. It appeared to be two stories, encircled by large arched windows that let out a warm glow of light, giving hint to the heavy drapery on the inside. The front lawn displayed perfectly trimmed hedges outlining the house. The lawn itself was flat, but raised from the driveway, and encased by a stone wall.

I swallowed hard, realizing I was in over my head. I was not just in a different world, I was in another dimension. I eyed Evan nervously.

He smiled and said, "Don't worry. It'll be over before you know it."

We pulled up along the circular driveway where we were greeted by a man with a black jacket and a bow tie. He opened Evan's door.

Evan leaned over before he got out and said, "Wait right there, I'll get you out." I didn't move. I actually didn't want to get out.

Evan walked around the back of the car and opened my door. He offered me his hand, to which I would have typically looked at him like he was insane, but with these shoes on, I gladly accepted the assistance. Waiting in front of the first set of stone steps were Evan's parents.

His mother was sparkling with her bobbed blond hair and bright blue eyes. She was covered in a fur coat and adorned with more diamonds than I'd ever seen on one person. She had soft, delicate features and looked very thin and breakable. She clutched a small black handbag that was sealed with more glitz.

In contrast, Mr. Mathews was a statuesque man, taller than Evan, but with strikingly similar features. He and Evan shared the same light brown hair and grayish blue eyes. His face was angular and serious as he stood in a long black coat, concealing a tuxedo.

I took a deep breath before approaching them. I tried my best to smile cordially while I was introduced.

"Vivian and Stuart Mathews, this is-

"Emily Thomas," Vivian finished, holding out her hand. I tried to conceal the shocked look on my face, especially with being called Emily by someone I'd never seen before today.

"It's very nice to meet you," I said, shaking her delicate hand. Stuart remained still with his hands by his side, making no attempt to acknowledge me, forget about shake my hand.

"Well, aren't you lovely," Vivian admired. "We never get to meet Evan's girlfriends." I knew it was coming, but my heart still leapt when she said it, sending a flicker of heat to my cheeks.

Evan rolled his eyes. "Mom, you met Beth, remember?" His tone was impatient.

"Maybe for a second as you were leaving the house," she countered. "Anyway, it's a pleasure to meet you, Emily. Shall we go in?" There was an air about her that made me stand up straighter and afraid to walk, knowing how clumsy I'd appear next to her grace and sophistication. I gave Evan a fearful glance as we approached the first set of stone steps. There were only three, but they might as well have been a flight.

Evan offered me his right elbow to clutch as I concentrated with each step. I don't think I breathed the entire time. His parents glided ahead of us as I carefully placed one foot in front of the other along the stone pathway. At the top of the second set of steps was an enormous wooden door that opened as Vivian and Stuart neared it. They waited for us before entering.

"Stuart, Vivian," the dual voices of a man and woman sang. "Welcome. It's so wonderful to see you again." Vivian and Stuart were warmly greeted by whom I presumed to be Mr. and Mrs. Jacobs, with a quick embrace that included a brushing kiss on their cheeks and a handshake.

"Evelyn, Maxwell, you remember our youngest son, Evan, don't you?" Vivian offered as they stepped aside for us to enter.

"Of course," Mr. Jacobs greeted Evan with a handshake.

"And this is his girlfriend, Emily Thomas," she introduced. I smiled politely.

"Thank you for joining us," Mrs. Jacobs said grasping my right hand between her two cool, soft palms.

"Thank you for having me," I replied.

Evan slipped my coat off and handed it to a formally poised man, dressed in a tuxedo.

I was too distracted by the grand foyer, with its huge crystal chandelier and expansive stone staircase with a large red carpet running down the center, to notice Evan staring at me. I glanced over at him with a start.

"What?!" I was afraid I'd done something wrong already.

"Another pink sweater, huh? You're killing me."

I looked at him with wide eyes, my face flooded with color. "Evan!"

He smiled as we followed his parents into a room to the right of the foyer. I wasn't about to admit that seeing him in the dark tailored suit was just as distracting.

We entered a large room that could easily contain the entire first floor of my house within its walls, with a ceiling that was easily two stories high. The windows along the front of the house were framed with heavy ivory scrolled drapes that were held open with tasseled ropes. The top half of the walls were adorned with soft coral wallpaper, set above ivory wood panels embossed with leafing scrolls. On the large wall across from the entrance, hung two large paintings of a garden and a woman dressed around the period the house was constructed, and another portrait of the mansion was centered on the wall opposite the windows. The remaining wall housed a stone fireplace that was as tall as I was. Hanging above it was a pewter framed mirror that duplicated the size of the massive stone structure.

As predicted, there wasn't anywhere to sit. There were several oversized antique chairs set against the walls, but they were obviously for appearances only. The only other piece of furniture was a large stone topped table with dark wood legs gathered in the center that rolled out into a round base. Set on the round surface was the biggest floral arrangement I'd ever seen. It looked like a tree of flowers with different colors and textures—it was absolutely amazing.

"Are you okay?" Evan asked, as my unblinking eyes scanned the room.

"Sure," I replied slowly, nodding my head. He smiled and grabbed my hand to escort me to the corner of the room.

"Evan," a deep, distinguished voice greeted. It belonged to a man of average height, much shorter than Evan, with dark wavy hair and a thick black mustache. "How are you? Stuart said you were going to be here this evening."

"It's great to see you, Mr. Nicols," Evan acknowledged, shaking his hand. "Mr. Nicols, this is Emma Thomas. We go to school together. Emma, this is Mr. Nicols. He belongs to the same firm as my father."

"Aren't you stunning," he observed, cupping my hand in both of his as his eyes rolled over me. I was taken aback by the greeting, and forced an uncomfortable smile. "Evan, you should bring your girls around here more often." He nudged Evan with his elbow. It took everything I had to keep an even expression.

After a few more exchanges about soccer and Evan's winter travel plans, Mr. Nicols excused himself. I let out the breath I'd been holding while in his presence.

"I am so sorry. I had no idea—well, I was afraid—but still didn't think anyone would actually be that rude."

"That was interesting," was all I could say.

"Want something to eat?" he asked, nodding toward a server dressed in a tux, carrying a silver tray of bite-sized food.

"I'm okay."

"This will be over before you know it," he promised.

"You keep saying that," I mumbled, but began to wonder if he was saying it to himself as much as he was to me.

At that time, Vivian approached us with a portly man wearing small frameless glasses. He had a ring of white hair that blended with his pale complexion, contrasted by his ruddy cheeks.

"Evan, you remember Dr. Eckel, correct?" Vivian presented the small round man.

"Of course. It's nice to see you again, Dr. Eckel," Evan said, gripping his hand.

"Dr. Eckel, this is Evan's girlfriend, Emily Thomas."

"It's a pleasure to meet you Miss Thomas," Dr. Eckel said, shaking my hand gingerly. I produced a small smile.

"Dr. Eckel is a professor of Bio-Chemistry at Yale," Evan explained.

"Oh." I nodded lightly.

"Are you and Evan in many classes together?" his mother asked.

"Evan's in most of my classes."

"So you're intelligent. That's wonderful," she concluded, smiling softly. I wasn't sure what to say to that.

"She's also a great athlete," Evan offered, trying to deflect the awkward comment. "The girls' soccer team won the state championship last night because of her." His acknowledgement didn't help. The sweater became unbearably stifling the longer they spoke about me.

"Congratulations," Dr. Eckel stated. "Have you started looking at colleges?"

"I haven't visited any campuses yet, but I've had a few college scouts come to my games. My first choice is Stanford," I shared. My voice sounded so small in the huge room.

"Really?" Vivian reacted in interest.

"What do you plan to study?" Dr. Eckel inquired.

"I haven't narrowed it down yet."

"She could choose anything," Evan boasted. "She's in all of the advanced classes and has a 4.0."

"Hmm," his mother responded, still intrigued.

"Well, I wish you the best," Dr. Eckel offered, shaking my hand once again. "Evan, it's always a pleasure." He and Vivian strolled to greet another face they recognized.

I turned to Evan, trying to recover from my elevated temperature. "Don't do that," I pleaded.

"I'm sorry, what did I do?"

"Talking about me like that—it's so uncomfortable."

"But I didn't say anything that wasn't true, and I didn't exaggerate. Sorry if it's hard to hear the truth."

I took another breath. "I'm just not used to this."

"I know," he said grabbing my hand and giving it a gentle squeeze. He didn't let go as I anticipated he would.

"My parents said you were going to be here," an excited female voice squealed. I watched a stunning girl, with long wavy blond hair, saunter toward us. She wore a strapless black cocktail dress that hugged her slender figure. I felt juvenile and plain in comparison – despite Sara's best efforts. She wrapped her arms around Evan and gave him a quick peck on the mouth. He released my hand to return the embrace. I became an invisible witness to this intimate greeting, holding my hands in front of me, preferring to look at the floor.

"Catherine, this is Emma Thomas. We go to school together. Catherine is the daughter of Mr. and Mrs. Jacobs," Evan explained.

She turned to me with a start, oblivious to my presence until Evan mentioned me. I understood why as she pressed her body against his side, with her arms wrapped around his arm.

"Nice to meet you," she acknowledged with the slightest nod.

"Catherine attends Boston College," Evan shared, obviously trying to make up for Catherine's disinterest.

"Do you like it?" I asked, thinking I should say *something*.

"I do," she answered shortly, barely glancing at me.

"Evan, I have a surprise for you," she announced, dismissing me completely. "Come upstairs so I can give it to you." She started pulling him behind her. My eyes widened, realizing I was being left standing alone.

Evan slowed Catherine's persistent pace and said something low into her ear. They stopped and she glanced at me with confused eyes. Evan said something else and she looked at him with a furrowed brow as she lightly ran her hand across his cheek. Her face dropped to a sulk. She whispered in his ear and took in his expression with a mischievous grin. He shook his head with an apologetic smile. She shrugged, gave him a quick kiss on the lips, and glided away. I wanted so much to blend into the wallpaper at that moment.

Evan returned to me, his cheeks flushed.

Before he opened his mouth to say anything, I blurted, "Don't, it's okay. I really don't want to know. It's actually none of my business."

He examined me cautiously and said, "Really? That didn't bother you?"

I drew my brow together. "Why would you ask me that?"

"Because what she did was completely offensive. I was bothered by it, so I can't believe that you weren't."

I shrugged slightly and dropped my eyes to the floor. "I'm really not sure what to expect."

"You should never expect that," he stated while taking hold of my hand and raising my chin with his other hand. I couldn't breathe when I turned my eyes up at him. "Okay?"

"Sure," I whispered, glancing away.

This was the strangest night of my life. I was in the most exquisite house I'd ever seen, surrounded by people who assumed they had the privilege to say anything they wanted, regardless of how distasteful, and Evan was talking and acting ten years older than he was. He was right—Jake's party was going to be easy after this.

We were greeted and I was introduced to more people throughout the longest hour of my life. They'd ask Evan a question and cut him off to talk about themselves. Finally, as I was becoming cross-eyed to feign interest in another mind-numbing story, a bell chimed and Mr. Jacobs requested that everyone make their way into the dining room for dinner.

167

I found that after all of this stifling drama, I was starving. We entered a long dimly lit room with the same large arching windows framed in dark red drapes that showcased the back terrace. The top half of the walls were covered in antiqued glass mirrors up to the ceiling, while the bottom half duplicated the ivory wood casings in the previous room. Another impressive stone fireplace centered the wall opposite the windows.

A long dark wooden table divided the room, with the windows on one side and the fireplace on the other. Complimenting the grand table were tall, straight-back chairs – closer to forty chairs than the twenty Evan guestimated. The table was set with delicate china bordered with gold scrolling, along with a collection of elegant glassware and flatware. Small silver cups of colorful flowers and glowing crystal votives were intermittently dispersed along the center of the table. A stunning crystal chandelier was suspended over us, creating a soft ambience enhanced by a crackling fire.

Evan pulled out my chair for me to sit before sitting to my left. To my changing fortune, Dr. Eckel sat to my right. He was the only person I'd met who was not self righteous and rude, but then again, he didn't say much at all. That was fine by me too.

However, keeping with the momentum of the evening, on Evan's left was Catherine, who scooted her chair closer to him. She took a sip from an oversized wine glass and leaned towards him.

"What Evan, not drinking tonight?"

"I'm driving," he explained.

"You don't have to," she whispered, still loud enough that I could hear her. My back straightened, and I tried to take a sip of water to distract me. I didn't dare look over at them.

"Evan, I've missed you," she breathed. I choked on the water, coughing mid-gulp. I couldn't stop coughing. Everyone stared at me as I tried to contain my fit in my napkin.

"Sorry," I whispered, looking around at the startled faces. My face was red, not only from choking, but also from the words I'd just overheard.

"Are you okay?" Evan asked, trying to turn his back to Catherine.

"Yes," I replied apologetically. "I swallowed wrong, I'm sorry."

A line of servers entered the room, holding shallow bowls in each of their hands. The bowls were set in front of every person simultaneously. It was very impressive to witness.

"Start with the silverware on the outside and work your way in," Evan whispered. I looked down at the lines of silver. How much could we possibly eat to need all of this?

"Evan, don't ignore me," Catherine demanded while we ate our soup. It didn't appear that anyone else could hear her whispers over the murmurs of conversation that bounced around the cavernous room. I heard her because I was sitting next to Evan, and Dr. Eckel was as mute as I was.

"I'm not ignoring you, Catherine."

"When are you visiting me in Boston again?" she asked. "We had so much fun the last time. Remember?" She released a high pitched giggle.

My head cocked in reaction to this artificial sound. Did she really force a giggle? Who does that? I tried to hold in my laughter and ended up coughing again, receiving a few more glances.

"I'm really busy right now," Evan explained, glancing at me. I couldn't look at him.

"But I haven't seen you since I started school in August. Don't you miss me?"

I couldn't wait to hear his response to this one.

"I had a good time."

Nice one, Evan.

"I can promise you a better time. Why don't you come up next weekend? "

"Aren't you on break for Thanksgiving?"

"Then come visit me here."

"My brother will be home. I think we're going skiing."

"Evan," she whined. "Don't make me beg you."

Was she serious? I took another gulp of water trying to suffocate my urge to laugh. I swallowed it without incident but found I was soon out of water. To my astonishment, it was quickly refilled by a body dressed in a tuxedo who appeared out of nowhere with a silver pitcher.

Catherine sulked during the second and third courses. I had no idea what I was eating because the courses didn't resemble anything I could conjure up as food. But I tried them and was pleasantly surprised to discover that I liked them.

"How are you doing?" Evan leaned over to ask me.

"I'm doing just fine, thank you." I grinned. I still couldn't look at him, because that meant I would see her too. I didn't know if I could do that and keep a straight face.

"How are *you* doing?" I inquired, still grinning.

"I'm ready to leave actually," he admitted. A smile broke out on my face with the escape of a small laughing cough.

By the fifth course, which I did recognize to be beef, I had consumed three glasses of water and really needed to use the bathroom. The thought of standing up in front of all of these people and slipping out of the room unnoticed kept me paralyzed in my chair. But the settling pressure made taking one more bite unbearable.

"I have to use the restroom," I whispered to Evan.

"I'm not sure where they are," he admitted. "But you can ask one of the servers, and they'll let you know where to go."

Thankfully, the entrance was behind us. I held my breath as I slowly slid my chair away from the table. A loud scraping sound filled the room, disrupting every conversation. I grimaced and looked around apologetically at the same annoyed glares I'd been receiving all evening. I slipped out of the chair, and with as much concentration and grace as I could gather, I walked toward the open door. Next to it was a woman in a tuxedo with her dark hair neatly tied back into a low knot.

"Excuse me," I whispered. "Could you please tell me where the restroom is?"

"Go right out this door, and you will find them tucked on either side of the staircase. It doesn't matter which you use."

"Thank you." I smiled at her and stepped out the door. As I crossed the threshold, the heel of my shoe caught on the lip of the doorframe, faltering my fragile balance. I took several stammering steps into the foyer, trying to prevent myself from falling on my face. I recovered and remained on my feet, but the hard steps echoed like thunder throughout the foyer.

Evan came rushing out. "Are you okay?" he asked, prepared to scoop me off the floor.

"I'm fine," I replied, standing up straight. I pulled my sweater taut over my hips and took a quick breath before continuing to the restroom. I remained in the small space for longer than was necessary, fanning my face in attempt to reduce the shade of scarlet to a less noticeable red.

When I returned to the table, my unfinished beef course had been removed, and a plate with small portions of cheese, garnished with a fan of strawberries and tiny grapes was set in its place. Catherine was hovering over Evan, whispering in his ear while stroking the back of his neck. I fought the temptation to glance over at him when I eased back into my seat.

Whatever Catherine was saying to Evan, she was saying it low enough that I couldn't hear. At the end of the course, Evan excused himself and slid out of his chair. I turned toward him to see his red face before he left the room. Catherine giggled, watching him go. I caught her eye and stared at her, questioning. She smirked with a raised eyebrow before taking a sip of wine. I looked away and placed a grape in my mouth, unnerved.

Evan entered through a door at the other end of the fireplace and leaned over to whisper into his parents' ears, who were sitting toward the head of the table with the Jacobs'. He tilted his watch and said something else. His mother gave him a quick peck on the cheek. Evan approached Mr. and Mrs. Jacobs to exchange a few words before shaking their hands. He exited the door and re-entered the one behind me.

"Ready?" he whispered, leaning over the side of my chair.

"Sure," I replied, setting down my glass of water.

He helped pull my chair out without making the same bellowing noise I did earlier. We walked into the foyer, and Evan provided a card to the same poised gentleman in the tux to retrieve our coats.

"Leaving so soon?" Catherine asked, as she sashayed across the marble floor.

"We have another commitment," Evan stated flatly.

"You will come back to visit me, won't you Evan," she demanded, rather than questioned.

I couldn't contain myself any longer. As Evan slid the coat over my arms, I started laughing. At first in spurts—because I was trying to hold it in. But then there were tears in my eyes, and I couldn't stop it from erupting.

"Are you laughing at me?" she asked.

"Actually, yes I am," I stated with my eyes watering. My face reddened as I covered my mouth to capture another bout of laughter.

Evan smiled wide and said, "Good night, Catherine," before escorting me out.

171

Once the door closed behind us, I couldn't hold back. I laughed so hard, I had to bend over to support myself with my hands on my knees. I couldn't see through the tears that were streaming down my face. I tried to compose myself, wiping the moisture from my cheeks, and took a couple steps forward.

Then I thought of her whine and giggle, and lost it again. I collapsed onto the top stone step, holding my stomach as I convulsed with laughter. After it was too painful to laugh anymore, I took a deep breath and wiped my cheeks again. Evan stood at the bottom of the stairs, watching me with an amused expression.

"I'm glad you found that funny," he observed with his hands in his pockets.

"Please don't mention it," I groaned, trying not to laugh. "I can't laugh any more. It hurts. Let's just say we're even."

19. NOT LAUGHING

"READY FOR JAKE'S PARTY?" EVAN ASKED FROM THE DRIVER'S SEAT, easily releasing the formal disposition I'd witnessed most of the evening.

"After that, I'm ready for anything."

"We'll see," he grinned. "Maybe I'll be the one laughing at the end of the night."

"What's that supposed to mean?" I asked, suddenly nervous.

"Nothing," he replied, continuing to grin.

When we pulled into Jake's driveway, there were already a dozen or so cars lining it, making us the last vehicle to fit before the street. Evan kept watch outside the car while I changed into a pair of jeans and more manageable shoes.

"So much better," I breathed when I stepped out of the car.

"You still look good," Evan remarked with a half smile. I ignored him.

I kept the same guard while he changed from his suit into a pair of jeans and a sweater.

"Whenever you want to leave, we leave," Evan told me as we approached the front door. "Don't feel bad either. He invited you, this isn't for me. I'm just here because you are."

"Okay," I agreed, trying to read into his warning. He'd been acting strange about this party since I'd mentioned it. But I couldn't figure out why.

I rang the doorbell since it seemed more appropriate than just walking in. It wasn't the loud scene we encountered at Scott's party. Jake answered the door with a huge smile.

"Emma! You're here! Sara said you'd be here soon," he said opening the door wider for us to enter. His welcoming smile faltered when he found Evan behind me. "Oh, you brought Evan." Evan gave him a quick smirk.

"Nice to see you, Jake," Evan said, patting his hand on Jake's shoulder as we passed him to enter. Jake shut the door and turned to Evan.

"Sorry, man. You may be outnumbered tonight," Jake informed him with a snide grin.

"I'm not worried."

I had no idea what they were talking about, but could definitely sense a little tension. I studied Evan's face for a sign, but he just smiled at me.

"You can hang your coats in the closet." Jake pointed to the door next to the entrance.

The small foyer led down a hallway. As we followed Jake, I noticed an entrance on the left that opened into a living room with an overstuffed couch and a large flat-screened TV. To the right was another room with a long leather couch and a desk, presumably an office.

The rooms were dimly lit by flickering candlelight. There were only a few people in each room, quietly conversing. A soothing jazz tune with a soulful trumpet blaring carried throughout the house. The end of the hall revealed a set of carpeted stairs and then it opened up into a kitchen. The kitchen was bright with the overhead lights gleaming off the white surfaces.

Sara was leaning against the island laughing at something Jason said. She looked up when we entered the room.

"Drinks are downstairs," Jake offered. "Relax and have a good time. I'll be right back." He disappeared down a set of stairs that connected with the stairs leading up.

"Emma, Evan!" Sara exclaimed. "How was dinner?"

"Filling," I replied, with a quick laugh. Evan pressed his lips together and scowled at me.

Sara examined us with her brows pulled together, trying to decipher our exchange.

"I'll tell you later," I said quickly, still grinning. "When did you guys get here?"

"We haven't been here that long," Sara admitted. "I was going to give you a few more minutes before I called."

"Where is everyone?" I asked, looking around then picking up on the small grin that Evan wasn't doing a very good job of hiding.

"I honestly don't know," Sara confessed, looking around too. "We really did *just* get here. I think everyone must be downstairs, but I don't think there's a lot of people here."

We were interrupted by the ringing of the door bell. Jake bounded up the steps and strode down the hall. Six more people I didn't know entered the house – they looked like seniors.

"I think everyone's here," I overheard Jake tell one of the guys when they neared the kitchen.

"Emma Thomas?" the guy whispered, in shock. I tried to pretend I didn't hear him.

"Don't even think about it," Jake whispered firmly, leading the group down the stairs.

Evan pressed his lips together to keep from laughing. I narrowed my eyes, knowing something was up. He raised his eyebrows and shrugged, looking away to avoid my glare.

"Do you want to go downstairs?" Sara asked, as it was obvious we were the only ones upstairs, except for the few people in the front rooms.

"Might as well," I agreed.

Sara and I walked down together, while Jason and Evan followed behind us discussing a football game or something.

We entered the shadowy basement with its low ceilings. At the base of the stairs was a long dark bar, with tall black leather chairs pulled up to it. There were a few people sitting on the chairs, talking. When I scanned the wide "U" shaped space, I estimated about fifteen people dispersed throughout it.

Besides those at the bar, there were others sitting on a sectional couch in front of a suspended television. The rest were clustered around a pool table across from the stairs or sitting on the black leather sofa tucked in against the wall. I was surprised that no one was playing pool or watching TV. The same sultry soulful music piped through the speakers down here

175

"Want a drink?" Jake offered as we congregated at the end of the bar.

"Do you have soda?"

"Sure, it's in the fridge on the other side of the basement. There's a door over there—help yourself."

I cut through the sectional area, through the door he indicated into the unfinished side of the basement. Against the wall was an old white refrigerator filled with bottles and cans of a variety of sodas. I grabbed a bottle and returned to Evan, Jason and Sara, who were still standing at the bar.

"What do you think?" I whispered to Sara, who was sipping something red from a glass. "Does this feel weird to you?"

"I have a feeling I know what's going on," she admitted. "I've always wondered what Jake's parties were all about, but I had no idea. Guess he never wanted to invite the judge's daughter for a reason."

Before I could ask what she was talking about, Jake approached again.

"Evan," Jake beckoned, "I want you to meet a couple of people I don't think you know."

Evan looked at Jake curiously. He hesitated to say, "I'll be right back," before walking away. I nodded, not really concerned. I had no idea why he was acting so weird, but this party wasn't nearly as intimidating as the last. I wasn't worried about being left alone. There really wasn't much going on.

"I wish we could play pool or something," I told Jason and Sara. "It feels strange just standing here."

"It's not that kind of party," Sara whispered with a knowing grin.

"What do you mean?" I was so confused and kinda bored to be honest.

"Hey," a small brunette exclaimed walking down the stairs. Sara turned toward her and smiled.

"Hey Bridgette!" Sara returned enthusiastically.

Bridgette was followed closely by one of the guys from the soccer team. She greeted Sara with a quick hug.

"I didn't know you were going to be here," the petite brunette said to Sara in surprise.

"We came with Emma," Sara explained. "Emma this is Bridgette."

"Hi," I said softly. She smiled politely, casually eyeing me. The guy's hand slid around the Bridgette's waist, resting low so it was practically holding her ass. I looked up at her face, pretending not to have noticed.

Jason started talking to him, apparently they knew each other too. The entire time, the guy's hand remained attached to Bridgette. It was almost as if he were claiming her or something.

"Did you just get here?" Bridgette asked.

"Not that long ago," Sara replied.

"I didn't realize you were interested in Rich," Sara whispered, nodding to the guy with the branding hand.

"I figured, why not?" Bridgette declared with a shrug.

Sara tightened her eyes at the response but didn't inquire further. Instead, she and Bridgette began talking about their mothers, who apparently knew each other, and other subjects they had in common that I knew nothing about. I pulled out one of the black leather bar chairs to sit and half listened as I fiddled with the soda bottle.

"We're going upstairs," Sara said after awhile. "Will you be okay? I promise I'll be right back."

"Sure." I nodded with a reassuring smile.

"Don't go anywhere," she warned, leaving me even more confused.

I scanned the room but couldn't locate which group Evan was in with the lights so low.

"Left alone?" a voice asked from behind me. I turned to find a dark haired guy with vibrant bluish-green eyes leaning against the chair next to me. I recognized him as one of the guys who arrived after we did.

"For now," I said with a small shrug.

"That's not good."

"How do you know Jake?" I asked.

"We're friends – we're both seniors," he explained. "You're Emma Thomas, right?"

"Yeah," I said slowly, trying to figure out if I should know who he was.

"I'm Drew Carson. I realize you probably don't know me." But something made me wonder why I did. His name sounded so familiar, but I couldn't quite place it.

"But you know who I am?"

"Of course." He laughed. "That was a great game last night. I heard you have scouts looking to pick you up."

177

I blushed. "Yeah. So you were at the game?"

"Who wasn't?" His sincerity made me smile.

"Why do I recognize you? I know I've seen you," I struggled, "but I can't place it."

"Basketball probably," he offered. That was it. Drew Carson, captain of the guys' basketball team this season. That made sense with his lean built frame. How had I not noticed him in school? But then again, it seemed I didn't notice anyone in school unless they threw themselves in front of me.

"That's it. Sorry."

"That's all right. I should have tried to talk to you before tonight," he admitted. "But I'm glad you're here. I'm surprised you're here, but whatever." He revealed a sparkling smile as his cheeks creased with deep dimples. Honestly, how did I not notice him before—he was beautiful.

"I like your sweater," he said, after a few seconds of silence.

"Thanks." I blushed again. I was searching for anything to say that wouldn't sound forced. "Do you ski?" I had no idea where the question came from, but it was the first thing that came out of my mouth. Could I be any more pathetic?

"Yeah, I'm going to Vermont next weekend with my family. Do you?"

"Actually, I don't." We both looked at each other and started laughing at the awkwardness. Our laughter was loud against the murmuring voices, invoking a few annoyed stares.

"Oops." I smiled, covering my mouth. "I didn't realize we were *supposed* to be quiet."

"Don't worry about it," he said, smiling back. "They're just taking this way too seriously." I was confused by what he meant, but most of tonight seemed confusing. I'd figure it out eventually, hopefully.

"Do you do anything else besides play basketball and ski?" I asked, still trying to keep the conversation alive, but not as stressed after our outburst.

"I surf and try to go white water kayaking when I can." Then he continued to talk about the best waves he'd ever surfed – in Australia. I listened and was soon engrossed in his story.

We continued back and forth until it occurred to me that it had been a long time since Evan, Sara and Jason disappeared. I glanced around casually while contributing to the conversation but was unable to make out any of their faces in the dark corners.

"I'll be right back," I announced. "I'm going to get another drink."

"I need to run up to the bathroom," Drew said, pointing up the stairs. "Meet you back here?" He actually wanted to keep talking to me?

"Sure," I agreed.

I walked through the space with the sectionals again, discretely trying to look at the faces to find Evan or Sara. I was shocked to walk in on a few couples kissing—heavily. It didn't seem to bother them that I was there or that there were other couples next to them doing the same thing. I kept my eyes to the ground until I heard the heavy breathing and walked faster.

When I was behind the closed door, I tried to figure out how I was going to get through there again. I inspected the other side of the basement, hoping there was a door that connected to the pool table side, but was disappointed. The only other door was a bulkhead that led to the backyard. Was I that desperate?

"There you are." I spun around and found Jake closing the door behind him.

"Hi Jake," I responded casually, trying to conceal my anxiety.

"I've wanted to talk to you all night," he confessed while approaching me. "But I didn't really want to do it here." He presented the dingy surroundings, sounding overly cocky. "Let me show you around the house, and we can find somewhere private to..." he paused before adding, "talk." He smirked like it was an inside joke. Everything suddenly made sense. I remained still, catching myself before dropping my mouth wide open in shock.

"Uh, well..." I stumbled, looking past him to the closed door. "Thanks, but I don't need a tour. We can talk at the bar?"

"I was hoping for some place with less people." He winked. No way, again?! I couldn't help myself; the words were coming out of my mouth before I could stop them.

"Who are you?" I questioned, aghast at his boldness.

"What?" he questioned in shock.

"This is a hook up party, isn't it?" It came out more as an accusation than a question. I couldn't believe how long it had taken me to figure it out.

"Whatever happens, happens," he said with a devious smirk. I remained dumbfounded by his arrogance.

"And so you decided to invite *me*?" I questioned, unable to imagine how that made sense.

"Why not?" he asked, not catching on, still overly confident.

"You obviously don't know me," I bit, unable to conceal my disgust. "Why would you think I'd want to hook up with *you*?"

"Ouch," he replied, not looking pleased anymore.

Before I could say anything else that would make me not want to show my face in school again, I hurried past him to discover that the door was open. Evan stood in the frame, with his hand still on the handle. I didn't know how long he'd been listening, but it must have been for most of it because he greeted me with his amused grin.

"You are so dead," I threatened as I pushed past him. It only added to his amusement as he let out a small laugh.

"Hey, Emma," Drew started when he saw me approaching. Then he looked at my face, which hid nothing, and asked, "What happened?"

"Were you in on this too?" I bit.

I didn't wait for his answer as I rushed up the stairs and found Sara and Jason talking in the kitchen with their jackets on.

"Can we please go?" I pleaded. "This is too weird."

"We were just coming to get you," Sara admitted. "I was wondering how long it was going to take for you to want to leave. Let's go back to my place."

"Sure," Evan agreed from behind me.

I turned sharply and snapped, "I don't think she was inviting *you*." Sara's eyes widened at my attack. I continued down the hall to retrieve my jacket from the closet.

Sara and Jason headed to Sara's car while I paced myself a step ahead of Evan to his.

After he shut his door, he said, "I should have warned you. I'm sorry."

"Evan, you knew, and you still let me come here?" I yelled.

"I knew nothing was going to happen. I wasn't afraid you were going to do anything, and I hoped that you'd let Jake see you're not into him – which you definitely did. I'm so sick of hearing him talk about…" He stopped himself.

"I'm sorry, really." His face was serious and his eyes soft, forcing my anger to dissipate.

"Fine, you can come over to Sara's." I still found it difficult to be upset with him for very long.

After we pulled out of the driveway, my stomach shot out a charge that caused my heart to stammer. "Evan, where were you? *And* you said you've been to one of his parties before. Are you serious? Did you... who... no way." My voice grew louder with each unfinished question.

Evan laughed.

"Forget it, it's none of my business," I murmured quietly, looking out the window. I was tormented by the possibilities.

"Relax. Jake was trying to keep me *distracted* by introducing me to some girls, so he could talk to you. He was pissed that I was there. He knew you'd bring Sara, and she'd probably bring Jason, but he wasn't expecting me. So I was just *talking*—like you were with Drew Carson, right?" My heart skipped a beat.

"I've only been to one other party of Jake's, and I didn't know what they were all about when I accepted the invite. I didn't..." He had a hard time finding the words. I turned to look at him, realizing he couldn't tell me what he'd done.

"Really?" I accused in shock.

"It's not what you think," he defended. "I'd rather not get into details." We were quiet for a moment. I stared out the window at the silhouetted trees and the occasional up-lit house.

"Does that really bother you?" he finally asked.

"What?"

"That I may have kissed a girl or whatever at one of Jake's parties?"

I hesitated before answering. "I didn't think you were like that," I replied softly.

"I'm not," he claimed emphatically. "That's why I've only gone to the one party, and I didn't do what you probably think I did. That's not what interests me. It's too important of a decision to pick someone at random, in someone else's house."

I let out an awkward laugh and tried to catch myself before I let out another.

"What's so funny?"

"I can't talk about this with you." I let out another uneasy laugh. "It's too weird. Sorry."

"You think talking about sex is weird?"

"No. Talking about it with *you* is weird," I emphasized. "Can we please change the subject?"

"So, you've never..." he started.

"Evan!" I yelled.

"Of course not," he concluded quietly.

"And you have?" I asked before I could shut my mouth.

"I thought we weren't talking about it."

"We're not," I said, turning to look out the window again. We didn't say another word until we pulled into Sara's driveway.

"Do you still want me to come in?" he asked.

"Do you still want to?" I asked in return.

"Of course I do."

"Then come in."

We followed behind Sara and Jason into the house. Sara let her parents know we were home before we headed up the stairs.

"Would you mind if Jason and I watch a movie in my room?" Sara whispered as she and I followed a few steps behind the guys to the third floor.

"Are you serious?!" I asked. She begged with her widened eyes. "Fine." I conceded. She smiled gratefully.

Sara bent over the couch as Jason sat down and whispered in his ear. He grinned and followed her into the bedroom. Evan looked to me, trying to interpret what just happened.

"They want alone time," I shared. He nodded, suddenly understanding.

"What movie are we watching?" I inquired, sitting on the opposite end of the couch.

"Are you going to stay awake this time?"

"Yes," I stressed, appearing offended.

Evan selected a movie about a small town, where people were inexplicably disappearing.

After a while, the exhaustion started pulling at me, so I grabbed a pillow and curled up in the empty space on the couch next to Evan to continue watching the movie – still committed to staying awake. I began fighting with my eyelids as they attempted to glue themselves shut every time I blinked. Finally, I gave in.

"Emma," Sara whispered, gently shaking my shoulder. She sounded distant as I struggled against consciousness – I was too comfortable. "Em, you know it's two o'clock in the morning, don't you?"

Her whisper was louder, coming in more clearly. I groaned to acknowledge I heard her. Then I felt the weight around my waist and warmth against my back. I blinked my eyes open, attempting to focus. I heard the rhythmic breathing behind my ear and felt the warm breath upon my neck. My eyes grew wider.

"What are you doing?" Sara demanded. I glanced behind me in surprise.

"Sara," I whispered emphatically, "how could you let this happen?" I carefully removed the arm from around my waist then slowly slid off the couch. I looked at Sara with huge eyes and my mouth open accusingly.

"Me? I didn't do anything," she whispered firmly. I crept over to the stairs; Sara followed.

"I fell asleep," I whispered vehemently. "I had no idea he was still here; forget about *that*." I pointed to his position on the couch.

Sara tried not to laugh. "Em, you two looked so cute." I swatted at her arm.

"Knock it off Sara," I demanded, still whispering. "What am I supposed to do now?"

"Wake him up and kick him out."

"Why can't you?"

"He's all yours." She laughed and went to her room.

"Sara," I yelled in a whisper at the closed door.

I sighed, looking over at the couch. He did look so peaceful lying curled up on his side. I folded my knees into me as I scrunched at the end of the couch next to his feet. I watched him sleep for a minute, trying to build up the nerve to wake him.

I kicked the back of his thigh gently with my foot.

"Evan," I called softly. He didn't respond, so I pushed a little harder, rocking him. "Evan, you need to wake up."

"Hmmm," he groaned, peeking out from under his long dark lashes. He peered up at me and grinned. "Hi." He stretched his arms above him and turned onto his back so that he could face me.

"Hi," I whispered.

"What time is it?" he asked with a groggy voice.

"Two in the morning."

"No way," he replied in disbelief, pushing himself up to sit. "Why did you let me fall asleep?"

"Me? I think I fell asleep before you did."

"Yeah," he remembered, "that's right. "

"Are you going to be okay to drive home?"

"Why? Would you let me sleep here?"

"No," I admitted. "I was just trying to sound concerned." He smiled—finally fully awake.

"Did I kick you off the couch?" he asked, trying to take in the scene.

"I slept just fine," I admitted, avoiding his question.

Evan stood up and stretched again. He found his shoes and slipped them on his feet.

"Will I see you... today, actually?" he confirmed, grabbing his jacket from the back of the chair.

"I have to be home by four, so I need to be back here by three. Would you rather sleep?"

"No, it's Sunday. It's my day – so, I'll pick you up at ten, okay?"

"Can we make it eleven?" I countered, thinking about how late Sara and I would sleep in, and that we still needed to compare stories.

"Really?" he pleaded. "Ten-thirty?"

"Sure."

I stood from the couch to walk him down the stairs. We snuck to the first floor, careful not to wake Sara's parents. I stopped on the bottom step as he went for the door. He turned to look at me without saying a word. I stood with my arms crossed, bracing myself against the cold air seeping in through the open door. His lingering made me nervous, igniting a tingling in my stomach.

"Good night," I finally whispered, trying to urge him to leave.

"Good night," he replied and walked out the door.

I locked it behind him, and quickly ascended the stairs to Sara's room. She was waiting for me in her bed.

"Did he kiss you?" she inquired eagerly.

"No! Sara, you can't ask me questions like that—like you're hoping he has—and then try to tell me we can't date."

"You're right," she admitted with a sigh. "I promise to try to be more consistent. But I really want you to kiss him."

"Then keep it to yourself. Good night, Sara."

I slipped under the covers after preparing for bed, compelling sleep to find me again, so I wouldn't think about if I wanted Evan to kiss me.

20. THE ROOM

"ARE YOU AWAKE?" SARA ASKED FROM THE BED ACROSS FROM ME.

"Uh huh," I grumbled from under the covers. "I'm awake."

"You need to wake up so you can tell me about dinner last night."

I rolled over to face her. She was definitely more awake than I was, propped up on her elbow, waiting for me. I stretched and yawned loudly. I propped the pillow against the headboard and pushed myself up to sit.

"How was dinner? I can't wait any longer," she insisted.

I provided the details of the other dimension, including descriptions of Evan's parents, the rude guests and how different Evan was around these people. I left Catherine for last. When I was done, Sara was laughing hysterically, not quite as hard as I did when it happened, but she did wipe tears from her eyes.

"I cannot believe you said that to her," she finally managed to say.

"I couldn't contain myself," I confessed. "I guess it warmed me up for Jake's party."

"Wait, what happened at Jake's party, besides everyone hooking up?"

"Let's see—I met Drew Carson, and I thought he was such a nice guy until I realized what the party was all about, and then Jake followed me into the other side of the basement and tried to get me to go somewhere alone with him."

"What did you do?" she asked, looking horrified. "I warned you not to go anywhere."

"Sara, I had no idea what you were talking about. But when I finally got it, I basically told him there was no way in hell I was hooking up with him and came upstairs where I found you and Jason. Sara, Evan knew what kind of party it was when Jake invited me, and he didn't warn me. He's been to one before."

"Seriously?" she asked in disbelief. "Wow, I didn't think he was like that."

"Neither did I," I agreed. "And he swears he's not and that he didn't *do anything*. But he couldn't tell me what he did. Maybe I really don't want to know."

"I do," she exclaimed.

"Sara!" I looked at her, astounded. "He can do whatever he wants with whomever he wants. It's none of our business." Needing to change the subject, I asked, "What's going on with you and Jason? How was your *alone time?*"

Sara sighed and fell on her back. It was not the reaction I was expecting.

"What?! Tell me!" I demanded impatiently.

"You and Evan did more on that couch last night than Jason and I have. Well, except we've kissed and even that took forever," she confessed in frustration.

"What do you mean?"

"I know what you think of me," she glanced over at me and my eyes apologized again. "But I don't care; I like sex. He won't touch me. I don't know what to do. I don't think he's into me." The sorrowful disappointment resounded in her voice. I wasn't sure how to console her.

"Do you still like him?"

"I'm not sure of that either." After a moment in silence, she cautiously brought up, "So, we never got to talk about what happened the other night with your mom showing up at the game."

"I'd rather not," I blurted. "It's just too much to think about." I didn't want to let myself go back there to that night, or any other that involved my mother. It was too painful.

Sara respected my withdrawn response without a word. She glanced at the clock next to her bed and asked, "What time is Evan picking you up?"

"Ten-thirty," I told her and then glanced at the clock too. "Sara, he's going to be here in an hour. I need to take a shower. But we're not done talking about you and Jason. We'll talk about it tomorrow, okay?"

"Okay," she sighed.

Evan arrived at exactly ten-thirty – I was barely ready.

"What are we doing today?" I asked, feeling the warm November sun on my face through the car window as we drove away from Sara's.

"Don't worry, I'll show you."

When we pulled into his driveway, I was surprised to find a silver BMW parked there as well. I'd never seen another car in his driveway before. Then it struck me that someone else was home. Could I possibly face his parents after my humiliating performance last night?

"Who's home?" I asked, hoping he'd tell me, *no one.*

"My mom. Don't worry, we probably won't see her."

The words were barely out of his mouth when the kitchen door opened and his mother stepped out to greet us.

"Or maybe you will," Evan corrected in surprise.

Vivian was dressed in wide legged black pants with a fitted blue turtleneck sweater that flattered her petite figure. I couldn't get over how refined she looked, even without all the glitz.

"Emily," she said with a smile, "it's nice to see you again." I smiled cautiously, not understanding the warm reception. Even Evan was scrutinizing her greeting.

We met her at the bottom of the porch steps and she gave me a brief embrace. I froze, unable to return it since it happened so quickly, and I honestly wasn't expecting it.

"I understand you and Evan have planned to spend the afternoon together. I think that is wonderful," she glowed.

"Mom, what's wrong with you?"

Vivian looked at him disapprovingly.

"Evan, I'm happy to see Emily again, that's all." She smiled at me apologetically for Evan's rudeness.

"We're going in the garage," he told her, eyeing her suspiciously.

"It was great to see you," she said. "Perhaps you could come over for dinner sometime."

"Um, that would be nice," I answered in shock. I replayed our interaction last night, not understanding why she was being so nice to me.

I followed Evan into the garage, but instead of going upstairs to the rec room, he opened the door leading into the other half of the garage. When we were behind closed doors, he paused, his eyes flickering in deliberation.

"What's wrong?" I asked.

"I have no idea why she's acting so strange, and it's making me really nervous. I'm trying to remember if I said something, or overheard anything to explain it. I'm sorry if it made you uncomfortable."

"I was actually trying to come up with the same answer," I admitted. "I was expecting her to despise me after my humiliating clumsiness last night. Besides, I thought for sure Catherine would've said something."

He smiled, remembering my departing comment.

"Oh, I'm sorry about that by the way," I told him, looking at the floor.

"What are you talking about?"

"I should have helped you out more than I did during dinner, instead of laughing. I really wasn't laughing at you. I felt bad that you had to put up with her. I was laughing at how ridiculous she was."

"Don't worry about it. You definitely helped in the end with that priceless exit." He smiled, and I smiled back.

"Okay, what are we doing?" I asked, looking around the expansive space. There were two ride-on lawn mowers, a jet ski and some other recreational vehicles parked in the otherwise empty space.

Evan walked over to a black dirt bike and handed me a red helmet.

"We're going for a ride," he said, kicking up the stand and rolling it toward the large door at the other end. He pressed a button and the door rolled open.

I watched him, not sure if my legs could move, let alone about walk.

"Evan, I'm not sure that's a great idea."

"Trust me, you'll love it." He fastened a black helmet on his head. I warily walked out to him and slid the helmet on my head. What the hell was I doing?

Evan helped me fasten the strap and showed me where to sit and place my feet. He explained that the path was pretty flat, but to expect to bounce a little. Great, not only was this my first time on a bike, but this one could potentially throw me off!

Evan kicked the starter and the dirt bike revved to life. The explosive rumble caused my heart to falter. It didn't help when he throttled it a few times. He motioned for me to get on. Before I could talk myself out of it, I climbed up and threw my leg over the seat. I slid closer to his back and put my hands on his waist. He grabbed my hands and pulled them around him. Once we started, I understood why.

We sped off through the back field, toward the woods. My heart pounded against my chest. I gripped him tighter as we entered the woods and the terrain became bumpier—I could feel the seat give with each divot and root, still too scared to enjoy the experience.

Eventually, I became accustomed to the uneven ride and loosened my death grip. I still kept my arms snugly around him, knowing that one unexpected bounce and I'd be airborne. I focused on the trees streaking by and the sun fighting through the tops of the evergreens. It was brighter in the woods than I expected, probably because most of the trees were bare, preparing for winter—despite the unseasonably warm day.

Evan eventually slowed and crawled to a stop. He shut off the bike and took off his helmet. I sat up and attempted to do the same. I couldn't figure out how to take it off, so I climbed off the bike and asked him to help me. My legs trembled beneath me.

"Well?" he asked, after removing the helmet from my head.

I shrugged. "Not bad."

"What?" he questioned. "You loved it, admit it."

"Not really."

He shook his head and smiled.

"This is nice." I nodded toward the glistening clearing with the sunlight dancing along the swaying overgrown blades and the brook along the bottom of a small hill, bubbling over rocks before disappearing into the woods.

"I've taken some amazing pictures out here."

"I don't think I've ever seen your pictures. Well, except for the newspaper and the one you submitted for the calendar."

"I can show you when we get back if you want."

"Sure."

We walked to the brook and sat at its edge, mesmerized by the water rippling over the stones.

"My mom showed up at the game the other night," I blurted, staring into the water. I wasn't prepared to say that, and honestly, I thought I was past it until I inadvertently found my thoughts drifting there again.

"You must have been happy to see her."

I let out an uneasy laugh. "I don't know about that."

Evan remained quiet, waiting for me to continue.

"It was awkward," I confessed.

"I'm sorry," Evan replied, not knowing what else to say. I shrugged dismissively, afraid to reveal more.

He casually took my hand, making my heart trip. We sat in silence, caught up in the glistening flow of the water.

"I'm still trying to figure out what my mother's up to," he finally said. "Or it's possible she could actually like you."

"Thanks," I shot back sarcastically.

"You know what I mean," he offered, trying to make me feel better. "It's not like you talked to her very much last night. She's never been this... accepting of anyone before. She's really hard to please."

"I can see that," I recognized with a slight nod. "Speaking of which, you were so different at the Jacobs' house. It was a little strange."

"How?"

"You seemed... older. You talked more proper and were almost stiff," I shared, hoping I didn't offend him. I looked over at him to see his eyes moving, considering my words.

"I guess I never thought about it, but you're probably right. It's most likely from years of having to go to those things – they're rubbing off on me. That sucks."

I let out a short laugh.

"I guess you'll have to come to more of them to keep me real," he suggested, gently nudging my shoulder with his. I caught my breath at his touch, my mouth posed in a shocked smile with thoughts of future dinners.

Then I heard a buzzing and a distant chime. Evan reached in his pocket and took out his cell phone. He read who was calling on the screen and grinned at me before answering.

"Hi Jake," he answered. My mouth dropped open. Evan smiled. He listened for a while, but couldn't keep the smile off of his face, occasionally glancing at me.

"Sorry I didn't tell you I was showing up with her. I didn't think it mattered." He listened again for a minute.

"I understand, but I warned you she wasn't like that." He looked at me with a grin. My eyes grew wider—I could only imagine what was being said on the other end.

"No, I don't think you have to worry about either of them saying anything. No, Jason won't – I talked to him about it last night.

"Yeah, I'd say she wasn't interested either." Evan smiled wider – heat flashed across my cheeks.

"Don't worry about it; it's fine. I'll see you tomorrow." He laughed as he pressed *End*.

"You'd better tell me what that was all about," I threatened.

"He was pissed that I was there, thinking that's why you acted that way. And he wanted to know if I thought any of you would say anything. The parties are handpicked for a reason – no one talks about what goes on there. There are rumors, but no one ever admits to anything. But the good news is that you won't have to worry about him hitting on you – I think he got the hint."

"Well, that's good," I admitted. "He really is so full of himself. I can't believe you're friends with him."

"I wouldn't say we're friends. I met him before I moved here. His mother and mine were on a fundraising committee, and I met him at the dinner. When he found out I was moving here, he invited me to one of his parties to *introduce* me to people before I started school." I really wanted to comment about his "introduction", but the thought of it made my stomach flip. I forced out the stray thoughts.

"Besides that, we have soccer in common, and we've hung out a few times with other guys. But I would never call him up and ask him over. He's a lot to take by himself. I'd hate to be the girl he's focused on – you have no idea what he says…" Then he stopped to look at me apologetically.

"Evan, are you serious?! He's said things about me to the soccer team?" My stomach turned in disgust.

"He doesn't when I'm around because he knows it pisses me off, and I have no problem telling him that. He's an ass, don't worry about it. He's not lying and saying that you've gotten together or anything like that." I knew he was trying to make me feel better, but I was fuming at the thought of being the topic of anything that came out of Jake's mouth.

"We should head back," Evan said, pulling me back from my angry thoughts. I followed him to the bike where he helped me with my helmet before we climbed on. The return trip didn't seem as long, thankfully. Can't say the bike was my favorite adrenaline rush.

Evan parked the bike in the garage before leading me upstairs. Upon entering, he selected the music of a guy with a smooth voice, strumming a guitar to an easy rhythm, singing about being under the stars—it reminded me of being on the beach.

"Are you hungry? I can run down and grab us a couple of sandwiches," he offered.

"Sure." He left while I sat on the couch, enchanted by the optimistic melodies. I barely heard Evan run back up the stairs.

"Here you go," he announced. I jumped.

"You don't pay attention very well, do you?"

"I didn't hear you," I defended. He let out a quick laugh. He placed a plate on the table in front of me with a bottle of root beer.

"Is your mom still here?"

"Yeah, she just gave me a hard time about taking you out on the bike. I assured her you weren't that breakable." I tightened my lips to hide a smile. I couldn't imagine his mother being so concerned about my well being. She barely knew me.

When we were done eating, Evan asked, "Do you want to see the pictures I was talking about?"

"Definitely."

I followed him as he opened the door behind the foosball tables into a rustic room with exposed wood beamed walls. There were two small windows on the other side of the room, overlooking the drive way. Two twin beds with navy comforters sat along one wall, and a long desk with pictures and photography equipment sprawled across it ran along the other. There was a simple, doorless closet on the same wall as the entrance with shelves of clothes, books and photography equipment.

One of the first things I noticed was Sara's white scarf hanging on the back of the rolling desk chair. Evan caught my eye and pressed his lips together.

"Yeah, you forgot that in my car. I keep forgetting to give it to you." I nodded, not sure what to make of it, so I decided to dismiss it.

Evan started pointing out different pictures of scenic landscapes that were pinned to the wooden beams above the desk, explaining where he was when he took them. I was easily lost in the detail of each shot, transported to the location as if I were there standing next to him when he took them.

I began flipping through the loose pictures scattered on the desk. Evan commented on some of the shots then became silent to let me look on my own. I couldn't say anything – I was speechless. I knew he was talented when I saw the results for the paper, but I had no idea.

I opened a black bound book, causing Evan to take in a quick breath. I hesitated, uncertain if he wanted me to look through it.

"That's my work for Art class," he offered. It didn't explain his reaction.

"Can I look through it?" I'd never seen him so tense before.

"Sure," he breathed, remaining uneasy, standing perfectly still.

I turned the pages and studied the art that he captured through his lens. The portfolio contained scenic pictures, sports action pictures, and abstract pictures of unidentifiable objects with smooth lines and intricate curves. Then I flipped the page and stopped. I could sense Evan stiffen even more when the image caught my breath.

I examined the black and white angled profile of the girl. The soft lines of her face filled most of the picture, her pale skin providing dramatic contrast with the dark background. A thick wet strand of hair clung to her subtly parted full lips. Drops of water scattered on her smooth skin, dripping from her sloping nose. Her almond shaped eyes were smeared with black, framing their haunted depths as she focused on a place far removed from the picture.

"It's beautiful," I breathed, admiring the powerful emotion and truth frozen in the single shot.

"I love that picture," he admitted softly. "I think it's because I love the girl in that picture."

I turned slowly to face him, confused by his words feeling my stomach twist.

"What?" The strangling spread to my chest. I could feel my heart beating in my throat.

"You don't remember when I took that picture?"

I stared at him, unsure of what he was talking about.

"You were so quiet for so long. You didn't say anything when I came back to check on you. So I left to get my camera, thinking I could get shots of people at the party and give you time alone since you didn't seem to want to talk." I was afraid to hear more. My heart beat louder, and my head felt light – I could barely breathe.

"By the time I got back, it had started to rain. I saw Sara in the house—I told her where you were, and that I'd meet her outside. You looked so amazing in your stillness, sitting in the rain; at the same time, you looked displaced – like you were a million miles away. I had to capture it. I tried to talk to you, but you wouldn't say anything. So I sat next to you and waited. You finally stirred from wherever you went and realized it was raining."

I heard every word he said, but I couldn't comprehend a single syllable. Then I stared into his stormy blue eyes and saw what he was saying. My knees buckled—I inhaled several fast breaths. I slowly lowered myself onto the chair at the desk, staring at the floor, my breath lost.

After a few minutes of deafening silence, Evan asked, "Are you okay?"

"No," I mouthed, shaking my head slowly. I looked up at him. "Evan, you can't say that. You can't mean it."

"That's not quite what I hoped you'd say," he responded, the disappointment evident in his tone.

"I'm sorry…" I started.

"Don't be, it's okay," he replied quickly, suddenly trying to downplay the situation. Then he thought better of it, and asked, "Are you really telling me you don't feel the same way?" I held my breath, and my heart ached.

"I can't, we can't," I stammered. "You don't understand. It doesn't matter how I feel, it just can't happen." He stared into my distraught eyes and shook his head in confusion.

"I *don't* understand. What are you talking about?"

"Can't we please just stay friends?" I begged.

"But you're not denying that you feel the same way."

"It's so much more complicated than that. If we can't be friends, then –" I couldn't say it. "*Please*, can we just be friends?"

He didn't respond. The silence was disrupted by the vibration of his phone. He pulled it out of his pocket and looked to me. "I've got to take this—it's my brother."

I nodded and he left the room. Soon after, I heard his footsteps on the stairs.

I became aware that I was strangling my shaking hands, and released them, but was unable to loosen the knot in my throat or calm the throbbing in my chest. I took a couple breaths in attempt to push it away. I stood on my rubber legs, taking another breath before walking out of the room, closing the door behind me.

21. JUST FRIENDS

"WE CAN BE FRIENDS," EVAN SAID WHEN HE RETURNED TWENTY minutes later. He sat next to me on the couch and grabbed my hand. The warmth of his hand sent shivers up my arm. I searched his eyes, wanting to believe him.

"I mean, we're already friends, so nothing has to change." The disappointment and confusion were replaced by a comforting smile. He *appeared* to be sincere. "Okay?"

I had no idea what had happened in that twenty minutes, but he was not the same as when he left.

"Yeah, okay," I said slowly. I tried to smile back.

I was so afraid of seeing him in school on Monday, expecting an awkwardness between us. However, there wasn't the tension or avoidance I anticipated. Everything was back to the way it was before the weekend ever happened – then again... it wasn't.

I noticed his presence so much more than I had before. Every time he brushed alongside my arm when we walked down the hall, or leaned in close to whisper to me in Anatomy, it sent thousands of sparks flying through my body. I found myself smiling more and caught up in his gaze longer. It was like I was noticing him for the first time, all over again. But this time, I knew he noticed me too.

Evan sat closer, walked nearer, and looked longer. He started storing his books in my locker in between classes, placing his hand on the small of my back when reaching over me to retrieve them. These subtle touches would ignite a warmth in my chest, and release tingles up the back of my neck. He didn't hold my hand in school, but he always found a way for the backs of our hands to lightly touch when we were near enough.

We were engaged in a very intricate dance of touching without touching, knowing without saying, and feeling without expressing. We were friends walking along a ledge, a very thin ledge—and I was too caught up in my heightened awareness of his existence to realize how close the ledge was to crumbling beneath my feet.

"What's going on with you?" Sara asked during our ride to school on Wednesday. I hadn't told her everything when I returned from Evan's that Sunday afternoon. I told her about the dirt bike ride and Jake's call, but I left out *the room*. I couldn't bring myself to say the words out loud, and since we agreed to be just friends, there was no point in saying them at all.

"What do you mean?"

"You and Evan have been acting really... different the last couple of days. Did something happen that you're not telling me?" She glanced over at my avoiding eyes and declared, "Something *did* happen! Em, did he kiss you? I can't believe you didn't tell me!"

"No, Sara, he did not kiss me," I said emphatically.

"Then what? You two are almost too... close, or something. I can tell it's not the same. So, what happened?"

"We're just friends," I emphasized.

"Did he say something?" she shot out in excitement. I couldn't conceal my pink cheeks. "Omigod, that's it. He finally told you how he feels about you. You have to tell me what he said."

"Sara, it doesn't matter," I retorted, getting redder as I remembered exactly what he said. "We're only going to be friends, so I'm not going to talk about it."

Sara didn't continue her interrogation, but a knowing smile crept on her face.

"Is Carol getting out of work early today, too?" Sara asked when we pulled into the parking lot.

"She actually took the day off so she could go shopping with her mother and start prepping everything for tomorrow. I guess her sister and her kids are getting into town tonight, so she wants to be there for that too." The thought of Carol in the kitchen *cooking* was laughable. I knew she wasn't going to measurably contribute to the Thanksgiving meal, but would gladly accept the unearned praise.

"So you can't go home after school, can you?"

"I think I'm going over Evan's," I replied, as casually as I possibly could.

"Yeah, and I'm coming with you," she insisted. I knew there was no point in arguing with her.

"Sure." I smiled slightly, trying to hide my disappointment.

To my surprise, Evan seemed perfectly accepting of gaining a chaperone. When we arrived at his house after a useless half-day of classes, I discovered why. Alongside his mother's BMW was a silver Volvo with New York license plates.

"Your brother?" I concluded.

"He got in late last night."

The side door opened as it did before, and Vivian exited wiping her hands on a white apron tied around her waist – evidently she *did* cook. She was stunning once again with her hair twisted neatly off of her face. She wore a full black skirt that fell below her knees and a pair of black boots that rose to meet it, along with a tailor fitted white blouse.

Behind her was a tall blond who was obviously her oldest son and the opposite of Evan in just about every way. Jared had shaggy blond hair that flipped out at the tops of his ears. His features resembled his mother's soft lines and thin lips, with her sparkling blue eyes. Jared was slightly taller than Evan, with a broader, more muscular build.

"Who's that?" I heard Sara whisper in my ear as they approached.

"Evan's mother and brother," I said quickly.

"Emily, how are you darling?" she asked, giving me the same embrace but adding a peck on the cheek. I still had a hard time returning the gesture due to its brevity.

"It's nice to see you again, Mrs. Mathews."

"Vivian, please. We are already acquainted, so we can forego the formalities," she insisted, smiling brightly.

"Jared, this is Emma," Evan declared proudly.

"Hi, I've heard a lot about you," Jared replied, extending his hand. I gave Evan a brief questioning glance, he responded with a quick rise of his eyebrows.

"This is my friend, Sara," I introduced, after she nudged my elbow for the second time.

"Sara, it's very nice to meet you. I met your parents. They are wonderful people," Vivian welcomed, shaking her hand. Before Jared could say anything to Sara, Vivian turned to me to ask, "Will you be staying for dinner?"

"Mom," Evan stressed, alarmed by the invitation, "it's the day before Thanksgiving. I'm sure Emma needs to get home to *her* family."

"Well, another time then," she said, ignoring his curtness.

"Of course," I promised.

"We're going upstairs to play pool," Evan announced before his mother could make any other impromptu invitations. He grabbed my hand and escorted me to the garage.

"It was nice seeing you again," I blurted quickly as we passed Vivian.

Sara and Jared followed behind us.

While Evan turned on the music and got us drinks, and Jared collected the pool balls on the table, Sara cornered me.

"*What* was that about?" she demanded. "His mother is practically gushing over you. Not to mention that he's holding your hand like it's the most natural thing in the world. Forget about dating—are you having a wedding you forgot to invite me to?"

"Sara!" I exclaimed a little too loudly, shocked by her words. Her eyes widened at my volume, and we both glanced around to make certain the guys hadn't overheard.

"Stop being stupid," I whispered. "I met his mother at the dinner, remember? And he grabbed my hand to drag me away before she said anything else that would embarrass him."

"Whatever you say," she replied, not convinced.

"You two ready?" Evan called from the pool table.

Evan and I were a team against Jared and Sara. Throughout the game we engaged in casual conversation about Cornell, soccer, the upcoming basketball season and Thanksgiving plans. I could feel Sara boring holes through me every time Evan leaned over me with his hand on my hip, adjusting my angle for the tougher shots. Then again, the searing heat could have been my heart pressed against my chest.

"So, what's with mom?" Jared asked when Evan was taking his shot. Evan waited until he knocked the nine ball into the corner pocket before he answered.

"You mean downstairs when we got here?" Evan confirmed.

"Yeah, that was strange," Jared noted.

"Um, actually, I didn't get to tell you this either, Emma." I raised my eyebrows when he looked over toward me. "I told you that Emma went to the Jacobs' with us for dinner last weekend, right?"

"Yeah, and I am so sorry you had to suffer through that," Jared empathized. I grinned in acknowledgement, too anxious to hear what Evan had to share to say anything.

"Well, it turns out quiet Dr. Eckel likes to gossip," he looked at me with a grin. My eyes widened, catching on. "Emma was sitting next to Dr. Eckel, and I guess he overheard Catherine's…"

"Pathetic charm," I interjected. Evan smiled at my choice of words.

"Sara you know about this, right?" Evan assumed. She nodded, trying to suppress a smile that drew color along Evan's neck. "Anyway, he also heard Emma's not so subtle reactions to some of the things she said."

"Noticed that, huh?" My face instantly felt warmer.

"I think half the table noticed, but only he knew what it was about since everyone else was talking. So, when we made our escape, he *happened* to be on his way to the restroom and witnessed your gracious exit."

"No way," I breathed, my mouth open.

"Don't worry; he thought it was pretty funny. He and my mother survive these dinners on gossip, so he told her what happened. My mother can't stand the Jacobs, including Catherine, and was impressed by how you subtly put her in her place."

"She's impressed with me because I laughed at Catherine Jacobs? That was not very subtle," I stated, dumbfounded.

"Well, you don't know Catherine. She's probably still trying to figure out why you were laughing at her," he said with a quick laugh. "But my mother thinks you showed a lot of restraint, considering." His mother must have misinterpreted my rudeness for something even I didn't understand.

"Huh," Jared mused, before taking his shot.

"Are you two going skiing this weekend?" I blurted in order to change the subject.

"Yeah, what are we doing this weekend?" Jared asked, directing his attention to Evan. "I want to get the snowboards out. We can go up Saturday and stay the night."

"Don't we have plans Sunday?" Evan turned to me for the answer.

"We could go out Friday instead," Sara quickly threw in. I almost forgot she was behind me, she'd been so quiet. "Em, you can say you and I have to work on the Journalism assignment together. You can lie and tell them it's due Monday, and since I won't be around for the rest of the weekend, Friday is the only day available. Then we can all go out to a movie or something. Jared, you're welcome to come too if you want."

"You're good with the lying to the parents' stories, huh?" Jared observed, sounding impressed.

"I've had four years of practice," she admitted, making me laugh.

"Sure, we can go out Friday," Evan responded tentatively, looking to me for approval. I nodded in agreement.

"That sounds good to me," Jared confirmed.

"Wait, what about Jason?" Evan asked, realizing that he was missing from the plan.

"Yeah, well, we won't be seeing much of Jason anymore," she confessed.

"What happened?" Evan countered.

"Um, he was just so… quiet," she said with a smile. I knew what she really meant and let out a quick laugh.

"He was really nice," she backtracked, "but I need a little more… spontaneity." She smirked at me.

"Huh, I'm sorry to hear that it didn't work out," Evan offered.

"Thanks," she replied, uncomfortable with the condolence.

We played a few games of pool and a couple rounds of darts before I realized that I needed to leave, so I could be home before George.

"I'll be right back," Evan told Jared, grabbing his coat.

"Oh, I'll drive Emma," Sara told Evan. Evan stopped with one arm in his sleeve and looked at me, questioning Sara's offer. I shrugged.

"Okay," he said reluctantly. "Then I'll see you Friday."

"I'll call you to confirm the time," Sara replied. "It was great to meet you Jared." I lingered, not sure if Evan was going to walk us down. Sara noticed my hesitation and grabbed my hand to drag me down the stairs.

"Bye." I waved before I disappeared.

"You are so full of shit," Sara accused when we pulled out of the driveway. My jaw dropped. "If there was any more sexual tension in that room…"

"What?" I interrupted with a laugh. "You are definitely seeing things that aren't there."

"Am I?"

I couldn't straighten the smile from my lips.

"Yeah, I didn't think so," she concluded from my lack of defense. "Emma, just be careful, okay?"

"I don't understand you," I confronted. "You keep saying how cute we are together and antagonizing me with questions about whether he's kissed me – and now that... well, you're not reacting the way I thought you would."

"I was stupid for teasing you about kissing him. I'm sorry," she admitted. "But now that I see your new *friendship*, I'm really afraid for you. If you can't hide it around me, then Carol is going to destroy you if she picks up on it."

"Don't worry, Sara, nothing's going to happen."

I didn't have to sit on the steps very long before George arrived home. It was easy to ask him if I could stay over Sara's on Friday without Carol around. He agreed to the plan, reminding me I had to be home first thing on Saturday to do my chores. He had to work for a few hours on Saturday, so he warned me not to upset Carol while I was home alone with her. I promised, knowing that just breathing would upset Carol, and there wasn't anything I could do about that.

I survived Thanksgiving at Janet's by not existing. I blended into the background as best as I could. When it came to cleaning up, Carol glowered at me in expectation of making myself useful, but Janet wouldn't hear of it. Carol did everything she could to keep from blowing up, so I stayed out of her way in the living room, coloring with the kids while they watched the first Christmas movie of the season.

I drove home with George while Carol and the kids spent more time with her sister and her two daughters who were visiting from Georgia.

∽✕∾

Sara picked me up in the morning so that we'd have the day together before we went to the movies. She wanted to go to the mall, but I begged her not to make me suffer through watching her try on a million pieces of clothes on the busiest shopping day of the year. She conceded to my pleading but still had to get a couple of things done before we went to lunch.

203

We stopped by a jeweler, so Sara could buy new earrings, then the seamstress, to pick up new clothes Sara had tailor fitted, and finally Sara splurged on pedicures for the two of us. It was Sara's idea of the perfect girl day, minus the clothes shopping. I was just along for the ride, getting a glimpse of what it was like to be Sara McKinley.

We walked quickly to the house in the cold with flip flops on our freshly pedi-ed feet. Anna admired my light pink toes and Sara's contrasting hot red while we sat and chatted on the couch. She was preparing a list of recipients for Christmas cards, so she could send them out the next week. I watched as Sara and her mom discussed their family and laughed about her dad's side. I smiled at their connection, feeling like I was looking through the windows of the ideal family. It also ached at the same time, knowing how frigid it was on this side of the window.

"What time are the boys meeting you?" Anna asked.

"We're going to an early show at six and then probably getting something to eat. We'll come back here and hang out after," Sara informed her mom, and me as well. This was the first time I was hearing our plans.

"Sounds great," Anna replied.

"Let's go figure out what I'm going to do with you," Sara said, pulling me off the couch.

I sat on her bed as she sorted through her closet.

"Sara," I called nervously. My tone made her stop what she was doing and step out of the closet so that I had her attention. "I don't think I can afford dinner and a movie. I've stashed some money, but not enough to do both."

I hated having to admit when I couldn't afford to do the things she had in mind for us. And she knew I hated when she offered to pay for things. It was hard enough borrowing her clothes; forget about having her extend her wallet to entertain me.

"Don't worry about it," she said nonchalantly. "I have movie passes that I have to use, so you can save your money for food. The passes include drinks and popcorn, so it'll work out. I actually have four, so the guys will use them too. Honestly, Em, they'll probably want to pay for dinner, feeling bad that I'm supplying the movies."

"Are you sure?"

"Definitely," she confirmed dismissively. "I have the passes, so we might as well use them." She ducked back into the closet, continuing her search.

"Do you have any more pink sweaters?" I yelled to Sara when I heard her groaning in frustration through the open door.

"No more pink sweaters for you," she hollered in return. Then she poked her head out and said, "I should make you go in sweats actually." I scowled at her.

"But you know I couldn't do that. I love dressing you up too much," she said with a smile. "Oh, I have it. I have this black shirt that will look amazing with dark jeans and wedged heels." She revealed a scooping black top that looked like it was too small.

"No heels," I protested.

"Uh, that's not going to work," she groaned. "Wait—what about boots. They have a thicker heel, so they won't be so hard to walk in." I shrugged in defeat. "Then I'll pull your hair back in a curly ponytail and you'll be adorable – to go to the movies with your *friends*." I picked up on the sarcasm and stuck my tongue out at her.

My hair bounced in the ponytail as I descended the stairs with Sara. She had her long locks in a high ponytail as well and wore a sapphire blouse that showed off her eyes. She looked like she was going on a date, despite the supposed casualness of the evening.

I met Evan's eyes and grinned back when he came into view at the bottom of the stairs.

"Don't you two look nice," Carl observed from the sitting room.

"Thanks, Dad," Sara said, giving him a peck on the cheek and grabbing our jackets. "We'll be back later."

Jared's silver Volvo waited for us in the driveway. Jared opened the passenger side door for Sara. She was heading toward the back door with me when the gesture caught her by surprise.

"Oh, thanks," she said, slipping onto the passenger seat.

Evan opened the back door for me, before he went around to the other side and slid in next to me. He had my hand in his before we even left the driveway. My lips curled up at the warmth of his touch. As we drove, the proximity of our bodies gradually became closer until the sides of our jeans were gently touching. I couldn't say that either of us moved intentionally, but there was a gravity that drew us together. My heart murmured in content.

In attempt to make up for her silence at Evan's the other day, Sara did most of the talking, with Jared being her main audience—although she kept turning around to include us. I knew she was doing it to prevent us from doing anything in the dark of the backseat. Jared was an endearing captor to Sara's charm. He laughed at the right time and commented intelligibly – I was relieved he was with us instead of Jason.

"No more pink sweaters?" Evan whispered while Sara discussed one of her favorite restaurants in New York, which coincidentally was one of Jared's as well.

"I've been banned," I whispered in return, nodding toward Sara. He looked from Sara back to me with his eyebrows pulled together. "Don't worry about it."

"Okay." He shrugged.

"But you still look great," he whispered leaning in so that his breath tickled my ear. He lingered for a second. I knew all I had to do was turn my head, and he would be right there. I took an even breath, allowing it to swirl in my head before slowly turning to meet him.

"Does that sound good to you?" Sara turned toward us. I quickly faced her, and Evan sat back against his seat. She shot me an accusing look.

"Sorry, what did you say?" I asked. Evan gave my hand a tight squeeze in frustration.

"For dinner," she emphasized, "is Italian okay?"

"Sure," Evan agreed.

We pulled up to the theater and Sara practically pulled me out of the car, putting her arm through mine while forcing us to walk together toward the entrance. The guys followed.

"Em, you are in so much trouble," she whispered. I could only grin in recognition of the truth.

When the guys found out Sara was taking care of the tickets, they insisted on paying for dinner – as Sara had predicted. After getting our drinks and popcorn, we made our way into the crowded theatre to see the newly released action movie.

I could tell Sara was angling to sit in-between me and Evan, but I slipped in behind him before she could enter the row – so Sara sat next to me and Jared was next to Evan. Evan easily found my hand again once the lights dimmed. I don't know if I could've recalled a single scene from the overly explosive flick. Not with Evan slowly brushing his finger tips along the inside of my hand, tracing delicate circles that made my entire body tingle.

Every so often Sara tried to distract me and pull me toward her with a comment about the action star and an unrealistic leap, or that he should have been dead within the first five minutes of the movie. When I leaned in to rest my head on Evan's shoulder, she finally gave up, shaking her head in frustration. I couldn't concentrate on anything except for his breath next to my ear and his cheek against the top of my head as he casually breathed me in. The star could've died in the first five minutes—I would have had no idea.

When we stood up to leave, my legs were weak and my head was spinning. Evan kept his hand on my waist, holding me next to him while we made our way up the crowded aisle. I placed my hand over his, securing him to me. As soon as we were in the main hall, Sara caught my arm.

"We'll be right back," she announced, pulling me away from Evan's wrap and toward the bathroom.

As soon as we entered, Sara whipped around to face me, demanding, "What are you doing?" She didn't pause to let me answer. "If you tell me one more time that you're just friends, I'm going to kill you. Do you want this? Because all you have to do is tell me and I'll leave you alone. But you were the one who convinced *me* this couldn't happen, and now look at you – you can barely see straight.

"Just think about it clearly for one minute and let me know if you want more from Evan than just a friendship. Forget about what you're *feeling* – *think* about it. Think about Carol."

I shuddered at the mention of her name.

I stood there for a minute, taking in her passionate expression and was overwhelmed with the situation. I couldn't think. My body was so mesmerized by the trance of his touch that my mind wasn't working. I couldn't answer her.

"I don't know what to do," I confessed quietly, "but don't worry about me Sara; it will be okay. I promise."

"You know you can't promise that."

I shrugged.

"Do you want me to interfere, so you can decide what to do?"

"Maybe," I agreed. I recognized her logic, but the swirling in my head was not allowing the rational thought to penetrate. "But don't be so invasive, okay? You and I can sit in the backseat together, but let me sit next to him in the restaurant, alright?"

"I can do that."

The guys were waiting for us patiently. I took Evan's hand and walked to the parking lot.

"I'm going to sit in back with Sara, okay?" I whispered as we neared the car.

"Sure," he said pausing to look at me. "Are you okay?"

"Yeah." I smiled back, putting him at ease. "It's a girl thing." He raised his eyebrows and nodded to indicate that he understood. I wished I did.

After a talkative dinner, we headed back to Sara's, still in the agreed upon seating arrangement. I was intoxicated by him as I gazed at the back of his neatly trimmed hairline and the linear muscles that ran down his neck to his back. I wasn't fighting against the pull of him anymore, and it felt so invigorating. I didn't want to pretend I didn't feel my pulse quicken every time I was near him. I wanted to feel it – I deserved that much, right?

"Sara, would you be okay with Jared if Evan and I watched a movie in your room?" I whispered in her ear. Her mouth dropped open, and for the first time, Sara was speechless.

"Are you sure?" she asked cautiously.

"Yeah, I'm sure." I smiled, the glow radiating from my cheeks.

She smiled back and whispered, "Okay." Then quickly added, "I want details." I laughed and Evan turned to find out what was so funny.

I looked at him and smiled, biting my lower lip. "Nothing," I assured him. Then I heard Sara gasp.

My eyes followed hers, looking past Evan, and froze, seeing exactly what had caused her to breathe in so sharply.

"Oh no, Sara… it's *her*." In that one breath, the ledge disintegrated from under my feet.

22. REVEALED

"GET DOWN," SARA INSTRUCTED FERVENTLY, PULLING ME ONTO THE seat.

"What's wrong?" Evan inspected our sunken silhouettes with concern.

"Evan, turn around," Sara demanded. He recognized the terror on my face and did.

Still facing forward, he asked, "What is going on?"

Before she could redirect him, Jared pulled into her driveway. Sara unfastened our seatbelts so we could slide to the floor behind the front seats.

"Shit," she whispered and pulled out her phone. "Jared, shut off the car. Hi mom. Listen, Jared – please listen to this Jared – is going to come to the front door and you're going to answer. He's going to look like he's asking if we're home, and you're going to shake your head and look like you're telling him we've already gone to bed.

"Jared, please go."

Jared, definitely perplexed by the situation, obeyed as directed.

Anna said something to Sara. I clutched my knees, staring at her as my body shook and my stomach turned.

"Mom, I promise I'll explain when I get home. Keep the back door unlocked. Bye."

She hung up the phone and watched the exchange at the door from between the seats. From my position on the floor behind the passenger seat, I was unable to see what happened, but it was brief. Jared was back in the car within a minute, awaiting further instructions.

"Pull out of the driveway and drive back to the main road at the end of my street," Sara guided him. "Take a right on the road, and then the first road on the right. Jared, let me know if that Jeep follows you."

After a stomach wrenching eternity, he said, "No, it's still parked across from your house."

Sara let out a sigh for the both of us. I couldn't tell if I was actually breathing.

"Are you going to tell me what's going on?" Evan demanded, growing more frustrated.

I couldn't bring myself to talk. I could only stare at Sara and shake my head.

"Who's in the Jeep?" Evan inquired.

"My aunt," I whispered, finding my voice. The admission of her presence made me feel faint. What was she doing here?

"Are we on the other street yet?" Sara asked.

"Yeah," Jared answered.

Sara sat back up on the seat, but I couldn't bring myself to move.

"It'll be okay," Sara consoled, pulling me up by my hands and urging me to sit on the seat. I slid onto the leather and sat with my head in my shaking hands. "There's no way she saw us. We noticed her from the top of the hill, before she could see in the car."

Evan turned around. "Are you not supposed to be out?"

"I'm *never* supposed to be out," I quivered. I couldn't look at him. I leaned against the window and nervously pulled at my lower lip with my fingers.

"Stop at the blue house that's still under construction." Sara leaned over the seat to point it out to Jared. "Do you have a flashlight that I can borrow?"

"Sure, it's in the trunk."

They got out of the car, leaving Evan and I alone.

"What's going to happen?"

"I don't know," I whispered, shaking my head.

"You're going to be okay, right?" he asked, the concern resounding in his voice.

Before I could answer, Sara opened my door and pulled me out by my hand. Evan opened his door to follow. I fought to find my feet beneath me, and leaned into Sara for support.

"Sara, what's going to happen?" Evan questioned.

"We have to go. I'll talk to you later," Sara blurted over her shoulder, escorting me along the dirt path that would eventually be a driveway, heading towards the construction site.

"Emma," Evan yelled. But I didn't turn around. I allowed Sara to hurry me along into the darkness.

I didn't remember our trek through the woods from the back of the unfinished property, to Sara's expansive backyard. Fear had a way of making time disappear, and the images came in flashes. I remembered walking through the downstairs door, the sight of Anna's concerned face, and Sara laying me in the bed. I couldn't close my eyes, and stared blankly at the dark sky through her skylights.

My head spun rapidly, trying to figure out how she knew. Had she followed us all night? Eventually, the fear subsided into a manageable place. I sensed Sara sitting next to me, watching me nervously.

"Did she leave?" I whispered.

"Right before we came into the house, my mom said."

"Do you think she knows?"

"I can't see how. My mom said that she called around seven and asked to speak with you. She told Carol we went to get something to eat and asked if you should call her when you got back. Carol said no. My mom doesn't remember when the car showed up across the street, but noticed it about fifteen minutes before I called her."

"What does your mom think?"

"She knows, Em. She doesn't know everything, but she knows how impossible they are. She would never say anything, I swear."

I believed her.

"Does *he* know?"

"He's called a couple of times. All he knows is that you're really freaked. I wouldn't tell him why, and he got angry with me. He wanted to come back over, but I told him he couldn't, so he asked to come by in the morning. I convinced him that there wasn't enough time since I had to get you home by eight."

"She won't do anything will she?" For the first time since we saw Carol's car, Sara sounded scared.

"No, I'm sure she'll just accuse me of whatever lie she decides on, insult me a lot, and send me to my room." I looked up at Sara and realized I couldn't let her know how truly terrified I was to go home. I pushed the fear away so I could put on a reassuring face for Sara's sake.

I propped myself up to sit against the headboard.

"I really freaked out, huh?" I tried to let out a laugh, but it sounded wrong.

"Em, you were so pale, I was afraid you might pass out."

"I thought for sure that she saw us, that's all. I was expecting her to confront me and didn't know if I could face her." I was hoping to downplay my paralyzed reaction in the car.

"My mom offered to try talking to her," Sara stated half-heartedly.

"You know that won't work," I replied, trying to control the panic in my voice.

"I know," Sara agreed with a defeated breath.

"I can't believe I reacted like that," I blurted, replaying my horrified reaction in my head. "Evan's probably wondering what the hell's wrong with me."

"He's just worried," Sara tried to soothe me. "He doesn't think any less of you, honestly."

I took a deep breath, trying to regain control over my quivering body before Sara noticed. What I couldn't tell her was that if her mom called, it would be the worst thing that could happen. What I couldn't show her was that I was petrified and didn't know how I was going to walk into that house in the morning. I knew Carol didn't need proof that I disobeyed her. She just had to believe I did.

~⚬~

I sat straight up, heaving and covered in sweat. I looked around the room, trying to place where I was. I recognized Sara and eased my fists from their white knuckled grip of the blanket.

"You sounded like you couldn't breathe."

"Just a nightmare," I explained, trying to relax my erected posture. "What time is it?"

"Six-thirty," she reported, still concerned by my appearance. "Do you want to talk about it?"

"I really don't remember it," I lied. "You should get some more sleep. I'm going to take a shower, okay?"

212

The smell of the earth still lingered in my nose as did the burn in my lungs from the weight of the dirt on my body, pressing the air out of my chest. I shivered and pushed the nightmare away.

Sara didn't go back to sleep. She was on her bed, waiting for me with a silver box in her lap.

"This was supposed to be a Christmas gift, but I can't wait another month." Her face was too serious to be presenting a gift.

"It's not as big of a deal as you think, but I really need you to have it before you go home today."

Her choice of words struck me. I glanced at the silver package with apprehension. Sara handed it to me with a stiff smile.

"Thanks." I tried to smile back, but couldn't get past her odd behavior.

I opened the box and unwrapped the tissue paper, and a silver cell phone fell onto my hand. Why was Sara so uncomfortable giving it to me?

"Thank you, Sara. This is so great. Is this a prepaid phone?" I asked, trying to sound as happy with the gift as I was.

"It's actually on my family's plan. Don't worry; it didn't cost anything to add you."

"Wow, that's perfect. I'm not sure how often I'll be able to use it, but this is so great." I was genuinely appreciative, but her cautious tone kept me from being able to express it. Then I found out why.

"You have to promise to call me when you get home and let me know that you're okay," she requested delicately. "If I don't hear from you by the end of the day, I'm calling the police."

"Sara," I implored, "don't do that. I promise you, I'll be fine."

"Then call me," she pleaded. "I have phone numbers already programmed." She showed me how to quick dial her cell and her home phone. There were two other numbers set in the memory as well.

"911, really Sara?" I questioned incredulously. "You don't think I could manage that one on my own?"

"One button is faster than four," she explained with a slight grin. I pulled up the fourth number and looked up at Sara in disbelief. She shrugged with a small smile.

"I set the ringer to vibrate so no one will hear it in your room. There's a charger in the box too."

"Sara, I'm not having it on in my house," I stated emphatically.

"You have to. I swear I won't call you, and no one else has the number. You have to promise me that you'll have it on." Her request sounded so desperate, I couldn't argue.

"Okay, I promise." I decided to keep it in the inner pocket of my jacket so it wouldn't be accidentally discovered. "We should get going."

I didn't know how I convinced my body to cooperate and walk down the stairs with my bag in my hand. But my legs failed to move when I opened the front door and saw the Jeep parked on the side of the street.

"Oh, Emma," Sara whispered in alarm behind me.

"Hi Sara," Carol bellowed with sickening charm. "I was driving home from my mother's and thought I'd pick up Emily on the way. Thank you for letting her stay with you." I felt Sara squeeze my arm, her panic was obvious. I kept staring at the woman with the wide smile, unable to breathe.

"Come on, Emily, don't just stand there." I stumbled down the front stairs, afraid to look back at Sara, but feeling the weight of the cell phone in my jacket pocket. I let the car devour me as I shut the passenger door, staring straight ahead. My body tightened and shrunk away from her, trapped in the confined space.

Silence stung my ears, as I waited for her words, her accusations and insults. But there was nothing. Then again, she didn't need words when my head collided against the side window with a sudden thrust of her hand. My head rung with an involuntary grunt of pain.

"You don't breathe unless I tell you you can. You seem to have forgotten whose house you're living in. You've pushed it too fucking far, and it's over. Don't go behind my back again."

We were pulling into the driveway before I could let her words sink in.

When we entered the kitchen, Amanda, our thirteen year old neighbor, said left the kids playing upstairs and went home.

I continued down the hall and stopped, staring at the door leading to my room. The door was closed, and it was never closed when I wasn't home – one of Carol's irrational rules. I approached slowly and cautiously pushed the door open, letting out a defeated breath. I faltered through the doorway, looking around in horrified dismay.

The closet door stood ajar, and the crawl space in the back was a vacant hole. Remnants of what it once protected were spewed at me feet.

"You think you're so smart," Carol accused. My back tensed as every nerve hummed beneath my skin. I turned to find her leaning against the door frame with her arms crossed, and I instinctively took a couple steps back, my bag sliding from my shoulder, dropping to the floor.

"I can see right through you, and you're not going to divide us." I was perplexed, unable to make sense of her accusations. "He will always choose me. I wanted to remind you of that."

"Carol," I heard George yell anxiously from the back door.

"I'm here," Carol hollered back with a distraught voice. She backed away from my door and caught George in an embrace. I watched the drama unfold, unable to predict the ending.

"George, I don't know what got into her," Carol flailed, burying her head in his shoulder. George attempted to peer around Carol to see into my room. "She burst in yelling that she's tired of being here, and how horrible we are to her. Then she locked herself in her room. That's when I called you. She was scaring me and the kids."

What?! What was she doing?

"I finally convinced her to open the door and ... well, you can see for yourself." Carol released him from her desperate grasp, allowing George to enter. His concern changed to anger as he viewed the repercussions of *my rage.*

He looked from the destruction of my things to my stunned face and back down again. I thought I caught him wince when he saw the shattered glass and torn picture of him and his brother crushed on the floor. I couldn't move as I watched his anger grow.

"What did you do?" he bellowed. "How could you do this?" My mouth dropped, shocked by his reaction. How could he think I did this? His face turned red as he scanned my torn canvases, along with shreds of smiles and small chubby baby hands and feet strewn everywhere.

George moved to me before I could react. He grabbed my arms and started shaking me. He struggled with the words between his clenched teeth, gripping my arms tighter. The tears flowed down my cheeks as I tried to speak.

"I...," I wept.

I was interrupted with a startling sting on my cheek. The force knocked me to the floor. I grabbed the spot where his hand had connected and looked down at the floor, stunned.

"If you weren't my brother's daughter, I'd…" he began. I tilted my head up toward him. His face was so red, it was almost purple as he shook with fury. Behind the rage, I thought I recognized sadness in his eyes. "You are not going anywhere for the next week. No sports, no newspaper, nothing. I cannot believe you did this!"

His sorrow broke through when he murmured, "He was my brother." Carol watched him leave in confusion, or perhaps it was disappointment when his reaction wasn't as severe as she'd intended. As soon as he disappeared, she peered down at me and grinned in contempt.

"This is not over," she threatened. "Clean this up, and get your chores done before I get home."

She shut the door, leaving me with the destruction of her hate. Everything I had that was mine—that was truly mine—was in pieces around me. I picked up the images of my parents and baby pictures of me and tried to find a way to fit them together. I let the broken pieces fall through my fingers and collapsed into a fit of tears. This pain was sharper than any slap or blow. She had taken the evidence that there was a time when I was happy and obliterated it, leaving only the memories.

I sat up when I heard a knock and looked to the door, but the sound wasn't right – it was more of a tapping. I looked around and found that it was coming from the window. No, please don't *tell me*. I closed my eyes as the tap hit the window again. I wiped my face and rushed to open the window before the tapping repeated, and they heard it.

"You can't be here," I whispered desperately.

"What happened? I wanted to make sure you're okay."

"Evan, leave." My voice was urgent as I pleaded with him to go.

"Why is your face red? Did he hit you?"

"You can't be here," I stressed. "Please, please just go." Tears rolled down my cheeks as I frantically looked from his face to the door, expecting it to open at any minute.

He gazed past me, extended onto his toes, to see into my room.

"What happened, Emma?" he gasped at the devastating scene.

"You're only going to make it worse. *Please* leave." I tried to position my body between his eyes and my room.

"I'm picking you up Monday so that you can tell me what this is all about," he insisted.

"Fine, just leave," I begged.

Evan finally acknowledged the pleading in my eyes and the urgency in my voice and backed away from the window. He hesitated, but I closed the window and pulled down my shade before he could say anything else.

I turned back to my broken world and knelt amongst its remains. I heard Carol say she'd be back soon and knew I didn't have time to mourn. I found a backpack in which to place the fragments of my pictures and letters from my mother, refusing to throw them away. I tossed the broken frames and sliced canvasses in a trash bag.

I mindlessly performed my list of chores. I was secured in this desolate state when I retreated to my room. I slid onto the floor with my back against my bed and stared at the blank wall across from me. The ache in my chest was curtained behind the numbness.

If I hadn't been able to admit it before now, I knew in this moment that I hated Carol. I clenched my jaw, pushing away the destructive screams that raged in my head. My nails dug into the palms of my hands, wanting so much to release the emotion. Instead I gasped and collapsed into chest-heaving sobs.

Her malevolence threatened to penetrate the only sanctity I had left, and I moaned in pain at how close she had come to crushing me. Was I really strong enough to not let her break me? Six hundred and nine days suddenly felt like a life sentence. Would I be able to recognize myself when I was finally released?

I sat in the closet and dialed Sara's number.

"Em, are you okay?" Sara asked in a single breath.

"Yeah, I'm fine," I whispered.

"You sound so sad. What did she do?"

"I can't talk about it right now. But I wanted you to hear from me like I promised."

"Evan came over this morning."

I didn't say anything.

"He was really upset and wanted to know what was happening, and if you were being hurt. He was basically screaming at me to tell him. I didn't, I swear, but he's insisting on picking you up on Monday. I wanted to warn you. I can be there too, so you can go with me instead if you want."

"No, it's okay," I mumbled. I knew I'd have to face him eventually.

"Emma, whatever happened there this morning, I am so sorry," she said softly.

"I'll see you Monday," I whispered and hung up the phone.

I didn't leave my room except to sneak out to use the bathroom. I heard the murmur of voices and the glee of the kids in the dining room. Not too long after, singing carried through the wall from the television followed by a quick rap on my door.

"Your uncle and I would like to speak with you." I watched her leave as I sat at the desk, hovering over my Chemistry book. I pushed the chair back and allowed my legs to carry my shell to the kitchen.

George and Carol stood on one side of the island, waiting for me. The remnants of grief remained in George's eyes while the smirk of victory reflected in Carol's.

"Your uncle and I wanted you to know how heartbroken you made us when you chose to act out and destroy your things. We are sorry you don't feel happy here since we've done everything to provide you with whatever it is you've asked. You play sports and are part of the school's clubs. We think we've been very accommodating.

"I thought we should ban you from all of your privileges for the remainder of the year." My eyes widened, and my throat closed.

"But your uncle has decided to be generous and allow you to be a part of the school activities, hoping it will make you a better person. But you will not be doing anything at all for the next week. You'll have to find a way to explain this to your coach and other teachers, and we better not hear that you've blamed us in any way. This is your own doing, and you need to own up to that.

"Since we aren't able to trust you to be home by yourself, you'll go to the library after school. You can have whoever it is who's chauffeuring you around these days drop you off at the house. You can ride your bike to and from the library. I arranged this with the head librarian, Marcia Pendle, this afternoon. She will sign you in and out every day. She has a desk for you to use, so you're in her sight the entire time. Don't even think about trying anything. If we hear that you weren't there or didn't cooperate, you *will* lose basketball for the season. Do you understand?"

"Yes," I murmured.

"Your destruction has hurt your uncle a great deal, and we think it's best that during the next couple of weeks, you allow him to find a way to forgive you. So you should stay out of sight while you're in the house. I'll let you know when we're done with dinner, because you are not getting out of your obligations. We'll have a plate set aside for you to eat before you do the dishes. But other than that, you will stay in your room. Understood?"

"Yes."

"Now, what do you have to say to your uncle?" She pursed her lips to try to conceal her smirk. I tightened my eyes in disgust before I could mask my loathing. "Well?"

I whispered, "I'm sorry you were hurt."

I wasn't lying, but I wasn't apologizing for something I didn't do either. He only nodded in acceptance.

I was banned to my room for the remainder of the weekend. As uneventful as it was, it was better than being anywhere near Carol. It gave me time to think about what I was going to say to my basketball coach and the other teachers. I couldn't come up with anything other than a vague explanation of obligations at home that I hoped they wouldn't question too much.

I couldn't think about Evan, and what I'd say to him on Monday. Every time I thought of him, and what he'd seen on Friday night, and then again on Saturday morning, I felt miserable. He saw a glimpse of *my* world, and I didn't like how it reflected back in his eyes.

23. SILENCE

I REMAINED SILENT IN THE PASSENGER SEAT. I COULDN'T EVEN BRING myself to look at him.

Evan drove to the end of my street before he asked, "How are you?"

"Humiliated," I answered, looking out the window.

The quiet settled in again for a few minutes before he asked, "Are you mad at me for checking on you?"

"You shouldn't have," I answered honestly.

"You're not going to tell me what happened, are you?"

"I can't. You saw more than enough."

He pulled into the same drugstore parking lot as before, and parked the car.

"Evan, I really don't want to talk about it," I insisted, finally looking at him.

"That's what's bothering me. Why can't you trust me?" His troubled eyes searched mine for an explanation.

"That has nothing to do with it."

"That has *everything* to do with it," he said emphatically. "I thought we were past that."

"I'm sorry you thought that," I said stoically. He pulled back as if my words burned him.

"So, you don't trust me to know what's going on with you at home?" After hesitating for a moment, he added, "You never planned to let me in did you?" His voice grew stronger as he spoke, almost angry.

I couldn't find the words to agree with him, knowing it would only make him more upset.

"What was I thinking?" he asked himself in a whisper. "I thought you were stronger than this." His words bit, and my heart flinched. "I can't believe you let them treat you like this."

After a minute of unreturned response, Evan murmured in sinking disappointment, "You're not who I thought you were."

"I knew that," I whispered.

"So I don't really know you, do I?"

I shrugged. He exhaled quickly and shook his head, frustrated with my unwillingness to answer.

"Does Sara?" he asked. "Do you trust Sara more than me?"

"Leave her out of this," I shot back.

"I don't get it," he said to himself, looking at the floor. Then he turned to me and asked, "Does he hurt you?"

"George?" I questioned, shocked by the accusation. "No, George wouldn't hurt me."

"Then, she just doesn't like you, is that it?" he pushed.

"Evan, I can't and don't want to talk about what happens behind the closed doors of my house. And you're right, I'm not that strong, and I'm not the person you thought I was. But I've been trying to tell you that all along. I'm sorry that you're disappointed now that you finally figured it out. But I'm never going to be able to tell you what you want to know."

His face turned red, but I wasn't certain what emotion fueled the heat.

"I'd really like to get to school now," I demanded.

Evan pulled out of the parking lot, and we drove the rest of the way in silence.

The silence lasted for a long time.

Sara tried to talk to me about it, but it took me a week before I could repeat the words said in the car that day. She never brought it up again and tried not to mention him at all.

We co-existed within the same halls of the school and the walls of our classrooms. We didn't speak to each other, even in Anatomy class where we sat a few feet apart. In the rest of our shared classes, we sat at opposite ends of the room.

This didn't mean I didn't notice him. I noticed him until I convinced myself that I couldn't anymore. I accepted the truth that I'd been avoiding all along – it could never work. It never had a chance. My aching heart had a hard time giving up hope, but I found a way to tuck that deep inside as well. I faded into the walls like I had before Evan Mathews walked through the doors of Weslyn High—except, I didn't completely disappear.

The week after Thanksgiving, when I was caught up in being angry and disappointed with Evan – angry that he forced his way in and disappointed that he didn't like what he saw when he got there – I was taken by surprise.

"I know what you probably think of me," Drew Carson said, joining Sara and me at our lunch table that Wednesday afternoon.

I glanced from Sara to Drew, not understanding what he was talking about or why he was sitting at our table.

"At Jake's party," he explained, "I saw how you looked at me before you left. I'm not like that."

"Really, then why were you there?" I was too annoyed with thoughts of Evan to hold back my candor. "Isn't that what all the guys were there for? You even admitted you're friends with Jake."

It was obvious he wasn't expecting my biting words either, but he didn't give up.

"You're right, I knew what went on. But whether you want to believe me or not, that was the first time I've shown up at one of his parties." I let out a skeptical laugh. Sara remained still, like she was watching a movie, her wide eyes shooting back and forth between Drew and me.

"I swear I only knew about them because Jake kept asking me to go. But I didn't give in until that night. But only because I heard you were going to be there."

He saw my eyes cringe in disgust, and quickly added, "I just wanted to *talk* to you, honest. Like I told you that night, I should've talked to you before then." I didn't respond.

"I was hoping to convince you to give me a second chance, that's all. I don't want you to think I'm *that guy*."

Before I could say anything, he got up from the table. Sara was left staring at me with her eyebrows raised. I read her thoughts, sighed in exasperation, and left the table as well. It wasn't worth discussing.

I missed the fall awards night because I was officially grounded. Sara let me know that she, Jill and I were next season's captains of the girls' soccer team. She also told me I was chosen as the team's MVP, along with making the All-State and All-American teams. There was a dinner in January recognizing the athletes. I knew I wouldn't be attending that either.

Soon after, the letters from the colleges started to arrive. I suspected there would have been phone calls as well, but our number was privately listed, and only a hand full of people in the world were privileged enough to have it. Carol dropped the pile of packets on the floor of my room each day. There were letters from coaches and athletic directors, hoping to set up a time for me to see their campuses and meet with them in the spring. I didn't know most of the colleges were interested in me until I received the letters.

This burst of mail gave me that something I needed to keep me looking forward, instead of continuing to be mired in the present. As long as I had the hope of escaping, I was convinced I could recover from Carol's glares and Evan's avoidance. I had to have something to hold on to as I hung from my ledge.

I didn't receive as much grief as I expected from my basketball coach or other teachers for taking the week off. I was technically supposed to try out for the basketball team before being placed on the roster, so Coach had me "try out" during a couple of study periods during the week. He deemed that it qualified me to start as point guard. I was expected to fill the position, so it wasn't a controversial decision.

Sara played volleyball during the winter, so Jill drove me home on the nights Sara had practice after us. Jill was happy to drive me, however, I got more out of our time together than I was prepared for. She was a little too up to date on the latest gossip, eager to contribute to its circulation. I really didn't want to hear it.

"Did you know that Evan went on a date with Haley Spencer on Saturday?" Jill asked after my first official practice with the team on Monday — perfect example of why I didn't want to hear it. "I really thought you and Evan were going to be together. What happened?"

I shrugged, unable to speak. Haley Spencer, really? A hot flash of anger and jealousy streaked through my body. I forced it away as fast as it made its appearance.

When Sara picked me up the next morning, I confronted her. "You knew about Evan and Haley, didn't you?"

Sara pressed her lips together and exhaled, contemplating what to say.

"I didn't think it was worth getting you upset over. Let me guess, Jill told you, right?"

"Sara, I was going to find out eventually, and it would have been so much easier coming from you."

"You're right. I'm sorry." Then she glanced at me, trying to read my face. "I bet he did this to get to you."

"He can do whatever he wants," I huffed. "I really don't care."

"Sure, whatever you say," Sara said, mocking me. "Em, even *I'm* upset that he went out with Haley Spencer. Come on, *Haley Spencer*—could he have picked any one more shallow and superficial? She's the exact opposite of you." As soon as the words left her mouth, she bit her lower lip.

I snapped my head over to gape at her. Her eyes softened as she offered a silent apology. She and I both understood the truth in her statement, and that truth turned in my stomach the entire ride to school. That was the day I finally returned Drew Carson's peace offering.

Drew had been persistently, but subtly, trying to get me to talk to him again since that day in the cafeteria. During lunch and at the end of the day, he made sure our paths crossed. He'd glance at me and say, "Hi, Emma." I would ignore him and keep walking.

Until the day I finally responded, "Hi, Drew." The sound of my voice stopped him mid-step, causing the person following him to the cafeteria to walk right into the back of him. I let out a small laugh and kept walking. I didn't see him again until I was walking up the stairs from the locker room to go to the gym. He was outside the gym's entrance talking to another guy when I caught his eye.

"Good luck in your game today."

I hadn't noticed him at first. I was too consumed by my thoughts of the game to notice anything. Hearing his voice snapped me back into the halls of the school with the sneakers squeaking and the dribbling of basketballs coming from the gym. That's when I saw Drew standing by the entrance. The guy he was talking to said he'd see him later and left us alone.

"Thanks," I responded. "What are you guys doing for practice today?"

"We're practicing tonight, after your game," Drew explained. "I'm thinking about showing up early so I can watch."

I wasn't sure what to think about his interest in our game. Was he coming to show support for our team, or was he coming to watch me?

"How do you think you'll do? I heard you've missed some practices."

My face turned red at this acknowledgement. "I was able to go over the plays with Coach Stanley, so I'm pretty sure I'll be fine."

"I believe it," he said with a smile. "I'll see you after your game." I smiled back.

It was impossible to deny that Drew was incredible looking, with his boyish face and deep dimples. It was easy to get lost in his breathtaking tranquil green eyes. They peeked out from under his black hair, which always looked like he just came from the beach. Knowing how much he loved to surf, he probably had. I stood in the doorway staring after him, even after he was out of sight.

"Emma, you ready?" Jill asked when she walked past me, snapping me out of my daze.

"Yeah, ready."

Just as he promised, Drew was waiting for me after I grabbed my things from the bench.

"Good game," he congratulated me. "You have a great outside shot."

"Thanks." I took a swig of my sports drink before gathering my gear from the bench.

"I'm glad you're talking to me."

"I figured everyone deserves a second chance." I grinned, and he returned the expression.

"I should get to practice." He nodded toward the court, where some of his teammates were dribbling and taking shots. "I'll talk to you tomorrow?"

"Sure."

With that second chance, Drew Carson would change everything. The rest of that week, I found our paths crossed more often. I invited him to sit with us during lunch, which I thought was going to cause

Sara to fall out of her seat. We found a few minutes to talk before or after our practices. Then I discovered he was actually assigned to my study period. As a senior privilege, if any of the students had study as their first or last class, they could opt to come in late or leave early. I never saw Drew in study, because he hadn't been there. But after we started talking, he decided to show up.

Sara didn't say anything about my sudden interest in Drew. She was friendly and accepting of his presence during the times that she and I usually had alone. I hoped she found his company as refreshing as I did. Drew was charming – helping me to recover my smile.

When I saw Drew at the end of each day, it was a way to recuperate from being exposed to Evan's evasive presence all day. It was easy to carry on conversations with him about anything and everything, but never anything too personal. He didn't push me to reveal more about myself than I was willing to share, which was a comforting relief. When I was with him, I found myself laughing—really, honestly, enjoyably laughing. He was a breath of fresh air after the heart wrenching storm that had engulfed me.

When I was with Drew, I wasn't thinking about Evan. I couldn't keep the two images in my head at the same time, so I pushed Evan's out. I started not to notice where Evan was, and I didn't flinch at the sound of his voice as often. I wasn't allowing space for him anymore.

Instead, I found myself focusing on Drew, who responded with full attention. I didn't expect it to be the same, and it wasn't. My heart didn't flutter or murmur whenever Drew sat next to me. It stayed deep within my chest, thumping at its consistent pace. I wasn't disappointed – I was relieved.

I didn't talk to Sara about Drew, and she didn't ask. But I wasn't expecting her to reaction when I asked if we could meet him at a bon fire on a private beach after the game that Friday.

"Em, I don't think that's a good idea," she insisted. "Maybe we should stay in and watch movies. It's only been a few weeks since the incident with Carol. You're lucky she's letting you stay over again."

I knew there was something more to her hesitation than she was admitting.

"Sara, are you telling me *you* don't want to go to this bon fire? I've heard who's supposed to be there, and it's a pretty decent list."

"Yeah, me too," she admitted reluctantly. "Em, you promise you won't do anything stupid, right?"

"What is that supposed to mean?" I asked, offended.

"I haven't said anything because I think you really *do* like him, but I'm worried about where you're headed with Drew."

"I don't know what you mean," I denied, but I had a feeling I knew where this was going.

"Just don't do anything you typically wouldn't if you weren't trying to get over Evan."

I didn't say anything. She knew I understood what she meant. Sara agreed to go to the bon fire after my basketball game Friday night, and I convinced myself that I didn't do anything that weekend that I didn't want to do. That was until I heard the accusations of what I did out loud.

"You *kissed* Drew Carson?!" Evan practically yelled as he stood next to me at my locker.

It took me a second to believe he was standing next to me, forget about talking – well, yelling at me. His face was flushed, and his jaw was tight. He leered at me from behind my locker door, holding it open with his hand. I glanced around the empty halls to see if anyone heard him.

"How did you hear about that?" I asked. Not only was I stunned to see Evan at my locker, but I was shocked that Drew had said anything.

"Don't worry I didn't hear it from Drew, he doesn't talk. But his friends do." He was fuming and seeing his reaction only ignited my anger. What gave him the right to be upset with me?

"I'm surprised you could hear with Haley Spencer's tongue in your ear," I shot back. His face turned a different shade of red as the surprise reflected in his eyes. "Yeah, I heard about that too."

"It's not what you think," he explained, still angry, but the bite was absent from his tone. "We went out once."

"Oh, is that why I saw you together at the bon fire?!" I yelled back. Now, I was the one infuriated as I recalled the image of Haley nuzzled into Evan's arm across from me at the bon fire.

"You were there?" he asked, dropping his attack.

"I left pretty much after I saw the two of you. So don't you dare try to make me feel anything remotely like guilt for kissing Drew." The heat spread across my face as I abruptly closed my locker, holding my backpack and duffle bag in my hands.

"But you hardly know him," he rebutted. "What, you've talked to him for a week and that makes it okay to kiss him the first time you see him out?" His voice escalated again.

"Oh, and you're so much better?! Had you ever talked to Haley before you did whatever you did with her at Jake's party that first weekend?"

His eyes widened as he leaned back from my blow, confirming what Haley had told me earlier that day.

"Yeah, it was really great to hear it from her too, Evan," I snapped, trying to hide the hurt in my voice, while recalling her snide remark about how interesting it was that she and I were seeing the guys that we met at Jake's party. I thought I was going to fall over when the words came out of her mouth before she walked away with a smug grin.

Evan struggled to find the words. "I didn't do…" His eyes pleaded. "It's really not like that. Can I explain?"

"No." The edge dropped from my voice, releasing the anger with it. I became emotionless, pushing away the pain and sadness that threatened to seep up from where I hid them. "I don't want to know."

I walked past him towards the stairs.

"I trusted you," Evan bellowed, as the distance grew between us. I stopped and turned back around. He walked towards me until we were only a foot apart. "I trusted you, and you couldn't trust me."

I stared back, watching the hurt reveal itself in his eyes. My heart ached in return.

"I unpacked for the first time ever – for you. I was honest with you about *everything* – even with the truth about how I felt about you. I've never been that honest before. I trusted you." His voice drifted into a whisper as he leaned closer to me. "Why couldn't you trust me?"

I swallowed the lump in my throat with tears welling in my eyes. My heart reached for him, begging me to touch him, as I absorbed the pain in his stormy eyes. The seconds lasted for what felt like minutes, and then I tensed my body and walked away.

I went through the doors leading to the stairs and hurried down them.

"I'm still in love with you," he yelled from the top step. I froze as the first tear rolled down my cheek. "Please don't walk away from me."

The tears streamed silently down my face—I couldn't move. My heartbeat thumped forcefully in my chest, and for a second, I almost turned around. Then the image of Evan and Haley together in front of the bon fire, with his arm around her shoulder, flashed through my head, and I found my feet moving in a rush down the stairs.

I made it through practice that afternoon, although I don't remember much about it. Forcing myself to dribble, pass and shoot kept me from replaying the confrontation with Evan. By the end of practice, I was too exhausted to think about anything.

As I was heading to the locker room, the junior varsity guys started warming up on the court for their game. Drew waited for me at the end of the bleachers, in front of the entrance to the guys' locker room.

"Can you stay for my game?" he asked.

"Sorry, I don't think so," I admitted with a frown. "Good luck though."

"Will I see you tomorrow night after your game?"

"Yeah, I'd like that. I just have to check with Sara to make sure she doesn't have anything planned."

"One of the guys from the team is having a few people over and I'd like it if you and Sara came too."

"I'll see," I promised, but I was pretty sure I wouldn't make it since I had to be home by ten.

Before I realized what he was doing, he leaned over and kissed me softly on the lips. My body stiffened, as I remained stunned, unable to breathe for a brief moment. Drew looked up and said, "Hey, Mathews."

"Hi Drew," Evan returned with a bite. I only caught a glimpse of the bag over Evan's arm as he walked past us toward the locker room.

My heart crashed into my stomach. Did Evan just see Drew kiss me?

"I'll see you tomorrow." Drew smiled and brushed his hand along my cheek.

I nodded and forced the faintest hint of a smile. He walked through the doors to the locker room after Evan.

I knew what Evan just witnessed between Drew and me, especially after what had happened at my locker, was worse than anything I'd seen between him and Haley. I suppressed the twisting storm of guilt that threatened to consume me. I waited until I was alone in my room that night before I unleashed it and cried myself to sleep.

24. FALLEN

"EMILY!" CAROL HOLLERED FROM THE KITCHEN. MY HAND HOVERED above my duffle bag, grasping the sweater I was about to pack. Panic set in as I tried to think of what I could've done. My chest felt tight when I entered the kitchen.

"Yeah?" I responded cautiously, my voice getting caught in my throat.

"Do you know who I just got off the phone with?" she yelled, revealing the strained vein along her temple. I glanced around, recognizing George and the kids were gone. Fear gripped my heart, and my head felt tight. I shook my head.

"Of course you don't, right? Because you *never* do anything wrong, do you?" I was past trying to understand her illogical questions, and braced myself for her wrath. "That was someone from Stanford –"

Oh no! My eyes shot up at the sound of the school's name.

"Oh, you *do* know what this is about?" she accused, still boiling. "Do you know how stupid I felt when this man was going on about your visit in the spring, and I have no idea what he was talking about?! Why did he have our phone number?!" I remained quiet. "You didn't really think we were going to let you fly to California, did you? How the hell did you convince him to invite you – did you blow him?"

Shock splayed across my face.

"You think you are so much better than me, don't you? That you can do whatever you fucking want?!"

"No," I whispered.

"That's right—not in my house! You drove your mother to drink, and now she's a useless whore. I'm not going to let *you* destroy my family too. You're fucking worthless. What school would possibly want *you?*"

Carol's face was scarlet while her voice grew louder. "How did you ever expect to pay for these schools? You're not that special that they're going to let you in for free." She waited, as if expecting an answer. "Well...?"

"They have scholarships," I said lowly. She scoffed. "And I was thinking I could use my dad's social security money."

"Huh. Did you think I was going to let you live here and not get anything out of it?" She let out a spiteful laugh. I glowered at her; the hate slowly crawled under my skin. That money was because my father died too soon, and she was going to strip me of the last connection I had to him?! I was so furious, I couldn't see straight. I turned to walk away with my jaw clenched.

Then I heard the scraping of metal and her amplified rage, "Don't you turn your fucking back on me!"

A piercing flash of light screamed through my head as something hard hit the base of my skull. I stumbled forward and reached for the support of the wall, but I couldn't find it in time. My legs gave out, and I collapsed on the floor.

"You are ruining my life," she grunted through clenched teeth. "You will wish you never set foot in this house." I pressed my shaking hands against the floor to push up while attempting to focus through the blur. I let out a breathless grunt as my chest was forced back down against the hard wood, and my arms collapsed beneath me when she swung again. The repeated impact left me fighting for my breath, as the sharpness settled between my shoulder blades. The room teetered and blurred around me as I searched for the direction of my room, knowing I needed to get there to escape her. Still gasping, I groped at the floor, urging my body forward while sliding on my elbows and pushing onto my knees.

Her vulgar grunts and grumblings were incoherent. Then I heard her growl, "You will learn to respect me. You owe me your life for everything I've given you. For everything you've destroyed."

The force of her swing ripped through my lower back – I screamed out in agony. The searing bolt of pain wrapped itself around my spine and spiked through my head. I released a broken moan before

231

sprawling on the floor. The room dimmed in a blur of light as I fought for consciousness.

I didn't know how long I'd been on the floor. I became aware of the loud stomping above me as she muttered to herself. I blinked my eyes open. The floor rippled before me. I closed my eyes to fight against the dizziness so that I could push myself up on my hands and knees. The tender muscles between my shoulder blades twisted into a burning knot as I strained to get up. I peered through my lashes and reached for the wall to steady myself on my knees. I tried to focus through the haze, my head bobbing heavily and my body swaying. With a grunt of effort, I lifted myself up to stand, leaning against the wall. I remained pressed against the wall breathing heavily as I waited for the room to settle and listened for her movement. A severe sharpness shot up my spine, leaving me breathless.

I took a deep breath to settle the nausea, determined to get out of the house before she came downstairs. I stood still for a moment with my eyes closed, steadying the spin of the earth. Convinced I had control of my equilibrium—I crept into my room and gingerly closed the door. The flight instinct kicked in and the blood raced through my body, overriding the pain. My heart pounded in my chest as I threw a few more items in my duffle bag. I opened my door to listen. She was quiet; the only sound I heard was my rapid pulse. I decided to take a chance and left my room. I cautiously took each step that brought me closer to the door. My ears hummed, anticipating the slightest sound.

I held my breath as I turned the handle of the door and didn't release it until the door was closed behind me. I hugged the side of the house, so she couldn't see me from her window. Once I reached the end of the driveway, adrenaline shot through me, and I ran. The pain in my back and head didn't exist while the road passed under my feet. I kept running until I was in the coffee shop a few blocks from the house.

I could only imagine what I must have looked like to the patrons and staff of the intimate café when I entered with the duffle bag over my arm, covered with sweat, and gasping for breath. I slid onto a chair at a small table in the corner and pulled out my phone. I pressed Sara's number and listened to it ring, hoping she'd pick up.

"Emma? What's wrong?"

"Come get me," my voice cracked.

"Omigod, are you hurt?"

"Sara, please come get me as soon as you can." My voice quivered as I fought to hold back the tears.

"Where are you?" she inquired urgently.

"At the coffee place near my house." I took a calming breath to keep from losing the little composure I had left.

"I'll be there as fast as I can."

I hung up the phone.

I spent the time it took Sara to arrive, staring at my hands, willing them to stop trembling. My breath shook with each pass through my quivering lips. I didn't dare look around the shop; instead I stared out the window, searching for Sara's car. When I saw her pull in, I rushed to meet her before she had a chance to get out.

I winced as I settled onto the passenger seat, the pain streaking up my entire back. I closed my eyes and let out a shaky breath. The tears found their way down my cheeks as I swallowed against the lump in my throat.

"Where are you hurt?" Sara asked, her voice unsteady.

"My back," I quivered, with my eyes still closed.

"Do you need to go to the hospital?"

"No," I shot back quickly. I attempted to release the tension in my shoulders and opened my eyes. I wiped away the tears and searched for my voice. "No hospital, okay? Just... do you have anything to help, aspirin or something?"

Sara rummaged around in the compartments of the center console, then handed me a white bottle of Advil. I spilled some pills onto my hand and swallowed them dry. Her forehead creased, mirroring the pain that was evident on my face. "Do you want to go back to my house?"

"Can we just stop there so you can get me a bag of ice? Then let's go somewhere where I can walk around."

"You want to *walk?*"

"If I stay still, I'll get stiff. I need to keep the blood flowing through my muscles so that I can play tonight."

"You think you're going to play basketball?! Em, I'm still trying to decide if I should take you to the hospital. You're pale, and you can't hide how much pain you're in. And if *you* can't hide it, then it must be pretty bad."

"It's because it just happened and my body's still in shock. I'll be fine, I promise." But I knew I was lying. I was far from *fine.*

Sara drove to her house and I waited in the car until she came out with a small cooler filled with ice, some storage bags and a couple of waters. She handed me a water when she entered the car.

"Let's go to the high school, and we'll walk the track," I suggested before taking several long gulps from the bottle. "I only have to waste a couple of hours before the JV game."

"Are you sure?" Sara asked, still uncertain with my decision.

"Sara, I swear, I'm okay."

I eased my body into a controlled place where the quivering hid beneath my skin. There was a deep ache in my head that trailed all the way down my back, but the piercing pain was gone—as long as I kept still.

We drove to the high school and parked near the football field. The parking lot only contained a handful of cars since it was still too early for anyone to be here for the game.

I took the cooler with me as I delicately lifted my body out of the car, gritting my teeth through the searing pain that made my stomach flip with nausea. Sara followed me to the field. I filled the bags with ice and lay on my stomach. Sara placed the bags along my back and sat next to me on the grass. We were silent for a few minutes as I lay with my eyes closed and my head resting on my folded arms, while Sara plucked the grass from the frozen field. I barely registered the cold December air with the ice on my back.

"You're shivering," Sara noted.

"I have ice covering my back, and it's thirty degrees out here."

"How long do you want to keep the ice on?"

"Fifteen to twenty minutes, then we'll walk around for a while before we do it again."

After another few minutes of silence, Sara asked, "Are you going to tell me what happened this time? Em, I promise not to say anything."

"I'm not sure if I should. I don't want you to feel guilty if you need to lie to your mom or anyone else for me."

"I'll find a way around answering," she promised.

"Stanford called," I started.

"Oh no," she gasped. "You didn't tell her."

"Yeah, I didn't tell her," I breathed. "Then she told me I didn't have access to the social security money from my dad for college; that it was her compensation for letting me live there. I got so pissed that I had to leave the room. That's when she hit me."

"What did she hit you with?"

"I'm not sure. Probably whatever she could get her hands on." I recalled the hard object crashing into my back and shivered.

"You can't go back there," Sara insisted.

"I really don't want to think about that right now. I just want to focus on being able to play in the game tonight."

"Em, I'm not sure that you should."

"Sara, I have to. She's taken everything else from me, including what I had left of my dad. I'm playing in this game tonight," I stated definitively. Sara didn't argue.

We walked briskly, until I couldn't handle it anymore. Of course, I didn't tell Sara this. Then I'd lie back down to be iced. I was desperate to defeat this pain. I was going to play in this game – nothing was going to stop me.

When cars started showing up for the JV game, Sara followed me into the building. We stood by the bleachers and watched until halftime when I had to change. I blared my music so loudly in my ears, I couldn't concentrate on anything else. Every so often, I'd pace in the hall to keep the blood flowing through my muscles, mostly because it hurt too much to stand still, and I needed to escape it any way I could. I swung my arms over my head and turned my neck side to side to keep my muscles from stiffening.

None of the girls questioned Sara when she followed me into the locker room to change. She snuck into a curtained shower stall with me to help me change. She carefully pulled my shirt over my head, and I clenched my teeth. My entire back screamed when I raised my arms. Sara questioned my well being again, but I ignored her. I was counting on adrenaline to make me oblivious to the pain once the game started.

The adrenaline did tunnel my focus when I was finally on the floor, helping me disconnect from the pain. I refused to concede to my burning muscles and the lightning storm in my head as I dribbled down the court, calling out the next play. Passing to the open teammate, squaring up to take a shot, following through with a rebound, and charging back to switch to defense, where the bodies bumped to gain position: that was all I concentrated on as the time ticked away.

I was surviving on adrenaline, and that would only carry me so far. As the second half progressed, it became harder to concentrate. I wasn't reacting as quickly to passes or charging for the steals as I usually did. I passed off the ball more, instead of taking the shot. During a timeout, Coach Stanley asked if I was okay. I explained that I fell on some ice earlier, and it was bothering me a little. He suggested taking me out of the game. I adamantly assured him that I was fine and could keep playing.

It was a close game. Probably closer than it should have been, and I blamed myself for that, knowing I had no right to be on the court. But I was afraid to find out what would happen if I stopped.

There was under a minute left in the game, and the lead kept changing by one with each possession. After a timeout and about thirty seconds on the clock, we had possession of the ball and were down by one point. I dribbled down the court, sending the offense in motion. I passed to Jill at the top of the key, who dribbled to the center of the paint and bounced it to Maggie along the baseline. Maggie noticed my clear shot from behind the three point line and popped it back out to me where I squared up to the basket, jumped, and let the ball roll off of my fingers. The defender jumped alongside me, swiping at the ball, which barely sailed over her fingertips. Her arm landed on my shoulder hard, knocking me back so my heels were no longer beneath me when I came down to land.

My breath rushed from my lungs when the floor made contact with my back. My head bounced back, colliding with the waxed surface. The cheers faded, and the images on the court blurred. I blinked my eyes as the colors ran together until there was only black.

I was moving quickly, but my legs were still. There was something around my neck, and I couldn't move. I heard the murmuring of voices but no words. My eyes wouldn't open. The cold air hit me, sending a shiver through my body. I was enveloped with the piercing bolt that ran along my back and into my head. Then I fell into the darkness again.

"Emily, can you hear me?" the soothing male voice asked.

I pulled back from the blinding light as I felt a cool touch on my lid.

"Emily, can you open your eyes for me?" the voice requested.

I blinked my eyes open, squinting to keep them protected from the bright light above me. I glanced around at the faces above me. There was something beeping over my head, and a hum of voices surrounded my space.

"Emily, I'm Dr. Chan," the soothing voice said. I focused on the gentle, round face of the man leaning over me. "You're in the hospital. You took a fall during your basketball game and hit your head."

I groaned in admission to the pain.

"My back," I whimpered.

"You're back hurts?" he confirmed

"My back," I whimpered again, the tears rolled across my temples. I couldn't turn my head with the brace holding it in place.

"We're going to take some x-rays to see what's going on," he informed me.

"Sara?" I searched for her amongst the faces.

"Who's Sara, honey," a rosy faced nurse leaned over to ask.

"My friend, Sara McKinley," I whispered between moans. "I need Sara."

"Your aunt and uncle are on their way," she assured me.

I groaned louder.

"Sara, please," I begged.

"I'll see if I can find her," she comforted me.

There were more voices, and then I was moving. The fluorescent lights blurred above me as I was wheeled through the maze of corridors. There was a figure at the end of my bed, but I couldn't see a face. The tears continued rolling down the crevices of my eyes and into my ears. I made an effort to contain the moans, but they escaped every so often on their own.

A team of bodies wearing blue and white lifted me onto a hard platform. As I was rolled onto my back, I screamed out in agony. There was *nothing* that could hold it back. A nurse gently turned me onto my side to examine the source of my torturous cries and let out a breath.

"Her back is badly bruised," she reported.

"Prop her on her side," Dr. Chan directed from my feet.

I slid into a tube and closed my eyes, concentrating on breathing evenly to cope with the suffering. The corners of my eyes were raw from the never ending seeping of tears. I remained in that area of the hospital for a time I could not judge, with the rolling, and the clicking, and the doors opening and closing.

Eventually, the hands of the team eased me back onto the forgiving cushion of the bed, supported on my side to provide some reprieve from the torment that had overtaken my body. Exhausted, I closed my eyes.

"We're waiting on the results of her x-rays before we know if there's any damage," Dr. Chan explained to someone. "You're welcome to stay with her, and I'll be back when I have the results."

"Sara?" I whispered through the grogginess. I opened my eyes when we rolled to a stop. A curtain was pulled around me, concealing the people on the other side.

"Hey honey," the soothing voice of the nurse greeted me. "Your aunt and uncle are here." I averted my eyes, not finding the comfort she hoped that news would provide me.

"Sara? Did you find her?" My tone was anxious, and her concerned expression recognized it.

"She's right outside," she promised. "I'll go get her."

"You can't keep me from seeing her," an irate voice yelled. "She's my daughter."

My heartbeat accelerated, picked up by the quick beeps on the machine above my head.

"Relax, Rachel," George instructed firmly.

"What's wrong with her?" she demanded heavily. I recognized her slur. My jaw tightened. What was she doing here? How did she even know?

"I don't think this is the right time to be talking to you," George responded.

"You can't keep me from her. She's my daughter," my mother declared. Then she went on to berate George and Carol about how they didn't love me, with expletives only my drunken mother could come up with.

"M'am, I need to ask you to come with us," a deep masculine voice demanded.

"Get your hands off me. You can't touch me. I need to stay here with my daughter. Get off me." The angered voice trailed away, until it was cut off completely when a pair of doors closed further down the hall.

"Emma?" Sara whispered, peering in through the curtains. My flittering eyes found Sara's pale face and her red rimmed eyes.

"Sara!" I wept, lifting my head. The movement forced me to moan in pain, causing Sara to wince.

"Ow. Try not to move," she whispered, pulling up a chair to sit beside me. She pressed her lips together and the line between her eyes deepened as she searched my agonized face. "I'm so sorry."

Her eyes filled and she quickly swiped away the tears with the hand that wasn't holding mine.

"I'm glad they finally let me see you. It felt like I was waiting forever." Her voice quivered. "You scared me." The tears welled in her eyes again, and she looked away to conceal them.

"I'll be okay," I assured her, but I knew seeing me on a hospital bed wasn't very convincing.

"You didn't look okay when you were lying lifeless on the floor of the basketball court. I don't think I've ever been so scared in my entire life."

"I slipped on ice and fell down the stairs at my house," I told her quietly.

"What?" Her forehead crumpled, not understanding.

"How I hurt myself," I explained. "I fell down the stairs on some ice."

"But Em, everyone saw you fall during the basketball game—I mean *everyone*," she explained, still confused.

"Look at my back," I encouraged.

Sara walked around to the other side of my bed and gently lifted my basketball jersey.

"Oh!" Sara exhaled upon seeing the bruising. "I knew you shouldn't have played. Have they given you anything for the pain?" She returned to the chair to hold my hand, her face paler than when she entered.

"Mm mm," I indicated in a negative through my pressed lips, trying to hold back the groan that would give away just how miserable I was.

"Okay, Emily," Dr. Chan declared, pulling back a section of the curtain.

"Hi, I'm Dr. Chan," he introduced himself to Sara.

"I'm Sara McKinley," she offered in return.

"Is it okay if she stays in the room while I go over this with you?" he asked me.

"Yes."

"Well, it looks like you've had a couple of injuries today, huh?"

239

"Yes," I whispered.

"The good news is that there's nothing too serious. You do have a concussion on the back of your head, but there isn't any bleeding. The x-rays of your spine came out clear, but you've bruised your tailbone. Unfortunately, there isn't anything we can do for that, and the best thing to do is to let it heal on its own. We're going to take the neck brace off, and give you something for the pain. You'll need to stay inactive for the next two weeks at least."

My eyes widened, not prepared for his prognosis.

"Sorry, but that means no basketball during that time. You won't be up for it anyway. We'll give you something to manage the pain, but you should schedule an appointment with your doctor in two weeks to follow up.

"Do you have any questions?" he asked.

"No," I whispered.

"Now, can you tell me about the bruises on your back?"

I hoped the machine wouldn't start beeping profusely when I lied, "I slipped on some ice outside my back door and fell down the stairs."

"Did you fall onto your back?"

"Yes."

"How many stairs did you fall on?"

"Four or Five."

"Okay," he sighed. "Sara, could I please have a moment alone with Emily?" I panicked when Sara left the room.

Dr. Chan sat down in the chair so that he was eye level.

"I'm concerned with your bruising," he said solemnly. "The images showed that you have a recovered contusion on the front of your head as well.

"Emily, I want you to please tell me the truth, and know that I will hold this information in the utmost confidence. How did you get the bruises on your back?"

"I fell down the stairs." I tried to sound as convincing as I could. I didn't know if it worked, but he nodded and stood up.

"You could have received those injuries in a fall, and I can't dispute that. But if you didn't, I hope that you would be able to tell someone.

"You're going to stay here for the night so that we can keep an eye on you and give you something for the pain to help you rest. If you need anything, or feel like talking, have the nurses page me."

"Can you please send Sara back in?"

"Sure. I'll have the nurse get her."

Sara came back into the room not long after the nurse removed my neck brace and cut off my clothes so she could slide on a hospital gown. I tried to get her to slip my game shirt over my head, but the movement caused me to holler, so she opted for scissors.

"Someone will be down shortly to transport you upstairs for the night," the nurse explained. "I'll be right back with something to help the pain."

"Thank you," I whispered, finding some relief already with the brace removed.

After she left, I noticed Sara appeared nervous, like she wanted to tell me something, but she kept stopping every time she opened her mouth to speak.

I watched her struggle through her silent debate until I finally demanded, "What aren't you telling me?"

She pressed her lips together and looked around for the words. "Um, Evan's outside. I didn't know if I should tell you while you were still coherent or wait until you were drugged."

I remained quiet.

"He wants to see you."

"No, Sara," I shot back urgently. "He can't see me."

"I knew you'd say that, but I promised I'd ask. Just so I can say I did, no Drew either, right?"

"He's here too?"

"There are a lot of people here, actually. Well, except for your aunt and uncle, who left after the doctor told them you were staying the night."

"No visitors," I pleaded. "*No one*, okay?"

"Got it," she affirmed.

"Sara, what happened when I fell?" I asked, not sure if I wanted to hear this but also surprised by the multiple visitors in the waiting room.

Sara looked at the ceiling, trying to force back the tears.

"Um, after you took the three pointer and it went in –"

"It went in?" I tried to remember the moment, but I couldn't get past the pounding in my head.

"Yeah, it did. The crowd was so loud, it was crazy – but in an instant it went dead silent. You were lying on the floor, and you weren't moving. Coach went out with the trainer to wake you, but they couldn't." Sara paused to take a calming breath, trying to control her trembling voice. "They called for the ambulance. The gym was so quiet while we waited for you to wake up. I tried to get down to the floor, but the coaches and some other adults were keeping people back.

"You still didn't move when they put you on the stretcher. Em, I was so scared. I got to the hospital as soon as I could, but they wouldn't tell me anything, no matter who I asked. Between Evan and me, I think we asked every person in a white jacket or blue scrubs who walked through the waiting area. Then everyone else started arriving to wait with us—first Drew with some of his friends, then your coach and other girls from the soccer and the basketball teams – I'm not sure who else.

"You're aunt and uncle finally arrived, and they were let in to see you. I was going crazy because they got in, and I couldn't, until the nurse finally came out and said you were asking for me."

I listened to her words, unable to account for a single second of that time, until I was in the hospital. It was surreal thinking of my unconscious body on the floor of the gym, with everyone staring at me. The fear and concern that came through in Sara's voice tore at me. I glanced at Sara's hand shaking on her lap. I hadn't realized that the hand holding mine was trembling since mine was as well.

"I'm sorry I scared you," I whispered.

"I'm just relieved to see that you're awake and moving," she said with a small smile, but the sadness lingered in her eyes. "I should go let everyone know how you are, and that you're staying the night, so they can leave. I'll be back before they move you."

The nurse entered with a syringe. Soon after she administered the clear liquid into my IV, the pain subsided, and the room swum around me as I drifted to sleep.

25. INEVITABLE

I DIDN'T RETURN HOME WITH GEORGE AND CAROL DURING THE TWO weeks of intense recovery. I didn't spend Christmas at home either. My only disappointment was not seeing the kids' faces on Christmas morning. I had always loved writing the letter to Santa and setting out the cookies with them, and watching them open their presents. I wondered what they were told when they asked for me.

Staying with Janet was... quiet. She didn't ask questions about what happened to me, or about anything at all for that matter. She gave me my space in her spare room, periodically checking on me to make sure I was comfortable and had plenty to eat and drink.

The first week was excruciating, and the slightest movement was debilitating. I relied upon the prescription pain pills to cope, which usually meant sleeping. As the second week crept by, the sharpness subsided, and the aching dwindled. My muscles were stiff from underuse, and my tailbone still reminded me of the impact whenever I'd sit—but at least I had some relief. I spent my days reading, sleeping and texting Sara.

Over the school break, I received daily texts from Sara checking in on me, then providing brief accounts of her day and updates on the basketball team. I missed seeing and talking with Sara despite our daily communication—it wasn't the same. I finally got up the nerve to ask Janet if Sara could visit the Saturday before we returned to school. Janet didn't even hesitate to say yes, so I probably could have asked her sooner. It was strange how unlike Carol she was.

Sara tentatively entered Janet's small one-story house. She was not her usual overly exuberant self, although I could tell by the spark in her eye that she wanted to be. Janet found the need to go to the store soon after Sara arrived. I knew it was her way of giving us time alone to talk.

"It's so great to see you!" Sara exclaimed, giving me a gentle hug. "You look good. So, do you feel better?"

"Yeah, I'm fine—just bored out of my mind." I allowed a smile to relax on my face – it had been so long since I'd felt the tightness in my cheeks. "Tell me what's been going on. I could only get so much from the abbreviated texts, and some of it I didn't understand at all."

Sara let out quick laugh. "Okay, so you know about basketball, right?"

"Yeah, I read about it in the paper too. That sucks about the two losses, but at least they won the other two."

"They're looking forward to having you back, especially Coach Stanley. I went skiing with my parents, Jill and Casey, but you knew that. What else?" Sara flicked her eyes toward the ceiling, thinking of other news she needed to catch me up on. "Oh, um, I guess Drew gave me flowers to give to you. But... I forgot them. Just make sure you thank him so he doesn't know I failed."

"Oh," I said quickly. Having had this time alone, I had the opportunity to consider what was happening between Drew and me. It was a whirlwind relationship, and it was difficult to recall how we had gotten to the point where he'd want to give me flowers. I could have convinced myself that we were friends, except for the kissing part. I couldn't get around that.

"He asks about you whenever I see him leaving practice. We haven't had practices after them for a while, so the guys are gone by the time the volleyball team gets on the floor. But he waits for me just so that he can check on you."

"That's sweet," I replied honestly. "I feel bad I haven't been able to talk to him."

"Are you still interested in him?" she inquired, doubt lining her voice.

I let out a guilty breath, avoiding Sara's eyes.

"What?!"

"Something happened that I didn't get to tell you because I got hurt," I confessed. She raised her eyebrows, vehemently urging me to continue. I took a second to decide where to start. It was a scene that

I'd been tormented with for the past two weeks—only second to the nightmares that made sleeping through the night impossible.

"Evan found out that Drew and I kissed." I hesitated to allow her to react.

"I figured," she replied with a slight shrug. "Everyone else in the school knows too."

"Seriously?" I groaned

"His friends have big mouths. That's something you really haven't been a part of yet, huh?"

"What do you mean?"

"Gossip. Everyone knows what you've done before you do. I've heard enough about what I've supposedly done over the years – it's so stupid. Funny thing is, they don't know the half of it. Anyway, there was talk about you and Evan before, but since no one knew anything to keep the rumors going, the fascination died. But you and Drew are a *big deal* for some reason."

My stomach turned. Hearing this only added to my guilt.

"That's not something I needed to hear," I sulked.

"Sorry. Why, what happened?"

"Evan and I were yelling at each other in the halls after he found out about Drew, and then I was yelling at him about Haley. He didn't realize I knew about them, and he wanted to explain, but I wouldn't let him. He shouted down the stairs that he still loved me, and I kept walking. To make it worse, he saw Drew kiss me after practice that night."

"Wow, I missed all that?" Sara digested my story and shook her head. "That explains the tension in the waiting room, I guess."

"What are you talking about?"

"When we were waiting for you in the hospital, Evan and Drew stayed on opposite sides of the room. Evan kept glaring at him, until Drew finally called him out on it."

"Please don't tell me this happened in front of everyone?" I sunk into the couch and put my head against the floral printed cushion, looking up at the ceiling.

"Sorry," she cringed. "The guys didn't *say* anything specifically about *you*—it was more that Drew was fed up with Evan's unwarranted hostility, and it gave Evan the chance to get in his face."

I groaned. This was difficult for me to imagine. Neither guy seemed the type to pick a fight. I knew Evan was mad at me, and unfortunately Drew was the conscious one he could yell at.

"So, what are you thinking?" Sara asked, examining my guilt ridden face.

"I feel horrible about Evan seeing Drew kiss me, especially after what happened right before that. But I was just so angry at him for trying to hide the fact that he was doing the same thing with Haley."

"What do you mean? He and Haley aren't seeing each other." Sara sounded so sure of her words. My heart skipped a beat.

"Sara, I *saw* them at the bon fire," I stated adamantly. "Evan had his arm around her. That's when I walked away with Drew, remember?"

"Em, you were on the other side of the fire. I was near Evan and he did *not* have his arm around Haley. She came over to him, said something stupid, like usual, and hugged him. He patted her on the back, humoring her, and then walked away. She went off and started flirting with Mitch. You must have only seen part of it."

That couldn't be true, could it? If it was true, then I would have never walked down the beach with Drew, and I wouldn't have been so distracted that I allowed him to kiss me. This whole mess was unraveling around me, and I knew I was at the center of all of it. What did I do?!

"But she said she was seeing him," I whispered. "I was so pissed when she told me at my locker that day."

"I would have a hard time believing *anything* she has to say. You know she hates you, right?"

"But, why?"

"Please don't make me say it," she huffed.

"Sara, did I totally screw this up?" The aching returned, but it was inside my chest, instead of my back.

"What do you want? You know that you and Evan stopped talking before Drew and Haley ever came into the picture – it had nothing to do with them."

"But I didn't help it any." I sunk further into the couch.

"What about Drew?"

"I don't know, Sara." I was so confused about what I wanted and what was best, I couldn't think straight. "He's so nice and, come on, just *look* at him." Sara smirked in agreement.

"But?" she encouraged.

I didn't say anything for a minute. I was tormented by the thought of never talking to Evan again, but that wouldn't change until I told him the truth – and that would never happen. So, where did that leave Drew? For some inexplicable reason, and without me realizing it was happening, Drew liked me. I couldn't deny that, despite my inability to understand it.

"Being around Drew makes more sense," I finally said.

"That's the strangest reason to date someone that I've ever heard," Sara responded.

"We're *dating*?" I asked in disbelief.

"Em, he's kissed you in public, he bought you flowers, and he calls me to check in on you – yeah, I'm pretty sure he thinks that."

"He calls you too?!"

"Oh, yeah, sorry – I forgot to mention that. You're right—he's sweet, thoughtful, and beautiful." She paused.

"But…" I waited.

"I'm not even going to finish that sentence."

"Sara!"

"Why do I have be the one to say it out loud?!" Frustrated, she finally exclaimed, "He's not Evan."

I instantly recognized the truth in her words. But I also knew that the truth didn't matter.

"Can we talk about something else?" I pleaded.

"You can't avoid this forever," she warned. "We're going back to school on Monday, and they're both going to be there."

"Sara, Evan doesn't want anything to do with me."

"I don't know, Em," she said, reluctant to say anything more, but I saw it in her roaming eyes.

"Just tell me, Sara."

Sara took a breath, pausing before she revealed, "Evan was really upset at the hospital. I talked to him alone for a while. He was hurt when you didn't want to see him. He thinks he cares more about you than you do about him. I could tell he wasn't comfortable talking to me about it, but I think he just needed to tell someone, if he couldn't tell you. He wished things were the way they were before that weekend we went to the movies."

So did I.

"Emma, he's not stupid. He pretty much knows what's going on at your house. You should have seen the way he looked at Carol and George when he realized who they were. He still cares about you. I think if you just talked to him…"

"I don't think I can, Sara," I whispered. She didn't respond, but when she dropped her eyes to the floor, I knew that she didn't like my decision. I still wouldn't be able to tell him the truth, and I didn't foresee that ever changing. I couldn't hurt him again. We sat silently for a moment.

"Speaking of the unspeakable," Sara said lowly, unable to meet my eyes. "Do you have to move back in with them?"

"Yeah," I breathed.

"We have to stop her,' she insisted. "There has to be a way without hurting the kids."

"I don't know…" I started, but was interrupted by Janet slowly opening the front door to give us plenty of warning that she was returning home.

"So, what else do you have to tell me?" I asked over emphatically to cover up the serious conversation.

Sara shrugged. Then her eyes got big. She hesitated, tormented whether she should tell me.

"Just tell me."

"I went out on a couple of dates with Jared this week," she blurted. She watched for my reaction, anticipating the worst. I wasn't sure what to say.

"Okay," I said slowly. "That's great, right?"

"It was *really* great," she glowed.

"How did it happen?" I asked, trying not to think of our night at the movies and how they hit it off, because then I'd have to think about that night with Evan – and how I'd never get it back.

"I called to return his flashlight. We started talking. Then he called me later that night, and we talked some more. He asked me out and I said yes."

"Leaving out the details?" I noticed. A vague account of dates wasn't Sara's style.

"I didn't know if it was going to be weird for you since he's Evan's brother. But I had to tell you, or else I was going to burst. I can leave out the other stuff if you'd rather not hear it."

"No, I want to hear everything," I replied honestly.

Sara went on to talk about their dinner date in Boston and another in New York. Her eyes sparkled as she gushed about her time with Jared. As much as I was happy for her, this strange hollow sensation filled my stomach. Was I jealous? I pushed away the selfish emotion and smiled.

"And the second night, he kissed me. It was the most amazing kiss ever. I thought I was going to fall over." Sara beamed as the memory danced across her eyes.

"What are you going to do now? I mean, he's going back to New York, right?"

"Yeah, he left this morning," she sighed. "It was the best time I've ever had, but he goes to college in New York." She shrugged, smiling contently.

"That's it?"

"Yeah, that's it. Honestly, I didn't expect anything else. I knew when I went out with him that that was probably going to be it."

"Then why'd you do it?" I questioned in confusion.

"Why not?!" she answered enthusiastically. "I'd rather have these incredible memories of the two nights I spent with him, knowing that I probably won't go out with him again, than not to have had them at all."

"Huh," I pondered, intrigued by Sara's perception. Her words sat with me long after she left that afternoon.

I continued thinking about what she said when I lay in bed that night. Was it better to get as much out of the moment as possible, knowing it could slip out from under you in a second? Was the actual experience better than the inevitable conclusion? I guess I had to decide if the conclusion was a broken heart, or a broken bone, in order to weigh the risk.

I didn't sleep well that night. My dreams swirled together in an incoherent jumble of images. I'm certain my restlessness was provoked by the conversation with Sara. Then again, I knew George was picking me up in the morning.

George and I sat in silence for the first part of the car ride – I stared out the window and he kept his eyes glued to the road.

"It would be best if you weren't around Carol very much," he finally said. His voice drew my attention. I wasn't surprised he refused to look over at me. "She's been under a lot of stress, and the new medication she's on is affecting her moods. You can stay in your room and eat after we do, like you did before, but I'll take care of the dishes. You just worry about getting your Saturday chores done while she's out shopping.

"I spoke with the McKinley's. They're willing to help us out by letting you spend Saturday's there, after you do your chores, and any Friday nights when you have a basketball game. They're sympathetic to Carol's stress and are very thoughtful to have offered. So please don't make this any more difficult. Sunday's you can spend at the library, like you have been. Emma, I don't think I have to remind you that what happens in our house, stays in our house."

I didn't react to his subtle threat. He had just taken away the remnants of the only family I had – regardless of how dysfunctional. I knew I wouldn't be able to spend time with the kids, and he'd speak to me even less now than he did before – it sunk in that I was truly alone.

My world was delicately balanced, but the scales never hung even. When something improved, something else had to crumble. Accepting this would be the hardest thing I'd ever have to learn, and even when I came to know it as true, it still crushed me.

26. BROKEN

"You bitch," Haley Spencer sneered from beside my locker. "What did you say to him?"

"I don't know what you're talking about." I knew she was obviously talking about Evan, but I had no idea what was going on.

"You must have said something to him to make him to leave," she insisted.

I heard her words, but I couldn't comprehend what she was saying. I stared back, stunned.

"He left!" Haley exclaimed. "He moved back to San Francisco, and I know it was because of you." Before I could respond, she stormed away.

I stood in her wake, unable to move. My books slipped from my hands and fell to the floor. Was she telling the truth?

"Here you go," a voice said, handing me my books.

"Thank you," I murmured, absently taking them without looking at the face.

There's no way she could be telling the truth. He had to be here. He just wasn't in school today. That was evident by his absent seat in English class. He couldn't have moved.

"Em, I just heard," Sara said from behind me. "I am so sorry. I didn't know."

"It's true?" I asked, turning to meet her sympathetic eyes.

"Yeah, I heard it from one of the guys on the basketball team."

Sara stood in front of her locker, contemplating my expression. She waited for me to react. But I couldn't. I didn't want to believe it. How could he be gone?

Then something broke. Sara saw it the second it happened and rushed alongside me, guiding me to the girls' bathroom. The halls were relatively empty since everyone had already gone to class, so there weren't many witnesses to the dramatic scene.

The pain crushed my heart. I sank to the floor, sliding my back down the cool tile wall. I didn't cry, and my eyes didn't fill with tears, although my insides felt like they'd been shred. I stared straight ahead, unable to focus on the wall across from me. We sat in silence for a time. I heard Sara breathing next to me, quietly witnessing my slow acceptance of the truth.

"He's really gone?" The words were caught in my throat, and I breathed them out in the faintest whisper.

Sara remained by my side without a word, holding my hand. The truth sank in deeper and my heart released an aching sob. I collapsed onto Sara's lap and gave in to its grief. My chest heaved as I gasped for air. Sara stroked my hair to sooth me while I cried into my folded arms.

"He can't be gone," I wept, wishing that saying it out loud, would make it true. I released another cry of pain.

Exhausted and raw, I laid my head still against her legs while the tears dried upon my face. My eyes stung from the tears, and my throat ached from the cries. My mind swirled with thoughts of why he left and questions of how he could have done it so suddenly. The more I thought about it, the more the pain turned to anger.

"I can't believe he left without saying anything." I pushed myself up to sit, the tension drawing back my shoulders. "He couldn't even say good-bye? Who does that?"

My rapid succession of emotions left Sara speechless, unable to find the words to answer. I stood up and began pacing, clenching my fists as I fumed at the thought of his selfish escape.

"Did the thought of being around me infuriate him so much that he couldn't even return to school? He had to run away to the other side of the country just to avoid me?! He's the one who stopped talking to me! Was I not supposed to get over him? Did he really want me to continue waiting for him to forgive me for something I didn't do? I'm sorry if he didn't like seeing me with someone else – but to pick up and move because of it!"

I grunted in frustration. My mind raced while I continued my pacing, unable to release my closed fists. I huffed and lost the words to continue my rambling rage. I breathed in, considering his actions with my heart strangled in my chest. The ire slowly subsided into a begrudged acceptance.

"Fine, if that's how he felt, then he should've gone. He obviously couldn't stand to look at me, so why should I care if he left?! Now I don't have to worry about him yelling at me, or making me feel guilty for my decisions. I don't care if I ever see him again."

This was almost convincing, but my heart stuttered in panic at the thought of not seeing his face in the halls.

"Do you really believe that?" Sara asked tentatively. I blinked at her, recognizing that she was in the room. "He didn't hate you, Emma."

"You don't know that, Sara," I shot back. "I hurt him. I couldn't trust him enough to let him in. Then I accused him of things he didn't do. To top it all off, I shoved it in his face by kissing another guy right in front of him. Of course he hates me, and maybe he should. He couldn't even be around me anymore. He absolutely hates me."

Sara remained silent as I convinced myself of this. The words stung, and the anger settled. It was no longer directed at Evan but at myself. I looked at my reflection in the mirror above the sink. The pain and anger flickered in my eyes as I realized that it all circled back to me. Now I was left holding the pieces of my heart, crushed by my own hands.

I shook my head in disgust at the image in the glass. I stared at the dark eyes, my jaw tightening, allowing the anger and revulsion to grow. I accepted the blame for forcing him away. He had every right to hate me, just as I hated myself at that moment. My stomach turned to ice, and I looked away from the accusing eyes.

Taking a deep breath, I pushed the pain deep down, but I let the guilt and self-loathing fester as a punishing reminder. I took another quick breath before facing Sara. She remained a silent witness, concern etched in her eyes. I was exhausted by the gut wrenching turmoil and couldn't feel anything anymore.

"I pushed him away, so he left," I confessed quietly, submitting to the final truth. "I don't have anyone to blame but myself – and now he's gone." I shrugged my shoulders dismissively. Sadness settled in Sara's eyes.

"Don't worry," I assured her. "I'm okay."

"No you're not," she whispered with a small shake of her head. After a brief silence, she said, "I think this period's about over. Are you going to your next class?"

"Sure," I shrugged. "Why not?"

We walked back to our lockers. My locker stood open, with my books casually tossed in the bottom. I grabbed what I needed as the bell rang.

"I'll see you back here before lunch?" Sara confirmed quietly, the worry still heavy in her eyes. I nodded.

I lingered at my locker for a second after Sara headed to class. I knew what was waiting for me, and as much as I tried to convince myself I was ready, I knew better. Smothered by anxiety, I couldn't loosen the tightness in my chest as I walked to Anatomy.

I sank onto my seat at the black table; the empty chair next to me screamed at me the entire class. I couldn't concentrate on the lecture. I kept glancing over at the crushing reminder of his absence.

By the end of class, I was irritated with my sorrow. I didn't have any right to grieve for him. I was the reason he was gone. But it didn't matter how much blame I took for forcing him to leave or how much effort I made to push it away – I was broken.

"Are you still in pain?" Drew questioned when he sat next to me and Sara at lunch.

I'd almost forgotten he was joining us, until he pulled out the chair. The guilt of being distracted by Evan washed over me with Drew's words. I obviously was not concealing my misery very well.

"No, I'm fine," I assured him with a forced smile. "It's just weird having everyone staring at me all day, that's all."

This wasn't completely a lie, although it had nothing to do with my pained expression. Everyone had been staring at me since I arrived at school that morning. I expected some stares and whispers, especially after Sara's account of the last time they saw me at the basketball game. But I wasn't expecting so many gawking faces. It was as if I'd returned from the grave. It was unsettling.

Drew's relief was evident when I saw him in the parking lot that morning. I was too preoccupied with searching for Evan's car to notice him approaching with a huge smile on his face. I suddenly caught sight of him and found his greeting too contagious not to return. He startled me when he wrapped his arms around me and held me gently against him. I hesitated before hugging him back. Sara watched in amusement, knowing I was freaking out on the inside.

I was more concerned that Evan might see us than I was about being in Drew's arms. It wasn't really a horrible place to be. I glanced around at the eyes that turned our way as they walked by. I was still trying to accept that Drew really did care about me. More importantly, I was trying to figure out how I felt about him.

So, as he sat at the lunch table asking me if I was still in pain, I decided I wasn't going to *think* about it anymore.

I leaned over and kissed him firmly on the lips and said as I pulled away, "I feel much better, thanks."

A grin emerged across his face and a subtle flush rose to his cheeks. Behind me, Sara started choking. I turned toward her convulsions.

"Sorry," she whispered, her face bright red. "Some bullshit caught in my throat." I raised my eyebrows at her words, hoping Drew hadn't heard.

"Are you playing in your game Wednesday?" Drew asked.

"It depends on how practice goes today and tomorrow," I replied. Drew moved his chair closer and rested his arm along the back of my chair. I could feel his heat radiating along my side, but the proximity of his body didn't ignite the tingling I was searching for.

"I'll definitely play Friday," I said, casually leaning closer so my shoulder touched his. I urged my heart to take notice, but it was too busy moping and wasn't about to be forced to flutter.

"Do you want to come over after the game to watch a movie?" he asked. Suddenly realizing Sara would be there too, he looked at Sara to include her in the invitation. "Or hang out or something?"

"There's a party Friday night at Kelli Mulligan's beach house," Sara informed him.

"Oh, you have plans?" Drew recognized in disappointment.

I shrugged apologetically, unaware of Sara's plans for us on Friday night. I was still trying to get used to the idea that I had a *Friday night*. When Sara found out that I was going to be staying with her on the weekends, all of her worries about my returning home rushed away. In their place was a revelation that she finally got to bring me to all the things I'd been missing out on. So my schedule defaulted to hers on the weekends – which was a little overwhelming.

"I have computer class with Kelli during second period; she invited us this morning. We're probably staying over," she informed us.

I raised my eyebrows in surprise. Not only did I have plans on a Friday night, but my sleep over had a sleep over? The thought of a party sent a familiar sensation surging through my veins – panic.

"She mentioned something about it to me last week after our basketball game. I didn't really consider it at the time. Is she letting anyone sleep over?" Drew asked.

"I don't know," Sara answered. This was not what she expected him to say, and I could tell she was bothered. I grinned.

"Do you want to go to the party?" My invite caused Sara to kick me under the table.

"I'll make sure it's still okay with Kelli. I have class with her next actually."

"Great," Sara forced. Her false enthusiasm was glaringly obvious to me, but Drew didn't appear to notice.

The lunch bell rang and Drew walked us into the hall.

"I'll see you before we leave for our game?" he confirmed.

"Yes," I replied with a small smile.

Drew put his hands on my waist and pulled me to him. The chatter of voices and shuffling of feet surrounded us, but I didn't resist his advances. His soft lips were warm against mine as he held them there for a prolonged moment. My heart refused to flutter, but I couldn't deny the warmth that spread through my stomach and the swirls that danced in my head. I decided I could live without the rush, since kissing him was by no means uneventful.

"Bye," he whispered with a small smile before walking away, leaving me looking after him.

"Ready?" Sara asked, snapping me back to the noise of the hall. She stared at me with wide eyes.

"Don't look at me like that."

"What are you doing?" she demanded incredulously.

"I don't know what you mean. Aren't we supposed to be *dating*?"

"I just sat with you for an hour in the girls' bathroom –"

"Don't, Sara." I turned at the top of the stairs to face her. "This has nothing to do with *him*. I like Drew."

Sara raised her eyebrows, challenging my statement.

"Really, I *do* like him," I insisted and continued walking toward our lockers.

"Fine, maybe you like him," Sara conceded. "But it still doesn't feel right to me. I don't care how amazing you think Drew is, he's not –"

"Don't say it, Sara," I threatened. "Stop mentioning *him*. He decided to leave and I have to move on."

"Just like that?" she challenged. I shrugged. "Don't do anything stupid, okay? You can't kiss your way through this." I rolled my eyes and left her at the lockers to go to Art class.

This ended up being harder than Anatomy. Ms. Mier asked us to create an art piece depicting an emotion. She challenged us to unleash an emotion that could be felt through our artistic interpretation. A thousand different emotions surged through my head. I was fearful of exploring any one of them individually. Anxiety set in as I gathered a canvas and tried to select some colors to begin.

"Having difficulty deciding?" Ms. Mier inquired. "Or are you afraid of tapping into that emotion?" I glanced at her, recognizing her knowing words.

"I'm sorry you have to feel it," she continued, "but I think you can create something amazing if you let yourself explore it. It may not help you heal, but it may help you process it."

She paused, gently placed her hand on my shoulder, and whispered, "It's okay to miss him," before walking away.

I swallowed hard, pressing my lips together. I grabbed shades of red and orange and returned to my easel to begin *processing*.

During the two weeks of that assignment, I allowed myself to tap into the raw pain and drip it onto the canvas. I was true to myself with each stroke. It was a draining process, but the release was therapeutic. On several occasions, I fought to focus through blurred vision as I added layers of color, developing the pain with each shade. When I cleaned my supplies, I forced it all back into the shadows. By the time I returned to the halls, nothing remained—except for the aching murmur that took over my heart the day he left.

I moved on. I returned to playing basketball, only sitting out half of the first game after my return. I continued focusing on my academics, and found it easier now that I could escape to my room each night without the suffocating tension. I had the attention of a great guy, who easily distracted *my* attention whenever he was within sight. And I had guaranteed time with Sara. I was surviving as I promised I would.

27. WARMTH

I CAUGHT A GLIMPSE OF HIS TOUSLED GOLDEN BROWN HAIR IN THE SEA of people. I followed after him, squeezing through the bodies, forcing myself to move faster. No matter how fast I tried to move, I couldn't reach him. The bodies became solid and I was pushing through branches that raked my skin. I could still see him up ahead, but he didn't look back. My legs refused to cooperate and run faster. It took every effort to propel myself forward. I couldn't let him get away. My heart raced as I feared losing sight of him.

Suddenly the ground slid beneath me, and I didn't see him anymore. The crumbling rocky surface continued to roll away. I tried to stop, but it was too late. I grabbed at the rocks and the loose dirt, my legs scraping along the rough surface. My fingers curled around the edge and my legs hung, suspended above the darkness. Panic enveloped me as I tried to pull myself up. The rocks started to break free from the ledge, and that's when I saw him standing above me. I tried to reach for him, but as soon as I lifted my hand, the ground beneath the other hand gave way. I didn't see his face when I fell. Just before I hit bottom, I shot up in bed.

I was greeted by the familiar residuals of my active sleep – the racing pulse, heavy breathing and sheen of sweat – but this time, there were tears running down my cheeks. I fell into my pillow and cried, giving way to the ache in my chest until I was too exhausted to hurt anymore and drifted back into a restless sleep.

"You look tired," Sara observed when she picked me up the next morning.

"I haven't been sleeping very well," I confessed, pushing away the unsettling images of the nightmare that still clung to me.

"Are you going to last for the party tonight?"

"I'll be fine," I promised. The thought of spending the night at Kelli Mulligan's beach house was enough to jolt me to attention. I wasn't concerned I was going to fall asleep – I was more concerned about going to my first party with Drew since the bon fire.

"Ready for the party tonight?" Drew asked when he met me in the parking lot.

Seeing him brought a smile to my face, as it had every morning that week when he found me at Sara's car. Although Sara wasn't blatantly rude, she wasn't making any attempt to accept Drew. It was uncomfortably out of character for her. I mindfully ignored her and fell under Drew's arm as he wrapped it around my shoulder.

"Yeah," I responded with a forced hoorah in my voice. Why was I stressin' over this party so much?

"It's going to be a good one," Drew said, pulling me against him.

Before we parted ways in the hall, he quickly brushed his lips against my cheek and whispered, "I'll see you at lunch." I smiled at his touch.

"Maybe that's what happened," Sara concluded as we walked to our lockers. "Your concussion must have left you confused and delusional."

"What are you talking about?"

"The fact that you continue to ogle at Drew like he is *the guy*."

"What's wrong with you?" I couldn't understand the motive for her bitterness.

"I just don't like *you* with Drew," she stated blatantly.

"What? You think I'm different? What have I done wrong?" I questioned in alarm.

"You didn't do anything wrong, really. You're just not the same, like something's missing." She shook her head slightly in deliberation. "I don't know how to explain it."

"Sara, why are you making this so hard? If there's something I'm doing that I don't know that I'm doing, please tell me so I can fix it. But if I'm not doing anything wrong, then I don't understand why it's so difficult to see us together? I'm *trying* to be happy, and Drew makes me happy. I'd be a lot happier if you weren't so critical of me. I want to have a good time this weekend. We're finally getting to spend weekends together without fear or having to lie. Aren't you excited at all?"

"I am," she replied quietly, then forced a smile on her face. It was a start. "I'm sorry. A lot has changed lately. I think I'm having a harder time adjusting than you are. I'll try to be happy for you."

She hesitated, like she wanted to add something, but thought better of it. I waited, letting her gather her words.

"I won't second guess you anymore. I trust that you know what you're doing, and I'll support you. So, yes, I promise by the time we leave today, I will be excited. Okay?"

"Thank you." I flashed her an appreciative smile before she headed to class.

By the time we met for lunch, Sara didn't show any visible signs of having reservations about Drew and me, and she was her exuberant self once again. She talked about Kelli's party and who was supposed to be there, noting who was sleeping over. Since the house was just twenty minutes from Weslyn, there were only a few invited to stay the night, and they were exclusively girls.

Sara's good mood held up for the remainder of the day. She even had an actual conversation with Drew. He talked to her like there wasn't ever anything wrong, but her efforts didn't go unnoticed by me. I was grateful that she was finally giving in to the idea that *he* was who I was with.

I knew that being with Drew was going to be different, and I wasn't going to feel the same. I shouldn't, right? So when he pulled me into the vacant trainer's office before I left for my game, I wasn't expecting his send off or how he'd make me feel.

"I'll meet you at Kelli's around eight?" he confirmed.

"That's about right," I recalled.

I knew he was going to kiss me when he leaned over, but I was surprised when he slid his hand behind my neck and wrapped his arm around my waist to pull me to him. His warm breath released into my mouth as he parted my lips with his tongue. The connection ignited a heat in my stomach. I released a shocked breath of excitement. Our bodies pressed firmly together, and our wet lips slid over the other's urgently. When he released me, I exhaled a quivering breath.

"Wow," he breathed.

"Yeah," I responded softly.

My entire body was pulsing, a sensation I'd never experienced before. I needed to steady my breath and the swirling in my head before I could move.

"I should go," I whispered, pressing my lips together. They still lingered with the remnants of our kiss.

"Okay," he replied with a grin. He met me with another kiss, initially meant to be a soft kiss good-bye. But as soon as we touched, we fell into the frenzied passion again. Before I could completely lose myself in the moment, I pulled away.

"Yeah, I really have to go," I breathed.

He smiled back before I slipped out the door.

"Why are your cheeks so red?" Jill observed as we walked together to the bus.

I put my hand to my face, registering the warmth with a smile.

"I had to run to get here in time," I lied. "I was talking to Ms. Holt about the paper."

The warmth and pulsing lingered for most of the bus ride. I sat in the back, resting my head against the window, staring at nothing. I barely heard the music blaring in my ears as I replayed the kiss in my head. My lips turned up at the corners, as I inhaled deeply.

"What's going on with you?" Jill questioned curiously from beside me.

I removed an earbud so that I could hear her.

"You don't look as focused as you usually do before a game," she noted. "Are you okay?"

I shook off the buzz.

"Yeah," I stated soberly. "I'm fine. I was just caught up in something else."

"I'm sure I know *who*." She grinned. I ignored her and put the earbud back in, forcing my mind to prepare for the game.

Sara picked me up at the school after we returned.

"You win?" Sara asked.

"Of course," I confirmed with a smile.

"My mom has dinner in the oven for us when we get home, so we'll get ready to go to Kelli's after we eat. I've already picked out your clothes."

I smile, having expected nothing less.

"Should I be nervous?"

"I think you may be."

I groaned.

I groaned again when I saw it.

"A dress, Sara?!" I discovered in dismay, staring in shock at the blue and green flirty strapless dress paired with a blue cardigan.

"No heels this time," she pointed out, hoping it would make up for the lack of material, but I couldn't take my enlarged eyes off of the dress.

"Just go take a shower and let me worry about the clothes," she demanded.

I obeyed.

I started buttoning the sweater, wanting to conceal the fact that nothing was holding up the dress. Sara removed my hands from the buttons, shaking her head. I examined the dress; it swayed a little too far above my knees in the mirror, and I gave Sara a worried glance. The dress kept me from being concerned with the large curlers in my hair.

"Relax, it looks great," Sara assured me. "I promise it isn't going to fall down. It fits perfectly."

"I don't understand how, considering how much bigger your chest is than mine."

"That's why I never wore it," she confessed. "Don't envy having a bigger bra size. It's more of a pain in the ass than you realize."

I let out a short laugh, skeptical of her self-criticism.

Sara removed the cooled curlers and released soft waves of hair that she tousled with her fingers. It was more volume than my hair had ever seen, and took me the entire car ride to get used to it.

"Stop playing with your hair," Sara reprimanded as we pulled into Kelli's driveway.

The Mulligan's beach house was spectacular. The house shined like a beacon at the top of the long inclined driveway when we pulled up. It was a modern two-story structure set on a cliff. The entire ocean side of the top floor was lined with windows that let off a distinct glow against the darkened sky.

Sara and I gathered our overnight bags and followed the stone driveway to a narrower walkway with our heels clicking along the hard surface. My stomach turned in anticipation of what awaited us behind the large white doors when Sara rang the bell.

"Hey Sara! Emma!" Kelli yelled in excitement when she opened the door. "Come on in."

We entered the small foyer which was illuminated by a large spiny light fixture suspended above our heads. We followed Kelli up a short flight of stairs that opened into a space so expansive it made my jaw drop. A sleek white and chrome kitchen with a massive cooking island and bar connected with a spacious living area that had an amazing view of the ocean. A fire flickered in the large stone fireplace along one side of the open room, and a chic chrome table with a glass top was centered along the glass wall. Another sitting area focused around a sophisticated entertainment unit on the other side. I recognized most of the forty, maybe fifty people scattered around.

We followed Kelli through the kitchen and down a long hall. She opened the last door. We walked into a bright white bedroom with a glass wall looking out at the ocean. There were two full sized beds adorned with white and blue pillows, a small fireplace across from a chaise, and its own private bathroom.

"This is where you'll be staying for the night," she announced as she walked in. She handed Sara a key. "So you don't have to worry about anyone wandering in here later." She grinned. "Come out whenever you're ready and help yourselves to anything."

"Nice, huh?" Sara admired after Kelli disappeared down the hall.

"Unbelievable," I gaped, watching the dark waves crash against the rocks.

After abandoning our bags in the room, we joined the party. This party was much different than the other two parties I'd been to. Everyone here was dressed like they were going out to an expensive restaurant, or maybe a nightclub. The girls made a point to show off skin, accented by something sparkly dangling from their ears or necks, while the guys made an extra effort to wear fitted clothes and style their hair with more product than I owned. Sara's dress now made sense, except that I was covering it up with the sweater, and I wasn't about to take off.

"How was your game?" Drew asked, sliding his arms around my waist, and giving me a quick kiss on the lips. The warmth rushed in at the touch of his lips, instantly reminding me of our connection earlier in the day.

"We won," I responded with a smile, accented by the red of my cheeks.

He took my hand and escorted me to the kitchen. Sara was already there greeting everyone as we made our way through. She picked up a glass of champagne, and Drew grabbed a beer. An uneasy twinge passed through my stomach.

"What do you want?" Drew asked, pulling me towards him so he could talk in my ear.

"I think I'm okay for now," I responded nervously. I glanced around and noticed most people holding some type of glass, presumably containing alcohol. An anxious flood surged through me, fearing more awkward exchanges with inebriated people. This was going to be interesting.

"Are you sure?" Drew confirmed. "I don't need to drink if it makes you uncomfortable."

I didn't know what to say in response. Of course it made me uncomfortable. I'd witnessed too many moments when my mother failed to function while intoxicated. Even though alcohol seemed to be at every party I'd been to so far, it didn't change my aversion to it. Could I really ask him not to drink?

"Are you driving?" was the first thing that came out of my mouth.

"No. I'm staying in the guest house tonight with a couple of the guys."

He's staying over? I held my breath at the thought of having him here all night, especially after the kiss we shared earlier. I could handle this, right?

"I don't drink," I shrugged apologetically.

"That's fine," he acknowledged, setting down the bottle. "I don't have to either." Then he kissed me softly on the lips, and whispered in my ear, "I don't need the alcohol to give me a buzz." My face grew hot. I let out a quick breath, not convinced I could handle it anymore.

I didn't know where Sara disappeared to, so I followed Drew to the sitting area where a few of his friends were talking about surfing. I stood next to Drew, with his arm around my waist, listening to their animated stories – which were more entertaining than I anticipated.

I spotted Sara with a few girls from soccer near the kitchen, so I told Drew I'd be right back.

"Hi," I said as I approached the small group.

"Hi Emma," Katie welcomed. "You look really great."

"Thanks," I replied awkwardly. "So do you." I noted the strapless white top, the form fitting black pants and the strappy black heels—with more inches than I could manage, but she pulled them off like she wore them every day.

"Where's Drew?" Sara asked.

"Talking to some friends." I nodded toward the group of laughing guys.

"Are you two officially together?" Lauren asked.

"What does that mean exactly?" I questioned, not understanding the "officially" part. Dating had rules that I evidently was not aware of.

"Are you seeing other people?" she clarified.

"I'm not," I answered, then glanced over at Drew who was completely engaged in a story. Did Drew want to see someone else? If he did, would that be okay? The thought of it triggered an unexpected twist in my stomach.

"We haven't talked about it," I confessed.

"Em, you should ask him what he expects," Sara advised. The other girls nodded.

"You don't want to assume anything and then get burned later," Jill added. "Drew doesn't kiss and tell, but you never know what he may have going on on the side." My eyes flashed toward Katie when her eyes averted to the floor and her cheeks turned a slight pink.

"That's why I was surprised when I heard he kissed you," Lauren noted. "I never hear about Drew."

"I think it's because it was her," Sara concluded. "It was a bigger deal, so I'm sure he couldn't keep that to himself."

The conversation regarding Drew and I was making me uncomfortable. I really wanted to change the subject.

"Are you staying over?" I asked the girls, but they were too entrenched in analyzing my relationship with Drew to hear me.

"I know how his friends are," Katie finally added, "so don't assume he's as innocent as you think." She wasn't talking to me directly, but I still heard the warning in her tone. I studied her suspiciously—she still refused to look at me. Sara picked up on the intonation as well.

"Katie, what do you know?"

"Nothing – I've just hung out with them before, when they went surfing in Jersey. I watched them *all* flirt with the girls there. I went with Michaela once when Jay invited her, right after they hooked up. When we got there, he barely paid any attention to her. He was too busy hitting on another girl from the city. He didn't even think twice about it, and then he didn't understand why Michaela was upset when he came back around and wanted to get with her later that night."

"That doesn't mean they're all like that," Jill argued. Katie shrugged. I recognized she wasn't telling us everything.

"Em, come with me," Sara requested. "I need another drink."

I pulled a bottle of sparkling water out of the refrigerator while Sara topped off her glass, awaiting the real reason she pulled me away from the girls.

"I think Katie may have had something with Drew," she warned. "Or still does."

"You think so?"

She shrugged. "Maybe. There's something definitely up. I know he's been with at least two girls here."

"Don't tell me," I pleaded.

Knowing Drew's history of girls was more than I could take; the thought of it caused my stomach to twist tighter. I glanced over at him again, but the guys had dispersed. I scanned the room and found him talking to Kelli and another girl I didn't know. The twist morphed into an unwelcome streak of jealousy. I forced myself to dismiss it, convinced I was overreacting. The girls had gotten to me, and I needed to shake off the insecurity.

"Just talk to him, so you're on the same page," she insisted. "Do you want to date him exclusively?"

It was a question I hadn't given much thought to. I'd allowed Drew to slip in when I wasn't paying attention, and now that I *was* paying attention, I didn't know what to think. I took seeing him every day for granted, unconcerned if he had an interest in anyone other than me. But looking around the room and seeing the options, I understood the temptation, and it made me question what was happening between us.

"I don't know," I answered honestly. "I've never really thought about it."

"I didn't think so." I was prepared for her to say more, but she didn't.

"Hey Sara," Jay approached us. "It's cool to see you here."

"Hi Jay," Sara acknowledged.

"Are you two up for going surfing with us this spring?"

The invitation to be a part of Drew's future was suddenly too overwhelming. I really had been living in the present. So all the talk about declaring my intent with Drew and surfing with him and his friends months from now, was too much to absorb all at once.

"We'll see," I remarked with a casual shrug.

"Come on. You'll love it," he insisted.

"A lot can happen between now and then," Sara answered, reading into my abbreviated response.

"True," Jay agreed. "But no matter what, I'd love to get you on a board—or see you in a bikini." He laughed. I stared at him with widened eyes, while Sara rolled hers.

"I was just kidding," he defended.

"Hey," Drew said, coming up behind me, slipping his arms around my waist.

"I was just talking about taking them surfing with us this spring," Jay told Drew.

"Really? You want me to teach you how to surf?" Drew came alongside me so he could see my face.

"Maybe," I shrugged, not wanting to mislead him about our potential future.

"She doesn't think you guys will last until the spring," Jay laughed.

"Jay!" Sara exclaimed, hitting his arm.

"Ow!" He flinched, holding the spot where she made contact. "What?!"

"She never said that," she bit back. Then she looked to Drew, rolling her eyes. "He's an idiot."

Drew observed me cautiously, trying to read my face.

"Are you ditching me already?" he questioned in concern.

"No!" I declared. "I never said anything like that. Thanks a lot, Jay!" Jay put his hands up in defense, which was obviously a common pose for him.

Drew took my hand and led me down the hall, away from the noise. My stomach turned, nervous to have this conversation right now.

"What's going on?" he asked

"Nothing," I assured him, but my voice lacked the confidence needed to set him at ease.

"I'd rather not talk right here," I stated, glancing toward the voice filled room, with the attentive ears and subtle glances in our direction as we attempted to isolate ourselves.

Drew's eyes tightened. I must've said something wrong. This wasn't going very well, and I couldn't figure out what I was saying that kept upsetting him.

He led me across the room, down the stairs, and out the front door. I shivered, wrapping the sweater around me to brace myself against the cold wind.

"Where are we going?" I asked, continuing alongside him across the driveway.

"Some place we can talk."

Through a break in the trees was a small cottage. He took out a key and unlocked the door. The small house was one large room with an eat-in kitchen, a sitting area, two queen sized beds on the far side, and a ladder leading up to a lofted bed. It was decorated in a typical New England nautical theme, with shells and pictures of sailboats, in complete contrast with the chic, modern design of the main house.

Drew shut the door and turned toward me. I was not prepared for the concerned look on his face. The misunderstanding evidently had gotten to him, and I was failing at saying the right thing to make him feel better. Now I was worried about what to say next.

"Tell me what that was all about?" he requested anxiously.

"I'm sorry." Panic streaked across his face. Wrong words again! What was I doing wrong? "The girls were trying to give me advice, and I let it get to me. It was stupid, really." I hoped he would find some comfort in my dismissive tone, but he remained tense.

"What did you want advice about?"

"I didn't," I said quickly. This was harder than I thought. "They asked me if you and I were *officially* together, and I said we hadn't really talked about it. So they told me I should, that way I'd know in case you were seeing someone else. It was ridiculous, and I shouldn't have listened to them."

"Huh." I waited as he processed what I said. The tension let up in his shoulders, but his eyes remained uneasy.

"So, are we together?" he finally asked.

Not what I was expecting.

"What does that mean exactly?"

Wrong question again. His eyes flinched in alarm.

"Do you want to be with anyone else?" he inquired cautiously.

My heart stammered at the question. I couldn't force the words out to tell him that there wasn't anyone else, so I shook my head. My heart continued to stutter at the untruth.

"Do you?" I returned anxiously, having already considered the reasons he may not want to be exclusive.

"No," he denied quickly. "So why don't you think we'll last until the spring?"

We were back to this question again? I took a breath, stalling before answering.

"I never said that," I promised.

"Do you think we will be?"

Now how was I going to answer that without it coming out wrong? I looked into his nervous bright green eyes and smirked. I decided to do the only thing I could to avoid answering. I took a step toward him and put my arms around his neck, pulling him toward me. He didn't resist when I kissed him.

Drew smiled softly, revealing his dimples. He leaned in to find me again with his soft lips, causing a warmth to surge through me. His mouth rushed to find mine over and over again as he pulled me closer. I could hardly breathe with the pulsing heat capturing my lungs.

His firm body pressed against mine. Small excited gasps escaped as he tightened his hold around my waist. We slowly moved across the room, keeping up the frantic kissing and breathing until my legs bumped up against something. He guided me onto my back on one of the beds. My head was caught up in the swirl of quick breaths, unable to process where this was leading. Then his hand slid along the back of my thigh and he pulled my leg around him. A sobering flash tried to register in my head.

Drew ran his lips along my neck, sending another whirl of excitement through my body, crushing the warning before it developed. The warmth of his tongue traveled down my neck as he proceeded to peel my sweater back to reveal my bare skin. I let out a small moan of pleasure as the swirl consumed me. He made his way back to my mouth and began running his hand along my outer thigh, then slid it in between my legs.

The sobering crash resounded in my head, at the same time a cold draft caught me.

"Whoa," a voice said from the door.

"Jay, get out!" Drew yelled, still pressed against me with his head turned toward the door.

I shot up from under him, pulling my dress down, and adjusting my sweater. Drew was forced to sit next to me on the bed.

"Sorry, man," Jay offered with an annoying smile. "I didn't know."

"Just get out."

"See you inside," Jay laughed, closing the door behind him.

"Shit," Drew whispered, falling on his back. "Sorry about that."

From a distance I could hear Sara's voice. "Jay, have you seen Emma?"

I jumped up from the bed, and proceeded to straighten my dress.

"She's in there." Jay laughed again.

"What's wrong?" Drew questioned in alarm, propped up on his elbows on the bed.

"Sara's looking for me," I explained, smoothing my hair in the mirror.

"Do you want to go back inside?" he inquired, the disappointment heavy in his voice. He stood up as Sara as knocked on the door.

"Emma, you in there?" Sara beckoned from the other side.

"Come in," Drew yelled back.

Sara peered in cautiously. I rolled my eyes at her suspicious entrance. She looked from me to Drew, and back to me again, then glanced at the rippled bedding. I knew I was in for a drilling later.

"Um, we were going to..." she faltered. "I was just looking for you."

"I'll be right there," I promised, unable to leave just yet with the bright red running from my cheeks down to my chest.

"Okay, I'll see you inside," she responded slowly, closing the door behind her.

"Sorry," I said to Drew. "But we should go back in before *everyone* starts looking for us."

"I could lock the door," he offered, pulling back the sweater and kissing the top of my shoulder. Before the swirls regained their momentum, I laughed nervously and backed away, covering my shoulder with the sweater. Drew conceded reluctantly, "Fine, we'll go back in."

We were welcomed with suspicious glances and assuming smiles that made my chest tighten when we entered the house. Maybe my face was still flushed, so they knew what we were up to just by looking at me. I searched the room for Sara and found Jay with the dumbest smile that I had a strong desire to smack off of his face.

"I'm going to get something to drink," I told Drew, heading toward the kitchen area.

He walked straight to Jay and had him in a corner in conversation before I made it to the kitchen.

"I guess you're official now," Jill said with a laugh.

"What?!" My worst fear was realized as she gave me a knowing grin. The heat crept along my neck to my cheeks.

"Come on," she hinted. "Jay has a big mouth, remember?"

"Great." I huffed, shaking my head in humiliation. "I'm sure it was so much worse coming out of his mouth."

"I don't know if it could get any worse."

"What are you talking about?" I demanded, now confused.

She didn't respond for a second, and then she nodded for me to walk over to an empty corner next to the cabinets. My heart skipped a beat in panic.

"He said he walked in on you and Drew having sex."

"What?!" I yelled, much louder than I should have. I grabbed the counter to support me so I wouldn't fall over. The people closest to us stopped to listen.

"We were kissing," I assured her in an agitated whisper. "That's it. What an ass!" My stomach turned, suddenly realizing why we'd received so many stares when we came back.

"Sorry." She shrugged. "Jay likes his stories." I shook my head in disbelief.

Sara had slipped in beside us while I was explaining what Jay had *actually* seen.

"I knew you wouldn't do that." She sounded relieved.

"Of course not!" I declared adamantly. Drew seemed to be having a very similar conversation with some of the guys on the other side of the room. Jay continued to shake his head while turning his hands in the air in his infamous defensive pose.

"Please tell me there is something more interesting to talk about than what Drew and I *didn't* do," I begged, trying to settle the nausea in my flipping stomach.

"Um, well, Katie disappeared with Tim somewhere," Jill offered.

"Really?" Sara asked, intrigued.

If trying to guess what two people were doing alone together was a form of entertainment, then I didn't want any part of it – especially after I had been one of the people providing the entertainment. I slipped past Sara and Jill, while they continued to draw outrageous conclusions, and found an empty space on the couch in front of the fireplace to stare at the flames. I was struck with an unsettling déjà vu.

"I had him once," Kelli said, breaking my entranced gaze. I watched her scoot towards me, greeted by the sweet burn of liquor. I let out a heavy breath, preparing myself.

"You are sooo lucky," she slurred. "Drew is the greatest guy."

"Mmm," I agreed, humoring her.

"I only fucked him once," she confessed. My back tensed. "We never dated or anything." She shared this information as if it should put me at ease. "But he's amazing, isn't he?" I couldn't move.

"I'm so glad you and Sara are here," Kelli murmured, laying her head on my shoulder. "You are the nicest people I've ever met." I glanced over at her short brown hair that flipped up in the right places, and her thin strapped cocktail dress that exposed her cleavage.

Great, so he'd been with her, and probably Katie. Who else in this room had the privilege of a Drew experience? I knew I wasn't the first person he'd dated, like he was for me. But from the sounds of it, dating wasn't necessary to get to know him. I felt sick with the thought of the girl next to me in a compromising position with Drew. I knew I shouldn't allow it to get to me. But whether it *should* or not, it did.

I had preoccupied myself in order to avoid thinking about Drew's past, and I eventually lost track of the time. I talked to random people about nothing in particular. I even watched a couple of guys arm wrestle, which was ridiculously entertaining—especially when one guy kept cheating by standing up out of his chair. Sara checked on me a few times, but she became preoccupied with a local guy that Kelli had invited. By the time Drew found me, most people were starting for the door or going to their rooms.

"Sorry it's been so long since I've seen you," Drew said, sliding next to me on the couch and placing his arm around my shoulders. I was ready to go to bed, and I had hoped to slip into my room without being noticed. I was hesitant to lean against him so he could put his arm around me – still not recovered from the thoughts that had plagued me most of the night. "You okay?"

"Just tired." I played it off by stretching my back—feeling horrible that he had picked up on my evasion.

"Too tired to be alone with me?" he whispered in my ear. I grinned; the warmth of his breath erased every insecurity that had disturbed me throughout the night. I turned my head, and he met me with a gentle kiss on the lips.

"Well?" he urged. I continued grinning, allowing the warmth to rush through me. He kissed me again, lingering a little longer while wrapping his arm around my waist to pull me closer.

Someone cleared her throat behind us. I pulled back and looked toward the noise to find Katie standing a few feet behind us. I sat up in surprise.

"Drew, could I talk to you a minute?" Katie asked innocently, swaying slightly with her hands on her hips and a flirtatious grin upon her face.

Drew sighed and looked to me. I shrugged, allowing him to decide if he wanted to talk to her.

"Sure," he said slowly and got up to follow her to a vacant spot leaning against the window in front of the dining room table.

I sunk into the couch, my twisting stomach kept me from watching. After a few minutes, Drew returned appearing bemused.

"Everything okay?" I asked, without really wanting to know the answer.

"Just wasn't expecting that," Drew admitted, with a distant look in his eye.

I couldn't ask him to explain, but his answer was unsettling. Now I *did* want to know what Katie said. He noticed when I tensed away, and he reached for my hand.

"It's a long story," he said dismissively. That didn't help.

"I think a few people are going in the hot tub downstairs," Drew offered. "Are you interested?"

"Not really," I replied, wanting more than ever to put the twisting discomfort behind me and go to my room.

"You really just want to go to bed, don't you?"

"I do," I confessed. "Sorry."

"That's fine. It's really late." Then he hesitated before he asked, "Could I lay with you?"

I stopped breathing. I definitely wasn't expecting that.

"I don't think that would be a great idea."

"You're probably right," he conceded. "Can I at least tuck you in?"

I grinned at the offer. "I think that would be okay."

Drew followed me to find Sara so that I could get the key. She looked at Drew behind me and raised her eyebrows. I rolled my eyes and shook my head, dismissing her silent insinuation. I knew that anyone who saw Drew follow me to the room would assume the same thing. With everything that had already happened and been misinterpreted tonight, I was beyond caring about it anymore.

Drew sat in a white chair in the room, while I prepared for bed in the bathroom. I emerged with my teeth brushed, face washed, wearing a pair of striped boxer shorts and a fitted tank top. Drew grinned, probably because he was seeing more of me than he'd seen so far.

I slipped under the covers of the bed as he locked the door.

"So no one walks in and assumes anything," he offered in response to my inquisitive look.

"You're just tucking me in, remember?"

Drew smirked.

"Good night," he whispered, leaning over to kiss my lips. He hesitated ever so slightly before his lips touched mine so that I could feel the heat of his breath. I inhaled softly as the tickle of his breath started to rouse the swirls in my head. His soft lips pressed against mine, and he kept them there long enough for my head to fill with the whirling sensation before he pulled away. I kept my eyes closed and breathed the slightest audible moan, unaware that I'd released the sound.

Before I could open my eyes, he was there again, finding me, but with much more energy and need. I returned the enthusiasm, wrapping my arms around his neck, pulling him closer. He lowered himself over me, on top of the blankets, continuing to find my urgent lips. He kissed down the slope of my neck, and I arched to meet him. My body was so caught up in the intoxicating warmth and hunger that I couldn't think. I could only respond to the pulsing that pulled me to him.

My breath escaped in gasps as he slipped under the covers, and I could feel him so much closer. I tasted the salt along his neck, my lips finding the spot below his ear. His breath accelerated, and he pushed harder against me, sliding his hand under the back of my tank top. A sobering shock tried to wake me when his tensed body pressed into me, warning me to slow down.

Drew ran his other hand along the back of my thigh and stopped under my knee, hitching it around him. The excited warmth racing through me collided with the sobering alarm going off in my head. I pulled away and took a breath, trying to listen. He held himself over me, looking down in attempt to understand my withdrawal. He leaned in to kiss me again, but I turned my head.

"Need a minute," I explained.

"Yeah," he sighed, pushing off me and sitting on the edge of the bed.

He turned toward me and asked, "Do you want me to leave?" His green eyes searched mine eagerly. I grinned and shook my head.

I interrupted him as he was about to pull back the blanket, "But you should." He nodded slowly, his eyes sinking with disappointment.

"Goodnight," he offered, leaning forward to kiss me.

"I think you did that already," I replied with a grin, stopping him before he got too close. "Goodnight."

Drew slowly stood and went to the door. He looked back at me one final time, hesitating long enough for me to consider changing my mind, before he closed it behind him.

Waiting for my pulsing body to recover, I couldn't even think about sleeping.

Just as I was falling asleep, a thud on the door stirred me. Sara was adamantly saying good night presumably to the local guy she just met. I wanted to slink under the covers when I heard her sliding against the door with heavy breaths and moans. After a few more low thuds, Sara finally entered with a promise to call him. I had my back to her and feigned sleep. I'd *heard* enough of the details of her night and really didn't want to talk about mine, so I didn't respond when she asked if I was awake. Eventually, sleep found me.

275

In the early hours of the morning, I was confronted with the same images of Evan on the cliff. This time I saw his face before I fell, and he looked so angry. I pleaded with him as he drifted away.

"Em?" Sara groaned half asleep. "Are you crying?"

The room was dark, with daylight hidden behind custom blinds. I lay in the bed, my enlarged eyes frantically searching around the unfamiliar room. The tears slid along my temples, and sweat pasted the sheet to my body. I eased up to sit, my heartbeat slowing to its intended pace.

"You called out his name," Sara stated, rolling onto her side to look at me.

"Who's name?"

"Evan's."

The sadness of the dream returned to me. I wiped the tears from my face.

"You miss him, don't you?"

I didn't say anything.

"You could always call him, you know."

I shook my head. "No I can't," I whispered. I got out of bed and entered the bathroom, closing the door behind me.

28. THE TRUTH

SOMEHOW I LIVED THROUGH THE RUMORS OF WHAT DIDN'T HAPPEN between Drew and me. I was mortified when one of the girls from the basketball team asked, in front of everyone in the locker room, if Drew and I had sex at Kelli's. Jill tried to defend me, and it worked for the most part with my teammates, but it didn't have the same result with the rest of the school. No one else asked me to my face, but I heard the whispers when I walked down the halls. Sara's urging me to "just ignore them" only confirmed what they were whispering about.

I wasn't invisible anymore, and there was no point in trying to fade away again. More people recognized my promotion in the social hierarchy and were bold enough to try to talk to me. At first it was just small talk, to which I awkwardly responded with short answers. Then I was invited to parties and out with a group of people I would never have known if they hadn't approached me. I always deferred to Sara to plan our weekends.

I remained trepidatious with my ghostly comings and goings through the house. I didn't know how long my absence was going to be accepted without an explanation of where I was coming from and going to. My stomach still dropped at the sound of her voice, anticipating the moment she'd notice me again. But as the month progressed, I was still just an occupant in their home, without any expectations besides the Saturday morning chores.

I missed seeing Leyla and Jack. I heard their voices in the distance, but rarely saw them. I convinced myself that this was better for them—that way there wouldn't be a chance of my world disrupting theirs again. It made the hurt more bearable, especially when I'd hear Leyla's excited stories from behind the closed door of my room.

During the first week of February, Anna and Carl announced that they were taking Sara and I to California during our school break to visit colleges. My coach arranged meetings with a few schools that were interested in me. Carl spoke with George to approve the trip, which I'm sure raked under Carol's skin. I hoped retribution wasn't waiting for me when we returned.

Sara was beyond excited with thoughts of us going to college together in California. I was thrilled as well, doing everything to ignore the fact that we were going to be in the same state – actually staying in the same city—as Evan.

His nightly hauntings became less frequent. I would think I finally escaped him, just to cry out in the night, propelled back to the dark bedroom sobbing. Sara stopped asking about the nightmares. She'd silently watch me recover from the bed across from me.

It was hard to heal when I saw my brokenness in streaks of red and orange displayed on the wall of the Art room. Ms. Mier praised that it was my best piece yet and said she was proud of my honesty. I absorbed her words without reaction. I'd hoped that releasing it on the canvas would help me move on, but I knew I was never going to put him behind me.

I allowed my heart to remain silent. It continued to ignore Drew's touch. But I embraced the warmth he ignited within the rest of me and the enrapturing swirls of excitement that clouded my head whenever we had a moment alone together.

It was easy to get lost in the breathing and kissing. But over time, the urgency increased. His hands wandered more, seeking the touch of my skin, gradually inching up or down. I felt like I was constantly redirecting his creeping hands and trailing lips. He wouldn't say anything, but I knew he was hoping I'd just give in and stop resisting. Instead of talking about it, I started to avoid being alone with him.

My evasiveness roused a wave of guilt. I tried convincing myself that it was because I wasn't ready, and it had nothing to do with Drew. We didn't have another conversation about our relationship after Kelli's party. We never discussed our feelings or expectations.

I took what we had at face value. We liked to be around each other. We easily found something to talk about, and he still made me laugh without much effort. The public affection and the moments of breathlessness confirmed our attraction to each other. So what was there to talk about?

"You still like me, right?" Drew asked while we sat on the couch in Sara's entertainment room. Sara and Jill had gone to the store, and we were waiting for a couple of Drew's friends to arrive for a night of horror movies. We had decided to stay in since our flight left for California first thing in the morning.

"Of course I do," I answered in alarm, my stomach dropping at the unprovoked question. I gently pushed his foot with mine as I sat facing him on the couch with my back against the arm. "Where did that come from?"

Drew shrugged, but remained serious. I tried to connect with him, to make him smile, but he avoided looking at me. I was so confused.

"So, why don't you want to be alone with me anymore?" he asked after a moment of silence.

I sat up straighter, suddenly fearing where this was going.

"I don't know what you mean."

"You seem to always find an excuse. If you like me, then why don't you want to be with me?"

I didn't respond, knowing what he was really asking.

Drew leaned forward and grabbed my calves, pulling me across the couch, draping my legs over his. He put his arms around my waist and inched me closer until our faces were less than a foot apart. The entire move happened so quickly, I didn't have time to react.

"I want more from you," he stated softly, gently brushing his lips against mine. "I want you to want me too. I want you to need to be with me as much as I need to be with you."

He pressed his lips to mine, lingering. I could feel his breath quicken. I listened in shock to what he was really asking me, too panicked by his words to feel his lips.

"I know you want me," he whispered, our lips inches apart.

When I still didn't kiss him, he pulled his head back to look me in the eye. Concern washed over his face.

"You don't?" he asked cautiously, slowly sitting back against the couch.

I couldn't answer. My hesitation caused him to narrow his eyes, examining my stunned face. He looked away, not liking what he saw.

"Hey!" Jill exclaimed when she and Sara reached the landing.

I quickly pushed myself off of his lap and scooted to the other side of the couch. Drew forced a smile to greet Sara and Jill. Jill began loading the small upstairs fridge with beers. I stood from the couch and offered to help get things together in the kitchen. Sara tossed Drew the remote and told him he was in charge of picking the first movie.

"What happened?" she asked, sensing my mood change.

"He pretty much just asked me to have sex with him," I responded quietly as I dumped a bag of chips in a bowl.

"No way!" Sara exclaimed in shock. "What did you say?"

"I couldn't answer him," I confessed guiltily.

"You didn't say *anything*?"

"I was trying to figure out what the answer was when you two arrived."

"So now he thinks you don't like him at all, right?"

"I told him I liked him," I explained. "But he said he wanted more from me."

"Are you ready for this? With him?"

"I like him. But..." I shrugged.

Sara smirked, and said, "I know."

"What should I do?"

"Just treat him like you normally would, and try to avoid being alone with him for now. But you have to talk to him about it eventually. He's going to see right through you anyway when you keep rejecting him, and it won't matter."

I was confused. "What do you mean?"

She smiled. "If you don't know what I'm talking about, then I can't tell you."

"Sara," I pleaded, "you're not making any sense. What are you talking about?"

"Here, bring these bowls of chips upstairs, and kiss him or something so it's not awkward all night."

Jill entered the kitchen, and I hesitated before grabbing the bowls from Sara's hands, still trying to decipher her message. I climbed the stairs slowly, figuring out how to approach Drew. I decided aggressive and direct was best.

I set the bowls of chips on the table and intercepted Drew's view of the television screen while he flipped through movie titles. Reluctantly he looked up at me. I moved closer and straddled his legs, hovering above him. He raised his eyebrows in reaction to my forwardness.

"I want to be with you," I whispered, looking down at him. I placed my hands on the back of his neck, running my fingers into his hair. "But I'm just not ready."

He looked at me in confusion, obviously expecting a different answer. He was about to slide out from under me when I quickly added, "Right now—but, soon." I didn't know why I lied to him. It was easier than admitting the truth.

I leaned down and firmly pressed my lips against his. Before I could pull back, he had his hands on my back and he quickly flipped me over onto my back so that his body was on top of mine and my legs were wrapped around him. He continued to search for my lips as my breathing quickened. He tried to roll me on my side, but the momentum forced us to roll off the couch and onto the floor.

I started laughing, deflating the intensity, as he groaned beneath me. He looked up at me and smiled. I pushed myself off of him and slid back on the couch as the voices of the guys with Sara and Jill neared the top floor.

During the movies, Drew and I laid on oversized pillows on the floor, in direct sight of everyone, so he couldn't get away with too much. Everyone else was scattered on the couch and loveseat, making comments about the pathetic girls wandering alone in the dark and warning the guys to look behind them right before they were slaughtered. I had my head propped against Drew's taut stomach while he played with my hair. I fell asleep during the middle of the second movie.

"Evan?" the voice asked, instantly crashing me back to reality, releasing me from the vivid nightmare.

I shot up and looked around the dark room. I was on the floor, under a blanket and tried to place where I was. I was in Sara's entertainment room I realized—then I remembered watching the movies.

I felt him sit up next to me. I knew in that moment what had happened, and I was afraid to turn around. I wiped the tears from my eyes and slowly faced him. He looked exactly how I feared – hurt and confused. But he also looked pissed, and I wasn't expecting that. I stared at him, trying to calm my quickened pulse, but it remained heightened with the silent confrontation.

"Nightmare?" he finally asked.

I nodded, preparing for what was about to happen.

"About Evan?" he bit. I looked down, unable to meet his eyes.

"I get it now," he whispered in agitation. I glanced at him as he shook his head slowly.

"Drew," I pleaded. He stood to put his shoes on and grabbed his jacket. I couldn't find the words to make him stay. The truth was... I didn't want him to stay.

I remained on the floor, watching him disappear down the stairs. That's when I noticed Sara on the couch wrapped in the arms of an unconscious guy. Sara peered over the arm of the couch with sympathetic eyes, having heard everything. I looked away.

∞

"You did much better than I thought you would while we were in San Francisco," Sara complimented on our flight back from California. "I was waiting for you to lose it."

I was relieved I'd been so convincing. In actuality, I searched the face of every guy we passed, hoping to see him.

"I almost called him," I confessed, unable to look at her.

"I'm not surprised, but he wasn't there." My mouth dropped open as I turned to stare at her. "He's snowboarding in Tahoe with some friends for the week."

"How do you know?"

"I asked Jared," she confessed. "I called him when I found out we were staying in San Francisco for a few days, thinking maybe we could bump into Evan so you could get some closure. Don't worry; Jared promised not to tell him."

I didn't know what to say. When I thought about it, I wasn't exactly surprised that Sara did this.

I tried so hard not to think about him, but it was impossible not to when we were right there. It ate at me that he was so close and I could possibly see him at any moment. I picked up my phone probably a million times and hit *5*. Every time I saw the preprogrammed Evan displayed on the screen, I'd hit *Cancel*. Now those agonizing moments of trying to decide if I could push the *Send* button didn't matter at all. He wasn't even in San Francisco.

"Speaking of closure," Sara continued, "what are you going to say to Drew?"

"I have to say something, don't I?"

"Yeah, you can't avoid him forever. The school isn't that big." After a pause, she asked nervously, "You are over, aren't you?"

I let out a short laugh. "Don't worry, Sara, I won't continue torturing you. You don't have to pretend to like him anymore. It's over."

"I did like him," she said, then thought better of it. "You're right, I didn't like him. Mostly because I didn't –"

"Like me with him," I finished. "I know."

"He wasn't right for you."

"I know," I answered honestly. "Drew is *that guy*. I'm pretty sure he would've broken up with me when he realized he wasn't going to get anything. I think it's pretty obvious we're over."

"You still need to tell him," Sara urged. I didn't know what I was going to say. The unavoidable *talk* was weighing on me more than I wanted to admit.

But there ended up being no need to worry after all. The whole school knew we were over before we'd even returned from California. I found out when I heard, "I can't believe Drew dumped you for Katie," as soon as I walked into school on Monday. Jill stared at me waiting for my reaction. She wasn't expecting me to laugh.

It took a few weeks, but the rumors simmered, and I was able to return to my evolving world without any more distractions. Although the rhythm had changed since the beginning of the year, I was content with its predictability, and part of that was being alone – which I readily accepted. I also accepted the silence in the house when I retreated to my room each night.

I kept waiting for Carol to react in some way to my trip to California. But all I heard when I returned from Sara's was about the trip George had surprised her with to Bermuda. I had a feeling George hadn't told her about California. I had no problem putting up with her gloating; it didn't leave bruises.

I concentrated on my classes, continuing to push myself to meet my overachieving expectations. I performed on the basketball court, helping our team finish the regular season with only one other loss. I laughed with Sara more than I used to, now that we were "weekend sisters," as she liked to refer to us.

Even the pain that murmured in my chest and the nightmares that continued to wake me became a predictable part of my existence. I accepted them, and I moved on – I was still surviving.

29. FLUTTER

"STILL NOT DOING A VERY GOOD JOB FADING," HIS VOICE SAID FROM behind me.

The paintbrush froze in my hand mid-stroke and started shaking. My heart stopped in my chest. I didn't know if I could turn around to face him.

I forced my legs to swing around to the other side of the stool.

"Hi." He smiled. My heart released a brief flutter.

"Hi," I whispered, forcing myself to breathe.

"When you weren't in the caf, I figured you'd either be here or the Journalism room."

I could only nod, searching for my voice.

"What are you doing here?" I forced the words from my mouth. My question was barely audible since I still wasn't breathing properly.

"Looking for you," he answered with his familiar grin. My heart picked up its pace, filling my cheeks with a rush of color. All I could do was stare into his blue eyes, afraid that if I looked away, he'd be gone. *Please convince me I wasn't hallucinating.*

"Sorry to hear that the basketball team lost in the semi's," he offered casually. He's talking about basketball? I definitely wasn't hallucinating.

"Thanks," I said, forcing my lips to resemble a smile. *Come on brain, don't fail me now – say something!*

"Not sure what to say, huh?" He smirked, amused by my inability to form a cohesive sentence.

"I'm glad I can…" I threw my hands in the air, forgetting that I had a paintbrush in my grasp, the green paint flung across his grey t-shirt. He looked down at the streak with wide eyes. I held my breath, pressing my lips together. A stifled laugh escaped from behind my pursed lips. Then I started laughing harder.

"That's funny, huh?" I bit my lower lip, still smiling. "Let's see if you think *this* is funny." He leaned over my table and rubbed blue paint on his hands. Realizing his intention, I jumped off the stool to escape retaliation.

"Evan, don't," I pleaded.

I rounded the corner toward the dark room when he caught me around the waist, leaving blue hand prints on my shirt. When he grabbed me, he didn't let go. Evan turned me to face him. Still smiling, I connected with his blue eyes, unaware he was pulling me closer. Just before I registered what was happening, my heart ignited, fluttering franticly. My head swirled in a rush. He placed his damp hand on my cheek and leaned down toward me.

A paralyzing charge flashed through my body when his firm lips touched mine. I inhaled his clean scent, allowing the tingling to run through my head. When he slowly pulled away, his eyes searched mine cautiously. I blinked through the buzz, trying to steady myself.

"Emma?" Ms. Mier's voice rang from around the corner.

Evan raised his eyebrows in surprise then slipped by me, toward the dark room. I attempted to sober up before responding.

"Hi, Ms. Mier," my voice cracked, stepping around the corner to meet her. My face was hot with embarrassment.

"Oh, hi," she said with a smile of surprise. With the smile still lingering, she gathered some papers from her desk. "I needed to get a few things. Could you please lock up when you leave today?"

"Sure," I agreed quickly.

She smiled wider.

"That's a good color on you," she acknowledged.

My face grew even hotter, if that was possible. I looked down at the hand prints on my white shirt.

"No, the red I mean."

My eyes widened. I watched her walk to the door and turn the lock.

Before closing the door behind her, she glanced at me and said, "Tell Mr. Mathews I said welcome back."

I nearly fell over. I stood there for a moment, uncertain what to do next. I decided not to think about it anymore and to do what I should have done three months ago.

I walked into the dark room. Evan was drying his hands next to the sink. I closed the door behind me and leaned against it, unable to move. He threw the paper towel in the basket and looked up, hesitating for a second.

My chest moved with an exaggerated breath. My heart beat frantically against my shirt. He read exactly what I wanted him to in my widened eyes and stepped toward me. I wrapped my arms around his neck, and he pulled me into him. I stood on my toes, extending myself to find him. He held me closer as his lips parted, and I felt the warmth of his breath. My heart released a surge that caught my breath when I felt his soft tongue. His lips were firm but gentle, pressed against mine in a slow, breathless rhythm. Tiny sparks flew through my head and down my spine—my legs trembled beneath me.

I lowered my head to his chest before my legs gave out. He kept his arms wrapped around me, resting his chin on the top of my head, while I listened to his accelerated heartbeat and deep breaths. I wiped an escaped tear from my eye, trying to remember how to breathe.

"That was worth waiting for," he whispered and then added with sarcasm, "Missed me, huh?"

I looked up at his perfect smile and replied with a smirk, "I survived."

"I heard."

I pulled away and eyed him suspiciously.

"I still have friends here." He shrugged. Just then, the bell rang, declaring the end of the school day. "What do you want to do? Do you have to go home?"

"I'm actually staying over at Sara's tonight."

"You are?" Evan confirmed, raising his eyebrows with a deliberate grin. "Do you think Sara will mind if I kidnap you for a couple of hours?" He casually leaned against the doorway, as I went to the sink to scrub his handprint from my face.

My heart stuttered.

"Um, I think she'll be fine," I replied, turning to face him. "What are you thinking?"

"We have to talk. I mean, I couldn't have asked for a better way to be welcomed back, but I have some things I need to say before there are any more misunderstandings."

I winced. Couldn't we have left it at the perfect welcome? My stomach twisted, fearful of what he needed to say. I could only imagine; although it couldn't be worse than what I'd been saying to myself since he left.

"So, you're back?" I confirmed cautiously.

"Yeah," he grinned. "We'll talk about it."

"Great," I huffed, zipping my sweatshirt to conceal the blue hand prints and smear of green paint.

Evan laughed. "Don't be so nervous. I'm here, right?" He grabbed my hand, the warmth from his touch spread up my arm.

The halls were sparsely occupied, since most people had already left. The shocked eyes of those remaining followed us as we traced the familiar route to my locker.

"Mathews!" a few guys yelled out in recognition. Evan nodded in acknowledgment, continuing to walk beside me. I think I was as shocked as everyone else to see him next to me. His firm grasp of my hand was the only thing keeping me from believing that I was dreaming the entire thing.

"So, he found you," Sara observed when we neared our lockers. "I was getting concerned that you threw each other out the window or something—but I can see that didn't happen." She eyed our interlocked hands with a small smile.

"We're going..." I started. "Where are we going?" I looked to Evan for the answer.

"We need to talk," he explained. "So, can I bring her back to your house in a couple of hours?"

"My parents are going out *again*. You can stay and hang out with us tonight if you want. That is if you don't say anything that's going to devastate her more than she's already been for the past three months."

Evan's shoulders shot back as he received the blow. I stared at Sara with my mouth open, shaking my head in disbelief.

"What?!" she shot back. "I'm just saying..."

"Enough," I finished, "*more* than enough!"

I glanced at Evan; he looked pale. I turned to my locker to gather my books before he could read the truth of her words on my face.

"I'll see you later then?" Sara confirmed in her pleasant voice.

"Sure," I replied dismissively, still in shock from her honesty.

Sara walked down the hall, leaving Evan and I alone.

"What did she mean by that?" Evan asked slowly.

"She's just being ridiculous." I wanted him to dismiss her words, but they lingered uncomfortably.

"Huh," he exhaled. "I guess it wasn't any better for you here."

I didn't understand what he meant and looked to him for translation.

"We'll talk about it," he assured me. "Ready?"

"Sure," I said, closing my locker, his assurance filling me with dread.

Evan took my hand again and escorted me to his car. I didn't say much during the ride, too consumed with the pending "talk". I wasn't completely surprised when we pulled into his empty driveway. I couldn't think of another place to give us the privacy we needed for our confessional.

I turned to him in the car before he opened his door.

"Can't I just enjoy that you're here for one day before we make it uncomfortable?"

Evan found my plea amusing. Of course he did.

"I need to do this. I've had three months to obsess over this conversation, so I need to say what I have to say." He flashed a reassuring smile. "Don't worry; it'll be better once we talk."

I wasn't convinced.

I followed him into his house. I was confused when he kept walking down the hall and up the stairs to his room. I hesitated before entering his bedroom. Evan stood at the end of his neatly made bed, waiting for me.

"I wanted you to see that I'm really here."

I glanced around the room and noticed the shelves were full of books and other personal belongings. I didn't see any taped boxes.

"I'm completely unpacked."

With that, Evan walked out of the room. I continued to follow him through the house and into the barn. My stomach was tangled in nerves when I sat down to face him on the couch. I slid my shoes off and leaned back against the arm of the couch, resting my chin on my knees. I hugged my knees to my chest, prepared for whatever it was we had to talk about.

"What I have to say goes beyond the three months I was gone," he began, playing with the seam of the cushion nervously. "I should have said something the month we weren't talkng before I left." He hesitated and then focused on my eyes. He let out a breath and pressed his lips together. I waited anxiously, barely breathing.

"I love you."

My heart pounded loudly, having never been told those three words.

"I didn't handle things right. I shouldn't have gotten mad at you like that, and I'm sorry. I said some things I didn't mean, and I pushed you away. I practically hand delivered you to Drew Carson, which killed me."

I opened my mouth to disagree, but he continued before I could get a word out.

"I know I did, Emma. Don't feel bad about it. But what was worse than that was when I was waiting in the hospital, not knowing. I can't get the image of you motionless on the gym floor out of my head."

I shifted my gaze, unable to look into his pained eyes. I mindlessly picked at my jeans with shaking hands.

"It was the worst moment of my life. And then when you wouldn't see me..." Evan paused to take another breath. I glanced up at him, watching him run his finger along the seam of the couch again. "I knew I'd really screwed up. If I couldn't be there for you... if you didn't *want* me to be there for you, then I couldn't be here at all. So I left.

"But I couldn't do it. I'd still talk to some of the guys, and you'd come up every once in a while when they talked about what happened over the weekend. They'd mention they saw you at a party or they'd talk about basketball. They knew we were close, so they'd bring you up – and I wanted to hear about you. Well... except for that one time."

My eyes shot up and my stomach turned. He didn't look at me.

"Are you over him?"

"Drew?" I confirmed in disbelief.

"Yeah."

I released a brief humorless laugh, to his surprise. "Yeah, I'm completely over Drew."

"Didn't *he* end things with *you?*" Evan questioned, still perplexed.

"I let people think what they wanted," I confessed, meeting Evan's blue eyes. "Like someone else I know."

He obviously didn't understand what I meant.

"I ended things... well, actually you did," I stated, thinking better of it. I knew Evan still wasn't following. It was my turn to explain. "It became obvious I wasn't over you."

"So you didn't..." Evan examined me cautiously, not knowing how to finish the sentence. My eyes widened in shock, knowing exactly what he was asking.

"Have sex with him?! No!" I declared, aghast with color rushing to my face.

"Sorry," he said with a relieved smile. "I just heard..."

I sighed. "Yeah, along with the rest of the school. That was horrible."

Evan let out a brief laugh.

"It's great that you can still find humor in my social catastrophes," I snapped.

"Sorry. I was just imagining your face when you found out what people thought you'd done," he said with a chuckle. "It probably looked a lot like what I just saw, actually."

He let out another quick laugh. I tried to force a scowl, but I was having a hard time keeping a straight face.

"He wasn't your fault," I said softly, suddenly more serious than I wanted to be. Evan quietly listened. "I was angry. I assumed things. I thought I saw more than there actually was between you and Haley..."

"I..." Evan started.

"I know," I interrupted, "and *I'm* sorry for ever thinking you were interested in her. So much wouldn't have happened if I hadn't... I thought you hated me."

Evan's eyes got wider, alarmed by my words.

"I thought I forced you away when you saw me with Drew. I thought you couldn't stand to be near me," I whispered, fiddling with my jeans again. "I hated what I'd done, and I was so furious with myself. I could only imagine what you must have felt. I'm so sorry." I blinked away the tears welling in my eyes, recalling how my rage in the bathroom had continued internally since that day.

Evan slid down the couch, and drew my bent knees across his lap. He forced me to look into his reflective blue eyes.

"I didn't hate you," he stated softly. "I could never hate you."

He leaned in and gently pressed his lips to mine. It took me a moment to find my breath after he pulled away.

"So what now?" I whispered.

"I'm here, with you… if you want me," he offered with a soft smile. I shoved his arm. "What?! I just wanted to be sure."

"Of course I want you," I shot back.

Evan smiled.

"Then there's just one more thing." His tone became serious. "I know that you won't tell me what happens at home. I was wrong to try to force you, and I was wrong about what I said to you. You are so much stronger than I ever thought you were. I get why it's hard for you to talk about it. Sara told me that you don't even talk to her about it most of the time. But I know…"

I was having a hard time listening to his words. Ice began to build up in my stomach. I wished he hadn't brought it up.

"And even if you won't, or can't, tell me – I know. I do have to tell you that I can't ever sit in a hospital waiting room again."

"I fell –" I tried to explain.

"Don't," Evan urged. "I know. Without you or Sara telling me, I know. So, even if you can't tell me the truth, don't lie. Don't defend them like it's okay. Because it's not. I won't let them do that to you again. I'm just warning you, I'll make you leave with me if I think that…"

"Evan," I interrupted, "I'm okay. I promise. It's been pretty tolerable since that day, actually. They barely even notice me anymore, and I get to spend the weekends at Sara's. It used to be Saturday nights, but it's evolved to Fridays as well. It's not the same, so don't talk like that. Okay?"

He didn't respond.

"Okay?" I repeated, forcing him to look at me.

"Yeah," he whispered.

I put my hand on his cheek, wanting him to believe me. He took my hand in his and kissed my palm, sending shivers up my arm.

"So we're better?" I confirmed.

A warm smile spread across his face. "Yeah, we're better."

Evan leaned toward me again. This time, when he pressed his lips to mine, he stayed there. He slid me onto his lap as I put my arms around his neck. My heart convulsed in a flood of flutters, capturing my breath. His lips slowly slid against mine, parting in a gentle motion. I felt his hot breath against my lips, the flitter enraptured my head. I positioned my body to face him, straddling his legs. He pulled away and examined me with a smirk.

"What?!" I exclaimed, shocked by his withdrawal.

"It's only my first day back."

I bit my bottom lip with a guilty grin, color flooded my cheeks.

"Yeah," I breathed, looking down. "Sorry." I flipped my leg over and sat on the couch next to him again.

Evan laughed at my embarrassed retreat.

"Stop it," I sulked, gently kicking his thigh with my foot. "I've waited for forever to kiss you."

He laughed again. "You just surprised me, that's all." He continued to grin as he looked at his watch.

"We should get to Sara's before she believes we *did* push each other out a window. That reminds me…"

"Don't," I begged, not wanting to reflect on Sara's reference to my devastation. "Not now, okay?"

"Okay," he agreed hesitantly, studying me more intently than I was comfortable with.

"What do you want to do tonight?" I asked with bright eyes, trying to deflect the serious moment. "A movie at Sara's?"

"Are you going to fall asleep again?"

"Probably."

I was asleep an hour into the movie. I didn't remember falling asleep, with Evan laying behind me on the couch, his arm wrapped around my waist and my hand in his. I was actually convinced that I was going to make it through the entire drama when it started.

"I'm right here," he whispered in confusion.

I shot up at the sound of his voice.

"Emma?"

I sat with my feet on the floor, gripping the cushion on either side of my legs with my heart racing. His hand gently brushed along my back.

"Are you okay?"

"You're here?" I whispered in relief, squinting to look at him.

He examined my face in concern, gently wiping the tear from my cheek.

293

"Yeah, I'm here," he soothed. A pained realization flashed across his face. "I'm not going anywhere."

Still dazed from the abrupt arousal, I stared at him, uncertain if I was truly awake.

"Come here." He pulled me down to lie on his chest, wrapping his warm arms around me as I drifted back to sleep.

I awoke the next morning in the same clothes as the night before. I sat up in a panic.

"Relax," Sara urged from the bed next to me. "We're going to see him tonight. I convinced him to go to a party with us."

I lay back down with a relieved smile, her words confirming that I hadn't been dreaming.

"I don't remember going to bed," I pondered.

"You had some help," Sara explained with a grin. "I couldn't wake you when I got home, so he carried you in here."

My heart thrust to life as the image of Evan carrying me to bed flashed through my head.

"How was Maggie's?" I asked Sara, rolling on my side to face her.

"Good," Sara replied dismissively. "So… what happened? I've been waiting for you to wake up for a half hour. I was going to jump on your bed if you didn't wake soon. Did he finally kiss you?"

"Sara!"

"Finally!" she concluded, not needing my confirmation. "How was it?"

"Stop it," I insisted.

"That good, huh?"

"Would you stop assuming things without my answers," I demanded with wide eyes.

"Are you going to answer?"

I smiled, deliberating if I could say it out loud.

"Stop beaming and give me *details*. You swore a million years ago that it never happened if you didn't tell me."

She got me there.

"Fine," I conceded with a sigh, sitting up against the pillow and crossing my legs. "Yes, we kissed. Actually I think he kissed me before I completed a sentence."

"No way!" Sara exclaimed. "And…"

"I don't think I can find the right words to describe it," I said pensively. "It was better than I could have ever thought possible."

"Figures," Sara stated with an exaggerated breath. "It only took you forever to give in to it. If you'd listened to me, you would have found out before the soccer season was over."

"Thanks, Sara," I shot back sarcastically, throwing a pillow at her.

"What was the talk about?" Sara inquired, determined to hear everything.

"Basically both of us taking blame for his leaving," I replied. Then I continued to sum up the details, not wanting to think about the awkwardness of the conversation too much.

Sara laughed when I told her how I reacted when he asked about Drew—and what we didn't do.

"What is it with the two of you, finding humor in my horror?"

"I guess we both know how you react in awkward situations, and it can be pretty funny. Sorry." She smirked. "What's going to happen now?"

"Well, we agreed that we're okay, and he's staying. We didn't have the *relationship conversation* if that's what you mean, and honestly, I don't think that's something I need to have with Evan."

"Because he's already told you he loves you, right?"

My face reddened as I suppressed a smile.

"Right," she confirmed.

"So what did you say we were doing tonight?" I asked, interrupting her from answering her own questions.

"You and I are going shopping today," she explained. I groaned. "Stop,. My mother's given us both gift cards for the mall. I figured it was time you owned your own pink sweater."

I grinned in agreement.

"And then we're going to Alison Bartlett's party. It's supposed to be pretty big, just to warn you."

"Great," I grunted, but I was slightly comforted when she confirmed that Evan was picking us up so that we could all go together.

As Sara was contorting my hair into a loose curly knot at the base of my neck, I considered, "Sara, you haven't mentioned an interest in anyone lately. What's going on with you?"

"I don't know," she remarked with a sigh. "I'm tired of the games, I guess. I don't think I'm going to find a guy in our school. That reminds me, we're going to New York next weekend. We're staying with my cousin at Rutgers and driving to Cornell for the day on Saturday. Coach called my parents about meetings for you. So, who knows, maybe I'll meet a college guy!"

"We're what?!" I choked.

"Sorry, I forgot to mention it. Your uncle thinks my parents are coming. They're not, so don't say anything to get caught in a lie."

I gawked at her in disbelief.

Sara added with a heavy breath before I could even think it, "Don't worry. Evan's meeting us in the city Saturday night. I asked him last night."

"I didn't say anything," I defended with a smile.

"You didn't have to," she said, rolling her eyes. "Em, I'm glad Evan's back—you know that, right?"

"Yeah," I replied cautiously, concerned by her tone.

"I want to make sure that you're going to be okay if Carol and George find out."

"I dated Drew without them finding out," I stated, not understanding what she was worried about.

"That was different," she tried to explain. "It's harder for you to hide it when you're with Evan. It'll be obvious to anyone who sees you that there's something going on with you – you're glowing. So, I need to know that it's going to be okay?"

Sara's nervousness caused me to hesitate before answering. It was going to be okay, wasn't it? I had to believe it would be.

"I hope so," I answered honestly. "Sara, I listened to what you told me that time at Janet's, about why you decided to go out with Jared, and I think I need to do the same thing. I'd rather be with Evan, knowing it may cause me some stress at home, than to never have this chance to be with him."

"It's different for you," she responded, still concerned. "You're risking a lot if Carol finds out."

"I'll survive," I promised. She didn't appear satisfied with my answer but remained silent.

"You're not going to fight this and make it hard for me, are you?" I questioned.

"No," she said with a warm smile. "I'm happy for you — honestly. So, let's go. Let's let everyone know Evan's back and that you two are *finally* together."

"Yay," I groaned, as we walked down the stairs. "That's exactly what I want tonight to be about."

30. LIFE OF THE PARTY

A VIBRANT SMILE EMERGED ON EVAN'S FACE WHEN WE NEARED THE bottom of the stairs. I couldn't help but smile in return.

"That's definitely my favorite sweater," Evan confessed when I reached the bottom step.

"I told you!" Sara exclaimed, referencing my hesitation to purchase the pink sweater with a swooping neck line that was mimicked by a low back. The heat on my face crept to my ears and down my neck.

While we were putting on our coats, Evan asked Sara, "Do you mind if Emma and I go for a quick walk before we go? I have to ask her something."

Sara flashed me a glance and answered, "Sure. Come get me when you're ready."

My heart was paralyzed in my chest, unable to think of what else he might want to know. My fear was justified when the question left his mouth.

"So, the nightmares..." he remarked quietly. "That's what Sara was talking about yesterday, huh?"

I avoided his eyes, following the ground as we walked.

"I'm sorry," he said, forcing me to look up into his distressed eyes with the tilt of his head.

"It's not your fault," I whispered.

"I'll make it up to you, I promise," he offered with a soft smile.

Evan put his arms around my waist as I reached up on my toes and pressed my lips against his. He held me tighter and sparks ricocheted

298

through my body. I breathed him in with each slow, deliberate pass of our lips. My head buzzed as his rhythm quickened and our lips parted. I let out a quick breath, pressing against him. He lifted his head with a grin.

"Why do you keep doing that?" I demanded in frustration, not wanting it to be over.

"We're in the middle of the street," he noted, glancing around. I slowly sank to my feet, releasing my hold with a sulking breath.

He wore an amused grin as we made our way back to Sara's. I examined him curiously, silently demanding an explanation.

"Just not what I expected from you," he explained. My eyes tightened in concern to which he quickly blurted, "Oh, it's not bad, believe me. It's just... you *are* interesting."

We parked in a large field across from Allison Bartlett's house, which was already filled with cars. Her house was about a mile in from the road, with no neighbors in sight – probably why it was such a popular party. The noise of conversation and music carried across the field as we stepped out of the car.

"I'm not going to be the third wheel," Sara declared. "So I'm going in by myself, and I'll meet you in there."

"Are you sure?" I asked, surprised that she preferred to go in alone rather than with us.

"Yeah, definitely," she laughed. "Besides, I want to see everyone's reaction when you walk in."

I shook my head in disbelief as she walked toward the noise.

I nervously looked at Evan as he came around the car to meet me. He stopped in front of me and took both of my hands in his.

"Ready?" he asked with a half smile.

"Sure," I shrugged.

He leaned toward me and delicately grazed my lips with his. The tease left me breathless, burning for more.

"I keep having to remind myself that I can do that," he smirked. "I've been programmed that it was off limits for so long; now it's going to take some getting used to."

"You definitely have my permission," I breathed, leaning toward him again.

299

Just before we were able to connect, I heard, "Holy shit! Evan Mathews?"

I sank back to my flat feet with a groaning sigh.

"Wait. *And* Emma Thomas? This is crazy."

I turned to face the annoyance. Of all the people to find out first!

"Hi Jay," Evan said casually. I clenched my teeth together before I turned to face him.

"Hi," I said quickly, feeling the burning cover my cheeks—so much for subtle entrances.

"When did you get back?" he asked Evan.

"Yesterday."

Jay raised his eyebrows and looked back and forth between us, "Wasting no time, I see."

My eyes widened as my mouth dropped open, "Jay!"

"Just saying," he said in his all too familiar stance of feigned innocence.

"Going in?" Evan asked, ignoring his comment.

"Yeah."

Evan took my hand and we walked alongside Jay into the house. There were people scattered on the front lawn and steps as we approached. The open door released the blare of music and voices which became practically deafening as we got closer. I pushed out a quick breath through my pursed lips before we entered. Evan squeezed my hand and glanced at me with a grin. Jay squirmed his way in ahead of us.

It was as bad as I feared. There was gawking, whispering, and even some pointing as we made our way through the crowd toward the kitchen. The guys welcomed Evan back with enthusiasm, while the girls just stared in shock, whispering to each other as we passed. Why did I think coming here was a good idea?

"You made it!" Sara praised as we squeezed into the kitchen. "Well, *everyone* knows you're here now. Jay was seriously the first person you saw?" She shook her head in amazement. "You couldn't have made a quieter entrance, could you?"

Evan laughed while I groaned at her sarcasm.

"This is crazy," I yelled to Sara as I took in the shoulder rubbing mass of bodies that continued onto the deck. Sara nodded in agreement.

"Do you want something to drink?" Evan leaned in close to ask in my ear.

I nodded.

Evan walked towards the bar and within a few feet, he was completely devoured by the crowd.

"Emma!" Jill exclaimed as she wiggled through to get to us. She looked around, "Where's Evan? I heard you came here together." Sara laughed.

"He's getting drinks," I shouted back to her, resigned that this was probably going to be the topic of the night.

"I am so excited for you," she shrieked. "Finally! I heard he came back once he heard about you and Drew."

"What?!" I yelled, shocked by the latest rumor. "Where does this stuff come from?!"

Jill shrugged.

"You're together right?" she confirmed cautiously.

"Yeah," I said slowly and then added emphatically, "but Drew has nothing to do with it."

"Let the stories begin," Sara declared with an amused expression. I eyed her disapprovingly.

"Hi!" Lauren shouted with a huge smile on her face. "You and Evan, huh? That is so amazing!"

"Hi, Lauren," I greeted with a sigh.

"Where is he?" she asked looking around.

"Getting drinks," Jill yelled back.

"Is there anywhere we can go that doesn't require yelling?" I asked.

Jill pointed to the porch. I debated whether or not I should wait for Evan, but being jostled by the crowd and having to yell to be heard was wearing on me. I was convinced he'd find us. I nodded to the girls to head out the door. We held onto each others' arms so we wouldn't get separated as we maneuvered through the human maze.

I took a breath of the cool air, relieved to be away from the confines of the house.

"Great," Jill said facing me, "now we can hear all about it. When did he get back?"

I knew this was coming, but it didn't make the grilling any less uncomfortable.

"Yesterday."

"And…" Lauren encouraged. "What happened?"

I wasn't sure what to say as I looked at their eager faces.

"There you guys are," Casey exclaimed. The girls opened the circle to welcome her.

"Emma was just telling us about what happened with Evan," Lauren explained.

"Evan's back?" Casey asked in disbelief.

We laughed at her cluelessness.

"Where have *you* been?" Jill gawked.

Casey shrugged sheepishly.

"So…" Lauren pressed, looking back at me.

"Um… he apologized; I apologized, and that's it. We're… better." They looked confused, not pleased with the lack of detail.

"That's it?" Casey asked, still not understanding what was going on.

"What do you mean?" I asked innocently.

Lauren moaned in frustration. "I wanted to hear how he swept you in his arms, begging for you to take him back, and kissed you for hours." Her dramatization caused us all to burst out laughing.

"Sorry," I shrugged, still smiling. "It's not going to happen."

"Does he know about Drew?" Jill cringed.

"Yeah," I said quietly.

"Does he know *everything*?" Casey asked in shock. I rolled my eyes knowing exactly what she meant.

"Casey!" Sara exclaimed swatting at her arm. "You really suck with keeping up. That never happened!"

"Oh," Casey said apologetically.

"Just to warn you, he's here," Lauren said. "And he's not with Katie. They broke up Thursday night. "

"That's fine," I shrugged, not really concerned with seeing Drew with or without Katie.

"They broke up already?" Sara gasped.

"Definitely," Jill murmured under her breath. She looked around, realizing she was overheard and we were all waiting for her to continue.

"Jill, don't you dare hold out," Sara threatened.

"You have to promise not to tell *anyone*," Jill stressed, then continued without waiting for our commitment. "Drew got Katie pregnant."

"No he didn't," Lauren stated in wide eyed shock.

"Well, she's not anymore," Jill continued, loving that she was the one revealing the headlining gossip.

"Did she..." Sara started, but Jill shrugged before she could ask.

"Not sure what happened exactly. Either she lost it or her parents made her get rid of it," Jill explained dismissively, not really concerned with the truth. "But I think Drew just dated her because she was pregnant and broke up with her when he didn't have to deal with it anymore."

"Wait," I interjected pensively. "When did she get pregnant?"

The girls turned toward me with sympathetic eyes – wondering the same thing I was.

"Not while you were together," Jill offered. "I guess they hooked up over the holiday break before you were *official*."

"I can't believe she was pregnant," Casey mouthed again, still absorbing the news.

I felt bad for Katie, and the fact that we were standing in the backyard at a party talking about her most intimate secret made me feel guilty.

I wandered away from the conversation, not wanting to hear anymore. I scanned the crowd along the deck, looking for Evan. I saw him at the top of the stairs searching the faces below in the yard. Our eyes connected, and he grinned, making me smile in return.

"Hi," he greeted with a crooked smile when he approached. "I figured you wouldn't want to stay inside."

I shook my head, taking the bottle he handed me. He set his hand on my lower back, escorting me back to the girls. With the exception of Sara, they all looked at us, with ridiculous gawking grins. I rolled my eyes.

"Hi, Evan," Jill sang. "Welcome back." Lauren and Casey giggled.

"Thanks," he said politely, giving me a quizzical glance. I just shook my head and sighed.

Our small group stayed outside and talked about the latest gossip, usually inspired by the people passing by. Evan and I stood there quietly, his arm around my waist, forced to listen. There would be a periodic interruption when someone recognized Evan and would ask about his return.

"I'm going to the bathroom," I told the girls while Evan was talking to a guy from the soccer team.

"I'll go with you," Sara offered, grabbing me by the arm.

"This party isn't so bad," Sara said in my ear as we climbed the stairs to the deck. I shrugged, agreeing reluctantly.

We made our way through the kitchen and found the line for the bathroom.

"I hope you don't have to go that bad," Sara said, eyeing the wait.

"I can wait," I assured her, leaning against the wall.

"Tony Sharpa asked me out," Sara confessed casually.

"When did this happen?" I asked, trying to recall how long she was in here before Evan and I found her.

"Yesterday, during study."

"Why didn't you tell me?!" I asked in astonishment.

"It wasn't that important," she laughed. "Not with Evan coming back and everything. Besides, I said 'no'. He's *the games* I was referring to earlier."

"Yeah, didn't you like him when he was dating Niki, and then he liked you when you were with Jason?"

She nodded, recalling the bad timing of their interest in one another.

"So, what's wrong now? You're both single finally," I questioned, confused.

"I don't know," she sighed. "It feels forced now."

"That doesn't make any sense," I returned in confusion.

"I heard you were here," his voice said from behind me. My heart stopped and my stomach turned. I stood frozen, unable to turn around.

Before I could pull myself together to face him, Drew appeared beside me, leaning his shoulder against the wall. My nose scrunched with the burn of liquor floating on his breath. It appeared he needed the wall to keep from falling to the floor.

"Had a little to drink, Drew?" Sara accused.

"Hi, Sara," Drew slurred with a smile. "You didn't like me, did you?"

Sara smiled, amused by his drunken honesty.

304

"Still don't," Sara replied with a malicious grin. "Maybe you should leave us alone."

We were gaining an audience. Everyone around us quieted to listen. I glanced around, wondering how to get out of this without causing a scene.

"We need to talk... in private." Drew tightly gripped my wrist and dragged me stumbling after him into the bathroom, pushing past the person who was about to enter. Sara reached out to grab me, but the crowd closed in around Drew and me, barricading Sara as we moved past them.

He forced me ahead of him and shut the door behind us, locking it.

"Drew," Sara banged on the other side of the door. "Let her out."

"Leave us the fuck alone, Sara," Drew yelled back, agitated.

I scanned the large white bathroom, looking for another way out. Drew turned and leaned his back against the door, ignoring Sara's banging.

"What do you want Drew?" I confronted coolly, despite the tremors that were overtaking me.

"Just wanted to talk to you," he jumbled, taking a step toward me. I backed away from him, dragging my feet along the tile.

"Go ahead, talk."

"Don't be like that." He reached for me, trying to take my hand. I pulled it out of reach. The music stopped abruptly while more voices banged on the door, yelling for Drew to open it. It didn't seem to faze him as he slowly approached me. I ran out of tiles beneath my feet, my back bumping into the wall.

"I just wanted you to know that I forgive you." He dragged his hand along my cheek, snagging a few strands of hair with it. A cloud of liquor floated from his parted lips as he continued, "You don't have to be with him just to get back at me."

I was confused by his words and tried to look him in the eye. Except he couldn't focus on anything—his eyes twitched in a drunken dance.

"I'll take you back," he muttered, leaning down toward me. I turned my head—his wet mouth pressed against my cheek.

The weight of his body pinned me against the wall as he trailed his tongue along my neck. I tried to shove him off, but I was his wall now, holding him up. He held me to him, ignorant of my squirming. He groped my breast while grinding into me.

305

"Drew, stop!" I yelled, pushing him back with all I could. He held tighter, aggressively pawing at me like we were in some impassioned exchange.

There was a crash of splintering wood as the door burst open. Drew was pulled from me, and all I could see were faces, staring. There were a group of guys struggling to get in. I thought I saw a glimpse of Evan in the twist of arms and hands before Sara grabbed my arm, and we rushed through the gawking mob.

Scuffling could be heard behind us with girls screaming and guys swearing. I tried to look over my shoulder before we were out the front door. I could only see bodies pushing in a frantic wave, some to get away, while others were trying to move closer.

Not long after we reached the car, Evan caught up with us. He was breathing heavily and his shirt was crumpled. He pulled me toward him and held me. I tried not to reveal how shaken up I was.

I pulled back to look up at his face. It was still flushed. Sara was standing to the side, quietly watching. "I'm okay," I assured him. "He was just really drunk. He didn't mean it."

"Don't," Evan stopped me. "Don't make excuses for him. I can't..."

He took a calming breath.

"Let's just go," he urged.

People were still staring at us from the front steps when we got into the car. The party inside resumed, with the music turned up again and the volume of voices steadily increasing. Evan took my hand in silence as we drove away.

31. NOTICED

I BEGGED THE WEEK TO GO BY QUICKLY OR FOR SOMEONE TO DO something more catastrophic and humiliating so Evan, Drew and I would be dropped from the headlines. Then Katie returned to school, and I wished I hadn't thought that. Everyone stared, whispered and pointed, avoiding her like she carried a contagion.

I knew pity wasn't what she needed, but I didn't know what else to offer. If *my* secret were released to the masses, I'd want to drop off the planet. So, whether it was the right decision or not, I left her alone. I didn't avoid her, but I didn't go out of my way to make her feel better either. My ambivalence could've been considered cowardice. Yes, it probably was. I found Katie crying in the girls' room on Friday, and slipped out before she knew I was there.

"Things are going to change around here," the foreboding voice yanked me back from my thoughts of that afternoon.

I stood in the hallway motionless, with my backpack over my shoulder and duffle bag in my hand. I had just returned from my weekend in New York with Evan and Sara. Carol met me with a hardened glare. I hadn't heard her hateful voice in so long; I'd forgotten how debilitating it could be.

"No more Friday nights at the McKinley's. You got away with it for too long and sleazed out of your responsibilities too often. You're not getting away with your shit anymore. You *should* be shoved in a box, but..."

My pulse quickened in anticipation of what she'd say next.

"...your uncle seems to think it would help with the tension in the house if we had one day to ourselves. It's not worth arguing over. *You* are never worth arguing over. So, tell Sara she can pick you up at noon on Saturday's, however you will be in this house by nine o'clock on Sunday morning.

"But, not this weekend. You're staying here to rake my backyard and my mother's on Sunday. Speaking of Sundays..."

Please don't say it.

"... you'll only be allowed to go to the library, nowhere else. If I find out that you're anywhere other than where you say you are, you *will* be living in a box until you graduate." My stomach twisted. I remained frozen, hoping she'd slither away without leaving a mark. Not so lucky.

"Am I making myself clear?" she growled, grabbing my ear, making me twist my head to follow the tugging.

"Yes," I whimpered, straining my neck.

I stood in the hall with my hand over my throbbing ear, watching my freedom disappear with her. I threw my bags on my bed upon entering my room and began pacing furiously. Why was she doing this to me? Why couldn't she have left me alone like she had for the past three months? What was the sudden interest in where I was? She hated me. Why would she want me home?

My chest tightened as I fumed at the thought of having to be with her all weekend. And knowing that I wasn't going to see Evan this weekend was more upsetting than spending it with *her*. Well... maybe not.

Unbeknownst to me, Evan and Sara decided to split my pickups and drop offs, so I wasn't expecting to see his BMW waiting for me when I walked down the driveway on Monday morning. But I was too distracted by next weekend's impending doom to be as thrilled as I should've been.

"Good morning," he greeted warmly when I closed the door.

"Hi," I responded, unable to smile in return.

"Are you ever in a good mood in the morning?"

"What?" His question distracted me from my brooding thoughts. "Oh, sorry. I'm just angry with my aunt right now."

"What happened?" His voice was heavy with concern, more than it needed to be.

"Nothing that bad," I assured, trying to put him at ease. "She's making me stay home this weekend, and I'm pissed. Sorry; I don't mean to be miserable."

"Are you going to the library on Sunday?"

"No, I'm going to her mother's to rake her yard," I grumbled.

"So…" he said without needing to say any more.

"Yeah," I sighed. "I'm trying to figure out when we'll be able to see each other."

"There's always next weekend," he consoled.

"You're giving up that easy?" I shot back, questioning his resolve.

"No," Evan replied with a light laugh. "But what other choice do we have, besides you sneaking out of your house?"

A flash of cold nerves streaked through my stomach at the thought of trying to climb out of my window without being heard. But then I was overcome with a spike of adrenaline. Could I really do this?

"That may be an option."

Evan shot me a sideways glance. "You want to sneak out of your house?" he confirmed in astonishment.

"I can do this," I declared out loud, trying to convince myself more than Evan.

The repercussions of getting caught sent a wave of nausea through me, but the thrill of getting away with it convinced me that it was worth it. I wasn't going to allow her to control my life any longer. It was more important for me to try, than to not have the chance at all. Where had I heard that before?

"You are insane!" Sara exclaimed, when I told her what I was planning to do. "If you get caught, we will never see you again!"

"But Sara," I argued, "aren't you the one who said that it was better to try and fail, than to never have the experience?"

"That's not quite what I said," she corrected. "Em, this is so much different than having a date with a guy I may never see again. You could lose everything."

I looked down at my uneaten lunch, understanding her concern. If I were the same person I'd been six months ago, we'd never be having this conversation. Too much had happened, and I wasn't ready to go back.

"Sara," I explained lowly, "what do I really have? If it weren't for you and Evan, I wouldn't even exist, or I might as well not exist. I need more than school and sports to keep me wanting to move forward. I can't be that person anymore, not now that I know the difference."

Sara sat silently, breaking off pieces of her cookie without eating them.

"Are you sure there isn't a way for you to move out of their house?" she finally questioned. "If you get caught..." She couldn't look me in the eye.

"I won't get caught," I assured her. We sat in silence for a moment, picking at our food.

"Are you going to the award ceremony tomorrow night?" Sara asked, changing the subject.

"I put it on the calendar, and they didn't say anything, so I think so."

"Are you staying at school, or should my parents and I pick you up at your house?"

"I'll probably stay here. I have to work on the newspaper and my History paper, so there's no point in going home." There was never a point in going home, but it was unavoidable, no matter how much I delayed the return. I didn't have any other choice.

∽∘

"Congratulations," she offered as Sara and I walked into the cool spring evening.

I approached her but not with the shock of our first encounter. I wasn't surprised to see her, but I was surprised by her sobriety. My mother appeared uncomfortably nervous standing on the sidewalk. She had her hands in her jacket pockets, glancing from the ground to my face, awaiting my reaction.

Sara didn't continue to the parking lot but waited a short distance away to give us room to talk. I walked closer to the frail woman who I barely resembled except for her dark brown hair and the almond shape of her eyes.

"I am so proud of you," she said gently, glancing up at me. "Captain next year, that's great, Emily."

"Co-captain," I corrected. She smiled lightly as she held my gaze with her sparkling eyes.

"I saw you play." She smiled bigger.

310

"I know," I answered quietly. "I heard you yelling in the stands." My mother's bellows were unmistakable since she was the only one yelling "Emily" amongst the cheering crowd.

"I've decided to stop drinking," she declared proudly. "I haven't had anything to drink since December." I could only nod, uncertain if I believed her words. I had no proof of the alleged truth other than her current condition.

"I got a new job too," she continued. "I'm an executive assistant at an engineering firm a couple towns over."

"You moved to Connecticut?" I questioned, shocked by this revelation.

"I wanted to be closer to you," she told me with an eager expression. "I was hoping we could see each other... if you wanted to."

My shoulders pulled back at this request. "We'll see," I replied, unable to commit. She nodded with her shoulder slumped in disappointment.

"I understand," she whispered, looking at the ground. "Are you okay?" She looked up at me again, searching for more than the three words asked.

"I'm okay," I assured her with a tight smile. Her concerned eyes didn't release their scrutiny.

"Would you mind if I went to some of your track meets? I know they're usually during the week, but if you have a weekend meet, would it be all right?"

I shrugged. "If you want." I really wanted to tell her not to come—that I preferred not to see her again. But I couldn't look into her desperate eyes and reject her so blatantly.

"I need to go," I told her, nodding towards Sara.

"Hi." My mother acknowledged Sara with her charming smile. "I'm Emily's mother, Rachel."

"Hi," Sara responded with a kind smile of her own. "I'm Sara. It's nice to meet you."

"Well, you girls be careful driving home," she told us. My eyebrows pulled together in reaction to her words. The concern sounded strange coming from her mouth.

"I'm so proud of you, baby," my mother offered with welling eyes. I couldn't stand to see the sentiment—it contradicted everything I knew of her. She was the one who didn't want me. Why should she care now?

"Thanks," I said and quickly turned away, striding toward Sara's car. Sara was a few quick steps behind me, not expecting my sudden departure.

"Are you all right?" she asked when we neared her car. "Did she say something wrong that I missed?"

"*Everything* she said was wrong," I declared, slipping into the passenger seat stiffly.

Sara studied me carefully before pulling out of the spot. I knew she wanted to understand, but she couldn't find the words to ask me to explain. So I didn't.

"Do you want to come over to my house for a little while, or do you think they're expecting you home?" Sara asked. "My parents left from here to go to a dinner for my dad's company, so they won't be home."

"I should go home," I decided quietly, looking out the window. "She's acting strange again, and I don't need her saying anything to me tonight. I don't think I could let her get away with it."

I ignored Sara's shocked expression and continued to stare out the window.

∞

"So what's the plan?" Evan asked during our walk to the Art room.

"There's a park a few streets away from my house," I explained, having dwelled on the details all week. "Meet me there at ten o'clock."

"Will they be in bed by then?" I heard the unease in his voice.

"No, but if we wait that long it will be so late." I exhaled slowly, recognizing the risk of trying to slip out with them in the next room watching television. But I also knew that they never came into my room at night, so I was fairly confident they wouldn't check on me while I was gone. "It'll be fine."

"We don't have to do this," Evan offered.

"Are you backing out?"

"No," he said quickly. "I just don't want you to get in trouble."

"Don't worry about it," I assured with forced confidence.

"Okay." He released a heavy breath before kissing me on the top of my head.

With a promise of texting Sara on Sunday as proof that I still existed, I exited her car to begin my gut wrenching weekend with Carol.

The only thing that kept me from festering in fury was the thought of sneaking out to see Evan the next night.

I spent Saturday in the yard raking while the kids jumped in the piles of leaves. Carol was nowhere to be seen, so being outside, surrounded by their laughter actually made the day enjoyable. George arrived home soon after I was done bagging the last pile. For such a small yard, it was astonishing how many leaves sat under the snow all winter. While I was out there, I moved the trash cans on the side of the house so I had a clear spot to drop from under my window. I figured I could use the metal trash can to climb back through the window when I returned, as long as I remembered to stand on the rims of the can. I was also concerned about moving the heavy can without it making noise. My stomach turned just thinking about it. Of course we were the only family in America who still owned metal trash cans – just my luck.

I had no appetite for dinner. I forced each bite of the lasagna into my mouth. It wasn't horrible since it was one of the few dishes Carol could handle without disastrous results. Not wanting to draw any unnecessary attention, I finished the food on my plate. I gently pulled down my sleeve, reminded of what Carol's attention felt like.

Was it possible that I'd forgotten what she was capable of? The enflamed skin along my forearm was a brand, a reminder of her seething affection. Carol played off my contact with the searing lasagna pan as an accident, but I saw her eyes dance when I jumped back with a quick, pained inhale. Did I really dare to test the limits of her loathing by sneaking out my window?

My stomach turned anxiously as I stared at the painted sky while washing dishes. I only had a few more hours to decide if I was capable of doing this. I thought of Evan and whether I could disappoint him. I knew he'd understand if I backed out. Then I thought of how disappointed *I* would be, and whether I could live with that. I absently rinsed the dishes and placed them in the dishwasher, the movement of my shirt irritating the raw bubbling skin.

I slipped into my room after taking out the trash, checking the can placement once again. I considered burying myself in homework to persuade time to pass quickly. But I knew I wouldn't be able to concentrate.

I opted to lie on my bed and drown my nausea with music – it didn't help. A thousand incoherent thoughts raced through my head as I stared at the ceiling. I'd start to visualize my escape route and then get worked up about the potential disasters. Could I drop the distance from the window to the ground without making a sound? Would one of the neighbors see me and say something? What would I say if they discovered I was missing or caught me outside? My stomach turned and my palms dampened.

I picked up my phone to text Evan that I wasn't going to meet him. I had the words displayed on the screen and started pulling at my lower lip. Could I do this? I wanted to see him so much. I couldn't force myself to hit *Send*. I dug my teeth into my lip and hit *Cancel*. I still had an hour and a half to decide.

The seconds ticked away like minutes – I couldn't keep still. I tapped my foot rapidly in the air, contemplating my choices. Should I give in to what I wanted to do or to what I should do? But why shouldn't I get to see Evan? Why was I letting them decide what was right for me? It's not like I was sneaking off to get drunk or get into any real trouble. They never had to know. I swallowed hard and bit my lip again.

The last forty-five minutes were the worst. I thought the heat in my stomach was going to burn through my skin. I shut off the music and listened to the low talking coming from the TV through the wall. Eventually, I slid off my bed and walked breathlessly to my closet with deliberate steps. I removed the stuffed duffle bag from the closet, placed it on my bed, and folded my comforter over it. I knew it didn't look much like a body, but I couldn't bear the thought of having my bed completely flat in my absence.

I examined the façade for a minute, almost panting with anxiety. I ran through the plan in my head one more time and inhaled quickly, biting my lip. Should I leave the window open or will the cool air be noticed if they walked by my door to go to the bathroom? How would I close it? I'd have to stand on a trash can. I clenched my teeth and held my breath in agony just thinking about moving it while they were a window away. I removed the phone from my pocket and lingered over the buttons ready to cancel once again.

Didn't George just throw away an empty milk crate that used to have paint cans in it? That would be high enough for me to reach the window to close it. I put the phone back in my pocket. I shut off my light with twenty minutes left to wait. I sat on the floor with my knees drawn into me, staring up at the window. I watched the stars blink through our neighbor's swaying trees, allowing the last few minutes to tick away. *I can do this*—I had to believe it. I took a breath to calm the pounding in my chest.

My hands shook as I placed my thumb and finger under the ridge of the wooden frame along the cold pane of glass. I held my breath, giving it a forceful, but restrained, push. The frame gave way slightly, and the first gust of cool spring air blew against my legs. I stopped to listen, with my pulse beating in my ears. I could faintly hear the voices from the TV continuing to play in the background but couldn't sense any movement.

I held my breath again and pushed the window up further. I continued inching it up until it was completely open. With my heartbeat in my throat, I slid a leg out the window and laid my chest forward to slide my other leg through. I held on to the wooden frame to drop to the ground. I nearly yelled out when I felt the hands around my waist.

"Shhh," he whispered in my ear, lowering me to the ground. I leaned my back against the house, afraid I was going to collapse from heart failure. I stared up at Evan with huge eyes, my hands covering my frantic heart.

"Sorry," he whispered. I covered his mouth, silently begging him not to make any noise.

I searched around for the milk crate. It was difficult to find in the small dark path between the house and the fence, but I finally located the square shape along the fence and placed it under the window. Evan realized what I was doing and touched my arm to indicate that he'd do it. He stood on the crate to lower the window. I pressed my lips together, barely breathing as I watched him ease it into place.

He grabbed my hand after he stepped down, and we slowly made our way along the side of the house until we reached the corner. I heard the television through the closed window above our heads and stiffened. Evan nodded his head, encouraging me to follow him. I hugged the front of the house, under the large glowing glass that peered into the living room. I knew how close they were and held my breath.

Just then, a flood light lit up across the street, exposing us in the shadows of the house. Evan grabbed my arm and pulled me against him in the dark corner that connected with the wall of the front foyer. I heard his quickened breath, or maybe it was mine. I bit my lip, inhaling quickly when Carol peeked through the curtain to investigate. She let the curtain fall, uninterested when she saw the neighbor getting into his car.

Evan released me when the car drove down the street, out of sight. I let out a small burst of air. He smiled. I widened my eyes, shocked by his reaction. He pushed his lips together to keep from laughing. I hit his arm in frustration.

Evan grabbed my hand again and rushed across the front yard. We jogged past a few houses before slowing to a walk. I jumped when I heard his voice.

"You thought we were going to get caught, didn't you?"

"No," I snapped. "But I can't believe you thought that was funny."

"I wouldn't say it was *funny*," he stated. "Well... maybe it was. I've never had to sneak out before so I did find it... entertaining."

I was still trying to convince myself that I'd made it out safely. I wasn't as amused. Evan put his arm around my shoulder, pulling me toward him. I looked up at his calm grinning face and my anxiety melted away. I released a small smile and leaned my head against his shoulder.

"It's been too long since you've been exposed to something new," Evan noted, sitting across from me on the top of the twisted climbing structure in the park.

"This was something new. I've never snuck out before. I guess your bad influence over me hasn't changed."

The whites of Evan's teeth reflected in the subtle light.

"I still can't believe you snuck out of your house," he said with a chuckle.

"What other choice did I have?" I defended, still not as amused as Evan.

"You didn't have to see me."

"Yes I did."

He leaned forward to kiss me, and my heart skipped in anticipation of the touch of his lips. I leaned in to meet him. Before I could reach him, my legs slipped through the hole that they were dangling in. I fell to the ground, landing on my feet with a thud. I groaned in frustration.

"Are you okay?" Evan smiled, looking down at me.

"Yes," I huffed. He slid down, landing in front of me. Still grinning, he put his arms around my waist and playfully rocked my hips from side to side.

"That was pretty funny." He casually bent down to kiss me.

"Great," I grunted, turning my head away. It was impossible to remain frustrated with his teasing when I felt the warmth of his kiss on my neck. I inhaled as he pulled me closer, and I wrapped my hands around the backs of his firm arms.

The fluttering rushed from my stomach and through my head as I turned to intercept his lips. They delicately slid across mine, inching with a slow sensual pace, causing a warmth to spread through my chest. I slid my arms around to grip his back and pulled myself closer. He ran his fingers in my hair as his pace quickened with my breath. When he slipped away, I kept my eyes closed, resting my head against him while still holding him tightly. His chest moved beneath me as he attempted to catch his breath.

"What should we do next Sunday?" I asked, releasing my grasp and jogging over to the swings. My sudden departure must have caught him off guard, because he wasn't behind me when I turned around to sit on the plastic seat.

"Um…" he considered, walking toward me. "Let me think about it." Evan sat on the swing next to mine with a contemplative smirk.

"I wouldn't mind going back to the batting cages," I suggested. "But I'm sure you don't want to do that since you play baseball all week."

"I'll come up with something," he promised. "Speaking of going back, I think we're good enough friends now for you to tell me who your first kiss was."

My heart skipped a beat.

"You still want to know?" I questioned.

"He doesn't go to our school, right?" Evan inquired, answering my question with his.

"No." I shook my head. "I met him last summer, when I went to Maine with Sara. He doesn't even know where I really live."

"Nice," he declared with a smile. "You're first kiss is a guy who knows nothing about you."

"Well, I didn't lie about *everything*," I defended.

"Poor guy." Evan laughed. "But you just kissed him, right?" I recognized the concern wrapped in his question.

"You know that answer," I replied. "But, what about you? I mean, I know you didn't do anything with Haley, but you never said…"

I couldn't come right out and directly ask him if he'd had sex. Did I really want to know? That question left me torn – part of me was curious, while the other couldn't imagine him being with someone else.

Evan was quiet for a moment. I almost asked him not to answer – to forget I'd asked.

"She was my best friend in San Francisco," he confessed before I could withdraw my question. My heart tightened, not prepared for his answer. "We were really great friends for over a year before deciding to date. We trusted each other, and it eventually happened last summer. But it was never the same after. We should have just stayed friends, and both of us knew it—but it was too late."

"Beth?" I whispered, recalling him mentioning her the night I met his parents.

"Yes."

"Oh," I replied, looking down, unable to say anything else.

"Does that bother you?" he asked cautiously.

I shrugged. "I didn't know you, and..." I hesitated. "I guess it's still hard to think of you being with another girl."

"I know," he replied, relating to my discomfort. A twinge of guilt shot through me.

"Do you still care about her? I mean... did you see her when you went back?" The anticipation of his answer caused my stomach to knot up.

Evan stopped his subtle swaying on his swing and turned toward me with a calm, still face.

"I've never felt like I do for you... for *anyone*," he vowed. "Beth and I were friends. I cared about her, but I didn't... It's not even remotely the same."

I swallowed hard, unable to speak.

"She moved to Japan with her family in December, so no, I didn't see her." The silence that followed was more uncomfortable than I could bear.

"I have an idea," I declared a little too loudly, as I shot out of my swing. Evan sat up straight in response to my sudden burst of energy.

"Is your car parked here?" I asked, looking toward the street that ran along the park.

"Yeah, it's over there." He pointed to the silhouette of the sports car.

"Do you have a blanket or something?"

"I have a sleeping bag in the trunk," he offered suspiciously.

"Can you please get it?" I requested with a smirk. Without inquiring further, Evan ran to get the sleeping bag.

318

I took it from him and walked to the outfield of the baseball field to open it on the ground. Evan watched curiously.

"I know you're going to think this is strange. Sara and I used to do this all the time, and I love doing it, especially when the stars are so bright."

I stood a few steps away from the sleeping bag and looked up at the sky.

"You focus on a single star," I explained, as I searched for my spot. "Then you spin around, staring at that one star, until you can't stand anymore." I started spinning to demonstrate. "Then you lie down to watch the stars spinning above you while your star remains still."

I stopped, catching my step, searching for Evan. He observed my demonstration with an amused smirk.

"You don't want to try?"

"No, but you can go ahead," he encouraged with a small laugh. He sat down on the sprawled sleeping back to witness my ridiculousness. After spinning, I lay next to him to watch the stars circling above me.

"You're missing out," I told him, as the earth swayed beneath my still body. He laughed.

My view of the streaking lights became obstructed when he leaned over me. The earth remained whirling beneath me, but it had nothing to do with spinning in circles.

I walked along my dark street, having left Evan a few houses back. The grin on my face felt permanent. The buzz still lingered from our night in the park. I slowly looked around, recognizing I was only a house away from mine. I took a deep breath in attempt to sober up.

The dark windows reduced the fear of being detected as I crept along the shadows to the side of the house where the trash cans awaited me. I held my breath and grabbed the handles on either side of the metal cylinder, lifting it with more force than was necessary. The empty can gave way easily, causing me to stumble backwards.

I recovered before bumping into the bags full of leaves set along the fence. I gently placed it under my window and used the milk crate to step on top of the can. In my post-Evan delirium, I neglected to place my feet on the edges—the metal lid popped under my weight. The deep echo rang loudly in the night. I tensed, holding on to the window sill, listening.

After a prolonged ear numbing silence, I pushed the window up. My heart stopped. It wouldn't move. I swallowed. My stomach was in my throat. I pushed it again as hard as I could. I nearly fell from the can when the window gave way and slid up. I grabbed the ledge to steady myself. With my hands on the windowsill, I lifted myself and tilted head first through the open window. I walked my hands along the floor then slowly lowered each leg from the sill.

I lay on the floor of my room, panting in relief. After a moment of listening for a stir upstairs, I moved to close the window. I removed the duffle bag from my bed and set it gently on the floor of my closet. I hung my coat on the back of the chair at the desk and slipped my shoes off. I crawled onto the bed, sinking into the mattress with an exhausted sigh and a smile, easily drifting to sleep.

∞

"Let's go," Carol declared loudly.

I shot up in my bed, dazed and disoriented.

"Did you sleep in your clothes?" she observed.

It took a moment to fight through the lingering sleep to realize that she was standing at the end of my bed with the door open behind her. I lifted the comforter to examine my attire.

"Oh, uh," I stumbled. "I must have fallen asleep reading."

She eyed me suspiciously and glanced around my room. I held my breath, fearing she saw through my lie.

"Well, you missed out on your shower," she announced. "We're leaving in ten minutes. You'd better be ready." She walked out of my room, closing the door behind her. I sat in my bed for half a minute, releasing the pressure in my lungs. Then I recalled my night with Evan, and the smile resurfaced on my face.

32. THE QUESTION

"THAT'S A PRETTY NASTY BURN," COACH STRAW OBSERVED WHEN SHE saw me on the stairs leading to the locker room. I pressed my arm to my side to conceal the deep red streak that still had blisters along it.

"I guess," I mumbled, not looking up at her, wishing I had long sleeves to pull down over it.

Coach Straw paused to look at me. Her scrutinizing glare made my stomach turn anxiously. She slowly nodded her head with a "Hmph."

"I'll see you outside," she declared dismissively, passing me on the stairs.

I hesitated, considering her stoic response.

"Are you coming?" Sara questioned, sauntering past me.

"Yeah," I said, snapping back from my paranoid thoughts.

"I cannot tell you how relieved I was to get your text yesterday," Sara announced on our way to the track.

"I told you not to worry."

"Yeah," she teased, "and you saying it makes it that easy too."

I laughed, recalling the years I must have aged in the two minutes it took to escape my room. I shared the late night's adventures with Sara while we jogged our warm up laps around the track.

"Wow," she responded slowly. "I guess I shouldn't be surprised that he's had sex. But were you?"

"Sort of," I admitted. "It shouldn't matter. It's not like he has a list or anything. But it's still strange to think of him with someone else."

"You don't think he feels the same way thinking about you and Drew? And he has to see Drew every day."

"I know," I replied, overtaken by a swarm of guilt. "But I was never going to go *that far* with Drew."

"Do you think you will with Evan?" she asked, grinning in anticipation to my answer.

My face flushed just thinking about it.

"You've thought about it, haven't you?" Sara accused when I didn't respond.

I shrugged and pressed my lips together, fighting to conceal my embarrassed smile.

"We haven't been together that long," I replied when I found my voice again.

"But you've known each other just about all year," she argued. "And just because you didn't admit it, you were stupid for each other from almost day one. So even though you've been *dating* for a couple of weeks, you've been each other's person for a lot longer."

I didn't respond. We jogged in silence until the coach blew the whistle to have us gather around for further training instructions. I was distracted for the remainder of practice. Sara's question followed me to bed that night, causing me to lie awake in the dark, contemplating the answer.

∞

"Hi," Evan greeted me the next morning when I slid into his car.

"Hi," I said quietly, my cheeks effortlessly turning a shade of red. I looked out the window when he drove away, hoping he hadn't noticed.

"Bad morning again?" he asked in response to my silence.

"Mm mm," I declined, trying to clear my head of the pressing question.

"Okay," Evan replied, baffled. "Did I miss something then?"

"No," I said quickly, trying to bite my lip to keep from smiling.

I forced myself to look at him so he could see that I wasn't upset. My cheeks felt like they were about to burst from grinning. I redirected my gaze back out the side window as the heat crept up my neck.

"I *am* missing something," Evan concluded, examining my comical expression with narrowed eyes.

I let out an uneasy laugh, begging my brain to think of something else, *anything* else.

"But you're not going to tell me what," he added. "Does Sara have something to do with this?"

I laughed again. "Sort of. Don't worry, I'll get over it."

But I couldn't. As much as I wanted to be relaxed and not think about what fate had in store, I found myself staring at him in class, wondering. I was convinced that it wasn't happening soon—but would it... could it... with him? I couldn't deny how I responded to him when we were near each other. I felt his presence in the room even when he wasn't next to me.

Evan didn't kiss me openly in school or hold me in a way that obviously indicated that we were a couple. Our affection was subtle. It didn't mean my heart wouldn't flutter when he brushed against me or that I didn't shiver from the warm tingling along my spine when he whispered in my ear so close that his breath tickled my neck. He didn't need to touch me. His attention alone, recognizing my existence, sent a flurry of sparks through my body.

By the time we could steal a moment alone, my body was pulsing with an electric charge, built up from being exposed to him all day. I tried to contain my enthusiasm when I touched his lips or ran my hands along his back. But it was hard to fight the excitement and desire to be closer to him.

So when Sara sunk the impending question in my head, I suddenly found it difficult to breathe when he stood too close to me. I hesitated before touching him, fearing my eagerness would reveal the thoughts that were consuming me. The distraction lingered the entire week, regardless of how much I tried to push it away. But then I found it was easily forgotten when Carol walked into the room.

"Shut the refrigerator, you fucking moron" she snapped.

"Huh?" I glanced around the kitchen, realizing I had the refrigerator door open in my hand. I quickly grabbed the milk and closed the door.

Carol scrutinized my absentminded action while she leaned against the counter, drinking her coffee.

"Why is the screen open in your room?"

I swallowed hard, trying not to spill the milk as I poured it over my cereal, suddenly remembering that I never closed the screen after I snuck out.

"Um," I said, clearing my throat. "I had a spider in my room, and opened the window to dump it outside. I must have forgotten to close the screen. Sorry."

I scooped a spoonful of cereal into my mouth, avoiding her eyes. Besides saying, "You really are an idiot," she didn't inquire about it further.

"I have some boxes in the back of my car that you need to bring in the house before you leave this morning. You can put them in the dining room."

"Okay," I mumbled with my mouth full. I shoveled in more spoonfuls of cereal, needing to escape her presence before she could ask any more questions or read through my lies.

I rinsed my bowl and placed it in the dishwasher before heading out the back door to unload the boxes. When I opened the back of the Jeep, I found three large cardboard boxes. I had to use both arms to pick one up. The huge box blocked my view when I lifted it, but it wasn't as heavy as I feared.

"Be careful with them," Carol demanded supervising from the deck.

I tried to ignore her as I passed by her into the house. She just stood on the deck, watching me struggle with the awkwardly oversized box. By the third one, I thought she'd finally disappeared into the house. I should have been paying better attention.

I stepped up onto the second step with my right foot, but when I lifted my left to follow—it met the slightest resistance. With the giant package in my arms, it was enough to set me off balance. My right knee buckled beneath me and slammed into the corner of the next step with all of my weight behind it. I collapsed to my knees. The box landed firmly on the board above me, still clutched in my hands.

I clenched my teeth to keep from yelling out as the jagged fire shot through my leg.

"You fucking klutz," Carol scolded from behind me. "I hope you didn't break it or else you'll be paying for it."

She slipped past me and entered the house without looking back. I followed her with a seething glare, tightening my jaw to hold back my contemptuous thoughts.

I pushed the box onto the deck and tensed when I pulled myself up by the railing. My knee streaked with pain the moment I straightened it. I yelled out through my clenched teeth, instinctively shifting my weight onto my other leg. I hopped up the steps, picking up the box to bring it into the house.

I tried to shake off the throbbing pain. I knew Evan was going to be here any minute, and I didn't want him to see me limping. I grabbed my bags and hobbled out, leaving Carol upstairs getting the kids ready for the day. I was hoping the tenderness would ease up by the time we got to school.

I reached the end of the driveway to find Evan waiting. I made every effort to walk as normally as I could, but my knee wanted to crumble under my weight, and I wanted to scream out in frustration.

"What happened?" Evan questioned in alarm, stepping out of the car.

I shook my head with my lips pressed together, unable to hide my anger. "I'm fine," I replied dismissively, sliding onto the passenger seat. He ducked back into the car and closed the door, staring at me with his brows drawn together.

"Em, really. What happened?" Evan demanded. I knew he was worried, but there was an agitation in his voice that made me uncomfortable.

"I fell on the stairs," I explained. "I was carrying a box into the house and couldn't see where I was going. I tripped and hit my knee on the step. I'll be fine. I must've landed right on my knee cap, so it kills right now."

"You tripped?" he confirmed suspiciously, finally driving away from the house.

"Yes. I tripped."

I wasn't lying. I didn't say what or *who* caused me to trip. I wasn't certain he bought my explanation, but I wasn't about to volunteer that Carol probably tripped me. I pulled up my pant leg while sucking the air through my teeth to examine my knee. Evan peered over, trying to see for himself.

There was a red mark at the point of contact, but nothing else – not yet.

"See," I presented my knee, "I just hit it funny. It'll go away."

But it didn't. I had to grit my teeth to fight through the debilitating pain as the morning progressed. By the time I saw Evan again, I was unable to support my weight on my right side.

"You're not okay," he insisted, examining the pain in my eyes.

"Fine, I'm not okay," I agreed reluctantly. "I'll go to the nurse to get some ice. I think it's starting to swell."

"I'm coming with you."

"Evan, you don't have to. It's not that big of a deal, honestly."

"We'll see," he replied sternly, taking my books from my arms. I knew he would've carried me if I'd let him.

When I gingerly pulled up my pant leg for the nurse to examine it, Evan groaned behind me.

"Ooh, honey, that looks like it hurts," the woman with the short white hair and kind eyes stated at the sight of the large purple circle on my knee. It was so swollen that my knee cap could no longer be identified. "I'm going to have you ice it for a while and keep it elevated."

I raised my eyes to get a glimpse of Evan with his lips pressed together as he stared at the purple nightmare growing on my leg. When the nurse left to retrieve an elastic wrap from the trainer's office, he inquired ardently, "You swear you tripped?"

I looked up to connect with his troubled blue eyes and affirmed, "I tripped."

The nurse instructed me to ice it on and off for the rest of the day. To my horrified dismay, she insisted I keep my weight off of it and use a pair of crutches that she removed from the closet. Evan and I made our way back to catch the end of Trigonometry. Our entrance was, of course, a blush inducing spectacle with everyone gawking at my condition. I prepared myself for the whispering.

"You tripped?" Sara confirmed with the same doubt that I'd received from Evan. My leg rested on a chair next to me at the lunch table with a bag of ice on my knee. Evan sat down across from me with a tray of food for us to share.

"Why won't you two believe me?" I questioned in an agitated tone.

"Because, I know you're lying," Sara shot back, just as aggravated. Evan's head shot up, looking between Sara's face and mine.

"You're lying?" he uttered in disappointment.

"Of course she is," Sara answered for me. "She's not *that* clumsy. She usually has help."

"Sara, stop," I insisted, observing Evan's flickering eyes. "I *did* trip. I don't know what I tripped on, because I couldn't see over the box. She was around, but I have no idea what made me fall. I can't say she wasn't thrilled to see me on my knees on the stairs, but I *did* trip."

Evan's jaw tightened. Sara shook her head in frustration.

"You don't have to cover up for her with us," she retorted. "So that means she's paying attention again, doesn't it?"

I shrugged, suddenly unable to eat my lunch.

"Let's see if you can stay at my house tonight since we have to get up so early for the SAT's," Sara suggested. "I'll call my mom during study and have her ask Carol."

The thought of seeing Carol gloat as I hobbled in on crutches made my chest tighten.

"You *tripped?*" Coach Straw repeated as she and the trainer examined my purple, almost black, knee.

Why did everyone keep asking me this?

"Yes."

"It doesn't appear to be broken," the trainer concluded after maneuvering it slightly. "The ice should help with the swelling. Stay off of it for the weekend, and if it's still swollen or you can't put weight on it by Monday, go to your doctor to have him order scans."

I *needed* it to be better by Monday. Just the thought of visiting the hospital made me queasy; forget about asking Carol or George to drive me there.

"It looks like you won't be part of practice today," Coach Straw declared. "Are you going home with Sara?" Her knowledge of my life outside of track was a little disturbing.

"Yes," I whispered.

"Well," she thought for a moment, "you can sit on the bleachers and ice your knee while you watch the baseball game if you want."

"Really?" I tried to suppress my grin. I hadn't had the opportunity to see Evan play yet. Our schedules never worked out so that either of us was free on a day the other had a meet or game.

"Doesn't your boyfriend play on the varsity team?" Coach Straw confirmed. How did she possibly know so much about me?

"Yes," I answered quickly. "Thank you."

"So?" Sara demanded when I exited the office.

"I am watching baseball today," I announced with a wide grin.

"Great. But are you okay?" she reiterated impatiently.

"I need to stay off of it, ice it, and see what happens on Monday," I reported.

"You're all set to stay over tonight, but I have some bad news," she stated, pressing her lips together. "My grandfather's back in the hospital, so we're going to New Hampshire to see him after the SAT's. That means you won't be able to stay over tomorrow night."

"Oh," I replied softly. "I hope he's okay."

"He's fine," she assured dismissively. "He probably ate the wrong thing that backed him up or something. It's never anything serious. I'm really sorry."

"That's fine," I returned, trying not to appear disappointed. "At least I don't have to deal with her tonight."

Sara and I continued outside and then went our separate ways. She agreed to find me after practice if the game wasn't over. I hopped over to the bleachers next to the baseball field. The teams were still warming up when I sat on the first row of the bleachers. I settled onto the hard seat with my leg resting on the metal plank, excited to watch the game.

33. DISCOVERY

"YOU COULD STAY AT MY HOUSE ON SATURDAY," EVAN OFFERED
when I told him that Sara's wasn't an option. The three of us sat on the
bleachers after I watched Weslyn win their game.

"That could work," Sara agreed with a smirk. I gawked back at her,
unable to believe she was agreeing with him. "My parents won't say that
you weren't with me. Your aunt and uncle will never know. Em, you
won't have to go home until Sunday morning."

"My parents won't be home, so they won't say anything," Evan
added. This revelation didn't make my decision easier, it actually made
it harder.

I considered my options and reluctantly agreed to spend Saturday
night at Evan's.

"You are in so much trouble," Sara taunted when we drove to my
house to grab my clothes for the weekend.

"Shut up, Sara," I shot back. "You're the one who thought it was
such a great idea."

"You have to tell me every single detail."

"Stop it. Nothing's going to happen," I declared, trying to convince
myself more than Sara.

Sara accompanied me into my house to help carry my bag. I thought
it was best not to provoke the situation by using the crutches, so I
limped in, trying to creep unnoticed through the kitchen while the
family ate in the dining room.

Carol greeted us with a disturbing smile in the kitchen.

"Hi Sara," she beamed. It was nauseating to witness. "Emma, the nurse called. She wants to make sure you rest your leg this weekend and continue icing it. So, lie low, okay?" Her false concern made me cringe.

"Okay," I said, unable to meet her eyes, continuing to inch toward my door.

"Chores on Sunday morning, alright?" she sang in a sickeningly sweet voice. I nodded.

I didn't know who she was trying to fool. We knew the monster that dwelled under her façade.

"Good luck with the SAT's."

"Thank you," Sara replied politely. I turned to escape the bizarre exchange and headed to my room.

We packed silently, the tension thick, knowing Carol was within earshot. I'm sure she was dying to overhear me say something about her to Sara, but there was no way I was going to give her ammunition for her next ambush. I threw clothes on my bed, and Sara stuffed them into the duffle bag.

I breathed easier when I was back in Sara's car.

"She is so strange."

"I don't think that's the right word for her," I grumbled.

"Just you and me tonight?" Sara confirmed. I realized she and I hadn't had much time alone since Evan's return.

"Sounds perfect."

Sara and I watched a movie and ate pizza. I let her paint my toes a horrible shade of purple that resembled the color of my knee. We were in bed early for a Friday night, in preparation for the SAT's the next morning.

❦

"Don't even ask," I scowled at Evan, entering the halls after sitting for hours reading questions, writing essays, and filling in what seemed like a million little circles. My mind raced through question after question, second guessing and scrutinizing my responses. My head was spinning, and my stomach was upside down, knowing my future now rest in another's hands.

"Okay, I won't ask you how you think you did," Evan promised. "Let's get something to eat. Everyone's going to Frank's if you want to go."

"That's fine," I agreed.

"How'd you do?" Jill asked with way more energy than anyone should have after spending hours on tests that would decide her future. She slid in at the booth across from us, eagerly awaiting my answer.

I dropped my head in my arms and groaned.

"She doesn't want to talk about it," Evan explained.

"Come on, Emma," Jill exclaimed, "you of all people shouldn't be worried about how you did."

"It all ran together," I complained, my voice muffled since I refused to lift my head. "I don't remember any of it. I could have answered anything, and I would have no recollection of whether it was correct or not. I think I'm going to throw up."

"Relax," Kyle urged. I didn't realize he was sitting next to Jill. "It's over now, so it doesn't matter."

"Easy for you to say," I mumbled, peering up at him from my defeated position, "you've already been accepted to college." Evan flashed his amused grin, which didn't help my anxiety at all. Knowing my angst was entertaining only made it that much worse.

"Please don't tell me you're going to be in a bad mood all day?" Evan pleaded as I hobbled on the crutches to his car.

"I'll get over it," I promised with a heavy sigh. "What are we doing today?"

"Not much. You need to stay off your leg. I thought we'd play video games or something so you can keep your leg up."

"Is that going to drive you crazy?" I asked, concerned that my immobility was going to bore him.

"No," he replied with a grin. "I don't always have to be doing something. I can just hang out."

And that's what we did for the rest of the afternoon – hung out on the couch above the garage. I watched Evan play the video games more than I participated. I was too frustrated with all of the buttons and knobs, unable to catch on to what I had to press or turn and when. I opted to prop my leg on his lap, observing his gaming skills while I iced it. It could have been worse.

"Want to watch a movie?" Evan offered while we sat in the kitchen, eating one of his creations for dinner.

"You know I'll fall asleep."

"I don't mind," he smiled.

"Where do you watch movies?" I inquired, realizing the only televisions I'd seen were in the barn and in his room.

"My room."

A sudden streak of panic made me more alert than I'd been all day. I tried to appear unaffected by his response, but I was hyperventilating on the inside.

"Do you play the piano?" I asked, trying to think of something to do besides go to his room.

"A little," he admitted slowly, not expecting the question.

"Will you play for me?"

Evan's cheeks flushed, making me smile. It was something I didn't see very often.

"Now you *have to*," I taunted after seeing how uncomfortable my request made him.

"I'll try," he said with a deep breath.

After we—or I should say, Evan, since he wouldn't let me help—cleaned up, I followed him to the piano. Evan sat on the bench and I scooted in next to him. He looked at me hesitantly and poised himself to play. I was truly excited to witness another one of his talents. Before he pressed the keys under his fingers, he looked at me again and shook his head.

"No, sorry—can't do it."

"What?!" I exclaimed disapprovingly. "You have to."

"No." He shook his head again, "I can't. Let's go listen to people who actually know what they're doing."

Without giving me a second to resist, Evan scooped me up in his arms and headed for the stairs.

"Evan, you really don't have to carry me." Being held sent a rush of color to my cheeks. And knowing that he was carrying me to his bedroom didn't help cool them.

"It'll take too long for you to hop up the stairs," he countered.

He nudged the door open with his shoulder and gently laid me on the bed. I quickly pushed myself up to sit, my pulse beating a thousand miles a minute. Evan selected a song with a catchy beat. A distinct voice, singing about being alone with a girl. He turned down the volume so that we could talk.

"I have to ask you something," Evan confessed nervously, sitting next to me on the bed, "and I know you're not going to like talking about it."

I remained still, already not liking it.

"When Sara said that 'she's paying attention again,' was she right?" After a moment of silence, he added, "And please don't lie."

I looked from his desperate eyes to my lap, where I dug my fingernails into my thumb.

"I don't know," I whispered. "I don't understand her enough to even begin to know what provokes her. But I'm not worried, and I don't want you and Sara to be either."

I met his eyes and pressed my lips into the slightest smile, trying to comfort him. It didn't relieve his troubled expression.

"I was serious about leaving with you."

I smiled wider.

"You know that, right?" he confirmed again, more adamantly. "Just tell me, and we'll leave."

"It's not going to come to that," I assured him, still smiling at his commitment to rescuing me. "I can get through this, as long as you promise not to leave again."

"I promise," he vowed and leaned in to kiss me.

I surprised him when I immediately asked a question after his lips separated from mine, not giving us the option to get carried away. He asked me to repeat it, obviously not prepared to talk. I was determined not to give in to the craving. I was going to be in control… or asleep.

"Emma," Evan whispered in my ear. My cheeks tightened as I smiled at the tickling of his fingers along my neck. "You can stay in here if you want, or you can sleep in the guestroom."

My eyes shot open. Evan was looking down at me as I lay on his chest with my arm casually draped across him. I sat up and looked around the dark room. The only source of light was from the television airing a late night talk show.

"Um," I responded, shaking off the haze of sleep, "the guestroom is fine."

"I'll get your bag and crutches," he offered.

"I don't need the crutches. I think I can put some weight on it."

He examined me skeptically.

"Honestly, I think it's feeling better."

Evan disappeared down the stairs, after pointing out a door down the long corridor that led to the guestroom. In his absence, I limped to the door, slowly putting more weight on my injured leg. It was still sore but definitely better.

I opened the door to reveal a delicately decorated room adorned with several paintings of pink, yellow and blue flowers. I recognized Vivian's influence in the white duvet with pink roses embroidered around the edges. The cream colored walls brightened the space, in complete contrast to Evan's dark room.

"This okay?" Evan confirmed from behind me.

"Yeah," I replied, limping over to sit on the edge of the bed.

Evan set my bag on the floor and hesitated.

"Um, good night." I wasn't sure what I should have said, but I don't think that was what he was expecting.

"Oh, yeah. Good night." He gave me a quick peck on the lips and walked out the door.

I collapsed onto my back with my arms spread beside me, releasing an aching sigh. I did the right thing, right? I *should* be sleeping in here, not in his room. After prepping for bed in the private bathroom, I slipped under the world's softest sheets and shut off the lamp on the white pedestal table.

Eyes, please close.

Willing myself to sleep was not working. I stared into the dark, fighting the desire to go to him. The beating in my chest was loud and steady – I could feel it in my throat. I needed to fall asleep—or at least turn over so I wasn't staring at the door any longer.

"Em? You awake?" Evan whispered. I couldn't help but smile when I turned over to find his head peering through the crack of the door.

He smiled back. "Knowing you were right down the hall was way too hard. I couldn't do it," Evan declared, sliding under the covers next to me. "Hi."

"Hi." I smiled wider.

"How's your knee?" he asked with his head on the pillow next to mine.

"You did not come in here to ask me about my knee," I accused.

He shook his head with a smirk and pulled me toward him. Although his lips were familiar to me, I still lost my breath when we connected. I became entranced by their slow soft passes over mine. My mouth parted to his advances with a soft breath. His hands slipped under my tank top, along my back. He stirred a warm tingling within me when he delicately traced his fingers along my stomach. I released a quick breath and pulled him closer—then winced as my knee hit his.

"Are you okay?" he questioned, pulling away – too far away.

"I'm okay," I whispered. He didn't move. "I promise—I'm fine."

Reluctantly, Evan moved closer until we were touching again. I kept my right leg on the bed behind my left, to protect us from another painful interruption. I was easily lost in his warmth again. I slid my hands under his shirt, running my fingers along the smooth curves of his chest and down to his waist. He inhaled quickly. He reached around and pulled his shirt over his head. My heart stopped. I breathlessly observed the silhouette of his defined, lean muscles in the dark and bit my lip. He leaned in to drag his parted lips along my neck.

When I thought we'd stop, we didn't. There wasn't a warning in my head urging me to slow down. All I could hear was our quick breaths. All I could feel was his touch on my heated skin. My head spun, and my pulse quickened; eventually releasing a moan I didn't know I had in my depths. Our discovery of each other left my chest rising with long, drawn breaths. There wasn't a quick retreat but a slow and gradual withdrawal as his arms settled around my waist, and I nuzzled into his neck, brushing it softly with my lips.

"How's your knee?" he whispered, kissing the top of my head.

I'd completely forgotten about my knee, but now I recognized the throbbing that kept pace with my heart.

"I'll be okay," I assured him.

"I'm going to get you some ice," he insisted, moving away from me. I instantly missed the warmth of his body, watching him slide his shirt over his head to conceal his defined lines before stepping out the door.

I lay on my back, awaiting his return. My eyes were slowly blinking closed when I heard the distinct clinking of ice. Evan slid his pillow under my knee before setting the bag of ice on it.

"I'm going to my room, so I don't bang your knee while you're sleeping," he stated, easing the down comforter over me before kissing my forehead. "Good night."

"Good night," I murmured with a delicate grin, already drifting to sleep. I knew in that moment, I would never love anyone in my life the way I loved Evan Mathews.

34. PAYING ATTENTION

"WHAT DID YOU DO?" SARA EXCLAIMED MUCH LOUDER THAN necessary when we drove away from Evan's the next morning. "And don't you dare say 'nothing', because you are glowing."

I pressed my palms against my fiery cheeks, knowing she saw way more than I intended.

"Not what you think," I corrected. "But, it was... interesting." I couldn't hold the smile back. I stared out the window, unable to make eye contact with her.

"Uh, 'interesting' is not details," she said impatiently. "You're not going to tell me, are you?"

"Not today." I grinned. But I would eventually. Not in the explicit detail that she would have liked, but enough so that she knew.

I was so caught up in the mind buzzing thoughts that fueled my glow when I returned home, that I barely registered my discomfort as I limped around on my leg, completing my chores. I was also oblivious when Carol came up behind me while I washed the previous night's dishes.

The knife slipped through my soapy hands with a quick, forceful withdrawal.

I inhaled sharply at the sting of the blade against the inside of my fingers.

"Oh, did I get you?" Carol remarked snidely. "I needed it."

I held my fingers tightly, glaring at her while what I really wanted to say screamed in my head. The blood dripped through my clenched fingers and spread in the water below. She set the knife on the counter, with no intention of using it, and left the kitchen with a malevolent smirk.

I reached across the counter and grabbed a handful of paper towels, leaving a trail of red in my wake. I wrapped them around the padded section of my sliced fingers, right below my knuckles. The blood easily soaked through the papery material.

I cradled my hand and walked into the bathroom, turning on the water to flush out the wound. My fingers pulsed as the blood flowed freely, swirling with the water down the drain. I had to use a towel to apply enough pressure to stop the bleeding. I knew I'd have to do everything I could to remove the bloodstains later.

Within a few minutes of strangling my fingers, the gapes in the fleshy tissue only trickled instead of gushed. I wrapped them with bandages as tightly as I could to allow the slices to clot. I clenched my teeth, shaking my head in disbelief at her cunningness. I pressed my lips together, flexing my jaw. The anger she provoked was not as easy to push away anymore. I was overtaken by the fury, and it lingered long after it should have been tucked deep inside.

Sara and Evan both eyed my wrapped fingers throughout the day on Monday, but it wasn't lunch that Sara said something.

"Are you going to tell us, or what?"

I rolled my eyes at her insistence. "Cut my fingers washing a knife," I responded flatly.

Sara shook her head and folded her arms across her chest. "All four of them?"

"The truth," Evan demanded, not allowing me to get away with the weak explanation. I didn't like the accusing way they were both staring at me. This wasn't their problem. They didn't need to make me feel like I'd done something wrong.

"Listen, I'm not going to tell you what happened. If you don't like my explanation, then you can fill in the blanks as you see fit. I'm not going to tell you anything more. You know where I live, and you know who I live with. I don't need to relive it again by telling you." Aggravated beyond what I could contain, I pushed myself away from the table and walked, or slightly limped, out of the cafeteria.

Neither Sara nor Evan said anything to me during Journalism class. They allowed me to fester in my own space for the fifty minutes of class. But as soon as it was over, they bombarded me again.

"You can't be mad at us," Evan implored. I kept my back to them while sitting at the computer.

"Emma, you have a tendency to downplay your injuries," Sara added. "You have to understand that we're going to be concerned."

"I can handle it," I snapped, spinning around in my chair to face them.

"Didn't you tell me something similar that afternoon on the track, right before you ended up in the hospital?" Sara's raised voice cracked as she finished the sentence. I remained silent and stared at the floor.

Evan scooted a chair in front of me and gently held my uninjured hand in both of his.

"We know you can handle more than you should," he stated soothingly, "but this is making us... nervous. I really think we should..." I shot my eyes at him, becoming panic-stricken when I realized how he intended to finish that sentence. He didn't finish his thought. The silence said enough.

"You don't understand," I whispered, dropping my gaze. "I can't leave their house. Not yet. I don't want to risk ruining Jack and Leyla's lives. I could also lose everything I've worked so hard for. Besides, I have nowhere to go."

"You..." they both began.

"Nowhere that I could stay without it causing more problems or exposing my secret," I corrected. "Do you really think they'd let me leave quietly, or live in the same town, wondering what I was telling your parents? I would have to leave Weslyn, and then people would start asking questions. I have no choice."

They understood. I could see it in their broken expressions. I shared with them the thoughts I'd already processed a hundred times before in my head. They finally got a glimpse of the true threat in exposing my situation. We would all lose. I hoped I convinced them that the risk of staying was worth it.

"I promise you," I vowed, looking between Evan and Sara, "I will know when I can't do it anymore, and then we can go anywhere you like." I finished my sentence looking at Evan. Sara's eyes flinched in confusion, but she didn't ask for an explanation—she understood enough.

"Besides, I only have four hundred and eighty days left." I smiled, trying to lighten the mood. It didn't work.

The next two weeks passed without incident. It helped that we spent the Easter holiday with Janet, and then I spent most of the week of vacation with Sara. George and Carol took the kids to the theme parks in Florida, leaving me behind, of course. Little did they know, Sara and I escaped to Florida as well to visit her grandmother for four days on the Gulf Coast while Evan was in France snowboarding with a friend from San Francisco.

"I think that would be a great gift for his birthday," Sara confirmed while we lounged on the soft white sand, the warm breeze blowing through our hair.

"You don't think it's too..." I scrunched my face, trying to find the right word.

"No, it's perfect."

"I think Ms. Mier will let me do parts of it in class as an assignment too. You know I'm having dinner with his parents on Sunday, right?"

"No, you didn't tell me that," Sara exclaimed, sitting up to face me.

"Do you remember his mom asking me to dinner back in the fall?"

"Yeah," she recalled eagerly.

"Well, she's insisting it be this Sunday. I can't believe I didn't tell you this," I pondered. "Oh, and the worst part is that she invited Carol and George as well."

"She did not," Sara gaped.

"Well, I actually had to ask them since I can't give my phone number to anyone besides you."

"So they know about Evan now?" Sara concluded, still unable to close her dropped jaw.

"They were going to find out eventually," I returned with a slight shrug. "You should have seen Carol's face when she found out I was dating someone. I think her irises turned red. It was pretty creepy."

"Are they going?" Sara asked in horror.

"Of course not," I responded as if stating the obvious. "But George was okay with *me* going, despite Carol."

"Em, this is going to be so bad, isn't it?" I watched as Sara's posture sank with the realization that, after all we'd done to conceal Evan from Carol, she'd found out about him. I accepted this inevitability the moment we kissed in the Art room. I had prepared for it until my stomach turned inside out—hoping that I was ready. Sara, obviously, was not.

"What could she possibly do that she hasn't already done?" I offered Sara, trying to put her at ease—without success.

"You're going back home after the track meet on Saturday, right?"

"Yes," I answered suspiciously.

"You have to text me within an hour of being home to let me know you're okay," she demanded.

"Sara, stop."

She silenced me with a stern stare. I knew I had to give in to her demands or risk being ignored for the remaining two days in Florida.

"Fine," I promised with an exasperated sigh, "I'll text you."

Neither of us mentioned it again for the rest of the week. As Saturday approached, Sara became more anxious. Her nervous energy distracted me from being nervous myself. I focused on seeing Evan at the meet, and that was enough to keep from thinking of Carol.

35. SABOTAGED

"Don't forget to text me," Sara insisted for the twentieth time when she dropped me off after the track meet that Saturday. I waved in confirmation with a roll of my eyes and walked up the driveway.

I prepared myself for whatever waited for me inside as I ascended the steps to the deck. The dining room hummed with little voices. Carol's voice carried through the kitchen, talking to George, in a calmer than usual tone.

"Emma!" I was greeted joyfully by Leyla who attacked my legs before I could bend down to embrace her.

"Put your things in your room," Carol instructed passively. "We're about to sit down and eat."

The pleasantness in her voice caused me to pause. I glanced around, having a hard time believing that she was actually talking to me. I obeyed warily.

"How was your time with Sara?" she asked, glancing toward me when I sat in my usual seat where a plate of spaghetti with meatballs was already served at my setting.

"Fine," I replied cautiously, still uncomfortable with the attention.

"That's great," she smiled. The expression looked odd on her face, having never truly seen her smile at me before.

I waited for something catastrophic to happen. But nothing did. Carol redirected the conversation back to George. They discussed a trip to the hardware store the next day to pick out flowers and shrubs for the front yard.

∞

There were so many alarms going off in my head the second I walked through the door the previous night, but there was no way I could have known, or ever suspected her of being so cruel. Even when it became obvious that this was her doing, it was still difficult to understand what really happened.

"Well, I guess you won't be in any condition to go to your *boyfriend's* tonight, will you?" Carol jeered, poking her head in the bathroom the next morning. She closed the door behind her, leaving me in my misery.

A cold sweat broke out across my forehead and down my back, right before my stomach convulsed. My body quivered at the exertion that kept me up throughout the night. I collapsed on the floor, pleading for death, or at least sleep. How could I possibly have anything left in my stomach after being in here for an entire night?

"You should call them to let them know you won't be able to make it," Carol bellowed through the door. I glared in contempt at the closed door, wishing she'd fall off a cliff.

I pushed myself up to sit against the bathtub, covering my face with my shaking hands. I lifted myself from the floor and groaned when every muscle in my body screamed in agony. My stomach turned again, and I leaned over the toilet. Nothing happened, so I slowly straightened to walk to the phone in the kitchen.

The effort to move was unbearable. My head was unsteady on my shoulders as I dragged my body through the kitchen, cradling my stomach. When I reached the phone, I realized I didn't have Evan's number memorized. I groaned at the thought of having to get it from my room. Then I noticed a piece of paper on the counter that had "Mathews" scribbled in her writing. The phone number was written beneath it. How did she have their number?

I pressed the numbers on the keypad, anticipating the voice on the other end. The anxiety agitated my stomach; I clutched it with my free arm as it began to roll. The phone rang several times before it was picked up.

"Hello?" Evan answered on the other end.

"Evan," I said in a voice I barely recognized.

"Emma?" Evan confirmed, concern resounding in his voice. "Are you okay?"

"I am so sick," I rasped. "I have a stomach bug or something. I'm so sorry I won't be able to come to dinner tonight."

"Do you need me to come get you?" he offered in alarm, skeptical of my explanation.

"No, really," I pleaded. "I just need to go to bed." My stomach gurgled in warning, and I knew I couldn't stay on the phone.

"I'll see you tomorrow morning?" he confirmed softly.

"Mmm," I groaned in affirmation before hanging up the phone and rushing back to the bathroom.

There was nothing left in me, but my body was determined to purge any trace of whatever it was that had invaded it. The convulsions left me weak and trembling. By the time night came around, I was finally able to make it to my bed, where I curled up under the covers and wished I wouldn't wake up again if this was how I was going to feel. But I woke up anyway.

I somehow managed to prepare for school the next morning. I knew that I wasn't allowed to stay home alone, and the repercussions of having Carol or George miss a day of work were more than I could fathom. I showered and wrapped my wet hair in a low knot above my neck. I sipped a glass of water, hoping it would relieve the trembling, before making my way out the door.

I practically collapsed in Evan's car, wanting so much to be under my covers again. I pulled my knees into me and buried my face in my arms. He didn't say anything for a full minute after we pulled away from my house. But a minute was all it took for my stomach to register that I'd attempted to put something in it.

"Evan, pull over," I whispered with an urgency that he recognized. When the car stopped, I forced myself out and staggered to the back just before my body rejected the fluid. I took a few cleansing breaths, willing the spasms in my stomach to stop while I supported myself on the back corner of his car. I slipped back into the car and put my face in my hands.

"You're not going to school," Evan determined. I could only groan. I barely noticed where we were going until the car pulled in his empty driveway.

"Evan, I can't stay here," I argued in a rasp. "I will get in so much trouble for missing school."

"I'll have my mom call in to excuse us."

I gave in and opened the door, setting my feet on the ground and taking an uneven breath before forcing my legs to receive my weight. Evan hovered. I knew he wanted to help, but I shook my head to fend him off. I followed him through the house, allowing him to take off my shoes after I collapsed on his bed. My eyes were closed the second I was enveloped by the warmth of his blankets. His hand gently brushed against my clammy face right before I drifted into a comatose sleep.

My eyes fluttered open in the dark space. I glanced around without moving my head. I recognized the comforting scent and knew where I was. Then I remembered why I was there and I moaned. Did he really see me throw up?

I peeked next to me and discovered that I was alone in the room. I listened for the warning growls of my stomach, but my stomach was calm, and my head was clear. I pressed my dry tongue to the roof of my mouth, craving water. I pushed myself up to sit, grimacing at the soreness of my abused back and stomach muscles. At least the excruciating body aches had subsided.

I stiffly moved to the bathroom to investigate how horrible I looked. I wasn't disappointed when I observed the ghostly reflection staring back at me—I was a disaster. Was there any way I could slip out and have Sara pick me up without Evan seeing me?

I let down my damp hair and combed my fingers through it, and I immediately put it back in the elastic, horrified by the results. I rinsed my face and mouth, attempting to be recognized as human again. I took a dab of toothpaste and put in on my finger, rubbing it on my teeth and tongue to conceal the aftermath of a day and a half of throwing up.

"Emma?" Evan called from the bedroom.

I peeked out through the bathroom doorway.

"How are you feeling?" he asked cautiously.

"Like someone scraped me off the road." He smiled at my answer, the worry washing away. "Oh, and I look like it too."

"No you don't," he assured, meeting me with open arms when I stepped out of the bathroom. I allowed him to wrap me in his warm embrace. He kissed the top of my head. "You look better than you did this morning. I heard that people could look green, but I'd never seen it before."

I tried to push away with a huff, but he tightened his hold, letting out a quick laugh.

"You still look pale, though," he observed. "Do you want to lie down?"

I nodded. He released me, and I slipped back under the blankets.

"I brought you some tea to try to get some fluids back into you, and it shouldn't upset your stomach—or at least that's what my mother told me."

"Is she here?"

"No, but I had to tell her you were sick, so she would call the school for us. She's called a couple of times to check on you and to give me way too much advice on how to take care of you. I tried to explain that you were still sleeping, but that didn't stop her."

Evan sat on the bed next to me, with his back against the headboard. He eased me over so my head rested on his lap, then he drew his fingers along my hairline. I closed my eyes, soothed by the tingling that traced his touch.

"What time is it?" I whispered.

"After two."

"I can't believe I slept that long."

"Me either. I had to check a few times to make sure you were still breathing. You never moved."

"I'm still breathing," I assured him quietly, with a small smile.

"I'm glad you're feeling better." He ran his hand down the back of my neck. The warm chills continued down my spine.

I sat up and searched for the tea on the table next to the bed. I took the smallest sip and let the warmth settle in my stomach before I felt it was safe to drink more.

"You still have your state ID from your trip with Sara, right?" Evan asked out of nowhere.

"Yes," I answered slowly.

"Do you have access to your birth certificate and social security card?" he inquired further. I drew my eyebrows together and remained silent.

"I think you should try to get them – just in case," he explained.

I knew he was serious, and that's what made it so strange to hear. He really was prepared to escape with me.

"I can tell George I need them to apply to the camp this summer. You're really serious about this?" I asked, studying his face.

"Yes, I am." I dropped my eyes, struck with the understanding of what he'd be giving up too. Going into hiding would mean sacrificing his family and friends, not to mention dropping out of high school.

"Evan, it's not going to come to that. I mean, really – where would we go?"

"Don't worry," he consoled with confidence. "I've given it a lot of thought. Besides, it wouldn't be permanent."

I decided not to question him further in fear of hearing any more of his plan. I refused to admit that it would ever get so bad that we'd be forced to run away. Evan believed in this plan because it was the only thing that he thought he could do to help me. It wasn't realistic, but I wasn't going to tell him that.

I did get the documents from George. Evan was relieved. But I wasn't. I couldn't tell him that I was paralyzed with fear at the thought of leaving and that I wasn't convinced I could do it. He just had to believe I could—at least until I was forced to decide.

36. DINNER

"WHERE IS IT?" SHE SHRIEKED, STARTLING ME AS I POURED A CAPFUL of detergent into the washer.

Stunned, I watched her rush to the laundry area and begin throwing clothes around. The clothes started bouncing against my body. Of course they didn't hurt, but the ferocity behind the throws still made me flinch.

"What did you do with it?" she demanded.

"What?" I asked quietly.

"The fucking towel," she screamed. "The one you ruined. What the fuck did you do with it?"

"I don't know what you're talking about," I lied. I'd thrown away the bloodstained hand towel I used to stop my fingers from bleeding. But how did she know?

"You know exactly what I'm talking about, you worthless piece of shit."

She continued throwing clothes in my direction. She looked ridiculous in her fit of rage, creating a windstorm of clothes tossed about the basement. I straightened up, no longer cowering, and I looked at this pathetic woman for the first time. My stomach twisted in disgust and anger. I was fed up with her irrational tirades.

"It's just a towel," my voice bellowed over her screams. She froze, shocked by the strength in my tone.

"What did you say?" she hissed. I stared back, unwavering, even with her "how dare you" look. As I stood there, staring her down, I suddenly realized how much taller I was than her. I smirked at the thought of my shrinking cowardice.

"It's just a towel," I repeated calmly, but with a confidence that kept me extended above her. I turned to shut the lid of the washer.

"It's just a towel?" she grunted, shoving the softener bottle right in my gut when I turned around. The air rushed from me, bending me in half as I held my stomach. She raised the bottle again and came down on my shoulder, crumpling me to the floor. I wanted to run for the stairs, but there was one last blow to my left arm, and I folded against the washer. "Don't ever fucking talk to me like that again."

"Carol," George yelled down the stairs, "you down there? Your mother's on the phone."

Carol trod off, grumbling, "Clean this up," before she climbed the stairs.

I collapsed to the floor, still breathing heavily from getting the wind knocked out of me. My fists were clenched, my nails digging into my palms. I inhaled deeply to calm the fire. It didn't disappear completely, but it was enough so that I could pull myself up and begin picking up her mess.

"Emma," George knocked on my door. "Evan's here."

My throat closed – he was *in* my house? What was he thinking?

"Okay," I squeaked, unable to find my voice. "I'll be right there." Something rolled inside me as I grabbed my jacket and walked down the hall.

"Hi," I said with wide eyes. He ignored my anxiety and smiled back.

"It's great to finally meet you," Carol declared with the widest smile. It was torturous to witness.

"You too," Evan returned politely.

"Well... we should go." The words rushed from my mouth in a single breath.

"Ten o'clock, okay?" Carol confirmed in her sweet tone. I winced at the sound.

"Yeah." I tried to force myself to smile, but if felt more like a grimace.

Evan put his hand on my back to escort me out. I stiffened, knowing they were still watching us. I hoped she hadn't noticed that he was touching me.

"What were you thinking?" I exclaimed in a whisper while we walked down the driveway.

"Em, they knew you were coming over to my house," he explained. "I couldn't bring myself to just pull up and honk. It doesn't matter who they are; that's not who I am."

It was unsettling to see him in my kitchen – the place of so much pain. The two images fought in my brain, making the discomfort harder to relinquish.

"You don't have to walk me to the door tonight, okay?" I pleaded.

"Okay," he agreed reluctantly. "But can I at least kiss you goodnight?" A smile flashed across his face, relieving my anxiety.

"We'll see," I replied with a teasing grin.

When we neared his house, a new anxiety revealed itself. My chest closed in around my lungs.

"Are you ready for this?" Evan asked, pulling into the driveway.

"Sure," I exhaled, trying to force a composed smile. He laughed at my unsuccessful attempt.

Evan took my hand as we walked up the porch steps. I guess it didn't matter to him that his parents saw us touching. This was going to be so strange.

"Emily, welcome," Vivian greeted when we entered. She floated over to give me an embrace, I was finally prepared for, and I awkwardly returned the gesture.

An enticing aroma floated across the kitchen as we sat at the peninsula. I was still awed by Vivian's grace as she glided around the cooking space, stirring, chopping and mixing. I'd always associated the setting with Evan, but tonight, Evan sat next to me and observed his mother on the other side, with his hand affectionately on my back.

"Do you want me to do anything?" he offered.

"No, we're just about done," she announced. "Your father's removing the steaks from the grill, and I'm putting the salad together. Well, you could offer Emily something to drink."

"Oh, yeah, sorry," he fumbled, redirecting his attention to me. "What would you like to drink?"

"You know what I like," I responded. A small grin appeared on his mother's face with my response.

"I'm happy to see you're feeling better," she offered. "I understand you were rather ill last weekend."

"Yes, but I'm feeling much better now. Thank you."

"I hope the tea helped."

"It did, thank you," I replied politely, not recalling if I finished the cup. Evan tried to conceal his smile, probably realizing I hadn't.

"Steaks are ready," Stuart announced, walking through the door with a platter of small steaks.

"Perfect timing," Vivian declared. "Everything is ready. Evan, dear, would you please help bring the food to the table?"

"Sure." Evan found bowls and serving utensils to pair with the sides and carried them to the dining table. I hadn't noticed the set table with decorative china and sparkling flatware until I turned to follow him. In the center, an intricate candelabrum let off a dazzling glow. I wasn't prepared for the formal setting.

"Shall we?" Vivian addressed me as she walked toward the table carrying a bottle of wine.

I picked up my glass to follow her. She and Stuart sat on either end while Evan and I sat facing each other in the middle. Evan shot me a grin when we sat down. I gave him a panicked smile, which made him laugh. His mother looked at him, questioning his outburst. He attempted to conceal it with a clearing of his throat.

My stomach was twisting with nerves; I wasn't sure how I was going to eat. I practically force fed myself every bite, despite the fact that is was one of the best meals I'd had since... well, since Evan cooked for me.

"How was your visit to California?" Vivian inquired the moment I put a piece of steak in my mouth. My face turned red as she patiently waited for me to swallow so I could answer.

"I loved it," I finally responded.

"Are you still looking at Stanford as your first choice?"

"Yes, I really enjoyed the meetings with the coach and the advisor," I explained. "It's going to come down to my SAT scores and how I perform this coming soccer season. But so far, they seem very interested."

"Have you decided on a major?"

"That did come up, and with my strong science and math background, the advisor mentioned pre-med."

Evan's eyes widened in surprise. Yeah, I hadn't mentioned that to anyone before this moment.

"That would be wonderful," she acknowledged with a smile. "Evan, have you narrowed down your selections yet?"

"Mom, let's not do this," he begged. "You know where I'm looking. My mother wants me to go to Cornell with my brother," he explained to me, "and my father wants me to go to Yale like he did."

"Oh," I nodded, realizing both colleges were on the wrong coast.

"Well, I suppose California would make sense if Emily was there," Vivian admitted with a slight rise of her shoulder. Stuart cleared his throat. "Stuart, California has some excellent schools."

Hearing our future being planned before me was surreal. It wasn't that I didn't want a future with Evan. I honestly hadn't thought much about it until this moment. However, listening to his *mother* plan our future, didn't feel quite right.

"Mom," Evan stressed, obviously just as uncomfortable, "we have plenty of time to talk about it. Let's talk about something else, okay?"

"If you insist," she agreed with an endearing smile. "Are you looking forward to going to the prom next month?"

Evan choked on his water. I stopped breathing.

"What?" she questioned Evan's obvious disruption.

"We haven't exactly talked about it yet," he confessed, glancing at me apologetically. I looked down at my plate and moved the asparagus around with my fork.

"Evan," she scolded, "she needs time to pick out a dress. You should have asked her already."

I bit my lip trying not to smile.

"Well, if you would like some assistance in finding a dress," she directed her attention to me, "I would be happy to take you to this fabulous boutique in New York."

"Okay, thank you," I stuttered. Evan tensed at the offer. The thought of it horrified me. I could barely survive shopping with Sara at the mall.

"Since I seem to be suggesting the wrong conversational topics," Vivian declared, directing her words towards Evan, "what would you like to talk about?"

Evan looked up, recognizing she was addressing him.

"Dad, how's work?" he asked quickly. Vivian let out an exasperated sigh.

"Emily does not need to hear about his tedious cases," Vivian interrupted before Stuart could open his mouth. I wasn't sure if Stuart actually intended to open his mouth. "We're supposed to be getting to know her." No, that's not a good idea either.

She offered me a warm smile, which I attempted to return. My stomach churned in anticipation of her impending question.

"What does your uncle do?" she asked politely.

I swallowed hard. We were really going to talk about my family, weren't we?

"He's a land surveyor."

"That's wonderful," she replied. "I understand that your father passed away when you were young. What did he do?"

Evan gave me a worried glance. I took a breath and replied, "He was an engineer for an architectural firm in Boston."

"Mom, aren't you working on a charity event in Boston?" Evan intercepted before his mother could ask another revealing question.

Vivian beamed at the chance to talk about one of her projects. Thankfully, she went into enough detail about the event that the conversation lasted for the remainder of dinner.

"You and Evan should attend it with us," she decided as she set the dessert in front of us. Evan grumbled, not hiding his distaste of the invitation. "Evan, stop that. It's a wonderful cause and you'll be able to meet so many people in the medical industry since it's for the hospital."

"When did you say it was?" I inquired.

"The middle of June."

"Oh, I'm sorry," I replied, trying to sound disappointed. "I'll be away at the soccer camp by then."

"Evan, is that the camp you applied for, as well?"

I turned toward Evan, unaware that he had applied.

"Oh, yeah," he answered, meeting my questioning eyes. "Sara gave me the application a few weeks ago. But, I'm not sure if they have a spot open."

The thought of spending the summer with Sara *and* Evan produced a glowing grin. Evan smiled in response to my radiant expression. Vivian asked me to explain the camp while we ate dessert, which was finally an easy topic, having been an assistant coach there for the past two summers.

After dessert, Vivian excused us and escorted me to the sitting room. Evan warily watched us leave while he and his father cleaned up the dishes. When he eventually joined us, I knew why.

"You are not showing her my baby pictures!" He sounded horrified, which made me laugh.

"Come on, Evan," I teased with a laughing smile, "you were adorable."

"I know," Vivian acknowledged, not understanding his reaction.

"Okay," he announced, "I think you've had her long enough."

Evan closed the photo book that was on my lap and placed it on the table. He held out his hand to take me away.

"We're going to the barn before I have to drive her home."

"I suppose," Vivian said with a sigh. "It was so nice to finally get to talk with you." She gave me a hug and kissed my cheek. "I look forward to seeing you again."

"Good night," I said to Stuart as Evan led me through the kitchen.

"Good night, Emily," Stuart's bold voice returned.

"Was it that horrible for you?" I laughed while we climbed the stairs.

"I was going to ask you the same thing," Evan returned. When we entered the room, he turned to face me, looking all too serious. "I'm sorry about that. I tried to give her boundaries, but she doesn't listen very well."

"It was fine," I assured him. He wrapped his arms around me and kissed me gently.

"You're birthday's in a couple of weeks," I said, looking up at him from within his wrap. "What would you like to do?"

"Will you be able to do anything on the Friday of my actual birthday?"

I sucked in air through my teeth and shook my head apologetically. "Saturday?" I offered.

"Okay," he agreed. "So, I'll do something with the guys on Friday. Maybe go to the city or something. Then Saturday's just you and me."

"Dinner?" I suggested. Evan considered my offer, then smirked.

"Yeah," he said, grinning. "I have an idea."

"I'm missing something." I was mystified by the look in his eye. I knew he was contriving a plan that he wasn't sharing.

"No," he said quickly. "Dinner is perfect. But can I choose?"

"Sure," I agreed slowly, still not trusting his reaction.

Carol and George were waiting for me when I returned home. Well, they pretended to be sitting at the island talking, but I was pretty sure they wanted to see if Evan would walk me to the door. I was so glad I'd convinced him not to, even when he tried to change my mind on the drive home.

"How was your night?" Carol inquired, with an edge to her tone.

"It was nice," I responded quietly, trying to continue to my room.

"We need to lay down some ground rules," George declared, making me stop and close my eyes. I turned to listen to their determination to destroy my world even more.

"You cannot go to Evan's when no one's home," Carol demanded. "If we hear otherwise, you won't be allowed to see him anymore. And that means when you're at Sara's too."

"He is not allowed to drive you home after school," George added. "We don't care if he drives you to school, but you can only drive with Sara or one of your other girlfriends in the afternoon."

"And lastly," Carol stated with a cutting grin, "if we find out that you are having sex, you will not be allowed to take a step out of this house until you graduate, except to go to school."

I remained motionless while her threat turned over in my head.

"Why are you looking at us like that?" she griped. "Are we not making ourselves clear?"

"I don't understand why you'd assume I'd have sex with him," I replied, my voice sounding more accusatory than defensive. "You know nothing about me, do you?"

"We know enough," Carol bit. "We know you are naïve and can easily be taken advantage of. Don't think for a second he cares about you. He's just like every other guy who only wants one thing."

"You don't know anything about him either," I shot back, my voice growing stronger.

Carol raised her eyebrows at my reaction, while George's face tensed.

"Maybe we should reconsider whether you're ready to date at all," Carol threatened. My heart stopped. "Is there something we should know? Are you already having sex?"

"No," I answered quickly as the panicked heat crept up my neck.

"Then this conversation is over," George finally interceded. "You know how we feel, and that's it."

37. GIFTS

I FOLLOWED THEIR RULES FOR THE NEXT TWO WEEKS. NOT BECAUSE I wanted to, because it's just how it ended up. Evan and I didn't go to his house the following Sunday, we went to the sports complex where he talked me into the driving range instead of the batting cages. I concluded in frustration never to do it again.

I spent time in Art and part of study period preparing his birthday gift. Ms. Mier didn't know exactly what it was for but was encouraging as I completed each page. I had a feeling she knew more than she admitted, but then again, she always did.

When it was finally finished, I let Sara look it over to make sure I hadn't stepped over any lines that would make it too... much. She understood its entire content since I told her *everything*, so it was unnerving to watch her reaction as she scanned each page. She smiled at the end and shocked me by giving me a hug.

"Em, it's perfect."

"Really?"

"Definitely—he's going to love it."

"Then why do I feel like I'm going to throw up at the thought of giving it to him?"

"Because it's so personal and thoughtful. He has to love it."

I hoped she was right.

My stomach was in my throat the entire ride to school on Friday. I nervously wrung my hands in my lap. Evan finally said something when we arrived at school.

"What's going on?" He turned to face me after shutting the car off.

I took a quick breath. "I didn't know when was the best time to do this, so I'm just going to do it now." I reached into my backpack and pulled out the flat, wrapped square. "Happy birthday."

Evan produced an uncomfortable grin. "Thank you."

"You don't have to open it now," I blurted when he started to unwrap the gift. "You can look at it later, when you're by yourself."

He eyed me suspiciously and opened it anyway.

"Evan, really, you don't have to look at it now." Maybe I *was* going to throw up.

"Did you make this?"

I bit my lip and nodded.

To my horror, Evan started turning the pages of the ribbon bound collection of art. A smile crept onto his face. I held my breath, watching his bright eyes take in each moment captured by the stroke of my brush.

He turned to the page with the image of Sara's scarf and remarked, "I still have this, don't I?" He hesitated at the page with the blue hand print, smiling wider, which sent a warm chill through me. I took in his soft expression while he scanned the lyrics I transcribed from one of the songs he downloaded on my iPod, and he shook his head with a smile at the Jacobs' exquisite chandelier. Evan ran his fingers along the brook in the meadow, and he let out a light laugh remembering the cityscape from atop the apartment building in New York. His cheeks flushed at the sight of the pink roses on the last page, and he slowly closed the book with a deep breath.

"This is everything, huh?" he questioned, taking a hold of my hand.

"Only the good stuff," I corrected, my fiery cheeks now crimson.

"This is amazing. Thank you." He leaned over and found me waiting for him. My head was swirling already from not being able to breathe, but with the touch of his lips, the sensation escalated. He left me needing a minute to float back down before stepping out of the car.

Evan met me on the other side of the car and wrapped me tightly in his arms. My heart still hadn't recovered from the kiss and continued to falter when I looked up into his steel blue eyes.

"That is the best gift I've ever received," he grinned. He kissed me again, but with a little more restraint.

"Oh," I sighed when he finally released me. "I'm glad you like it."

"That was hard for you, wasn't it?" Evan noted, holding my hand as we walked into school. I hesitated, unsure of what he meant. "Having me look at it with you right there."

"You have no idea," I confessed. He smiled at my honesty.

"So tomorrow night's my turn," he declared with a slight squeeze of my hand, leaving me perplexed as he disappeared down the hall.

Evan wouldn't explain what he meant when I asked later that day. But, he did want me to wear his favorite pink sweater, which I agreed to do with a shrug – it was his birthday. He continued to avoid telling me what he meant by his statement, making me nervous. It made Sara giddy. She came up with a thousand reasons he was being so mysterious, but none of them were even close to what he actually planned.

"We're having dinner at your house?" I questioned in confusion when we pulled in his driveway. Evan grinned.

"Close your eyes," he requested.

"What?! Why?" I demanded in a rush. "Evan, what did you do? This is supposed to be *your* birthday, right?"

"Yes," he replied with a quick smile, "and this is what I wanted to do for my birthday. Close your eyes."

I swallowed the anxiousness and obeyed. Evan helped me out of the car and wrapped a silky fabric around my eyes.

"Are you serious?"

"I know you'll peek before you're supposed to."

"Evan, I have heels on; I'm going to kill myself."

"No you won't." He swept his arm under my knees, and I fell back, cradled in his arms. I yelled out in surprise and wrapped my arms firmly around his neck.

"That was not necessary," I scolded.

"Don't want you to kill yourself," he remarked, a smile in his voice.

I heard his feet crunching along the gravel that led to the barn and then the squeak of a door. I recognized the scents of the garage as he continued up the stairs. He pushed the door open and effortlessly lowered me onto my feet. I was afraid to open my eyes after he untied the fabric.

When I did, my mouth dropped open. The entire room was shimmering in a soft glow, with lines of candles on every surface. The couch was pushed toward the wall to allow room for a small table in the center of the floor, adorned with candlesticks and set for two. I recognized the soft whispery female voice floating through the speakers.

"Is this from my playlist?" I questioned.

"I told you it set a mood," Evan smirked, then examined me intently and asked, "So, how'd I do?"

"It's beautiful," I breathed. He stood behind me with his arms around my waist, bending to kiss the top of my shoulder.

Evan escorted me to the table and pulled out a chair for me. Even though I knew it was part of who he was, the chivalry still felt awkward. I smiled nervously as he sat across from me, a colorful salad in front of us.

"Is this weird for you?" he asked, observing my fidgeting.

"No," I answered reluctantly. "I'm trying to get over that you thought to do this."

"Thanks," he replied sarcastically. "You didn't think I had this in me?"

"It's not that," I corrected. "It's *your* birthday, so it doesn't feel quite right."

"This is exactly what I wanted to do for my birthday. So, relax, okay?"

"Okay," I breathed, searching for the appetite to eat the berries and greens before me.

"We *are* going to the prom together, right?" he confirmed. "I know I didn't officially ask you. Actually, I think my mother did."

I laughed. "Yes, Evan, I will go to the prom with you."

"Please don't tell me that you're going to go shopping with her," he begged.

"I could never afford any place she'd take me."

"Oh, I'm pretty sure she wants to buy the dress." My eyes widened in surprise. He added, "It would just be too strange having you and my mother alone together. I know she'd tell you things that would freak me out."

"Really?" I teased. "Maybe we *should* go shopping together." Evan shook his head as I laughed at the idea of bonding with Vivian.

After I got over the initial shock of the romantic setting and recognized that it was only Evan and I, everything felt comfortable again. We talked casually and laughed easily. It was perfect. I'd almost forgotten that we were sitting in the barn. The flickering light transformed the room, hiding the games and tables in the shadows. I was soothed by the candles and the music—lost in the soft light flickering in Evan's eyes. But, the anxiety returned when Evan set down a small blue box in front of me, instead of the dessert I was expecting.

I couldn't find my voice or even breathe. He smiled at me from across the table, watching me struggle for words.

"Don't say anything," he insisted. "This is what *I* wanted to do."

I stared at him, unable to bring myself to open the box.

"You have to open it," he pleaded. I looked nervously between him and the box. "*Please* open it. You're killing me."

I took a quick breath and slid the top off the box. I looked up at Evan with wide eyes, still unable to speak.

"I thought you should have one of your own to go with the sweater," he explained. "You like it, right?"

"Yes," I breathed, too overwhelmed to touch the sparkling rock inside the box. Evan stood behind me and removed it from the velvet to place it around my neck. I gently caressed it with my shaking finger tips as it lay against my skin.

I stood up to face him. "Thank you," I whispered. I wrapped my arms around him and extended on my toes to find his lips. My lips brushed gently against his, lingering for a moment before slowly pulling away.

Evan had his arms around my waist, holding me against him. The music settled in around us and we found ourselves slowly moving to the soothing seductive voice.

"Are we dancing?" I questioned with a smile.

"I think we are," Evan agreed with a slight nod of his head. "Is that bad?"

"No, just something else I've never done before," I admitted. I laid my head under his chin, allowing him to sway me.

The delicate strums and smooth melodies were mesmerizing, adding to the enchantment of the flickering lights and the warmth of his body. I searched his face as he gazed down at me with a soft smile. My stomach fluttered and my head felt light, I was completely consumed by him.

"I love you," I whispered – the words flowed effortlessly from my mouth.

Evan pulled me against him and pressed his lips to mine. The tender kiss soon turned urgent, sending electric charges throughout my body. His lips moved down my neck and his hands slid along my back under the sweater. I let out an excited breath as I ran my hands along his taught frame under his shirt. He pulled it up over his head. We separated long enough to allow him to drop it to the floor.

We were moving, still in our passionate exchange, in the direction of the room above the garage. I slid my sweater over my head and dropped it behind me. Evan stopped.

"Are you sure?" he questioned with a heavy breath, studying my face for a sign of doubt.

"Yes," I said in a whispering sigh, pulling him toward me again. He eagerly accepted me. I kicked off my shoes and unbuttoned my pants. Evan caught my hands.

"Really, we don't have to do this."

"Evan, I love you. I want to. But if you don't..." I started to zip my pants, and his hands caught mine again. We stood still for a second, staring at each other. Then he slid down my zipper and eased my pants over my hips. I stepped out of them and followed him into the room. He held me against his warm smooth skin before gently laying me on top of the comforter, his mouth trailing along my shoulders down to my stomach. He stood to remove his shoes and to slide off his pants.

I wrapped my leg around the back of his thigh as he eased himself over me. My mouth found his neck, and I traced my lips along his shoulder. Our frantic breaths revealed our excitement, as his fingers traced along my stomach, sending a thousand sparks shooting through my body.

Evan froze when the lights flashed through the front windows. My eyes widened in alarm, as I held my breath.

"Oh no," he exclaimed, jumping up to investigate. He grabbed his pants and quickly stuffed each leg into them. I propped myself up on my elbows, watching in shock as he hopped to put his shoes back on.

"Stay here," he instructed as he rushed out the door, closing it behind him.

"Evan, you up there?" I heard a guy's voice yell a few minutes later. You have got to be kidding me! The distinct thump of footsteps climbed the stairs.

"Oh," the voice exclaimed. "Are we interrupting something?"

A flood of light shone through the bottom of the closed door. I panicked. Someone was in the other room. My clothes were in the other room! I heard more footsteps and voices. I snuck off the bed and tiptoed to the closet to find something to throw on.

"No," Evan replied uneasily. "Um, I was just cleaning up."

"Had a good birthday, huh?" the voice asked with a laugh.

"Jared, what are you doing here?" Evan finally asked.

"Came here with a few of the guys to surprise you for your birthday. Happy Birthday."

"Thanks," Evan responded. Jared didn't seem to notice the tension in his voice.

"Let's turn on the music and play pool or something," Jared suggested emphatically. "Get whatever you want to drink at the bar."

"Sounds good," one of the other voices agreed. "What's with all the candles?"

"It's from earlier," Evan stated dismissively.

In the dim light, I made out a pair of jogging pants and a sweatshirt. I threw them on, folding the waistband of the oversized pants. The clothes hung off me, but it was better than being practically naked.

"I should bring these plates to the house," Evan told the guys. "I'll be right back."

The room on the other side of the door erupted with the bellows of a punk rock band and the crashing of pool balls.

I sat on the bed, having no idea what to do. I knew that there was no way I was going out that door while they were still in the other room.

"Emma?" Evan whispered. I jumped at the sound of the voice coming from the floor. I leaned over the edge of the bed to find Evan peering up through an open trap door in the floor. He was standing on a fold-down ladder that led to the garage.

"You can come down this way. They won't know," Evan explained.

I carefully made my way down the ladder in my bare feet, with Evan waiting at the bottom. He replaced the floor panel before folding the ladder back up. Without saying anything, he grabbed my hand. I followed him out the door into the cool moonlit night.

"I am so sorry," he stressed while we walked in the damp grass of the field behind his house. "I had no idea he was coming."

"It's okay."

"I hid your clothes in the closet before they came up. I promise to get them back to you."

"I'm never going to see that sweater again, am I?"

"Well, maybe after it stops smelling like you," he responded with a grin. Evan secured his arms around me. "We'll have other moments, I promise. I'm not going anywhere… well, not without you."

"I know."

"Nice outfit," Sara observed with a smile when I walked into her bedroom. "You have a story to share, that's for sure."

"How was your date with Tony?" I asked, trying to delay the inevitable conversation.

"Done," Sara declared casually, with a slight shrug. "Is that a diamond around your neck? Em, start talking."

I brushed over the more intimate scenes, much to Sara's disappointment, and when I was done with my account of the evening, Sara erupted in laughter. I slowly joined in.

"I can't believe you almost got caught *your first time!*" she exclaimed in-between fits of laughter.

"Shut up, Sara," I laughed, throwing a pillow at her. "It *wasn't* my first time. It didn't happen."

"You have *the worst* luck," she bellowed, tears rolling down her cheeks.

38. SHATTERED

"YOU LITTLE TRAMP," CAROL MUTTERED FROM BEHIND ME WHILE I swept the kitchen floor. I spun around at the sound of her voice.

"What did you have to do to get that?" she demanded, reaching for the necklace. I backed away, out of her clutches. Her eyes widened with shock.

"You can't honestly think he cares about you," she jeered. "He probably had that from the last girl he screwed."

The fire ignited within me as I stared in disgust at this pathetic woman.

"Shut up, Carol," I shot back firmly, towering over her.

"What did you just say?" she demanded, with a ferocity that could have blown the house to pieces. Her hand connected with the side of my face with a rocking force. The broom reverberated off the floor.

I turned my head back toward her. The fire fed every muscle of my tensed body. I raised my fist.

"What, are you going to hit me?" she smirked. "Go ahead and hit me."

My mind snapped back. I looked up at my clenched hand—appalled at what I was about to do. I pushed away the rage before it swallowed me.

"I have no idea why you're so twisted, but I'm not you," I spat. "You disgust me."

Carol stared at me with contempt. My insides twisted, instantly regretting my cutting statement. Fear started overtaking the anger, and my body began to quiver.

She grabbed for my arm, and I shoved her off.

"You fucking bitch," she grunted, coming at me with a force I wasn't expecting but should have prepared for. She pushed my shoulders to slam me against the door, but I slipped on the broom at my feet. Glass shattered around me, and fire shot through my arm when my elbow crashed through a panel of the door.

I screamed in pain, the jagged edges slicing into me. I cradled my elbow against me. Blood ran between my fingers, dripping onto the floor. I continued to groan through clamped teeth with the shards digging into my flesh.

"What the hell is going on?!" George exclaimed, running up the stairs to the deck. He froze outside the door at the sight of the broken glass and me on the floor, soaked in blood. His eyes trailed up to Carol, and he stared at her in abhorrent shock.

"George," she gasped, "it was an accident. She slipped, I swear."

"Don't just stand there," he yelled. "Get her a towel." Carol rushed to the bathroom, obeying his command.

George opened the door as much as he could with my collapsed body still in front of it, paralyzed with shock. He slipped through and bent down to examine the damage.

"I need to take you to the hospital," he concluded. "There's still glass in the cuts, and you probably need stitches."

Warm tears slid down my face. George lifted me just as Carol was returning with a towel. Her eyes pleaded with George. He grabbed the towel from her without giving her a glance and carefully wrapped it around my arm to catch the flowing blood.

"George, I'm so sorry," she whimpered.

"We'll talk about this when I get back," he snapped still unable to look at her. He opened the door for me, and I followed him to his truck wordlessly. He didn't say anything either as he opened the passenger door. I climbed in, exhaling with an aggravated grunt as the movement forced the splinters in deeper.

The silence continued until we arrived at the hospital. We were admitted immediately and enclosed by curtains in the emergency room. The doctor examined the cuts before numbing the area to remove the glass and assess which cuts needed stitches.

I sat on the bed mindlessly listening to the chunks of glass cling as they hit the bottom of the metal bowl. I couldn't stop the flowing tears that was dripping from my chin as much as I tried to swallow them away. I shivered when the doctor poked and examined the exposed tissue for additional slivers. I eventually surrendered to the nothingness while the needle pulled the torn skin together.

George tensed when the doctor asked me to explain how it happened. My lying had become more convincing over the past couple of months, so the story of slipping backward on the wet floor spilled out easily. I didn't care if the doctor believed me, but he didn't seem to doubt me. We were there several hours before we were finally on our way home.

"I'm going to take care of this," George stated lowly during our drive home. "Just go to your room, and let me handle it, okay?"

"Okay," I whispered.

"There has to be a way for the two of you to live together," he mumbled to himself.

I knew by his tone that he still believed I had as much to do with this, if not more, than she did. I clenched my teeth, clearly understanding that he would always side with her, and as long as he did, she would never stop.

I expected Carol's car to be gone when we arrived home. I didn't know why I expected it. Maybe I was hoping she would've left. But her blue Jeep sat motionless in the driveway when we pulled in behind it. I slid down from the passenger seat, careful of my bandaged arm, and lumbered silently into the house.

Carol had swept up the glass and taped a piece of clear plastic to the door, covering the hole the shattered pane left behind. She was nowhere to be seen as I walked to my room, closing the door behind me. My arm was still numb for the most part, but it was already starting to throb. I lay on my bed, staring at the ceiling, too exhausted to succumb to either anger or sadness. I allowed my thoughts to dull, enveloped by numbness that comforted me like a familiar blanket.

I heard a murmur of heated voices upstairs and the cries of Leyla and Jack. I closed my eyes to block it out. I thought I recognized her sobbing voice, pleading with him. Then there was silence. He came down the stairs and walked into the kitchen. The exhaustion eventually won over and I drifted to sleep.

I didn't wake until the morning. I blinked, realizing I was still dressed and lying on top of my bedding. I glanced at the clock; my alarm was ten minutes away from going off.

I propped myself up. The sharp fire shot through my arm. I bolted upright, drawing in a quick breath through my teeth. The doctor told me I couldn't get the stitches wet for the first twenty-four hours, and so the thought of how I would manage a shower made me collapse onto my back again with a frustrated sigh. Then I thought of how I still had to face Sara and Evan, and I groaned. Wasn't there any way I could avoid going to school today?

I opted for a sponge bath, to avoid the impossibility of a one armed shower, and put my hair up so it wasn't obvious that I hadn't washed it. I noticed the house was eerily still when I walked out of the bathroom. I paused in the hall, not hearing a sound except for the hum of the refrigerator.

I cautiously walked into the kitchen, listening intently. There was no movement in the kitchen or the dining room. A bag was set on the island with a note attached to it, next to a key.

This is the ointment to put on your stitches twice a day. Carol is staying with her mother for a few days. She just needs space. Everything will be different. Use the key to lock up when you leave.

I read the note over several times, shaking my head. He really believed it was going to be different? The tears welled in my eyes, forcing their way down my cheeks. I wiped them away and swallowed the lump in the back of my throat.

I put the bag of bandages and ointment on my desk and gathered my books before leaving the house to meet Evan. I locked the kitchen door behind me, struck by the distinct click of the bolt when I turned the key—a sound that I'd never made before. I continued to fight against the tears before clomping down the stairs.

"Is she here?" Evan asked quietly after I shut the car door behind me. I shouldn't have been surprised that he noticed. As much as I was hoping the long sleeved shirt would conceal my bandages, the bulky wrap left a distinct bulge. I suppose my sunken frame clued him in as well.

"No," I whispered, looking out the window. "She's staying with her mother for a few days."

"You can't stay here anymore."

"I know," I mouthed, unable to make a sound. My eyes stung as I blinked back the tears unable to look at him. My mind remained blank, not wanting to think of what his words really meant. We drove in silence the entire way to school.

When we pulled into the school's parking lot, Evan shut off the car and shifted his body to face me.

"Emma?" he beckoned softly, making me turn towards him. "Are you okay?" I shook my head.

His hand brushed along my cheek, and I collapsed into his arms, sobbing against his chest. He held me until I couldn't cry anymore. I brushed the tears from my face and looked up into his glassy eyes. Seeing the pain in them tore at my heart. He kissed me softly, keeping his eyes closed when I pulled away.

"Do you want to go *now*?" he asked, when he was able to look at me again.

"*Now*?" I choked.

"Why not? What are we waiting for?"

The understanding of what he wanted to do suddenly weighed heavily in my stomach. Images of packing my bags and escaping with him ran through my head, causing my throat to close and adrenaline to rush through my veins. It was too much for me to process.

"Tomorrow," I implored, needing one more day to collect my thoughts. "She's not staying at the house tonight. Let me have the night to pack, and we can leave tomorrow, whenever you want."

Evan studied my face as I pleaded with my eyes.

"No one will be home when you leave in the morning, right?" he confirmed.

"Right."

"Then when I pick you up tomorrow morning, have whatever you want to take ready, and we're gone."

My heart skipped a beat as I nodded. Could I really do this? Leave everything behind and risk my entire future to escape her? Allowing her to destroy me didn't seem right, not after everything I'd been through. I needed the twenty-four hours to decide what to do.

Evan and I missed homeroom and had to stop at the office for tardy slips before going to Art class. We were quiet while we walked the halls together. But he never left my side, holding my hand or wrapping his arm around me as I floated alongside him to each class. His strength kept me moving forward, and it was also tearing me apart.

"You're going to do what?!" Sara questioned fervently when Evan told her what we were planning. "How is that going to work? How long will you be gone?"

I could only stare at her since I didn't have the answers. She verbalized the same questions that ran through my head.

"I have a plan," was all Evan would reveal. "I'll tell you later, I promise."

Sara shook her head in amazement at what it had finally come to. She mimicked my every thought with her actions and words.

Before we could discuss it further, there was an announcement requesting my presence in the vice principal's office. Sara and Evan became still as a few heads turned toward me curiously. My stomach wrapped itself around a fiery ball of nerves when I stood to leave. Evan got up to go with me.

"It's okay," I assured him. "I'll see you in Journalism."

My feet felt heavy as they unwillingly carried my body down the hall to the vice principal's office. Mr. Montgomery was standing outside his door, awaiting my arrival. When I entered the room, my chest flickered with nerves as I glanced around at the faces seated along the conference table.

"Emily," Mr. Montgomery stated with a voice of authority, "please take a seat."

Still staring from eye to eye, I slid onto the chair at the end of the table. Why were they here? But I knew, clenching my jaw to fight the lump in my throat. I collected myself before their betrayal could completely break me. My back stiffened, preparing for what would come next.

"We're all here because we're concerned about you," Mr. Montgomery's deep voice boomed across the table, so stiff and diplomatic, without a hint of compassion. "We want you to explain how you get your injuries. Is someone hurting you?"

"No," I shook my head adamantly, my defenses kicking in.

"Emma," Coach Straw said, her approach warmer than his, but it still rang with an accusatory undertone. "We know you're not accident prone like you'd like us to believe. We just want to know what's going on."

"Nothing," I snapped back, overly guarded.

"We're not here to make things harder for you," Ms. Mier explained in her melodic voice, empathy pouring from her. "We're here because we truly care about you and want to help you."

Looking into her gentle brown eyes caused the lump to rise in my throat again. How could she have done this to me?! I swallowed hard.

"I swear, there's nothing to protect me from," I protested. My cracking voice betrayed me.

"Is Evan Mathews hurting you?" Mr. Montgomery interrogated. I widened my eyes, appalled at his accusation. Ms. Mier shot him the same look.

"Evan would never hurt me," I growled, infuriated by the allegation. My bite made them all sit back in their chairs.

"I know that," Ms. Mier soothed. "But someone is. Please tell us."

"I can't." I choked on the knot in my throat. I ground my teeth together, trying to fight against the tears collecting in my eyes with exaggerated blinks.

"Emma, I know this is hard," Ms. Farkis, the school psychologist interjected, "but we promise that no one will hurt you because you told us. We'll make sure of it."

"You don't know that," I whispered. They stared at me in silence, waiting. I clenched my fists against the table, needing to escape. "I can't do this."

I stood up and rushed out the door. I heard the screech of chairs when a few stood to follow me.

"Let her go," Ms. Farkis advised.

I ran down the hall in a blur of tears. I wiped my face and tried to breathe evenly when I approached the Journalism room. I didn't care whose attention I got first, one of them had to notice. Sara was staring out the small window of the door, so it was an easy choice. She excused herself to the bathroom and met me in the hall.

"We have to leave," I blurted, rushing toward our lockers.

"What happened?"

"They're trying to figure out what's going on, but I wouldn't tell them. Sara, I have to get out of here."

"Where do you want to go?"

"Let's go back to my house so that I can pack; then I don't care where we go."

"Do you want me to get Evan?"

"Not yet. Not until we can figure out where to meet him. They actually had the nerve to ask if he was hurting me."

"What?! Are they really that stupid?" she exclaimed incredulously.

We grabbed our bags. I didn't bother to put any books in it, not knowing if I would ever need them again. We flew down the side stairs, avoiding the main doors. Sara ran to get her car while I waited for her against the side of the building. My pulse raced, and my whole body quivered, unable to stand still while I kept watch for her car.

I ran to the car when she pulled around and sunk onto the seat, trying to find comfort now that we were driving away—but I couldn't. This all felt wrong, and it was happening way too fast. My brain couldn't make sense of it, and I was overwhelmed with fear. Was I doing the right thing, or was I overreacting?

Sara remained silent during the drive to my house. I was so lost in my questions and doubting thoughts, that I didn't realize when we had turned onto my street. Sara's pocket buzzed and she looked at her phone.

"Hi," she answered, glancing at me. "Yeah, we're going to her house to get her things."

She listened for a minute and pressed her lips together.

"Evan, I'm still not sure that's the best idea." She listened again. "Okay, we'll meet you there in an hour."

"What did he say?" I asked when she hung up.

"We're going to meet him at his house in an hour. Em, I'm not sure that you taking off to who knows where is the best answer. I still think there's a way out of this without you having to leave."

"I know," I agreed lowly. "But let's at least hear him out."

"Do you want me to come in with you?" Sara asked, glancing at the empty house.

"No, I won't be long."

"Emily?" George's voice hollered after I heard the click of the back door.

I continued throwing things in my bags, ignoring him when he walked into my room. He took in the bags on my bed with confusion.

"What do you think you're doing?! I received a call from the school saying you left upset and that they wanted us to come in to talk with them. What did you say?!"

"Don't worry, George," I turned to face him, raising my voice, "I didn't say anything to them! But I can't stay here and live like this anymore! I can't live with *her!*"

He flinched at the anger in my voice. The alien tone was as difficult for him to hear as it was for me to project.

"You're not leaving here," he stated sternly, between clenched teeth. "Listen, we will straighten this whole thing out, but you are not leaving this house. Do you understand me?"

The underlying threat in his voice knocked me back. Could I walk past him? Would he let me? Should I sneak out the window after he leaves me alone?

I watched his posture soften and sadness wash over his face. I silently took notice of the resigned transformation.

"I understand you're upset. And I promise you, we'll figure out a way to work this out. None of us can live like this anymore. But leaving right now is not going to help anything. Carol's staying with her mother tonight.

"We'll go to the school together tomorrow and straighten everything out. There's no need for anyone to get hurt by this. Just stay until tomorrow, and if you still want to leave after the meeting, we'll make arrangements. Okay?"

My mind raced. Did he mean it? Would he let me leave tomorrow? I wouldn't have to fly off to wherever Evan had planned to take me—I could stay here? Just one more night.

"Okay," I whispered.

"Why don't you go tell Sara that you'll see her tomorrow."

I slowly walked to Sara's car, still trying to decide if I was making the right decision. Something in the depths of my stomach was begging for me to leave.

"I'm going to stay," I told Sara quietly.

"What do you mean?" Sara questioned in a panic.

"She's not staying here tonight. We're going in to the school tomorrow morning to clear everything up, and he said that I could leave if I still wanted to after the meeting."

"You believe him?" she asked, still uneasy.

"I have to," I whispered, my eyes filling with tears. "He's giving me an out without having to hurt anyone or run away."

Sara got out of her car and hugged me. We wiped the tears from our eyes when we finally let go.

"I'll see you tomorrow, okay?" my voice rasped.

"Okay," she whispered, sniffling. "What do I tell Evan? He's not going to be happy when I show up without you. He's probably going to want to come here to get you."

"Sara, he can't," I pleaded. "Convince him that everything will be okay and I'll see him tomorrow. Please, can you do that?"

"I'll try."

"Make him listen. I promise everything will be okay."

39. BREATHE

I TRIED TO MOVE, BUT THERE WAS RESISTANCE. CONFUSED, I TUGGED at my arms—they wouldn't follow. I started to breathe quickly, through my nose—my mouth wouldn't open. I frantically looked around in the dark. Where was I?

Then I couldn't see at all. There was something over my face. My heart beat hysterically, like it was going to explode in my chest. I pulled harder at my arms which were strung above my head. I heard the jangling of metal as the sharp edges of the restraints dug into my wrists.

"I am not losing my family because of you," she seethed.

Panic consumed me. I started squirming, screaming as loud as the restricted covering would allow. The pillow pressed against my face. I shook my head back and forth vigorously, trying to remove it. It wouldn't shift enough to provide me air.

There was pressure on my chest. I tried to twist to get her off. That's when her cold hands gripped around my neck. I screamed louder, but my frantic pleas were muffled by the tape. I flipped my body back and forth—the restraints on my wrists and the weight on my chest wouldn't allow me to escape her strangling grasp.

This couldn't be happening. *Please someone hear me.*

I pulled at the restraints—the edges scraped away my flesh. I strained to pull harder, needing to be free of their hold. I couldn't find my breath as her grip tightened. I needed to cough, but the air wouldn't escape.

I pushed against the bed with my feet, arching my back. The strain of our weight pulled at my shoulders, and heard something pop; then a searing pain catapulted through my shoulder.

One of her hands released its hold. I sucked in a breath full of air, the effort burning my throat. I shrieked in agony when the bones of my ankle crunched with the impact of something she swung into it. I collapsed onto my back, my breath faltering. The darkness swirled as the torturous pain overtook me. I fought the pull taking me under.

The cold clutches returned to my throat, squeezing harder. I choked, trying desperately to breathe in. The air didn't come.

I needed someone to hear me. I swung my left leg toward the wall with all my force, pounding against it. The adrenaline and panic shrouded the pain.

The pressure in my head continued to build. My lungs burned. The claws around my neck crushed in deeper.

I pounded on the wall one more time. *Please someone hear me.*

I could feel it pulling me under. I couldn't struggle anymore. The burning was too much. I gave in, collapsing beneath the hands, and succumbing to the darkness.

EPILOGUE

IN THE UNEVEN BALANCE OF MY LIFE, I EXPERIENCED LOVE AND LOSS, more loss than I thought I could handle. But the love was unexpected. I almost missed out on it, too afraid and uncertain to give it a chance.

Love helped me live life instead of just survive it. It challenged my resolve, proving I was stronger than I ever thought possible. The comfort of it healed my wounds and caressed my scars. It gave me the confidence to stand taller than the inches within my body. In the dark, I searched for it, yearning for its reprieve, only finding that I was alone.

I couldn't feel the pain of my broken body. I couldn't hear the beats of my heart fading within my chest. I couldn't listen to the agonizing pleas as he clutched me against him. It was silent. All that was left was... me.

In the silence, there was peace. A peace that came too soon, but I sought refuge in its release. Release from the pain, the chaos and the fear. Being comforted by the unfamiliar calm would require a sacrifice I didn't want to make; but I didn't know if I had the strength to fight.

I knew time was slipping. I could no longer ignore the dwindling pulse. The thumping struggled to keep pace. The darkness pushed in around me. There was an ease to slipping away—giving in to the quiet and finding the resolution of nothingness. I was drawn to the resignation. I tried to hold on to the memories of my sacrifice—the warmth, the flutters, the truth in his eyes. Was life a choice?

In the balance of love and loss, it was love that made me struggle to... *Breathe*.

ACKNOWLEDGMENTS

to my original fans...

A ginormous thank you to:
my trusted friend, Faith,
for being the first to see every word and a voice of reason in my life;
my talented editor and friend, Elizabeth,
for having an eye for detail and a passion for the art of writing;
my most enthusiastic fan and true friend, Emily,
who at times believes in me more than I do of myself;
my honest friend, Amy,
for encouraging and believing in me throughout the entire process;
my insightful friend, Chrissy,
for teaching me the importance of getting to the point and that opening
up isn't a bad thing;
my Sara and sister in my life, Steph,
for always being honest, even when I'm not ready to hear it;
my sincerely genuine friend, Meredith,
for believing in my potential and the scope of my words;
my fervent friend, Nicole,
for living and breathing in Weslyn for over 400 pages, and sharing every
emotion along the way;
Amy, for seeing the "big picture";
Erin, for her refreshing candor;
Galen, for allowing my words to bond us;
Stephanie, for being a truly passionate fan from the beginning;
my sweet friend, Kara,
who had expectations of my success as if it had already happened;
my endearing friend, Katrina,
for nights of much needed laughter and words of encouragement;
Lisa, for the guidance that has left an everlasting impression;
Ann, for transforming an idea into an amazing book cover with not
much to work with—that is talent;
Dru, for challenging me to open my own doors;
and Dan, for our connection as you read this story.

ABOUT THE AUTHOR

Rebecca Donovan, a graduate of the University of Missouri—Columbia, lives in a quiet town in Massachusetts with her son. She recently released, *Barely Breathing,* the second installment of *The Breathing Series.* Rebecca is currently working on, *Out of Breath*, the series' conclusion.

Follow her projects on her website, www.rebeccadonovan.com and Facebook, www.facebook.com/ReasontoBreathe.

17859399R00223

Made in the USA
Lexington, KY
02 October 2012